HOLIDAY
Star

DR. MELISSA DYMOND

SOMETIMES THE HERO
IS THE ONE THAT NEEDS SAVING.

Illustrated and Photo Book Cover by Qamber designs

Formatting by KUHN Design Group | kuhndesigngroup.com

Copyedited by Dymond & Associates

Please visit the author's website at www.melissadymondauthor.com for character art, sales, book deals, writing updates, and more.

Connect on social media—let's be friends!
Instagram: https://www.instagram.com/melissadymondauthor/
Facebook: https://www.facebook.com/melissadymondauthor
Tiktok: https://www.tiktok.com/@melissadymond6

ISBN (eBook-clean/closed door) 979-8-9875850-0-9
ISBN (eBook-spicy/open door) 979-8-9875850-1-6
ISBN (Print-clean/closed door) 979-8-9875850-2-3
ISBN (Print-spicy/open door) 979-8-9875850-3-0
ISBN (photo cover-clean/closed door) 979-8-9875850-4-7
ISBN (photo cover-spicy/open door) 979-8-9875850-5-4

First edition 2023

To the cancer warriors of the world, this book is for you.
I hope we can fight this disease together. All of us united.

To those struggling, let your strength be a beacon for the rest of us.
For the lights we have lost, let us always remember them.

To my own personal heroes, Amelia, Chris,
and my dad Tony, please keep battling.

MUSICAL INSPIRATION:
"Dandelions" by Ruth B.

PROLOGUE

OHMYGOD! There he is," Jenny whispers in a high-pitched squeal, her hand on my arm, nails digging into my skin. I don't even bother to lift my gaze from my plate. I know who she's referring to. *Caleb Lawson.* He's the *only* thing she's been talking about tonight.

"I can't believe he's your cousin now." She rips a dinner roll in half, smears it with butter, and shoves it into her mouth, all without taking her eyes off the man across the room.

"He's *not* my cousin." I'm exasperated because we've had this conversation at least a dozen times. She's mostly kidding, but honestly, I'm tired of her bringing it up. "He's the son of my stepfather's sister."

My *new* stepfather.

I search through the crowded ballroom until I find my mother in her long white dress. She's beautiful, flowers woven into her hair, diamond earrings, an early wedding gift from her husband, dangling from her ears. Talking with some distant relatives, she waves her expressive hands.

As I watch, my new stepdad, Seth, comes up behind her. He winds an arm around her waist and joins the conversation. Mom leans into him, relaxing into that embrace like it's the most natural thing. She's happy today, on her wedding day.

I'm happy for her, too.

I'm just sad for me.

Which is a bad feeling, a selfish one. My dad passed away almost nine years ago, and Mom had waited a *long* time before she dated. She waited until my

7

older brother and I had moved out and my younger brother was a senior in high school, applying for college.

Once she finally started dating, she met Seth pretty quickly. When Mom knew she could have a future with him, she spoke to each of us individually, asking for our permission before they got serious.

It shouldn't bother me when Seth takes her hand and leads her out onto the dance floor. She deserves it, to be loved once again. I know this. I believe it wholeheartedly.

But, much to my dismay, it does bother me. Because all I can see is my father spinning her around our living room, dancing in the colorful glow of the Christmas tree. The sound of their laughter and how they stared into each other's eyes as if no one else existed.

I have to remind myself *that* is a memory, and *this* is reality.

Looking away from the dance floor, I take in the understated cream-colored ballroom. Simple flower arrangements of white roses and lilies sit on tables that are ringed by slip-covered chairs. Crystal chandeliers cast a warm glow over the guests as they chat and mingle.

Out of the window, it's a picture-perfect Santa Monica day. The Pacific Ocean glistens with white-capped waves. Surfers balance, arms outstretched, only to topple into the water as the swell they ride crashes into the sand.

Mom lets out a tinkling laugh, drawing my attention back to her. I watch as Seth twirls her around the dance floor, causing her white wedding dress to flare out into a bell shape.

I have a dress like that, too. It's in a garment bag, shoved deep into the back of my closet. Never worn.

"Do you think it's possible to be equal parts happy and sad at the same time?" I ask Jenny, fiddling with the place card in front of me. It has my name on it, in swooping cursive script.

Dr. Gwen Wright.

Before Jenny can answer, my older brother, Brandon, comes over. "You're up," he tells me. I rise and follow him to the raised dais in the center of the room, where a microphone sits on a stand, waiting for me.

Mom and Seth have finished their dance and taken their seats at the long, narrow table reserved for the wedding party. I glance over, and Mom gives me an encouraging smile.

Anxious, I rearrange the wide skirts of my lacy, blue bridesmaid dress. Next to me, Brandon taps a fork against a crystal goblet. The loud ringing sound echoes through the room, drawing everyone's attention. Brandon hands me the microphone and takes a step back, leaving me alone in the spotlight, a place that feels unfamiliar. Insecurity batters at me, chipping away at the confidence I've built over the years.

When I look into the crowd, my gaze snags on my younger brother Teddy, who sits two tables down with his suit jacket off and his tie askew. He gives me a cheesy thumbs up, trying to bolster my spirits. I send a shaky smile back.

After I clear my throat, I say, "Hello, everyone." The microphone lets out a high-pitched hiss of feedback. I readjust it and begin again, sounding unnaturally loud. "I'm Gwen, the daughter of the bride and also the maid of honor. Thank you all for joining my family and me today as we celebrate the marriage of my mother, Melinda, and Seth.

"As most of you already know, I have the best mother in the world. She puts her children first. Whether it was staying up late to help us finish a project for school or cuddling with us on the couch when we were sick, Mom was always there for us."

I pause, swallowing down the knot in my throat, anxious about the next part. I hadn't been sure how to address my father's death from colon cancer in this toast. If I should ignore it because it's too morbid or mention it as a way to honor him and to acknowledge all the hardships my family went through after he died. In the end, I included him. I still think of my dad every day and to leave him out had felt like a betrayal.

"After my father passed away, I worried that as much as she cared for us, my mom also needed someone to care for her. When she met Seth and fell in love with him, I knew I didn't have to be anxious about that any longer. She had found someone she could share her life with. Someone who loves her as much as she loves us."

I smile at Seth, my lips tight, and raise my glass to him.

He nods back at me, smiling pleasantly.

"Welcome to the family, Seth. Welcome also to his sister, Marjorie, and her family." I tip my glass toward the other side of the room, where Marjorie sits.

Marjorie beams, pleased to be the center of attention, just as I knew she would. I've only met Seth's sister a couple of times, but she struck me as shallow and pretentious. I figured she'd like having everyone's eyes on her and on the man sitting next to her, her son, mega-superstar Caleb Lawson. Her husband, Ben, sits meekly behind his wife and child.

"I'll end with a toast to my mother and Seth. I'm so happy that you found each other. Here's to a life filled with endless love. Cheers!"

I raise my glass high above my head and bring it to my lips, taking a sip of white wine. The alcohol washes away any remaining nerves.

Polite applause follows me back to my seat next to Mom.

She leans over and gives me a soft, perfumed kiss on the cheek. "That was wonderful, honey. Thank you."

I nod, knowing it's a compliment that she asked *me*, out of her three children, to give the speech. But really, I'm the obvious choice. Compared to my brothers, Brandon and Teddy, I'm the most stable. The most likely not to be overly stiff and formal like Brandon and not to be too informal and make inappropriate jokes like Teddy.

I glance at the place card in front of my mother's seat. It reads, *Mr. and Mrs. Peterson.* Now we don't even share a last name, my mother and me. It's official. She's moved on, and I'm still here. Stuck. Ever since her engagement, I worry that she'll keep moving on and leave me behind. That I'll lose her, too.

As best man, Caleb is up next to speak. His presence tonight has added an extra sense of excitement to the wedding. The guests have spent as much time gawking at his table as they have looking at the bride and groom.

The crowd hushes, watching him saunter up to the stage. Every eye is trained on him, reverent.

Most celebrities are disappointing when you see them in real life. You realize they aren't as tall as you expected or that they've been photoshopped on the magazine covers.

Not Caleb Lawson.

He's just as handsome in person as he is on the movie screen. He has every attractive feature you can think of: piercing blue eyes, chiseled cheekbones, a full pouty mouth. His hair is the color of sunshine. Like the hazy kind that warms your skin on a tropical beach. Not to mention the muscles. Good grief, those sculpted muscles.

It's all a bit ridiculous, really. That one person should get such a bounty of hotness. Not fair to the rest of us mere mortals.

Microphone in hand, Caleb smiles easily, brilliantly. His teeth are unnaturally white and straight. He's hard to look away from. Something shines out of him beyond his unbelievable good looks. You can see it on the screen when he acts, and it's even more apparent here, when he stands before us. A real-life flesh and blood star.

I'm not the only one who feels it. Women fan themselves in the crowd, and men sit up straighter, smoothing their hair over to the left, just like Caleb's.

I resist the urge to roll my eyes. I've never believed in the idea of celebrity adoration. As far as I'm concerned, movie stars put their pants on one leg at a time, same as the rest of us.

"Good evening, ladies and gentlemen," Caleb begins, voice low and husky. He pauses, runs his hand through his hair, and swallows. Then his smile widens, and he cracks a joke. "I know it's been an emotional day. The cake is already in tiers."

The crowd laughs uproariously, like he's on a stand-up comedy special.

Which he's not.

"My name is Caleb. Seth is my uncle and godfather. But he's more than that. Seth is my mentor, cheerleader, and conscience. I'm honored that he chose me to stand beside him on this momentous day. The day that he marries his best friend."

The guests all sigh out an "aww," and Caleb glances around the room, smiling sweetly, as if their response is unexpected and charming.

I scoff internally, not understanding why I'm the only one who sees it. That every word out of Caleb's mouth, every quirk of his eyebrow, every gesture of his long-fingered hand is calculated to bring out the most emotional reaction from his audience.

The man is a multi-award-winning actor, for Christ's sakes. Standing in front of a crowd, selling a story, acting. This is what he was raised to do since he was five years old.

Caleb continues. "Preparing this speech has gotten me thinking a lot about love. True love. What does it look like? What does it feel like? Now, I'm obviously no expert, as the tabloids have shown repeatedly." He lets out a small, self-deprecating laugh, and the crowd laughs along with him.

"After some thought, what I came up with is that true love is when someone loves you, even on the days that they don't like you. It's when someone is willing to stand by your side when you are on the top of the world and when the world has crushed you under its heel."

"It's someone who will be there with you for the big things—weddings, birthdays, funerals—and the small things too, taking out the trash, remembering if you prefer tea or coffee. Someone who will take care of you when you are sick or when your feelings are hurt. Someone to kiss away all those casual cruelties that happen in everyday life. Someone who shines a light into your darkness, and you do the same for them. That's what I think about when I say true love."

"Almost a year ago, when Seth first told me that he had found true love, I'm going to be honest with you, I was skeptical. I mean, the man is in his late forties and has never been married. Talk about a red flag!"

More laughter.

"But once I saw them together, Seth and Melinda. Once I saw the way they complement each other's personalities. Well, I don't need to tell you all, because it's apparent from the way they look at each other."

He gestures over at Mom and Seth, his eyes shining, like maybe, just maybe, he might shed a tear.

But he doesn't.

"This, ladies and gentlemen," pausing dramatically, he says. "*This* is true love, and I'm so incredibly grateful that my uncle has found it. May we all be so lucky. Cheers to the happy couple."

The room swells with applause, so loud that it makes the polite clapping I received seem pathetic by comparison.

Caleb grins widely, basking in his moment of glory, before he drains the last of the amber liquor in his glass and struts back to his parents.

The toasts complete, the DJ strikes up some lively music and couples make their way onto the dance floor. Mom and Seth go with them.

I return to Jenny at her table. "It's not fair," I gripe to her. "How am I supposed to compete with Caleb Freaking Lawson? Of course, he's going to give a better toast than I am. He probably had one of his screenwriter friends compose the entire speech for him."

I flop into the seat next to her, looking out the window at the cloudless summer sky. This close to the ocean, the Los Angeles smog gets swept away by the breeze off the water. Palm trees sway outside, teased by that same wind.

Jenny's not listening, too busy staring past me, her eyes wide. "He's coming over here," she says in a breathy whisper, her voice so strangled that I glance over to confirm she's still breathing.

She is. Just barely.

I lift my gaze to the man that has her so excited.

Sure enough, Caleb is walking straight toward us, his eyes fixed on me.

He marches to our table, then stays there, looming over us. I met him briefly before the ceremony, so he knows who I am, but he hasn't spoken with Jenny yet. I make quick introductions.

When he shakes my best friend's hand, she stares up at him unblinking, her mouth hanging open, awestruck. "H—h, h—i, hi. Hello. Hey," Jenny stutters out. I can practically see her brain melting into a puddle of goo. She holds onto his hand for an uncomfortably long time.

My gaze moves to the doors of the ballroom, where two burly men stand with their hands clasped in front of them. Caleb's bodyguards. Seth had warned us they would be here tonight.

I wonder what it's like to be famous, to never truly be alone. I can't imagine it's very pleasant, but it's all that Caleb has ever known. He must be used to it. Who knows? He probably likes it.

The bodyguards watch Jenny's interaction with Caleb closely. As she refuses to let go of his hand, they start to inch toward us. I'm about to warn Jenny when Caleb gently extracts himself from her grip.

"It's nice to meet you," he says smoothly. Then he turns to me. "My mom said I should ask you to dance, seeing how we're family now."

I raise an eyebrow at his request. "Do you usually do what your mother tells you?"

His mouth twitches into a tiny smirk. "Most of the time. I've found it makes my life much easier." He shoves his hands into his pockets, slouching casually, striking a pose like a model on the runway at fashion week. I can't decide if he does that on purpose or if he's truly unaware.

"Well, you can tell her that you asked and I declined," I say primly.

His laugh is startling in its loudness. He squeezes his eyes shut and throws his head back, exposing the long column of his neck, with all of its smooth tan skin. He laughs like I said something hilarious.

I glare at him, annoyed. I wasn't trying to be funny.

The laugh settles down to a chuckle. "That's cute. You obviously haven't spent much time with my mom if you think that's going to satisfy her."

He holds his hand out to me, letting it hang in the air between us, waiting for me to take it.

I don't.

His smirk widens, like he's enjoying the challenge I'm giving him. "I'm going to stand here until you say yes, so you might as well give in."

I hate giving in.

"Look, our moms are united against us." Caleb nods his head toward the other side of the room.

I follow the motion, and, sure enough, my mom stands next to Marjorie. They're staring openly at us. My mom's giving me a pointed glare. I can almost hear her voice in my ear, telling me to "behave."

Fine.

It's her wedding day.

I won't ruin it by making a scene. I take Caleb's hand and rise from my seat.

Leaving an envious Jenny behind, we go to the dance floor. It's a slow song, one that's been on the radio a lot recently.

Caleb tilts his head, listening. "I like this song." He sighs, as if the music pleases him.

He pulls me into him, guiding my arms up around his neck and placing his hands on my waist. I have to rise onto my toes to reach his height. His touch is warm, hot even. Which is weird because a shiver runs through my body at that moment.

We sway together, no fancy dance moves. Caleb is easy to dance with. He leads with expertise, gliding past the other dancers with a firm hand that slides from my waist to the small of my back, drawing me closer. He smells like a mixture of expensive alcohol, scotch or bourbon, and even more expensive cologne, with an undertone of something spicy. Cinnamon, maybe?

After a minute, he bends his head down, so I can hear him over the music. "I heard you're a doctor. That's impressive. Congratulations." He takes a deep inhalation and breathes it back out, tickling my ear.

"Thanks." I readjust my hands around his neck, loosening my fingers and then retightening them for a better grip.

In the past ten years, I've only seen a handful of movies. I've been too busy studying for medical school. But I did see one of his movies. It was a summer blockbuster. I don't fully remember the plot, just that he was a detective and there were a lot of exciting car chases and explosions.

A specific scene stood out to me. It's where he's pulling himself out of the pool. Water pouring off chiseled abs and down his perfect body...

"I heard you're an actor," I say, pretending like I wasn't just picturing his movie...and his body.

He nods, then chuckles darkly when he realizes I won't congratulate him the way he did me.

There's a beat of silence, which he fills by saying, "The ceremony was nice."

"Mmm. Yes. Lovely," I murmur absently, my mind returning to my dad. I wonder what my parents' wedding day was like. What songs were played? It was back in the 1990s, so probably some horrible grunge music. Did they dance together like this, my mother and father?

Caleb must sense my distraction. He pulls apart, just a little, and stares down at me with a quizzical expression, like he's searching for the things I'm not saying.

Up this close, his eyes are aqua blue. Such an unusual color that I search for the rim of contacts, wondering which parts of him are real and which are fake. No contacts that I can see. I squirm slightly, uncomfortable with his scrutiny.

"That was an excellent performance you gave earlier." Without warning, he spins me out away from him. Our arms stretch out taut between us, and then he twitches his wrist and I come back to him, spinning like a top. I crash into his hard chest as he pulls me close.

"Excuse me?" My eyes snap up to his, taking a moment to focus since I'm dizzy from all that twirling.

"The toast you gave. You're a good actress."

I bristle, offended. "That wasn't a performance. Those words were heartfelt and honest." I pull farther away from Caleb, reestablishing the space between us.

"Riiight," he says, making it sound like he means the exact opposite. Like he doesn't believe me. "You can't fool an actor, you know. I can tell you aren't thrilled about your mom marrying my uncle. Is it because you enjoyed having her all to yourself?"

What. The. Heck.

The audacity of this guy.

"First of all, I've never had my mom to myself. I'm the middle child. I always had to share her with my brothers and my dad. And then, after my dad died, I shared her with her work. I don't know what you're talking about, but if I did have any reservations about this wedding, it would have nothing to do with Seth."

I don't understand why I continue. I should stop my rant right there, but the words keep pouring out of me, like they're tired of being bottled up all night. "It's just hard to see her move on. Thirty years ago, my parents said forever in their wedding vows. My dad believed it, but it turned out that his forever was a lot shorter than Mom's, and that makes me sad."

To my horror, there's a prickling in the corners of my eyes, as tears gather there. I look to the ground, hiding them. Caleb's hand is under my chin, lifting it. We're not dancing anymore. Just standing still, staring at each other in the middle of the dance floor.

He's a talented actor, but the sympathy and remorse on his face as he gazes down at me looks awfully sincere. It spears me, the way he's looking at me right now. Like he *sees* me.

"I'm sorry. I'm a jerk," he says plainly, like it's a universal truth.

Which, for some reason, makes me laugh, because my emotions are all over the place tonight. Because in all the ways I imagined this wedding going, Caleb Lawson apologizing to me and saying he's a jerk wasn't one of them.

It's the first time I've laughed in a long, long while, and it leaves me feeling lighter. Like all my worries are bubbles in a champagne glass, rising to the top to burst and float away into the night.

"Whatever." I roll my eyes at him. "It's fine."

The song ends, as if it thinks we've said enough, and we pull apart.

"Well." There's a hint of awkwardness. "Thanks for the dance." He gives me the tiniest bow.

"Yeah. See you around." I don't know why I say that. He's a busy man. I'll probably never see him again.

We go our separate ways.

I very deliberately don't think about Caleb Lawson again for the rest of the night. And I'm sure he doesn't think about me either.

NEW MOON

1

SIX MONTHS LATER, NEW YORK

The hospital is the most depressing place to spend a holiday. Of course, it's worse for the patients who are sick and hurt, but it's almost as bad for the staff.

As a medical student, and now as a resident in the Emergency Room, I've spent countless holidays working in the hospital. The last two Christmases, last New Year's Eve, and today, Thanksgiving.

We try to make the best of it. There's a huge potluck dinner in the break-room. A smorgasbord of sliced turkey, stuffing, and store-bought pumpkin pie.

It's not the same.

I comfort myself, remembering that I just have to make it through this evening. One last shift here at my Manhattan hospital before my big one-month academic sabbatical, when I get to travel home to my mom's house in Los Angeles. I will finally spend Christmas with my family and work on the research paper I'm hoping to publish in the spring.

I can do it. A few more hours.

The automatic double doors that lead out to the ambulance bay slide open, letting in a flurry of snow and a stretcher with a thin woman strapped on it. She's unconscious, the EMTs working on her frantically. I run to her, my stethoscope banging against my shoulder with each step. Trampled snow-flakes melt into puddles under our feet.

The next few hours go by in a blur. There's a five-year-old with a ruptured appendix, a mother who burned herself pulling the turkey out of the oven, and, the craziest patient of all, a mall Santa Claus who's having a heart attack. Thanksgiving isn't even over yet, but already the Santas are out.

At around nine p.m., I get my twenty-minute dinner break. I rush to the doctor's lounge and make a FaceTime call to my family. My mom picks up on the first ring, like she was sitting there with the phone in her hands, waiting for me.

"Gwen! Happy Thanksgiving." She pushes her blonde hair, the same color as mine but shorter and with more curl, out of her face. Her voice is happy, relaxed. It still gets me to hear her this way, rather than the stressed clipped tone she had in the years after my father died, back when the money was tight and grief was thick around all of us.

"Hey, Mom. Happy Thanksgiving. How's it going?"

"Good, honey, but I miss you." A small pucker between her brows. Mom lifts her hand to the screen, almost like she wants to touch me through it.

"How's Pip doing with all those people in the house?" I ask about our tiny, timid Chihuahua. Pip is our nickname for her, short for Pipsqueak.

Mom laughs. "You know Pip. She spends most of her time cowering under the sofa."

We smile at each other, warmth and affection reaching through our phone screens. The moment is interrupted by the sound of a jackhammer in the background. Mom winces.

"How's the construction going?" I ask, then add, "I still can't believe you paid extra for them to work on Thanksgiving day."

The house that Mom and Seth bought together after they got married is a 1950s two-story bungalow in the suburbs of West L.A. I had been ecstatic when they got it because it's in the same neighborhood that my best friend, Jenny, lives in. Unfortunately, after they moved in, they discovered asbestos, a deadly material used to insulate older homes in the walls and ceilings.

This led to a whole-house gutting to remedy the situation. For a couple of months, they lived in a hotel because it was too dangerous to return home.

That part of the renovation is complete, and they have moved back in. Now they are in the phase where the house has to be rebuilt, including replacement of the outdated plumbing and electrical lines.

Seth and Mom had focused first on getting the master bedroom, kitchen, and living room into shape in time for Thanksgiving. The remainder of the house is still in shambles, forcing the rest of our family to stay at a nearby hotel.

Mom grimaces. "I know. I feel awful, asking them to work on a holiday, but we simply have to get this project finished. It's taking longer than expected since a lot of materials were on back order. Some bad news. We've been pushing the workers, but your room isn't finished." Her face falls in disappointment. "I'm so sorry, honey. I was hoping it would be ready. I even dug out the boxes that hold your old things so I could unpack for you and put up some of your posters on the walls, but it will have to wait."

"It's all right, Mom. No big deal."

"It *is* a big deal. I want this house to be like home to you, Gwen. I want you always to feel welcome here."

I nod, unable to tell her that there is only one house I'll ever consider my *real* home. It's the one that I grew up in. The one we had to sell in those dark days after my dad passed away.

In the kitchen now, Mom places her phone on the counter, leaning it against the wall, then steps back so I have a view of the entire room.

The kitchen has white cabinets surrounding a large island. A round table is off to the side, occupied by a partially finished jigsaw puzzle. It's a family tradition. We complete a new puzzle over each holiday break. From what I can see of it, this one looks like a complicated ocean scene, with lots of blue pieces scattered around.

The house is open concept. The kitchen flows into the family room, where a plush sofa, dusted with dog hair, sits in front of the TV.

My younger brother, Teddy, is sprawled out on the couch watching football.

"Hey, Teddy Bear," I call out over the phone and get back a grunt. He's in his freshman year at the University of Michigan, where he works as an RA in the dorms.

Marjorie and Ben sit in chairs next to the couch. They call out a chorus of hellos, which I answer back. Seeing Marjorie stirs an unpleasant sensation in my stomach. I remember how smug she looked the last time I saw her, sitting next to Caleb at the wedding.

My stepdad, Seth, walks into the kitchen. It's been six months since he married my mom, but whenever I see him, I get that old twinge of resentment. It's not fair to him. He's a great guy, but his presence is a constant reminder that life has changed in ways I still can't accept.

Mom worries about us and our lack of bonding. I can tell. When I came home for a short visit in August, she arranged little tasks for Seth and me to complete, like she's in HR and we're two employees whom she needs to work together. No matter what team-building activities she threw at us, we couldn't move past the stage of forced conversation.

Liv, my pretty sister-in-law, who I adore, is in the kitchen checking on something in the oven. My seven-year-old twin nieces, Brandon's and Liv's kids, Maddie and Megan, run through the house shrieking.

Seeing them all together makes me even more lonely. I wish I was there with them. I know exactly how the evening will go. Later tonight they will have Thanksgiving dinner, turkey paired with the quiet conversation of the adults as they catch up with each other. Dinner rolls eaten until there's only one remaining, which the twins will fight over. Left-over stuffing scraped into the dog bowl. After they finish eating, they'll work on the puzzle.

I'm going to miss out on all of it. The dinner. The puzzle. The warm hugs from my nieces and slobbery dog kisses.

It's okay, though. I'm flying home tomorrow. I won't see most of the family. They will all leave to go back to school and work, but at least I'll spend time with Mom and Seth. And everyone will be back together in just a month when we celebrate Christmas.

The pager at my hip vibrates at the same time that my phone, sitting on the table in front of me, pings. I check the messages.

"Hey, guys?" I say to my family. "I have to go in a minute. They need me back in the ER."

With my phone in my hands, I stand up and pull on my long white lab coat, its pockets gapping open, weighed down with my stethoscope, pens, and notebooks.

Mom comes into view, bending closer. There's worry in her brown eyes, a tightening around her mouth that I know all too well.

"Mom? What's going on?"

My stepfather walks up behind, placing a comforting hand on her shoulder. She glances back at him. A look passes between Seth and my mom. A silent conversation is occurring, only understood by the two of them. She presses her lips together, clearly apprehensive.

"I need to talk to you about something, honey," she says hesitantly. "Seth and I…we'll be moving to Japan for a little while."

"Japan?" I echo, reaching out blindly for a chair and falling into it.

"Seth has an amazing opportunity to head up a department there. They're doing some cutting-edge software development, and it's a big honor to be a part of it. We just found out about it a few days ago. I wanted to make sure it was really going to happen before I told you."

"You're moving?" The room is closing in around me.

"It won't be a permanent move. We'll keep this house and rent it out once the renovations are done. They think Seth's project could take one to two years. Then we would come back." Each word comes out faster and faster as Mom tries to explain.

"What about your job? What about us?" I think of my brothers and myself. The sting of betrayal hits when I see Brandon and Teddy in the living room staring at me with sympathy. They don't seem surprised by this news, which means they already knew. Why was I the last to find out?

Mom comes closer to the screen, blotting out the rest of my family. In her best soothing voice, she says. "They have an international school there. They've been searching for a math teacher like me. When we reached out, they were ecstatic. I've already got a job lined up."

Mom places her hand on top of Seth's and smiles at him. A look so intimate it makes me glance away. Her voice is choked, full of emotion. "It's almost like fate, how easily everything fell into place."

She sends a fond gaze to my brothers. "As for you kids, you don't really need me here anymore."

"*I* still need you." I sniffle, my throat tightening, hating this idea of my mom leaving me. Moving not just across the country, but across the world.

I've already lost Dad.

First with the marriage to Seth and now with this move, I fear even more that I'm losing my mother. The situation raises so many questions. Who will I have left now? Who will take care of me? Who can I take care of if all my family has moved on?

She smiles gently. "But you don't need me, honey. You've all moved out and started your adult lives. It's been a hard adjustment for me, too. Watching you grow." Mom takes in a shuddering breath, and her smile wavers. "When I'm in Japan, I'll miss you. I already miss you, but I'll just be a plane ride away. It's not like we won't see each other."

I want to tell her it's not that simple. That the airplane ride between New York and Japan is a whole lot longer than the one between New York and California. But how can I tell her that when, for the last two years, I didn't even make it home for Christmas? Do I expect her to just sit there and wait for me or my brothers on the off chance that we need her?

I rein in my desire to be selfish. To demand she stay here for me. Even though every fiber of my being hates this idea, I nod my head, still sniffling. "Japan sounds cool. I've always wanted to visit there."

There's relief in her eyes.

"When do you leave?"

"That's the thing, honey. What I need to talk to you about. We leave tomorrow."

2

omorrow!" I exclaim so loudly that the other doctors in the lounge lift their heads and stare over at me. "What do you mean? Tomorrow? I'm coming home tomorrow."

She speaks to me in a soothing tone, the one she would use when I was little, before I went to the pediatrician to get a shot. "I know, and I'm so sorry, but the project starts immediately. They want us to leave as soon as possible."

"There's more to tell you. We have to ask you for a huge favor. You're already set to come here, and we desperately need someone to watch over the work being done on the house. Not that you actually have to do anything with the construction. A foreman is on site who monitors everything. It's just that we're supposed to have a member of the family living here for liability purposes. Do you think you could do that? House sit for us? I know it's a lot."

I'm silent, stunned.

Mom is flustered by my obvious shock, rushing in to say, "If it's too much, I totally understand. I can stay back for a while, let Seth go to Japan without me. I'll just tell the school that I can't start yet. I—"

"No," I interrupt, my voice firm. There's no way I'll be responsible for keeping Mom from Seth. They've been inseparable since they got married. It's like Mom wants to spend every minute with her new husband, maybe to make up for all the time she missed out on with my dad.

"It's fine. You go, and I'll stay."

Mom looks skeptical, so I tell her, "*Really.* It'll be okay. I can watch your house by myself. It might even be better that way. I'll be able to focus on getting my research notes in order and write my article."

I don't believe what I'm saying, but if I show any misgivings Mom will feel too guilty to leave. She'll stay home with me and be miserable.

"What does this mean for Christmas, though? Are you coming back for that?"

Eyes glassy, Mom sadly shakes her head. "I'm sorry, honey, but I don't think so. We'll be too busy settling into our new place by then."

"What about everyone else? Is *anyone* coming home for Christmas?"

A heavy, awkward silence descends. On the verge of tears, Mom says. "No. There's no room for anyone here as long as the house is under construction. No one wants to get hotel rooms again. Brandon and Liv will go to Liv's parents with the girls."

This can't be right. We can't all be separated for yet another Christmas. It's been brutal starting a new life in Manhattan, battling against the rigor of residency along with missing my family. The anticipation of going home is the only thing that's gotten me through these past few months.

I raise my voice into the speaker. "How about you, Teddy? Do you want to come spend Christmas with me at Mom and Seth's house? We can have a sleepover like we used to when you were little. Spread out blankets on the floor."

Teddy sits up straight and scrubs his hand over his face, a gesture he makes when he's uncomfortable. "I can't. I got picked as the RA who has to stay in the dorms for winter break. You know, for the kids who don't go home. I'm sorry, Sissy."

He must really feel bad about it to use my old nickname. The one from when he was a toddler and couldn't pronounce Gwen. That name pulls on my heartstrings every time, reminding me of when he was a tow-headed little boy with cracker crumbs on his face and skinned knees. Those days seem so long ago.

I sigh, defeated. "Can you at least leave Pip, so I won't be totally alone? I'll send her back to you after Christmas."

"Of course, Pip can stay. We were debating what to do with her anyway." Mom still looks teary-eyed. "We'll all FaceTime together on Christmas, so it won't be like you're totally alone."

Everyone nods, and I nod along with them.

"Yes. That'll be fine." Forcing a smile, I lie and say, "Don't worry. It's going to be a great Christmas."

3

CALIFORNIA

Jenny picked me up at the airport. When I saw her waiting for me on the sidewalk with a sign in her hands, posterboard with glitter paint that read, "Welcome Home BFF," I dropped my bag at my feet, threw myself into her arms, and burst into tears.

Now, Jenny and I sit in my mother and Seth's empty house, sipping eggnog and working on the puzzle while I grumble to her. "I still can't believe they left me alone for Christmas. And what about next year? Where will we meet if Mom and Seth are still in Japan? At Brandon and Liv's place? Liv is great, but not really the Martha Stewart type. I can't imagine her hosting everyone for the holidays. Mom's the glue that holds us together."

"I'm sorry." Jenny's gaze is full of sympathy. "I know how much you were looking forward to being home. Are you sure you can't come with me and my family to Hawaii for Christmas? My parents would love to have you."

I sigh, simultaneously grateful for the offer and regretful that I can't take her up on it. "It's not an option for me to be gone that long. The construction crew is taking off Christmas day, but they'll be working every other day that week. Seth promised a bonus if they finish on time."

I already feel a little better, having poured out all of my fears and frustrations to Jenny. As usual, she understood exactly when to stay quiet and when to talk. Just being with her felt like my homecoming wasn't totally in vain. At least one person had been waiting for me.

We've been best friends since sixth grade, when she moved to California. Visually, we couldn't look more different. Jenny is tall and curvy while I'm short and slim. She has smooth dark skin, inherited from her parents, who immigrated from Nigeria when she was a baby. My skin is pale and lightly freckled, prone to flush and sunburn easily. Her eyes are brown like the center of a sunflower, while mine are such a light blue that they're almost translucent.

No matter how dissimilar we look, in my heart Jenny and I are one and the same. We like the same corny horror movies, romance novels, and boy bands. We like spending time just the two of us rather than in a large group, although if I was forced to choose, I'd say that she's the more outgoing one.

The only thing we disagree on is school. I always liked science while she was drawn to English and literature. At UCLA, where we went to college, I did biology as my premed major and Jenny studied journalism.

When I started medical school at USC, she had gotten a job as an intern at the *Los Angeles Times,* her dream newspaper. Even though she's been at it for four years, she still mostly fetches coffee for reporters and does research for them, but someday she wants to be an investigative journalist.

Another swallow of eggnog and then I refocus on the puzzle before me. My family hadn't made much headway on it before they all had to leave. It's only about 10 percent complete.

"Five thousand pieces might have been a bit ambitious," I gripe, scanning the nearly identical pieces spread out on the table and noting how every piece is the same shade of blue.

Pip lays in my lap, her body light as a hollow-boned bird. I can't stop petting her. My hand rubs from her forehead down to her feet. I scratch behind her ears, under her chin, and over her belly. She's in dog heaven, her tail thumping like a metronome against my thigh. I've missed her so much.

"I don't think this puzzle is so bad," says Jenny cheerfully.

She's crazy. For the past forty minutes, I've been working on a shark with rows of pointy teeth. "Hand me that one by your elbow," I tell her, gesturing to a puzzle piece that looks promising.

"What happened with that editor? The mean guy?" I ask as I fit together a portion of the shark's tail. When she doesn't answer immediately, I look over.

She's twirling a strand of her dark curly hair around her finger. I know that hair trick means she's nervous.

"Jenny? Is that editor still giving you a hard time?" I repeat, trying to get her attention.

It's been awful, being away from her, but we've talked on the phone almost every day, even if it's just for a few minutes while I change my scrubs or walk the short three blocks from my apartment to the hospital. At least I'm caught up with what's going on in her life.

"Yeah," she admits, looking my way. "He's still bossing me around. Yesterday, I pitched this idea to cover the jazz festival down in San Diego. Next thing I know, he's talking about it in our section meeting like it's his idea. There's nothing I can do, though. He's the senior editor of the entertainment section."

She taps her chin with a slim finger, musing. "You know, he kind of reminds me of Jax. They have the same curly dark hair…" Her mouth snaps shut, and her eyes cut over to me.

I bend my head to the puzzle and grind my teeth. Hearing my ex-fiancé's name knocks the wind out of me. Usually, Jenny is careful not to mention him. We have an unspoken agreement to pretend he never existed.

"Sorry," Jenny murmurs, guilty about her slip of tongue.

"It's fine," I reassure her even though it's not fine because now I'm thinking about his eyes, and how they crinkle in the corners when he smiles.

"At least we have almost a month together before I go." She changes the subject and snaps a puzzle piece into place. "I don't leave for Hawaii until the last week of December. I just wish we could spend the entire holiday with each other."

She pouts, sad I can't join her. But maybe that's not the only thing she's upset about because then she says, "Too bad your mom and Seth had to go. I was kind of hoping your special *cousin* might come visit for Christmas."

I roll my eyes. "Sorry to disappoint you, but I think Caleb's off filming a movie somewhere. I'm sure he's way too busy with his jet-set lifestyle to swing by."

Jenny scoots her chair closer to mine and lowers her voice to a whisper. "Did you hear about him and Lola Monroe?"

"Who's Lola Monroe?" I whisper back, not sure why we're whispering in an empty house. Okay, not really empty. The sound of hammering rings out, reminding me of the construction workers, but it's not like they can hear us.

Jenny's eyes widen like she can't believe I'm such a dunce. "Lola is the biggest, newest, most gorgeous actress in Hollywood. Come on, Gwen, you have to know about her. Six feet of pure hotness. She's on that new hit series, the one about the lady Formula One race car driver. It's on Netflix."

"Never heard of it or her."

Jenny looks scandalized by my admission. "Well, she and Caleb have been an item since he did a cameo appearance on the show. The tabloids have pictures of them draped all over each other in clubs, at parties, everywhere. They even walked the red carpet together at a charity event." She looks at me expectantly.

"This is important why exactly?" I ask, still not getting it.

"Because they broke up. It was on the radio this morning. Word is that she dumped him. How can you not know that?"

"Why should I? I don't follow celebrity gossip. Remember, we only met him that one time, at the wedding. And honestly, once was more than enough." I move the puzzle pieces in front of me, shuffling them around, hoping to finish off my shark.

Jenny carries on like she didn't hear me. "I bet she broke up with him because of that car crash a few months ago. He destroyed his Porsche on Pacific Coast Highway, right by the ocean. TMZ made it sound like he was drunk or on drugs or something, although he didn't get a DUI. The headline of the article was 'Lawson gets in trouble with the law.' Isn't that catchy?" The reporter in Jenny loves a good headline.

She scrolls through her phone and holds it out so I can see the photograph.

It's a harrowing image. All of the surroundings dissolve into the inky blackness of night. The asphalt is slick, darkened with rain. Shards of glass lay glittering in the road. Temporary lights have been set up on tall tripods to illuminate the car in the middle of the scene.

If you can call it a car anymore. I'm guessing it used to be a red sports car, but now it looks like it's been attacked and wrenched open by a wild beast. All that's left is a twisted heap of metal with jagged spikes rising out of the mess.

A sour twist of nausea in my stomach. I'm transported back to my shifts in the ER as I watch the car crash victims roll in on stretchers, their blood staining the cheap hospital sheets. I don't see how anyone could have walked away from a wreck like that.

"What do you think, Gwen?" Jenny asks. "He does drink sometimes, like at your mom's wedding, although he didn't seem drunk that night."

I tease her, "Oh, I'm sure you know exactly how much alcohol Caleb had at the wedding. You probably counted how many sips it took him to finish each one since you stared at him all night long."

Jenny doesn't argue. She really did stare at Caleb that entire evening. At least until he had to leave early. Marjorie had made sure to brag about how he was flying back to New York because he had an interview on Good Morning America the next day.

Jenny taps a finger against her lips, still fixated on Caleb, as she muses out loud. "I just wonder what happened. Why did he crash his car?"

The shark is almost complete. I sift through the pieces, on the hunt for the last portion of its dorsal fin, as I declare, "I don't know or care why Caleb Lawson does any of the things he does."

Any response Jenny was going to make is lost because I found the missing piece of my shark. With gusto, I slam it into place with my fist and cry out, "Done!"

4

A young Drew Barrymore holds a white telephone in one hand and a butcher knife in the other when the masked murderer grabs her from behind. She screams as he plunges a knife deep into her chest. Red blossoms, staining her sweater. *Blood.*

I jump, clutching my own chest, frightened even though I've seen the opening sequence of the first Scream movie at least a dozen times. I'm in the master bedroom, snuggled in Mom and Seth's enormous king-sized bed with its plush comforter and goose-down pillows. It's a far cry from the old futon I use as both a sofa and bed in my tiny Manhattan studio.

The bedroom is dark. The only light comes from the television and from the window, where occasional flashes of lightning illuminate the room. There's a storm outside. The wind wails along the eaves, and rain hammers angrily against the windowpane, demanding to be let in.

It's the perfect night to watch a scary movie.

With a shiver, I pull the covers up to my neck. On the TV, the parents of the murdered teen discover her body hanging from a tree. I shovel popcorn into my mouth and chew slowly, eyes glued to the grisly sight.

Pip circles three times beside me and curls into a furry ball. She's asleep before I am, snoring softly. I must pass out right after her, still trying to make up my sleep deficit from all those long ER shifts, because when I open my eyes the closing credits are rolling.

Blinking groggily, I wonder what woke me. Why am I suddenly, jarringly, wide awake? Staring into the darkness with my heart pounding like I've just run a mile.

I'm scared.

The clock by the bed reads 3:27 a.m. That's when I hear it. The thing that must have woken me. A sound from downstairs. There's a loud crash followed by a deep masculine voice cursing incoherently, like the man tripped over something metal. Maybe the pile of paint cans by the front door?

Someone is in the house with me.

An intruder.

My heart leaps into my throat, thumping under my jaw. I'm not just scared now, I'm terrified. With a start, I realize how stupid I am. My phone is downstairs, charging on the kitchen counter. Sometimes the hospital accidentally calls me, even when I'm off shift, so I don't leave it by my bed. This means I'm trapped alone in a house with a home invader between me and my phone.

No way to call 911.

No way to get help.

A million scenarios run through my mind and in most of them I end up dead. What if he has a knife? A gun? Is he going to rob me? Kill me?

I glance down at the still-sleeping Pip.

Not much of a guard dog, that's for sure.

Stealthily, I slide out of bed and tiptoe to the slightly open bedroom door. Pressing my ear to the crack, I hear the sound of cupboards being flung open and slammed shut.

The thief is ransacking the house.

I'm angry. An uncharacteristic deep rage washes over me as the need to protect my family floods my system. How dare he? What awful criminal breaks into someone's house and steals from them? My mom has had enough hardship in her life. I can't call her tomorrow and tell her that all of her valuables have been stolen. I won't put her through yet another trauma.

A steely determination grips me. I won't sit here and hide like some little mouse. I'm going to stop this intruder, get to my phone, and call the police.

I will *not* be the victim tonight.

Slowly, I ease the door open further and creep out into the hall. I remember a large wrench, red with rust stains, that a worker left in the hallway bathroom. Padding to that room, I grab it, liking the heft of it in my hands. The cool metal warms quickly to my touch.

Easing through each step, I creep down the stairs. In my old home I had known every loose, creaky floorboard, but I haven't spent as much time in this house, so I make my way gingerly. The last thing I want is to give the intruder warning before I strike.

Large wet shoe prints, slowly drying, lead from the front door to the kitchen. Judging by their size, the man must be huge.

I swallow thickly.

On the bottom stair, I see his shadow. It looks like there's only one culprit. I peek around the corner. He's in the kitchen, searching through the cupboards and drawers, with his back to me.

My stomach tightens in fear. I grip the wrench tighter, my palms sweaty.

Without warning, I leap into the kitchen, raise my arms above my head, and, using all my weight, swing the wrench at his head. I bring it down like it's a baseball bat and I'm going for the winning home run.

There's a loud thwack. The man drops heavily to the floor. He ends up with his head out of sight, hidden behind the kitchen island.

At that moment, a piercing whistle rings through the house, so startling that I drop the wrench. It lands with a clatter on the tile floor. I clap my hands over my ears and look around, trying to find out where the noise is coming from. It's painfully loud, wailing on and on.

My eyes land on the source of that terrible sound. It's a tea kettle, sitting on the stovetop with steam rising in a twisting white ribbon from its spout. Behind it on the counter sits a mug with a tea bag in it.

That's…weird.

I don't know a lot about criminals, but I doubt they make a cup of tea while they rob a place.

My gaze falls to the damp sneakered feet and the jean-clad legs of the intruder.

Slowly, I edge my way around the island to see who I've knocked out. Inch by inch, the man comes into view, starting from his legs and moving up.

Dark wash jeans accentuate a narrow waist.

A gray t-shirt that's ridden up, exposing a slice of tanned and toned six-pack abs.

Large hands with their fingers lightly curled.

Corded forearms that lead to broad shoulders.

A strong jaw, stubble coated with fair hair that glints in the kitchen lights.

Full pouty lips.

A straight nose.

Golden hair, turning darker from the thin trickle of blood that stains his hairline and runs down past his closed eyes to his razor-sharp cheekbones.

That's when I realize who I just knocked unconscious.

It's Caleb.

Caleb Freaking Lawson.

5

gasp, my hands flying up to my cheeks.

Uh oh.

I just assaulted America's favorite movie star.

Before I can fully freak out, I slip into doctor mode. Dropping to my knees next to him, I slide my fingers under his jaw, searching for a pulse.

It's there. His heartbeat is strong and steady.

Thank goodness.

Next, my hands move up to his head, palpating the goose egg that's swelling from where I hit him. As I lean closer to inspect the cut, some detached part of my brain notices that he smells nice. That spicy smell I noticed at the wedding, like cinnamon mixed with a hint of nutmeg.

Caleb wakes as I prod his wound, his breath becoming a hiss of pain sucked in through his teeth. He raises a hand and pushes my arm away.

"Wha…" A single aqua blue eye cracks open to gaze at me blearily. "Wh— what happened?"

Air gusts out of me in a sigh of relief.

He probably has a concussion, but I still don't know how bad.

I sink back onto my heels, watching closely. "What's your name?"

"Huh?" The other eye opens. His forehead wrinkles, obviously confused. "Gwen, it's me. Caleb. We've met before?" He's looking at me like I'm the one who got bonked on the head.

It's totally inappropriate, not the right moment at all, but a little part

41

of me, fourteen-year-old me, does a mental fist pump in the air and thinks, *Caleb Freaking Lawson just said my name for the first time ever.*

Fourteen-year-old me is so dumb. Twenty-eight-year-old me is *way* smarter. She chastises her younger self. *Who cares if he knows your name?*

I play it cool, waving my hands dismissively. "Yeah, I know. This is an exam. I'm trying to figure out if you're neurologically intact."

Those wrinkles in his forehead deepen. "I'm...what?"

"Neurologically intact. If your brain is working right. I need to ask you a series of questions. What year is it?"

His face screws up like I've asked him something hard. "2023?"

"Are you asking me or telling me?"

"Telling you, I guess."

I nod once, inspecting his pupils to make sure they're the same size.

Caleb tries to sit up, but I push him back. I'm not done yet.

"How many fingers am I holding up?" I put up two fingers, like I'm making a peace sign.

Caleb peers at them. "Two."

"Where do you live?"

He hesitates, "Um...everywhere?"

Okay, maybe that's a bad question for someone who travels so much.

I try again. "What city are you in now?"

"L.A." His gaze is clearing.

Good. So, just a mild concussion. I didn't give him permanent brain damage.

He touches his scalp. When he brings blood-stained fingers to his face, his eyes go wide. "What?" He struggles to sit up, and this time I let him. Hooking an arm around his shoulder, I haul him into a sitting position.

"What happened?" he asks.

"I hit you."

Caleb's brow furrows. "Hit me? Why?" He touches his head again and grits his teeth against the pain. "With what?"

"I thought you were a robber breaking into the house. I hit you," I wince as I say it, "with a wrench."

His voice rises in alarm. "A wrench!"

"Yeah." I bite my lip. "About that...Sorry."

Confusion hardens into outrage. "I can't believe you hit me." He clasps his head, blood seeping through his fingers. "Is this how you treat all of your house guests?"

"House guest," I scoff, adrenaline still pumping through my veins. The aftermath of fear leaves me shaky, ready to lash out. "More like a midnight murderer. Who the heck breaks into someone's house in the middle of the night like this?"

"Uncle Seth gave me a key. He said I could come anytime."

He's bleeding more briskly now that he's sitting. I jump up and grab a handful of paper towels off the counter. Crushing them into a ball, I knock his hand aside and press the wad of towels against the gash, using my other hand braced on the back of his head to hold him in place. His hair is silky soft against my palm.

"To most people, anytime means daytime. Not 3:00 a.m." I hurl an outraged glare at him.

"Well, excuse me. I just got off a flight from Paris, so I'm not exactly sure what time it is." He's all sarcasm and anger, like he has the right to be offended.

I press harder, putting pressure on the wound to stop the bleeding. I mimic his snark, matching it with my own. "We can't all be world travelers like you, but there is this new invention, it's called a clock. They even put it on the front of your phone for extra convenience. Maybe you should try looking at it next time. You know, before you break into a house in the middle of the night and scare the bejesus out of someone."

His face flushes red to match the blood that stains the paper towel. Furious, slowly enunciating each word, he grits out, "I didn't break in. I told you Uncle Seth gave me the key."

Annoyed, I press harder.

"Ouch." Caleb grabs my arm as if he wants to pull me away. He doesn't, though, just holds his position. His hand is so big that it completely encircles my wrist, his thumb and middle finger overlapping.

We sit in silence like that for a few minutes. Him on the floor and me kneeling next to him.

The quiet gives me time to calm down. "Don't you know? Seth and my mom are gone. They left for Japan yesterday."

"What?" His head jerks back, and I chase it with the paper towels. "I didn't know that. Why didn't anyone tell me?"

A bitter laugh leaks out of me. "Don't feel too bad. I just found out about it two days ago. It was all very quick. I'm staying here for the next month to watch the house and make sure the construction goes to plan."

"That's awfully nice of you."

I shrug. "I was supposed to be here anyway. There's this big research paper I've been working on. I've got time off from the hospital to finish it. I already have all the data gathered. I just need to do some analysis and write it up."

"I figured Uncle Seth would be here for Christmas." His shoulders droop. "Hoped we could spend it together." There's something young and wistful, almost boyish, about how he says the last part.

"Well," I tell him. "Sorry to disappoint, but the only Christmas gift you're getting in this house is me."

I ease the pressure on his head, and his hand drops from my wrist. Peeling the paper towel away slowly, I examine the cut. The bleeding has slowed enough to see the wound now. It's a deep, jagged laceration in the hair above his forehead, about three inches long, still oozing slightly.

"How's it feeling?" I ask, more quietly. "Does it hurt?"

"It feels like you hit me with a wrench." He pouts, sullen.

Okay. I deserve that.

One more peek at his wound. "I have good news, and I have bad news. The good news is that the bleeding has almost stopped. The bad news is that you need stitches."

Caleb lunges backward, shaking his head from side to side. "No. No. I'm not going to the hospital. Absolutely *not*."

I raise my hands, placating. "I'm sorry, but you have to. The cut is too deep. It won't close on its own."

He is adamant. "Nope. No. Nopity-nope."

"Nopity-nope." I laugh. "Is that even a word?"

"I don't care if it's a word or not. All words mean the same thing. The answer is no."

"Why not?"

"Because that's why I'm here. I'm hiding." Shadows flit over his face. A haunted look, or maybe hunted.

"Hiding?" I repeat as I take the bloody paper towels, stand up, and throw them in the trash. "Hiding from what?"

"Not from what. From who."

"From whom, you mean," I correct before I can stop myself.

Great, I'm the grammar police now. Way to go, Gwen.

Caleb raises a single eyebrow at me, a gesture that I've seen him do in movies and on magazine covers. He's known for that quirk of his right eyebrow. It's so famous that a cast member on Saturday Night Live has mastered it, mimicking it perfectly so he can spoof Caleb on the show. Now, he's using that single eyebrow against me while he sits blood stained on my mother's kitchen floor.

The absurdity of our situation hits me, but not enough for my eyes to stop tracing the arch of that stupidly perfect brow.

"Sorry." With effort, I pull my gaze away. "Who are you hiding from?"

"Everyone. The fans. The paparazzi." He sighs, eyes downcast. "They've been all over me recently. It's suffocating."

I wonder if he's referring to those tabloids Jenny was telling me about. The ones reporting on his recent breakup. His car crash.

Caleb continues, "This house is perfect, don't you see? With Seth gone. They'll never look for me here. Even my parents and PR team won't know where I'm at."

I lean against the kitchen counter, gazing down at him. The corner of the cool granite digs into my hip. "I thought you people loved that? All the adoration from the fans. The flashing cameras of the paparazzi. Any publicity is good publicity. That kind of thing."

"You people?" His mouth turns down, hard. I've offended him.

"You people, like famous movie star people. That's what I mean." I thought my explanation might help, but it doesn't. His frown deepens, and I almost feel bad about it.

I hate making anyone unhappy.

To make up for it, I offer him something precious. Something I usually reserve only for my immediate family and Jenny.

I offer him free medical treatment.

"I can sew it up for you." I gesture at his head. "If you want, I have suture in my suitcase upstairs. I even have some numbing medicine."

I always travel with it, ever since Jenny sliced open her foot when we were on spring break in Mexico last year. I had kicked myself so hard for not having it when I had to take her to a shady-looking urgent care that would only accept cash.

I watched them stitch her up, the suture lines uneven and the knots loose. It had taken all of my restraint not to elbow that doctor out of the way so I could do it myself. In the end, I had made so many suggestions and criticisms that the staff asked me to wait out in the hall until he was done.

My offer of free sutures does the trick. Caleb's frown disappears, replaced by something hopeful. "You can? That would be great."

Upstairs I fetch sterile gloves, a suture kit, and scissors out of my toiletries bag.

When I come back down, Caleb has moved to a chair at the kitchen table where he's staring at the puzzle with a perplexed expression. He looks up when I walk in. "This thing is a nightmare. Every piece is the same color of blue."

"That's exactly what I said!" I exclaim, feeling vindicated that someone else agrees with me.

I press a square alcohol pad against his skin to disinfect the cut. It must sting, but Caleb is stoic, barely flinching as I apply it to the wound.

It's oddly intimate, how I'm leaning in with my face so close to his. His breath ghosts over my cheek. A spicy warm breeze. I gently brush the hair off his forehead and out of my way. I wonder how many other women have touched him like this, felt these velvety strands run through their fingers. Wonder how many have kissed those full lips. Probably a lot. He is famous, after all.

Caleb holds still as a statue, with only his eyes moving. He watches me closely as I focus on his injury. When I shift my gaze to his, he stares at me unblinking with those ocean eyes for so long that it grows uncomfortable. Heat rises from my chest to my cheeks, staining them.

Stop staring and start suturing, I scold myself.

"This is going to hurt, just a little." I plunge the needle holding lidocaine into his scalp and inject tiny bits at a time, moving around to cover the whole area.

He stops looking at me and squeezes his eyes shut. A muscle ticks in his clenched jaw.

Once the skin is numb, I say, "There, the worst part is over."

He's gripping his seat, knuckles white.

"The rest is easy," I reassure him as I take the suture out of its packaging. The curved silver needle gleams in the overhead lights. Nerves get to me when I bring it to his forehead. I think about how his face is his living. About how it should be some high-powered plastic surgeon working on someone as famous as Caleb.

Not me.

Sensing my hesitation, Caleb opens his eyes and peers at me. He speaks softly, encouraging me. "It's okay. You've got this."

I nod, blow out my breath, and push the needle deep into his skin.

He starts to sway, looking woozy.

I pause, holding the suture steady. "Caleb? You all right? Just take some big breaths for me."

He makes a weird wheezing noise, his lashes fluttering and his gaze distant.

Uh oh.

"Caleb—"

"Yes ma'am, I'll have the fries," he slurs as his eyes roll until only the whites show.

In slow motion, Caleb slumps sideways off the chair. His arm flails out and sweeps the puzzle off the table. Sea-blue pieces fall with him as he tumbles to the floor, hitting the back of his head with a loud thump on the tiles.

He's unconscious. *Again.*

6

sew up the cut while he's passed out in a litter of puzzle pieces, not even trying to wake him. I figure it's better this way, with him motionless and unaware. Better for him to not have the memory of each stitch. Better for me to not have the pressure of his eyes on me while I work.

Suturing is my favorite medical procedure. I find it soothing. The repetitive dip and rise of the needle as it flows through the skin. Then, at the end, when I pull the thread tight and tie it off into a perfect square knot, there's something very satisfying about that moment, watching the laceration close like I'm zipping it shut. Seeing it disappear. It's magic with me as the magician.

As I work, I shake my head, thinking about all those movies where Caleb played the macho tough guy. The mobster. The cowboy. The superhero. How ironic that one stitch has him fainting.

Just goes to show, you can't believe everything you see on the screen. The real Caleb is obviously a different person from the roles he plays. It makes me wonder about what the true Caleb is like. The man behind the mask of fame.

Once I'm done closing his wound, I reach around to feel the swelling on the back of his head. There's a golf-ball–sized lump from where he fell the second time. It's going to hurt when he wakes up.

I rouse Caleb enough to move him over to the fluffy rug that lies in front of the sofa. He crawls over and flops onto his back, closing his eyes. "So tired," he mumbles. Before I can get him up on the couch, he's asleep, sprawled out on the floor, limbs spreading in every direction like a human starfish.

As I stand over him, I worry that he's tired because of his head injury, but then again, it could be because it's almost dawn. The light in the room is changing, first to gray and now to a rosy, yellow pink.

What should I do? I'm exhausted. My mother's bed is calling, but if Caleb has a concussion I should stay and monitor him. Make sure he doesn't wake up vomiting or slip into too deep of a sleep.

Resigned, I gather some blankets and pillows. Placing a pillow under Caleb's head and then one next to him, I lie down. The room has a chill to it, so I pull the blanket up to cover both of us. I roll onto my side, facing away from him, and close my eyes, falling quickly asleep.

It's a nice, dreamless sleep until it's interrupted by someone screaming.

7

My eyes fly open to find Jenny standing over us, her hands clamped over her mouth in an effort to contain the loud squeal that just erupted from it.

"Jenny!" I clutch the covers to my chest, my heart racing. "You scared me so badly. I—"

"OHMYGOD! You're sleeping with Caleb Lawson."

"Shhh," I shush her, getting up from the floor. A quick glance shows Caleb is asleep and, thankfully, still alive.

I grab Jenny by the elbow and lead her away before she wakes him. Quickly, I drag her up the stairs to the master bedroom. "I'm not sleeping with him," I hiss, maybe a little too vehemently. "I'm sleeping *next* to him."

I'm not in the best mood, having been woken abruptly twice now.

Her eyes are wide. "But what's he doing here?"

"Not totally sure," I admit. "He showed up in the middle of the night saying something about hiding. I kind of hit him," I wince, embarrassed to say it out loud, "with a wrench on the head and knocked him out."

"What?!" Jenny's voice rises in a near shriek.

I shush her again. "Yeah. It was a crazy night. Anyway, what are you doing here? How'd you get in?"

"We're supposed to go to Butt Camp, remember? I knocked and knocked. You didn't answer, so I used the key under the flowerpot. You know, the emergency one."

"Oh! With all the excitement, I totally forgot." Whenever I'm in town, Jenny likes to drag me to every bizarre workout she can find. The one she's referring to now is a boot camp workout. As a joke, we call it Butt Camp because when we are done our butts always hurt. It's basically torture with farm equipment. We do a lot of pushing around tractor tires and lifting bales of hay. I hate it, but Jenny adores it, so I go for her sake.

"Sorry. I don't think I have it in me to work out today. After being up half the night dealing with Caleb, I'm dead on my feet."

She smirks. "There's only one excuse I would accept from you to miss Butt Camp, and it's hanging out with Caleb Lawson." I grimace, which makes her laugh, and then she adds, "I wish you had kissed him, though."

"Yeah, right. Like that would ever happen." I roll my eyes at her fondly, ignoring the memory of how soft Caleb's hair felt against my palm.

"A girl can dream," she counters.

"My only dream right now is to go back to sleep."

"Okay, I can take a hint. I'll leave you to it." Jenny leans forward and wraps me in her signature so-tight-it's-almost-painful hug. It's perfect.

"We're still going to baby goat yoga on Wednesday, right?" she asks.

"That's a real thing? I thought you were joking when you told me about it on the phone."

"Of course it's real. You'll love it. All these adorable baby goats walking on you while you do yoga. It's relaxing." Jenny looks at me, her cheerful expression shifting into one full of concern. "You need that, Gwen. You're so stressed all the time. So serious. I know it's a lot, your job in the hospital. I know how hard you worked to get there. How you had to be so responsible, always studying, but those days are over. You made it."

"Hardly," I interrupt. "I still have two more years of residency to finish."

"I get that, but you know what I mean. It'll be good for you to get out. Do a little goat yoga and lighten up."

She means no harm. She only wants the best for me, but unknowingly she's hit a nerve. Someone else once called me too serious. Right before he broke my heart.

Maybe he had a point, and maybe she does, too.

Now that I've achieved my biggest goal of getting into an ER residency, I've had this dissatisfied feeling. I've found myself staring into my mirror lately, wondering if this is it. Is this all I am? All I'll ever be? Just serious, sensible, dependable Gwen?

That sounds so boring. I've always colored in the lines. After my dad died, *any* risk terrified me. I wouldn't even go on a roller coaster, too busy thinking of what it would do to my mom and brothers if an accident happened and the coaster went off the track.

But recently, I've been yearning for something more. To become unrestrained, let myself live more fully. For so many years, I focused on staying safe and accomplishing my goals. Spent all my time in the library studying, watching out the window while my friends had picnics together on the quad below. Helping them pick out dresses for parties I couldn't go to because I had an organic chemistry test the next day. Hearing about their adventures over the phone as I sat in my dorm room with a book in my hand.

I love being a doctor, but sometimes I feel like I missed out. It's left me a little lost, like I'm not entirely sure who I am or who I want to be.

As she turns to leave, I stop her. "Hey, Jenny, let's keep this between us. About Caleb being here. I'm not sure what's going on with him, but I suppose everyone deserves a safe place to crash. So don't tell anyone else. Okay?"

Jenny draws her fingers across her mouth in a "my lips are sealed" gesture. Then she pretends to turn the lock and throw away the key. That old motion, left over from our teenage years when I would make her swear to keep all my secrets, makes me smile. Of course, my secrets back then were that I had a crush on Tyler Hamilton or that I got a B in pre-algebra.

This secret is bigger, a grown-up secret. If I can trust anyone, it's my best friend.

8

sleep in the master bedroom until noon, surprising even myself. I can't recall the last time I slept in that late. Pip stays with me, tucked into my side.

When I wake, I make a quick phone call to Mom, checking in with her. Her voice has a slight echo to it, accentuated by the long distance. "Thanks again for watching the house while we're gone, honey. You don't know what a relief it is, knowing that you're there. There's no one I trust more. You're always so responsible. It's like how much you helped me when your dad passed. How you took care of Teddy while I worked."

Usually her praise would warm me, fill up all my empty spaces. But today it hits differently. The flavor of it tastes dull in my mouth. Sensible and responsible is an ugly echo of what Jenny said earlier. It sounds lackluster to me now. Not how I want to be described.

I don't tell her about Caleb and that he's staying here. It's not a conscious decision. I'm not trying to lie. It's more like I don't want to disappoint or worry her. I doubt she'd be too happy about me being alone in the house with a man I barely know, even if he is Seth's nephew. I don't want her to rush back here, thinking she has to chaperone us.

After I end my call, I go downstairs to find the puzzle pieces back on the table. Caleb must have picked them up off the floor. My eyes drift over to where he slouches on the couch, in the same wrinkled clothing from the night before. His hair is messy, and his cheek is stubbled.

Even disheveled, he's still handsome.

He's so focused on reading the book in his hands that he doesn't notice me. I give a start when I see the cover, recognizing it immediately. It's an old, battered copy of *Twilight* by Stephenie Meyer.

My book.

I know that crumpled cover and the coffee stain on the front. I remember how Jax spilled during a late-night study session. "Where'd you get that?" I ask, my voice sharp.

Caleb startles. "Oh, hi," he says when he sees me. "It was in a box over there." He points to a corner of the living room, where cardboard boxes are stacked neatly on top of one another.

I go to investigate. In the highest box, the one that's partially open, I see a bunch of my stuff. A random assortment of mementos left over from elementary school all the way to medical school. I hadn't known Mom kept so many of my old things. A golden tassel from my college graduation cap lies draped over a microbiology test. I smile at the A+ circled in red at the top.

There's the first-place ribbon from the science fair that I won in seventh grade. My father had been so proud of me that day. He'd called me his little genius. Said I was going to change the world. Make it a better place. Sometimes I wonder if anyone will ever have that kind of faith in me again, or if he was the only one who could sense the potential in me.

A set of watercolor paints rests in the corner of the box. I crack open its lid to find the small circles of paint so dried out that they have cracks across them, jagged lines that radiate out like the parched ground of the desert. I must have been in a purple mood when I last used them. That color is all gone, but there's lots of brown, blue, and green left over.

Back in junior high and early high school, before my dad died, I chose art as my elective. I had looked forward to that period, with its paint-spattered tables and the smell of turpentine. The painter part of my brain is already calculating which colors I would mix together to mimic the vivid aqua blue of Caleb's eyes.

I stop thinking about paint when I notice the clear plastic box buried deep beneath a pile of loose paper and other awards. It holds a carefully preserved corsage. Pink roses, now faded to brown, surrounded by fragile babies' breath pinned to a silver wristband.

I take out the box and crack it open. A whiff of rose scent, dulled with age, puffs out. The bitter sting of regret hits the back of my throat. The image of Jax slipping that elastic band over my wrist before prom overlaps with him slipping the diamond ring onto my left finger. There's a doubling of time, the flash of a camera on both occasions, as Mom took our picture, capturing those moments when I smiled up into his crinkled brown eyes.

"Are you turned on by men who glitter?" Caleb interrupts my sad memories.

"I'm sorry. What?" I shake my head, momentarily confused. The corsage goes back in the box, and I turn to find him observing me carefully.

He holds up the book. "The vampires in this novel—they sparkle in the sun."

Oh. Yeah, now I remember. The thought of a shiny vampire makes me smile. "Why?" I tease. "Are you planning on getting into my make-up?"

He makes a surprised noise, like that's not what he expected me to say, and then snorts with laughter. At that sound, a slow cat-like satisfaction curls up my spine. It's probably unwise to enjoy making him laugh like that.

Too much pressure.

The laughter fades quickly into his morose look. He sighs as if the burst of happiness took too much out of him and starts reading again.

I take in his appearance, cataloging the changes I see since Mom and Seth's wedding. This isn't the Caleb I met before. That confident, cocky Caleb is gone. Purple shadows lie like bruises under his eyes. He's lost weight, his muscles less bulging. Those cheekbones are so sharp they would slice open my hand if I dared to touch him.

"Last night you said you were hiding," I say, wondering what's responsible for this new Caleb. "What's going on?"

He shrugs, artificially nonchalant. "Not much. I fired my agent, canceled my upcoming projects, and mute all incoming phone calls." He doesn't even look up from the book he's reading.

Alrighty, then.

"You should try muting your cell phone." He gives a dismissive glance at my phone lying on the end table next to him. "It's liberating not to be tied to that thing anymore."

And miss texting with Jenny every five minutes? I don't think so.

As if on cue, Jenny's name lights up my screen. Her text message pops up. *What's he doing now?* I leap across the couch, almost landing in Caleb's lap, muting the phone before he can read what she wrote.

"No thanks. I'll keep my phone on." I slide it into the back pocket of my jeans as I eye him. "How's your head feeling?"

"Hurts." He sends me an accusatory glare.

I screw up my face, wrinkling my nose against a stab of guilt. "Sorry. I feel bad I hit you." It only takes a couple of steps to cross the room and move closer to him. "Now that you know Seth's in Japan, what's your plan?"

Caleb's still looking at his, or rather *my*, book when he answers. "Like I told you last night, I'm going to stay here as long as I can," he says with complete confidence. Finally, he raises his head to look at me. "I've got a couple of changes of clothing." He points to a small duffle bag I didn't notice before. "I'll have to do laundry, but I should be fine." A condescending smirk and then a wink before he returns to his reading.

Excuse me? Did he seriously just wink and then dismiss me?

I wait for him to say something more, to acknowledge that these plans involve me, since I'm also living in this house and I'm definitely *not* leaving. The way I see it, *I'm* the landlord and *he's* the squatter.

Caleb doesn't look up, though, borderline ignoring me.

It's extremely irritating.

"Oh-kay." I draw the word out. "What about me?"

Squinting, his gaze travels back to me, the book falling to settle against his broad chest. "What about you?"

"I'm living here too, you know. How are we supposed to share this space? With all the construction, it's tiny."

Only the kitchen, living room, master bedroom, and its bathroom are fully renovated. The rest of the house lies under huge sheets of semi-translucent plastic tarps, so thick I can barely hear the distant sound of hammering and the buzz of power tools. The plastic tarps are taped from the ceiling to the floor, cordoning off the other rooms from us like we've been exposed to an alien life form and are under quarantine. Any moment now, scientists in scary yellow hazmat suits should enter to examine us. That's how the house looks.

"Easy. I'll sleep on the couch, and you take upstairs." He answers like he's got it all figured out, which I highly doubt.

"How about the bathroom? You can only get to it by walking through the master bedroom."

This makes him pause. I resist the urge to say, "Told you so."

"I suppose we'll have to take turns in the bathroom." Caleb's trying to work it out in his mind. I can practically see the gears turning. Next thing I know, he'll come up with a shower schedule and then a chore chart. He lifts one shoulder and looks back to his book. "You doctor types are pretty efficient, anyway, so it shouldn't be an issue."

And now he's stereotyping me. Awesome.

Although, I guess I also did that a little last night. Stereotyped him.

I pinch the bridge of my nose and try again to voice my concerns. "I'm just not sure there's room for both of us. It is my *mom's* house."

He bristles, looking up. "It's my *uncle's* house, too." His hand comes up to run through his hair, tousling it and making it stick up all spiky.

We glare at each other, in a standoff, while I resist the urge to punch him.

It's Pip who breaks the tension. She ambles downstairs, taking each step slowly. She's my dad's dog, old now with white fur on her muzzle and her eyes cloudy. It hurts my heart to see the effects of time on her sweet face. When she wanders into the living room, she comes right over and greets us. Pip jumps up on the couch next to Caleb and gently sniffs his elbow, never quite touching her cold, wet nose to his skin.

Caleb reacts like a fire-breathing dragon had landed next to him. His eyes widen and nostrils flare. He scrambles backward on the couch away from her.

I call Pip over to me. She comes, tail wagging. I hoist her into my lap and let her lick my hand.

Caleb's lip curls, disgusted.

Guess he's not a dog person. Should've known. I've never trusted someone who doesn't like animals.

We ignore each other for the rest of the afternoon, with me working on my research at the kitchen table and Caleb reading on the couch. I assume he gives no more thought to our predicament. Probably he thinks that because he's famous he has a right to stay wherever he wants.

The pompous jerk.

By evening, my brain is fried. Tired of struggling through the complex statistics of my data, I set it aside and turn to the puzzle, focusing all my attention on it.

A hand enters my peripheral vision, making me jump. Caleb is leaning over my shoulder. He snaps a part of the puzzle into place. "There," he says with satisfaction, "the jellyfish is done."

He places a heavy hand on my shoulder, making it tingle, as he leans in farther to peer at my stack of research papers. "Yikes. That looks super-complicated." He inhales and then gives a sharp exhale, his breath stirring the hair on top of my head.

Then he's gone, moving into the kitchen. "I'm making a turkey sandwich for dinner. Want one?" He bends over, looking inside the refrigerator.

I try to ignore how fine his butt looks in that position.

It's not easy.

"Okay," I accept begrudgingly, wishing I could give him the silent treatment, but I'm not a good cook and a free meal is *way* too tempting.

He's in the kitchen for a long time, opening drawers and banging pots around. The sandwich he brings me looks gourmet, with soft white bread and thick-sliced tomatoes and lettuce peeking out of the sides.

My eyes close with the first taste. I bite back a moan. "Caleb, this is delicious." I lift the corner of the bread and peer inside. "What's this amazing sauce you put on it?"

"I made some garlic aioli. All the ingredients were in the fridge."

"From scratch? Where'd you learn to do that?" A sip of water washes down my next mouthful.

He shrugs, chewing his own sandwich slowly. After he swallows, he says, "There's a lot of downtime when you're shooting a movie. It takes a while for them to prepare for the upcoming scene or review the footage. During that time, I would hang out with the on-set caterers. I'd watch over their shoulders, get under foot. Eventually, they got used to me and showed me some tricks."

His eyes dip away from me, somewhat bashful. "I'm pretty good at it. Cooking."

Out of nowhere, he surprises me. "Don't worry. I won't be a total free-loader. If you grocery shop, I'll feed you. That's how I'll pay you for letting me be here."

So he *was* thinking about it.

I pause. There's something vulnerable about his offer. It's in the way he says it. Like he's trying to prove his worth to me. I understand that feeling. I recognize it. Because I feel that way too. All the time. Trying to prove that I'm good enough. Thinking that if I try hard enough, people will let me stay, that they won't keep leaving me.

Before I know it, I'm nodding my head, agreeing to this crazy plan. That's how I end up living with Caleb Freaking Lawson.

9

What's he doing now?

    Jenny's been texting me this question every hour on the hour. There's nothing new to report. It's been two days, and Caleb's spent most of the time on the couch. He gets up to eat and lays down to sleep, but that's about it.

Jenny texts me again. *You must have some interesting gossip for me. Pretty please?* I can practically hear her cajoling tone written all over the words. This is why she's a journalist. She loves knowing other people's business.

I pause, trying to come up with something juicy to give her.

I don't think he has the best relationship with his mom. I overheard them talking on the phone yesterday and it sounded strained, I text back.

My mind goes to that phone conversation. Caleb didn't hide it from me, keeping his phone on speaker while I sat, working on my research paper at the kitchen table.

You know his mom was his manager, right? From the time he was a little kid until he was a teenager, Jenny writes.

Ah, that makes sense, given how she had interrogated him. Even though he has professional managers now, on that phone call Marjorie had acted like it was still her job. She had grilled him about upcoming roles, contract negotiations, and collaboration opportunities.

Caleb answered her questions the way an angsty teenager would, with monosyllabic responses. Judging from what she said, Marjorie doesn't know about the…*ahem*…changes he's recently made to his career. I'm sure not going to be the one to tell her. I'd like to be in New York before that particular revelation hits.

Caleb had cut the phone call short, saying he had stuff to do, which was a lie because he went back to silently reading and munching on a gingerbread cookie that he had baked earlier.

"She doesn't know where you are? Your mom?" I asked him, wanting to confirm it, as I bit into my own cookie. It was delicious, soft and sweet.

"No, and I'd like to keep it that way." He gave me a slit-eyed stare as if I'd tattle on him.

"What about Seth? Did you tell him you're here?"

Caleb slumped deeper into the couch, his gaze darting left and right. "No, and I feel awful about it. Uncle Seth is one of the few people I trust. He's always stood up for me, but…" He hesitated. "I'm worried that if he knows, my mom will find out. She's good at getting everyone to spill their secrets, especially Seth. She can be very…persistent."

It hung there between us. If he's lying, then I need to hide the truth, too. This doesn't work otherwise. I already lied by omission the first day he was here, when I talked to Mom and didn't mention him, but would I continue to carry his secret? Should I?

Caleb watched me with wide, owlish eyes, waiting to see what I would decide.

"I won't say anything. To my mom or to Seth." I'm not sure why I agreed. I'm not usually a liar, especially to my family. But as much as he annoys me, there's something fragile about Caleb, something that makes me want to protect him.

His relief was palpable.

Other than that phone call, he's been pretty boring, I tell Jenny.

It's the truth. Besides that one rather heavy conversation, he isn't very communicative. He does small talk occasionally, but mostly he listens to music with his earbuds in or he reads. Already, he's made it through the first two Twilight books. He also scribbles in a black and white composition notebook that he stores underneath the couch.

"What's in there? What are you writing?" I've asked a couple of times, pointing at the notebook.

Whenever I bring it up, he gets a shifty, almost secretive expression. "Nothing."

"Come on. What's inside?" I stretch my neck, trying to peek over the top of the pages, but he jerks the book away. He holds it face down, tight to his chest, and glares at me.

He can look angry all he wants.

I'm not scared of Caleb Lawson.

"Tell me what it is," I badger him, almost enjoying the irritated way he narrows his eyes at me. He's fun to poke at, like a grumpy bear, and I'm bored, trapped in the house with this broody, uncommunicative man.

"Some notes. Flight times and other junk." Caleb relents and flashes the book at me, exposing it for a brief few seconds before ripping it away.

I get a glimpse of flight times written on one page, just like he said. The other page is covered by his hand, I think deliberately.

That's where he's hiding something. On that page.

Now I'm the one who's annoyed, but I let it go.

Caleb can keep his secrets.

10

'm at the box of memorabilia again. Sorting through it. Figuring out which parts of my past to keep and which to get rid of. I pick up the set of paints and stare at it, weighing it in my hand before putting it back down.

Grunting, I move the heavy cardboard box off the tall stack to access the one beneath it.

This next box is full of Christmas decorations. Mom probably got these out before she got the news about the transfer to Japan. Tinsel and garland tangle with a string of colorful lights. Plastic angels and snowflakes press together. A rosy-cheeked Santa Claus has a smattering of glitter in his hair.

Whoever packed this box must have been in a hurry. It's like they threw everything in here without thought, haphazard. I pull out the string of lights and untangle it from the garland. There's a complicated knot in the strand, where the bulbs have caught on one another. After several minutes of struggle, I still can't straighten them out.

Caleb has his earbuds in, jittering his leg and bobbing his head to whatever music he's listening to. When I walk over and tap him on the knee, he pulls the earphones out and looks at me questioningly.

"Here, make yourself useful." I toss one end of the lights at him. He's startled but catches the strand before it smacks him in the face.

"I need you to hold that part steady while I unwind this side," I instruct.

Begrudgingly, he holds tight, as I struggle to thread the wire through its snarled loops.

"Maybe we should decorate?" I muse out loud as I work. "There's a ton of stuff in this box. We could put it out. Make the house more festive." I look at him. "What do you think? Wouldn't that be nice?"

A shrug like he couldn't care less. "I guess so."

His apathetic routine is starting to grate on me. It's bad enough that I don't have my family here with me for the holiday, but now I have to spend my time with this Scrooge? I rub my fists into my eyes, feeling alone even though there's another person in the room. I had so looked forward to this vacation, but nothing is turning out the way I thought it would.

"What?" I demand, my voice cross. "Do you have something against Christmas, Mr. Grinch? Don't you put up lights and decorations at your place? Or are you too fancy for that? Let me guess, Christmas trees don't go with the minimalist chic aesthetic of your penthouse. Is that it?"

His anger matches mine. "You have a lot of preconceived notions about me."

"Like you don't have preconceived notions about me, too," I counter. "Let me guess, to you doctors are predictable and nerdy." I flinch internally, thinking this is exactly how I don't want to be described.

He crosses his arms over his chest, still managing to hold onto the lights. "I never said that."

"Yes, you did. That first night. You looked at my research papers and said they were boring."

"I did not!" His voice rises. "I said they looked complicated, not boring."

"Whatever. Stop changing the subject." I raise an eyebrow. "Am I right? *Do* you decorate for Christmas or *don't* you?"

"I don't." Before I can claim victory, he quickly adds, "Not because I don't want to, but because I'm never home for Christmas. I'm always traveling."

"Always?" I question, doubting. "Like every single year?"

"Always." He's firm. "I've never once been home for Christmas. Usually, I'm not even with my parents. They stay here in L.A. and celebrate without me."

Instantly, my anger evaporates. I cover my mouth with my hand. "Caleb! That's literally one of the saddest things I've ever heard."

He acts as if I've hit him with the wrench again, dropping the lights and bringing his hands up to ward off my sympathy. "Oh, no!" he exclaims. "Don't look at me like that."

"Like what?"

"Like you pity me. Just…stop it. Trust me, it's fine. I've spent Christmas in lots of cool places. On yachts. In airplanes. Once, I was in the Swiss Alps and it was snowing."

"That all sounds awful." I clutch my chest, remembering Thanksgiving, how lonely it had been, working in the hospital without my family.

It's like that for Caleb *all* the time.

His hands drop, and he gives me a strange look, like he really thought he could change my mind and now that he can't, he doesn't know what to do.

"Why?" he asks, his voice gruff. "What was your Christmas like?"

I brighten. Warm memories of my past Christmases flood me. "When my dad was alive, our Christmases were pure magic. He loved it even more than us kids. It was his special holiday." My eyes close as I picture it, all those perfect days. "My family would decorate the entire house together."

"Dad would string these lights," I hold up the ones in my hands, "along the eaves of our house. Mom would pace nervously below while he worked, worried he was going to fall off the ladder."

"As a family, we would go pick out a tree. The entire house smelled like pine. We put on this TV station every year. It had a picture of a yule log burning. We'd make hot chocolate with tiny white marshmallows."

I remember how, when I was little, I'd push those marshmallows down with my spoon, trying to submerge them, and be delighted when they would inevitably pop back up to the surface, where they would bob and float. That's how my family seemed in those days.

Unsinkable.

"After he died, Mom tried to keep the old traditions going. We all did, but it was never quite the same." I sigh, my joy deflating. "This year is the worst. Now it's just me. All alone." I drop my eyes to the bulbs in my lap, the corners of my mouth sinking down.

Caleb's voice sounds far away. I'm too wrapped up in my misery to fully process it when he says, "You're not alone."

"Huh?" I look up, wondering if I heard him correctly.

"I said you're not alone. I'm here." Grumpily, he concedes, "I guess we could put up *some* decorations."

My smile returns, sneaking back into the room like it's not sure if it should be there. I shake the string of lights, letting it unspool from my hands. While we were talking, I got the knots out.

His hand is up again, in a "stop" motion. "Just a few decorations," he amends, alarmed by my rising enthusiasm. "Not the whole box. And don't even think about asking me to get up on a ladder."

I don't pay attention to his words, too happy picturing our little space all cheery, full of Christmas joy. I clap my hands together excitedly. "Oh, Caleb, it's going to be so fun."

He looks doubtful.

I spring up and go to the box, leaning over until I almost fall in. As I dig through the items all the way down to the bottom, Caleb comes to stand behind me, bringing his cinnamon scent. It's from his toothpaste. I'd figured it out this morning when I saw the tube next to the sink in the bathroom. That's why he always smells so mouthwatering.

"Here's garland for the stairs." I pile the sparkly red material into his arms. "These snowmen figurines go on the mantle." I hand them over. "Oh! Look at this adorable bell Teddy made when he was in kindergarten." I add it to the stack.

By the time I'm done, Caleb's swaying, buried under an assortment of Christmas décor, only his eyes and the top of his head peeking out. I glance briefly at the cut in his hairline from where I hit him. It seems to be healing nicely, shouldn't leave much of a scar.

Working together, we wind the garland through the stair railing, passing it back and forth between each spindle. I decorate the kitchen countertops while he does the fireplace mantle.

Caleb finds Christmas music on his phone and plays it, the small speaker making it sound tinny and faint. Those old songs don't need to be heard clearly, though. I have them memorized with the many times I've listened to them over the years.

"Turn that up," I shout to him. Construction on the house continues, with a loud drilling noise coming from behind the plastic tarps.

Caleb cranks up the volume, and I hum along, doing a shimmy to Rocking Around the Christmas Tree. When I glance up, I see Caleb watching me, his lips tipping up into a bemused smirk.

"What?" I demand, hands on my hips.

He tries unsuccessfully to dampen that amused twitch of his mouth. "It's nothing."

At my insistent look, he lets out a deep breath. "It's just, you weren't kidding. You really do love Christmas."

"What's not to love? Everyone's together. There are presents. Yummy food and drinks." I spread my arms as wide as they will go and spin in a circle, waving to all the decorations we've put up. "Look at this place," I tell him. "It's merry and jolly and…and…" I struggle until I find the right word, "and happy."

Caleb takes a step back and lets his eyes slowly roam over the room, like he's trying to see it from my point of view. There's green and red everywhere. Little ceramic reindeer and white-haired Santas. Cotton balls stretched apart to make fake snow.

Finally, his attention returns to me. He stares at me with a focus that makes me self-conscious. "I suppose it does look like that, like happy," he says after a long pause. There's a flicker of light in his eyes that wasn't there before.

Just then, the doorbell rings, startling me. "Oops. I almost forgot. I'm going to the mall with Jenny."

"Have fun." Caleb waves distractedly as he moves back to the couch, picking up his book. The glimmer of light I had seen a moment before extinguishes like it never existed.

I'm putting on my sneakers when I wonder if he'll get lonely, in here by himself. "Do you want to come with us?"

"Oh please, no." He licks the tip of his finger in a way that catches my attention and holds it captive. Unblinking, I watch as he uses that dampened finger to turn the page of his book. There's a weird sensation in my lower belly, my stomach performing a slow flip-flop.

I avert my eyes, blushing and feeling stupid about it.

Breathe, Gwen, breathe. You are not *attracted to moody movie stars. That's not who you are.*

It's probably for the best that he's not tagging along. I'm clearly spending too much time with him if I find a wet fingertip so distracting. Besides, I can't imagine what a mess it would create, taking him to our tiny suburban mall. We wouldn't get past the entrance before a mob of fans would accost him.

The last thing I need to see is a bunch of women salivating over Caleb Freaking Lawson.

11

'm still thinking about that, picturing it in my mind, when Jenny and I sit down at the mall food court. Giant glittering snowflakes hang from the vaulted ceiling over our heads, drifting and spinning lazily. A fake Santa walks by, sipping iced coffee through a straw.

I dip my pepperoni pizza into a small cup of ranch dressing while Jenny twirls chow mein on her fork. "Do you think it would stink?" I ask her. "Being Caleb?"

She looks at me with wide brown eyes. "Are you kidding? It would be awesome being Caleb. Everyone loves him. He's rich, hot, and famous. What would stink about that?"

"Well, for one, he can't just stroll through the mall whenever he likes." I wave my pizza around, using its pointy tip to indicate the food court. "He can't pop in for an Orange Julius."

Jenny looks at our surroundings slowly, taking in the worn linoleum floors, overflowing trash cans, and sticky tables. "I'd give up this mall in a second if that meant I got to shop on Rodeo Drive like he does."

"That's the thing." I swallow a fizzy sip of Coke. "He can't do Rodeo Drive, either. The other day he told me some stylist buys all of his clothing, even his underwear."

I lean toward her and whisper sadly, "Do you know he's never had a real Christmas? Like never ever."

Jenny tilts her head and looks me over, all eagle-eyed. "Are you feeling sorry for him?" she asks suspiciously. "Because it's kind of ridiculous when celebrities cry and complain. Like, dude, a million people would happily trade places with you."

I sigh, frustrated because I'm not sure what I believe. I'm not even sure what I'm trying to say. "I get that, but I'm not convinced those people who want to trade really understand the situation they'd be getting into. That's all I'm saying. For all of its perks, his life also has a lot of limitations."

"Look at you," Jenny teases. "You were so determined not to care about him. You said you didn't even like him, remember? And now you're spending precious mall time worrying about Caleb Lawson."

"I'm *not* worrying about him," I mutter into the table. But she's right. I am worried about Caleb. That brooding man-boy who's crawled onto the living-room couch like a turtle into his shell. "He just doesn't seem very happy. Sometimes he is, but mostly he's not."

"Is there anything we can do? To help?" Classic Jenny, generous to a fault. That's why she's trying to get an investigative reporter job, so she can be a champion for the underdogs in the world. I picture her, hands on hips and a red cape flowing out behind.

I shake off a dollop of ranch before shoving the pizza into my mouth, mumbling around it as I chew. "He needs to get out of that house, at least for a little while."

Jenny props her head up with her hand. She's quiet, thinking. "Oh!" She sits up suddenly. "What about caroling tonight? My parents are both working so they won't be there, but we could go and take Caleb. It'll be just the three of us. We can wrap him up in a hat and scarves, so he won't be so recognizable. We could position him in the back row, away from the lights. What about that? It'll be fun."

Every year, people from Jenny's neighborhood, *my* neighborhood now, get together at the local park. The coordinators pass out Christmas sheet music to all the volunteers, and we stroll from house to house, singing carols. I always go with Jenny and her family. It's our tradition.

"Jenny," taking her hand and giving it a squeeze, "you're brilliant. It'll be performing, but not performing. Totally in his wheelhouse. It's perfect."

She squeezes my fingers back and dramatically flutters her eyelashes. "I *am* a bit of a genius," she brags.

"Yes, you are."

As I wipe my mouth with a napkin, my eyes scan the mall, searching through the holiday shopping crowd.

"You're looking for him, aren't you?" Jenny asks quietly.

Pretending not to understand, I respond, "Who?"

I should have known better. She's not fooled. "You know who." She sets her mouth in a thin line. "Jax, that's who."

"How'd you guess?"

Jenny gives me a knowing stare. "Because you're the most predictable person I've ever met."

Even though she's right and her words hold no venom, they still sting. I add her description of me to the one Mom talked about when I called her the other day. Dependable, responsible, and now predictable Gwen.

That's me. Yuck.

"Who knows if he's in town?" The memory of high-school Jax, god of Abercrombie good looks, grinning at me over his calculator, flashes through my mind. I blink that image away. "He's probably still in San Diego, teaching kindergarten. I'm not sure if they're out for winter break yet." I fold my dirty napkin into a square and then triangles.

A loud silence from my best friend. I look up and pin her with a stare. "Jenny?"

"Jax is home for Christmas," she admits reluctantly.

"How do you know?" I search the crowd in earnest now. As if my ex might suddenly appear. I'm usually good at not thinking about him, but whenever I'm here, when the possibility of seeing him becomes a reality, I can't stop looking.

It's not impossible, right? Maybe fate would throw him in my path again, except this time he would have broken up with Sophie. We could tell our children about how Mommy and Daddy would never have reconciled except for that day when Daddy was craving some frozen yogurt and decided to go to the mall. It would be our second "meet cute." Like in the romance novels I read. How the man and woman always meet in a cute way.

A better one, since I don't actually remember our first "meet cute." Jax had always just been there in the background of my life, ever since we were in the same preschool. Sure, I didn't speak with him until our senior year of high school, but I knew he was around. All those years, I kept him in my peripheral vision. Not daring to look at him directly.

Once I finally did talk to him, that had been it. Together for six years, engaged for one. I had believed it would last forever.

Stupid me.

"Sarah told me." Jenny answers my question. "Said he's been hanging out at Shooter's."

That's where I saw him the last time. Over two years ago, in that dump of a bar our classmates return to every holiday break. He had been sitting on a stool with a giggling Sophie in his lap. I had lasted all of five minutes as he whispered in her ear before I begged Jenny to leave.

"You've got to move on." Jenny uses her stern voice, bringing me back to the present.

"I have," I lie.

She looks like she wants to shake me. "You haven't. You've barely dated since you broke up, and the guys you've gone out with never get past a third date. It's been three years now. I know you don't always see it, but you're pretty, Gwen. I've seen a lot of guys check you out, but you ignore them."

"I've been a little busy, you know. Going to medical school and then getting into residency aren't easy. I had to do a lot of studying. You should remember. You were there for most of it." I cross my arms over my chest, defensive.

"Yeah, I do know. But somehow other people make time for romance. What about that girl across the hall from us? Back in the dorms? Diana, was that her name? She went on to medical school like you *and* had a steady boyfriend."

I don't bother telling Jenny that Diana was in an M.D.-Ph.D program yet still maintained a boyfriend. That information won't help my case.

Jenny's eyes bore into me. "You romanticize Jax. He wasn't as perfect in real life. Remember when your appendix ruptured and you were in the hospital for three days? He only came to visit you once."

This is a long-running argument. Jenny has never been a huge fan of Jax.

Even after all this time, even after his betrayal, I fall into my old role of defending him to her. "That's because he's squeamish. You know that."

I remember how I would tell Jax about a particularly interesting patient from the hospital, and he would ask me to stop because it made him queasy.

She's not done. "You're a doctor, Gwen. That's who you are. Didn't you worry that would be a problem? That he couldn't stand to be anywhere near a hospital? I'm just saying you put him on a pedestal he doesn't deserve. You use that false memory of him to keep other guys away."

"Okay. Okay, I get it," I grumble, wanting her to drop the subject. "Get over Jax. Love again. I'll be sure to add it to my list for Santa. I'll tell him the next time I sit on his lap."

don't want to," Caleb complains as I tug on his arm, trying unsuccessfully to pull him off the couch. "Why, Gwen? Why should I go caroling?"

That's the second time he's said my name. Not that I'm counting. There's just something nice about how he says it, about how his mouth rounds with the G and flattens out by the N.

G-w-e-N.

"You should go because it'll be good for you." I tug on an arm that feels like solid marble. Each muscle is defined beneath my hand, like it was carved with a chisel.

"You should go because you can't hide out in the living room forever." Another tug on his bicep. His skin is warm, hot actually. I have a flashback to the night of my mother's wedding when we danced. How his hands had slid from my waist to the small of my back, pressing me close.

"You should go because it's Christmas."

Tug and suddenly he's moving. Surging up from the couch to tower over me so fast that I fall backward, my arms windmilling, until he grabs my hand, sending a jolt of electricity up my arm. He holds on until I'm steady and then lets go. I stare at my hand, still buzzing from his touch, like it doesn't belong to my body. *What is wrong with me?*

"Well, it is Christmas, so I guess I have to," he says mildly. "Where are your scarves?"

Twenty minutes later, Caleb looks like a human snowman. A red knit cap sits low on his head, tugged down to obscure his famous eyebrows, and my mismatched midnight-blue scarf is wrapped around his neck, covering his chin. Brandon's old puffy jacket is too small for him, the fabric straining from all those muscles.

I step back, away from his delicious cinnamon scent, and purse my lips, surveying my handiwork. He's overdressed for the warm California winter, but it'll do. If you don't stare too closely, you won't recognize him. Only those aqua eyes give him away.

"How do I look?" He's been watching me, silent and still as a doll while I've dressed him.

"Meh." I put my hand out and seesaw it back and forth in a "so-so" gesture. "You look pretty average. Not great, but okay."

His smile is wide, the most pleased I've seen him so far. I should call him average more often. He seems to like it. Maybe if you've been called amazing your whole life, average starts to sound pretty good.

"Hmm," he hums. "Just okay, huh? I'll take it."

I pull away, about to walk out of the room, when, without touching me, Caleb leans forward, bringing his nose to my hair and inhaling deeply. I freeze, startled by his nearness, by the heat blasting off his body and how I can see the pulse in his neck, fluttering in time to his heartbeat.

"You smell nice," he murmurs in a low rumble that I feel all the way to my toes, "like strawberries."

Oh. That's what this is about. "It's my shampoo," My voice is breathy, weakened by his proximity.

"I know. I smelled the bottle in the shower."

There's a new awareness in me of how close Caleb is standing. He's still looking at me closely, like he's trying to read my mind. I grasp for words that will drown out the loud hammering of my heart. "We better get going," I finally say, overly cheerful. "Jenny's waiting."

Caleb nods once, and we go down the stairs.

The house is quiet now. The construction workers have gone home for the night. As we march downstairs, the silence makes Jenny's gasp of surprise at Caleb's ridiculous outfit even louder. Fortunately, Caleb hadn't been mad at me when I explained that Jenny knows he's here. I had reassured him over and over that she would keep his secret.

Pip sniffs around Caleb like she's never seen him before. He freezes and stares at the toy-sized dog with something like fear. I call her away from him, and Pip comes, trotting happily over to me.

Caleb flashes a grateful smile my way. The second smile I've seen from him today.

And that's when I realize what millions of adoring fans already know. That there's something special about Caleb Lawson when he smiles.

t's a warm, breezy night. I'm worried Caleb will overheat in all his winter gear, but he's not complaining. About thirty people meet up in the park across from our house. I greet neighbors and old friends that I know from having done this before with Jenny's family.

Several times as I move through the crowd, I glance up to see Caleb staring over at me. Which is to be expected, I guess, since I'm the person here that he knows best. When I catch his eye, I try to send him a reassuring smile, but he darts his gaze away like he didn't see me. I swear at one point, he even blushes when I catch him looking my way.

Whatever. Weirdo.

Jenny is talking to Caleb off to the side of the crowd. It makes me nervous, so I keep an eye on them while I mingle. I hope she's not telling him about how, when we were fourteen, she had a poster of him from *Teen Bop* magazine hanging on her bedroom wall.

I can still remember it. Back then, his left ear was pierced with a twinkling diamond stud. He's given up on the earring now, but I noticed the scar the other day when he leaned over to shove his notebook under the couch. A small dot of puckered skin, the single flaw on an otherwise flawless face.

He's only two years older than us, so that makes him sixteen in that poster. Only a teenager, but already oozing masculinity. Something about that bothers me now, how he was presented that way at such a young age. A product designed to sell magazines to impressionable girls.

That poster cheated us all. Made him a two-dimensional object. Made us believe that only perfect people deserve love and adoration.

Whatever Caleb and Jenny are talking about seems to be going okay. They look relaxed and casual. She hasn't fallen down at his feet to worship him, at least not yet.

The cheerful hum of conversation is interrupted when our neighbor and the organizer of this caroling event, Mr. Sanderson, stands up on a bench. He whistles loudly, getting our attention. We listen as his wife hands out sheet music.

"Howdy, folks. You all know the drill. We sing one song at each house, starting over on Myrtle Road and making our way to Elm Street. If we knock and they don't answer, we move on. No fuss. No muss. At the end, everyone is invited back to my place for hot chocolate." He raises his voice like a middle-aged, overweight cheerleader and yells, "Now, who wants to go spread some Christmas spirit?!"

A ragged whooping and cheering rises from our group. Even Caleb looks interested. En masse, we cross the street to approach the first house.

I hold back to let Jenny and Caleb catch up. "You ready for this?" I ask, grinning.

Jenny returns my smile as we stop at the large wooden door. I make sure Caleb is positioned in the back of the crowd, although I can't help that he's a foot taller than most of the people in front of us. He stays close to my side, his arm brushing mine.

At the first house there is a young mother, with her hair in a ponytail and tired eyes. A tiny baby sleeps, cradled in her arms. Moths circle lazily over her head, drawn to the light above the door. When she sees us filling up the walkway and spilling out onto the lawn, her eyes go wide.

Before we launch into song, Mr. Sanderson waves his hands over his head. "Song change. Song change, everybody. Let's sing Silent Night." We all look at each other in shock. This is unprecedented. Mr. Sanderson is a bit of a drill sergeant. He never changes the order of our songs.

It's not until the third line, when we sing the part about "round yon virgin, mother and child," that I see Mr. Sanderson's brilliance. Those words ring in the air as we serenade the mother and baby. It's such a tender moment. The young mom's eyes shine with tears. Several members of our group are openly crying.

A sniffle makes me turn my head, expecting soft-hearted Jenny to be sobbing. But it's not Jenny. It's Caleb. The scarf bobs as he chokes his emotions down. I nudge him with my elbow. He sends me a warning glare and whispers, "Not a single word." It would be intimidating, except that he has to break off his threat to swipe his hand quickly over his eyes.

I duck my head, letting my hair hang down to hide my smirk. My plan is working. Caleb is out of the house and interacting with the world. Mr. Moody Pants is experiencing actual authentic emotions, something that I'm guessing he doesn't get a lot of in Hollywood. I mentally congratulate myself for a job well done.

As we continue with Silent Night, I focus on Caleb beside me. He's regained control and joins the rest of us in song. Now that I single out his voice, I realize something astonishing. Caleb has an incredible singing voice. Not just good. Not just great, but absolutely amazing. It's better than anything I've heard on the radio or at a concert.

With each house we move to, Caleb grows louder and more confident. His voice is so strong that, halfway through the evening, more and more people are shooting looks over their shoulders, curious to know who sings so well.

On a front porch, where a father and his teenage daughter watch us, we start Joy to the World. By the last line, Caleb's voice carries over all of ours. He has a distinctive sound, husky and deep with huge range, hitting both high notes and low. Slowly, one by one, the rest of the carolers go silent and turn to watch him.

Caleb doesn't notice. He's lost in the moment, eyes closed and head back. The last line of the song lingers in the air like smoke when he opens his eyes and stares at all the admiring faces around him. Everyone applauds, hands clapping loudly. Caleb's scarf fell down while he sang, exposing his mouth. A shy, tentative smile grows there, along with another emotion that passes too quickly for me to define.

That's the exact moment when the teenage daughter shouts, "Hey! That's Caleb Lawson!"

14

The girl yells shrilly into her house, "Mandy! Get out here. Caleb Lawson is in our front yard!" Another teenage girl, this one slightly older, comes to the door. When she sees Caleb, she screams, clamping her hands over her cheeks. She looks at her sister and they both scream, jumping up and down while they hold each other's hands.

I expect Caleb to run. That's surely what I would have done, but he doesn't. Instead, he transforms from the broody grump of the past few days into the Caleb from my mother's wedding.

He slips his knit hat off, exposing hair that shines like spun gold in the moonlight. Holding his hand out and with an overly wide smile plastered on his face, he strides through the crowd toward the hysterical girls, who are now both crying and screaming. The carolers part for him like he's Moses and they're the Red Sea.

When he reaches the doorstep, he first shakes the bemused father's hand, giving it a firm pump. Then he turns his attention to the girls. Caleb bends down to their level. With his hands on his knees, he greets them, talking with a calm, soothing voice I've never heard before.

He moves slowly, reaching out and lightly hugging each girl. After they have calmed somewhat, there's a flurry of photographs and autographs. One sister has him sign her favorite shirt so she can "wear it everywhere, because nobody is going to believe you were at my house."

Eventually, once the girls have their slice of him, Caleb says good-bye and we continue on to finish the last of our caroling.

The evening is ruined, though. No one can seem to concentrate on singing anymore. They are too busy glancing back at Caleb or jockeying around each other, trying to get close to him as we walk between houses.

Songs fall flat, and our harmony is lost.

By the time we are done, the group is restless. When Mr. Sanderson asks Caleb if he's coming over for hot chocolate, Caleb shakes his head. "Thanks for the offer, sir, but I'm pretty tired. I think I'll just go on home." After he waves good-bye to the rest of the crew, he shoves his hands deep into his pockets, but not before I notice that they're trembling. He pivots and starts back toward our house.

Most people have moved on, already heading over to Sanderson's place for the post-caroling party. I pause, trapped between two choices. Stay or go.

It comes to me then, that flash of emotion on Caleb's face when he finished singing, right before he was recognized. I can name it now. That was the look of *hope*. A quick goodnight to Jenny and I run after him.

15

Caleb's almost at the house when I catch up. Wordlessly, he climbs the stairs to the front door, unwinding my scarf with each step.

Once we're inside, he goes to the refrigerator, takes out a beer, and holds it in his hand, staring dully at it. He must change his mind because he puts the drink back into the fridge and swings the door shut with a thump.

Caleb crosses to the couch where he flops down on his back with a loud sigh and closes his eyes, revealing delicate blue veins across each eyelid.

My gaze follows the length of his lashes, the line of his jaw, the bob of his Adam's apple, and something small stirs in my chest.

"I'm sorry," I say quietly. "That wasn't how I wanted it to go."

He keeps his eyes closed. "Don't be sorry. There's nothing to be sorry for." His voice carries a deep note of exhaustion. One that he kept hidden when he was smiling and flashing cheesy peace signs for all those photographs.

He's so silent and still that I wonder for a minute if he's fallen asleep, but then I notice his fingers twitching, lightly rubbing the yarn of my scarf between his thumb and index finger. He's upset, and I don't like how he's hiding it from me. I also don't like how much it bothers me to see him unhappy.

An idea forms. "Wait right there," I tell Caleb, an unnecessary statement since it seems like he plans to never leave the couch again. I run from the room and bound up the stairs toward the master bedroom, giving a sharp whistle as I go.

Pip responds to her call immediately, trotting over with her tongue lolling.

I pick her up, my hand under her soft belly, and hold her against my chest. Whispering into her bat-like ear, "Come on, girl. You've got work to do."

Caleb's unchanged since I left him, lying there with his eyes clamped down tight. I walk over and unceremoniously dump Pip into his lap. When her sharp little feet hit him, he rockets up into a sitting position with a yelp. He scuttles backward as Pip sways, trying to keep her balance and not fall off.

With a look of horror, he stares down at the tiny dog and then up at me. "Gwen! What the heck?"

That's the third time he's said my name.

I rise to my full height of 5 ft. 2 in. "Caleb, this is Pip," I tell him calmly. Then I address the dog, speaking to her the same way I spoke to him. "Pip, this is Caleb."

Caleb snorts in disgust. His eyes roll as he squirms, trying to dislodge her, but Pip holds on like a trooper, scrabbling her feet around for purchase.

"Caleb," I say more firmly, using a tone I learned from my tenth-grade trigonometry teacher. "You need to calm down. You're scaring her."

"*I'm* scaring *her*?" he exclaims loudly. "What about me?"

"Look at her. She's way more nervous than you are." I point to the dog, who's trembling, her tail tucked between her legs. Pip hates the sound of raised voices. She's a wimp that way. She's the one who taught us all to fight nicely in my family. When my brothers and I were kids, we learned not to shout in anger, not wanting to scare poor Pip.

Caleb pauses long enough to take in Pip's obvious terror. His movements slow and then still. Eyeing Pip, his lips pucker with disgust. "Ugh. She's a rat with fur." His beautiful blue eyes shoot up to me. "Why are you torturing me like this?"

"You're upset. Whenever something is bothering me, I cuddle with Pip, and it makes me feel better. I thought it might help you, too. You need to deal with your feelings."

"I was dealing. I was laying here quietly until you dumped this...," He looks down at Pip like he's at a loss for words. "This...thing on me."

"Shutting down isn't the same as dealing." I know it probably isn't my place to give advice, but it was my idea to go caroling and I feel guilty about how things turned out. I'm not good at walking away when someone is in pain. I want to soothe, to heal. It's a trait that drew me to medicine.

"What are you now? My therapist or something? I already have one of those." He lashes out, full of spite.

"Mm-hmm," I murmur, unmoved by his tantrum. "And what does your therapist say, exactly?"

I think back to *my* therapist. The one Mom dragged me to after Dad died, who always lectured me about shutting down. How she told me I needed to do a better job at processing my feelings. I tried to do what she asked, but I never really knew how. How to let my dad go without also feeling like I was letting my love for him fade.

There's a strained silence, then Caleb's breath gusts out and his shoulders slump. "She says I have a lot to work on...and that I need to stop blocking things out."

Pip must sense his surrender, because she circles twice and lays down on him, curling herself into a ball.

Satisfied that he's over his freakout, I sit on the edge of the couch down by his feet. "Why are you frightened of her, anyway? Pip's not going to hurt you."

Caleb's quiet for a minute and then he says, "You've met my mom, so maybe you'll understand. She's not like your mom. Your mom is a safety-net mom. Like if you need her, she'll catch you." He shifts, scooting his feet over so I have more room. "My mom loves me and all, but she's more of the push you out of the plane at 30,000 feet type of mom."

I raise my eyebrows, not sure what his mother has to do with Pip.

He leans on his elbows and directs his gaze to the ceiling. "Did you ever hear the story about how I got my first big break, the commercial?"

I think back. My family has talked about Caleb's career in front of me, but it's usually focused on his current projects. How he's in Africa filming an action-adventure movie or in Cannes at the film festival. I don't remember them mentioning how he got started. "No, I've never heard that one."

His voice is low. "I was five. It was a commercial for dog food, and the dog bit me. I've been scared of them ever since."

My head jerks toward him so fast I almost topple over. "I'm sorry, what?"

"Yeah." His chuckle has a hint of bitterness. "Crazy, huh? The dog bit me, and I didn't cry. I just kept on smiling for the camera. My theory is that they hired me so we wouldn't sue them, but my mom says it's because I was such a good actor that I didn't break character. I got three stitches in my hand." He holds up his right hand, where I can see the thin white line of a scar along the base of his thumb. "I fainted when they sewed me up that time, too."

I grimace. "That's all kinds of messed up." It makes sense now how he responds to Pip. A piece of his puzzle falls into place.

He rolls slightly onto his side, peering down at me. "Isn't it? You'd be surprised how many people I tell that story to and they're only impressed with the part about how I didn't cry. They totally miss the part about how I was only five years old." His voice is raised by the end of his tale, laced with an undercurrent of resentment and, maybe, betrayal. "My mom took me out for ice cream afterward, so I guess there's that."

Reeling from the awfulness of his story, I say, "I'm sorry. That must feel bad, like you can't totally trust your own parents."

"Mom always told me that everything she did was for my own benefit. When she quit her job and moved us to L.A. to pursue my career. When she pulled me out of school so I could spend more time auditioning." His forehead creases. "I don't know. My parents sacrificed a lot so I could be successful, but now that I'm an adult, it's confusing. To sort out which parts they did for me and which parts they did for them." He gives a tiny shrug, and I can tell that he's done talking about it. There's the sense of a door slamming shut. Me on one side of it and him on the other.

I have more things I want to talk about, though. "When we were out tonight, before the thing with those girls, you were singing…" I trail off, hoping he'll take it from there, but Caleb stays silent, staring at me as if he doesn't know what I'm talking about. He may be an actor, but he can't fool me. I swallow and continue, "The thing is, your singing. It was good. Like really, really good."

I lean toward him, elbows on my knees. "Please don't tell me you can dance too, because that would make you a triple threat if you can act, sing, *and* dance. That's too much talent for one person." I try to lighten the mood.

"I can't sing." He frowns down at Pip in his lap, but I doubt he really sees her. There's a distant look in his eyes, like he's looking more inward than out.

"Of course you can," I argue. "I just heard you. It was amazing."

A firm shake of his head. "No, I can't do it."

"Why not? Is someone stopping you? Who?" I ask, indignant. Maybe his studio contract prohibits him from doing anything outside of acting?

A sly smile. "Don't you mean whom?" His teasing loosens the tension in my shoulders. I know it means the worst of his anger and sorrow has passed.

"Actually, in that sentence it's who." Guess I really am the grammar police.

Caleb sighs. I don't think he's aware of it, but this time when he shifts on the couch, he puts his hand over snoozing Pip, holding her steady. He even leaves that hand there once he's found a more comfortable position. "It's not anyone stopping me. It's just me."

"You're scared of singing?" I clarify.

He nods and shrugs, all in one motion. "I can maybe do it with a small group of people, like tonight with the caroling. But a large crowd…that terrifies me."

"You're an actor. You perform to large groups all the time."

"I don't. Not really. There's not that many people on a set when I act. Plus, it's usually the same group. The lighting crew, sound engineers, make-up artists. Even when the movies change, a lot of those people stay the same. I've grown up with most of them, almost like family. The movie industry is a small community. We've been together so long that it's easy to say my lines in front of them. If I had to do it for an entire concert hall…" He lets the sentence trail off and shudders.

"You're telling me that one of the most famous actors in the world has… stage fright?"

"Kinda? I guess that's as good a description as any. It's why I usually avoid live award ceremonies. If I win, I send in a prerecorded acceptance speech. Sometimes I have to walk the red carpet, but I never enjoy it. Even giving that toast at your mom's and Seth's wedding was nerve-wracking. I had a moment there, at the beginning, where my mouth dried up. I had to fight past it."

I'm silent, struggling to absorb this revelation. "What is it *exactly* that scares you about singing in front of a crowd?"

"I'm afraid of disappointing so many people, of letting them and the music down. I'm a good actor. I understand how to do that, but I don't know *anything* about being a singer." He shakes his head. "The music means too much to me to mess it up." Caleb pins me with a hard stare. "You can't tell anyone about this, okay? Like *no one.*"

I roll my eyes. "Who would I tell?"

"Jenny," he fires back immediately.

Oh. Yeah.

He's right, I tell Jenny everything. I'll have to be careful and keep this to myself. "Fine," I huff. "I won't tell Jenny or anyone else about your big, dark secret. Do you want me to sign an NDA?"

He looks for a moment like he's actually considering it, but then he shakes his head no.

"Well." Caleb picks up Pip and gently places her on the cushion. She cracks one sleepy eye open, then closes it. "Tonight has been," he pauses and my heart sinks, knowing he is going to say something disparaging, but he seems to reconsider. "The part with the caroling, that was pretty great, so thanks for that. And the talking…that was okay, too." His smile is small, but I consider it a win.

When that smile disappears, his weariness is so heavy it bows his shoulders. "As for the rest of it, don't worry about that. It's just my life. I used to enjoy it, all the fans. Back when I was a teenager, it helped my insecurities."

I snort. "You? Insecure?" I can't picture that.

"I was more insecure than anyone. Do you know how few child stars transition successfully into teen and then to adult celebrities?"

When I shake my head, he says, "Hardly any. Most of the time, the public decides you aren't so cute anymore and they throw you away. Discarded at twelve years old. That would have killed my mother, so I tried my best. I started to weight train by age eleven. Got daily facials so I wouldn't get the usual teenage acne. Back then, a pimple felt like the end of the world. Those screaming fans made me feel better about myself."

"And now?"

He shakes his head ruefully. "Now…I know how bad this sounds. What a cliché I am. Another actor choking on his silver spoon. But now I'm so exhausted. It's all forced. I'm not connected with my fans anymore. That energy that they used to give me, I can't tap into the way that I used to. I hate being like this. It's not fair to them." My heart aches at the defeated look on his face.

"You could retire."

"And do what? This is all I've ever known since I was five years old. I don't have any other skills." Everything in him droops. His head. His shoulders. His full mouth.

I understand the trap he's in a little better then. The endless loop of despair, confusion, and insecurity.

"I'm going to brush my teeth and turn in." He stands up, his eyes flicking over my face and trailing down to my lips, only to jump back up so quickly I wonder if I imagined it. He scrubs his hand across his chin, hard enough for me to hear his stubble scrape.

"Good night, Gwen." The fourth time he's said my name, the most real I've seen him.

A few minutes after he's left to go upstairs and use the bathroom, Pip raises her head, blinking groggily. She stands up, gives herself a little shake, and jumps off the couch. I scratch her ears, and she scampers out the dog door into the backyard.

I can't fall asleep that night, going over and over my conversation with Caleb. On the one hand, he has everything anyone could ask for: fame, money, good looks. But the pain in his eyes is real, and it reminds me that true happiness doesn't come from any of those things.

True happiness is a mom who calls me honey, a friend to confide in, that feeling I get in the hospital when I know that I've helped someone. That I've lived a life of service to others. That's my happiness, anyway.

It's strange how drawn to Caleb I've become over the past week. I was determined to dislike him, assuming he was shallow and selfish. But he's not any of the things I thought he was. He's beautifully broken, and sad, and angry, and vulnerable. Maybe that's what I find intriguing about him. The need to heal people is why I went to medical school. Do I like him because I want to fix him? Is that fair to him? I wouldn't want anyone to fix me. Not that I need fixing. I'm fine…totally fine. I don't know. It's all a jumbled mess in my mind.

After hours of tossing and turning, I give up and go downstairs to get a glass of water. Caleb is asleep on the couch, an old quilt my grandmother made thrown over him. Only his head sticks out. I can't resist taking a peek.

His hair is tousled gold. In sleep, his face is relaxed and boyish. He looks like an angel, fallen from heaven. That's when I notice Pip, curled into his side, with his hand draped loosely over her.

"Good dog," I whisper softly.

16

Teddy calls me early the next morning, which is weird. He usually just texts. These days, he prefers short, superficial conversations about the weather.

We used to be so close, my baby brother and me. After Dad died, Mom worked long hours, trying to support us. We moved from one tiny, cheap apartment to another. Brandon was mostly gone, off to community college, which he hated.

It was just Teddy and me, left at home together.

I was seventeen, and he was twelve.

I was sad, and he was lost.

He needed my help. I had to make him talk about what we had been through. Eventually, I learned that playing ball with him was the surest way to get him to open up. It could be any sport, really, but basketball seemed to work best. Something about having a ball in his hands distracted him enough to remove the filter from his mouth.

When we played, all of his thoughts, fears, and dreams would come spilling out. Basketball is how I learned about how devastated he was by Dad's passing. It's how I broke through to the point that he could cry in front of me. It's how I found out that he feared losing the rest of us, especially Mom. He admitted that he had nightmares where she died in a fire, a plane crash, a robbery gone wrong.

Later, when his grief over Dad started to fade and he went to high school, we still played ball. Playing basketball was when he told me about his first crush, Julie, when he was a sophomore. And it was how I learned she had left him and broken his heart when he was a junior.

Teddy wasn't the only one who benefited from those long hours together. I was more than happy to bask in the attention he gave me on the court. Since Dad was gone and Mom was working, I was always looking for something or someone to distract me from my loneliness.

This year, once he left for college, all that changed. Now it's like he's pushing me away. Trying to keep his distance.

It hurts.

"What's up Teddy?" I attempt to sound casual. Worried if I put too much pressure on him, he'll shut me out completely.

"Not a lot," he replies evenly.

I wait, because clearly something is going on. Otherwise, he wouldn't have called.

After a long pause, he admits, "I don't think I like it here, in Michigan."

"What? Why?" I'm surprised. He's sounded depressed the past few times we've talked, but I assumed it was from the stress of his final exams.

"It's cold and lonely."

I remember back to how dreary New York had been when I left. How the snow had swirled in through the ER doors during that last shift.

"This is your first non-California winter, Teddy. That's all. You'll get used to it, eventually. Probably, it's extra hard because you're missing Christmas at home."

A beat of silence. "It's not that simple. I hate college. The classes are boring. Engineering isn't what I thought it would be. I want to solve complicated problems, build cool things. Instead, it's calculations and abstract concepts. That's all I'm learning about."

I hear voices in the background of wherever he's at. There's the sound of him moving around and of a door closing. Those outside noises fade. I'm guessing he's in the tiny dorm room he gets free as part of his payment for being an RA.

"Don't make fun of me, okay?" He coughs and then rasps out, "I miss home. I thought I could go far away, that it would be cool to experience someplace different, but walking to school through the snow every single day is awful. The sky is always gray. I mean seriously, I haven't seen the sun in weeks. Over Thanksgiving break, I was so happy to be in California. I didn't want to come back here."

Wow. This is a bigger deal than I realized. I get it, what he's talking about. I miss my family and Jenny too. Sometimes, when I first got to New York, homesickness had been like a ravenous animal, eating me up from the inside until I was left hollow, totally empty. It's better now that some time has passed, but maybe Teddy can't move past it, that feeling.

"What do Mom and Seth say? Do they think you should quit?" I'm surprised I didn't find out about this sooner.

"That's the thing." He sighs. "I haven't told anyone else yet."

"What?" I ask, incredulous. "Mom's gonna freak. You know how hard it was for her when you left."

Mom had taken it badly, watching her baby go off to college. She cried, said she wasn't ready to have an empty nest. It occurs to me now that might be part of why she was so eager to move to Japan. It's possible she needed a change of pace, something new, to help redefine herself.

I should do that, too. Redefine myself. Become someone more than just boring, predictable, sensible Gwen. Daughter of a dead man.

Teddy says, "That's why I haven't said anything. I feel guilty for putting Mom through all that. She was so upset." He pauses and I wait, sensing he needs to say something big. "Do you ever think our family is a little strange? Like how Mom babies us…and how sometimes we like that she does."

I'm quiet for a minute, astonished that Teddy is bringing this up. It's something we never talk about. "I mean, yeah, but after everything with Dad I think it's understandable that we're a bit dysfunctional. We had to cling to each other to get through that. Right?"

"Except for Brandon. He went the opposite direction, away from us." There's an undertone of resentment from Teddy. He had looked up to his big brother. It's crazy for me to realize it now, after so much time has passed, but in a way we lost our father, mother, *and* brother all at once. Who wouldn't be messed up after that?

"Brandon was mad," I remind him. "Angry about what happened. I think being around us back then was too painful. He's better now. Liv and the twins helped."

There's a long silence between us, not uncomfortable but full of unexpressed emotions. Mostly sadness. Grief is a rock thrown into a lake. Its ripples keep reaching the shore long after the stone has sunk below the surface.

"Anyway, about college," I say, bringing the conversation back to our original topic. "You need to talk to Mom. Delaying telling her won't help."

"I know. I'm waiting for the right time." A long, gloomy sigh. "Please tell me that you've done something worse, Gwen. Something that Mom was super-mad at you about, but she eventually got over."

I shouldn't tell him, but I'm so happy that he reached out to me with his problems. That after months of barely talking, he finally called *me* of all the many people in our family to talk to. I want to reward him, to reinforce this connection between us.

The words come spilling out. "Not sure if this counts, since Mom doesn't officially know about it, but I *have* done something she wouldn't approve of."

"Oh?" He's interested. I picture him pressing the phone closer to his ear.

I'm probably asking for bad karma, because a little thrill goes through me. There's something so delicious about sharing a secret, especially one you shouldn't. I lower my voice, which is dumb since I'm in the car by myself, but still I whisper. "Caleb Lawson is staying at Mom and Seth's house with me."

"What?!" His surprise is gratifying. It makes me laugh.

I laugh even harder at his next question, "Isn't he America's hottest man or something like that?"

I think about the rumpled grouch who never leaves the living room and have to admit that even grungy Caleb is kind of handsome.

But I'm definitely *not* going to tell my baby brother that.

"I don't see him that way," I say. "He needed a place to crash for a while. That's all. He wants to lie low and stay out of the limelight."

"Do you like it? Living with him?"

I tilt my head, considering. "It's okay, I guess. He doesn't do much. Reads and listens to music. He's an excellent cook, though. Oh! Get this, I had to teach him how to do laundry."

"What?" The volume of Teddy's voice goes up a notch. "Isn't the guy in his late twenties? What do you mean you had to teach him?"

"He only has four shirts, so he needs to wash them every couple of days. He didn't know the difference between dishwasher detergent and washing machine detergent," I say gleefully. "So he put one of those dishwasher pods into the washing machine. By the time I found out, bubbles had flooded out of the washing machine and were spreading all over the laundry room floor. It was a disaster!"

I don't tell Teddy how I went running into the laundry room, slipped in the water, and fell on my butt, right in front of Caleb. *Talk about humiliating.* I also don't tell him how Caleb had truly laughed for the first time since he moved in and how that sound, a low rumbling guffaw, had echoed somewhere deep in my chest.

Nope. No need for my brother to hear about that part.

"That's crazy," Teddy exclaims. "Every adult should know how to clean their own clothing."

"Right? He's been sheltered from real-world stuff like that. The other day he told me he's never made a dentist or doctor appointment himself. His mom or some staff always do it for him."

I laugh, but then become more serious, making my voice firm, imitating Mom when she's telling us to be home by curfew. "You can't let anyone else know about Caleb living with me. Okay, Teddy? I mean it. *No* one."

"Fine," he huffs. "I won't tell a soul. Promise."

"Good. When are you going to talk to Mom about college?"

"Not sure." He sighs so loudly that I flinch and pull the receiver away from my ear. "I'll get around to it, eventually. Just keep it between us for now, though. Okay, Sissy?"

Geez. Seems like everyone wants me to keep their secrets recently. Caleb. Teddy.

But this is my baby brother. I'd do anything for him.

"Okay, Teddy Bear."

17

The baby goat has hard, pointy hooves that dig into my back in just the right spot. I should enjoy the sensation, but I'm too busy worrying that it'll pee on me.

"Isn't this amazing?" asks Jenny next to me as she flows into downward dog like she was born without any joints. Her own personal goat prances for a minute and then settles, perched atop her as if she's the biggest peak of Mt. Everest.

"Yeah, amazing," I agree halfheartedly.

In the spirit of the holiday, our goats are made even cuter by the tiny Christmas sweaters they wear. Mine has a snowman on the front. Jenny's goat has an elf.

The yoga instructor tells us to roll onto our backs. Assistants remove our goats. I'm relieved to have the adorable creature off me, but as soon as the bumpy yoga mat is pressed into my spine, the baby goat comes back. They set him on my stomach, and air whooshes out of me as his weight presses into my soft belly.

I really need to strengthen my abs. Goat yoga won't be the place to do that, though. It's more about gentle stretching and slow movements, all designed not to knock off our horned companions.

"I still can't get over Caleb last night," Jenny whispers as we bring our knees into our chests. "His singing voice is phenomenal."

I nod, hoping she will stop talking, but knowing from years of experience that she won't. While I live in a constant fear of getting in trouble, Jenny thrives off it.

Once, when we were in high school, she got detention for speaking in class. She had walked up to Mr. Martin, the scariest PE teacher the world has ever known. A man rumored to compete in lumberjack contests where he chopped down hundred-year-old pine trees and carried them on his back through a six-mile course.

Jenny had walked up to *that* man and thanked him for the detention. Sincerely, not sarcastically, she gave him a big thank you in front of the entire class.

For a brief heart-stopping moment, I had been terrified that she would hug him or kiss him on the cheek, but she didn't. Instead, she traipsed out of the classroom like she was going to a party with fairy princesses rather than a room full of hardened teenage criminals. Later, I discovered that Lance Jones, her infamous crush, had also received detention that day. Thus, her overeager enthusiasm to join him.

In contrast, I have recurring nightmares where I get sent to detention because I forgot to put my name on a test. Even though in my dream I got an A on the exam, I lost all credit for it. I wake up, my body slick with sweat and my mouth dry.

Goat yoga finishes up. We pet our slit-eyed, coarse-haired friends goodbye and kneel to roll up our mats.

Jenny's still talking. "What's up with you and Caleb?"

"What?" I straighten to look at her. "Nothing."

Doubtful, she raises one eyebrow.

"I mean nothing romantic, if that's what you're getting at. He's got a lot going on, and I want to help him…if I can." I stand and shove the rolled mat into its bag, which I hang over my shoulder. Jenny does the same with hers.

She doesn't seem impressed. "Really? Because it didn't look like that to me."

"That's all there is to it, I swear."

"Gwen. Seriously. For such a smart person, you can be pretty dumb sometimes." Before I get offended, she goes on, "He watches you when you're not looking. I caught him doing it multiple times during caroling."

So she noticed it, too, but he was just looking at me as a friend, right?

"That's crazy," I scoff. "Goat yoga has made you delusional. There's no way Caleb thinks of me like that. He barely talks to me."

Except for last night when he told me things I doubt anyone else knows.

Jenny laughs, and even though I'm thrown off by what she just said, a happy Jenny always brightens my own mood. She's the sunshine to my rain clouds.

"He might be good for you." She quiets, growing thoughtful. "You need someone like him. Less structured, more willing to bend without breaking."

I don't know what she's talking about. I don't *need* Caleb. He's a mess. I'm fine. I don't need him or any man.

A baby goat wanders over for one last pat before we leave. Jenny bends down to it, blocking her face from my view, but not before I see her expression turn somber. "I know that it's been hard for you to trust, to love. Ever since your dad died. It's been hard for your entire family."

Jenny has lost it. The reason I haven't fallen in love for years now is because of everything that happened with Jax. It has nothing to do with my dad. Right?

I sigh. "You already gave me this speech, remember? At the food court?"

"I'm serious, Gwen. Don't blow me off." The goat wanders away, and she stands back up. "It's time to let someone in again. Why not have it be Caleb?"

Which is a ridiculous idea.

Utterly preposterous.

When I get home from goat yoga, I find Caleb at the kitchen table, working on the puzzle. One hand props up his chin and the other strokes Pip, who's lying in his lap, from snout to tail. Pip's neck is stretched out, her eyes closed and her tail thumping. Her expression is the picture of pure doggy bliss.

Without glancing up, he says, "Rat won't leave me alone," but there's no bite to his words.

A burst of sunlight slants in through the window and lands like a spotlight on Caleb, burnishing his golden hair, still mussed from sleep. He crosses one white-socked foot absently over the other.

It's the stupid socks that undo me. White ankle socks like a kid wears. There's something so simple and sweet about them. I wish I could take this moment and hold it forever. Lock it away in a room in my heart and keep the key only for myself.

Caleb must feel the weight of my gaze on him. He looks up and sees me standing frozen. I don't know what I look like, but something on my face makes his eyes narrow suspiciously. "What?"

"Nothing." I can't catch my breath. My traitorous heart has forgotten how to beat. It's terrifying and humiliating. I hate it, the riot of my emotions right now, so I turn and flee upstairs.

Away from my feelings and away from him.

avoid Caleb for the rest of the day, which isn't easy because I'm constantly walking through the living room.

"I'm going for a jog at the park," I tell him as I grab my sneakers from where they sit by the couch.

Caleb waves absently. "Have fun."

"Taking a swim," I sing out when I walk past to the backyard, making sure that my coverup is wrapped tightly around me, hiding my bathing suit.

Caleb looks up and nods slowly.

"Meeting Jenny to do some Christmas shopping." I pull my jacket off its hanger in the coat closet.

Caleb purses his lips, his eyes sharp.

"We're out of milk. I'll go pick some up." I almost make it out the door. *Almost.*

"Gwen," Caleb says my name for the fifth time, firmly.

I stop, drop my hand from the doorknob, and slowly turn around to face him. "Yes?"

"What's going on?" He puts his notebook facedown next to him and frowns at me, gaze heavy with suspicion.

"What do you mean?" I widen my eyes, full of feigned innocence.

Caleb stalks over to me, his shoulders set and jaw tight. Once he's right in front of me, inches away, he stops. His scent, cinnamon spice, follows him.

His eyes, more blue than the sky out of the window, drill into mine. It takes everything in me to hold still under that gaze. To not squirm or run out the door.

"You're acting weird," he says finally.

"Me?" I put my hand to my chest. "I'm not acting weird. You're acting weird."

Did I just say that? What am I? A nine-year-old?

Caleb searches my face, concern etching his features. "Are you okay? Did something happen?"

Yeah. I realized that you are a man, and I am a woman, and that we could kiss. Why did I just think that? Now I'm thinking about kissing him. I will myself not to look at his lips, which makes me look at his lips, which makes me lick my lips. Now he's watching me lick my lips. And everything is just so overwhelming. And so hot. Why is it so hot in here? I'm panicking, because it's so hot and I want to kiss him, so I say, "My research paper just got preliminary approval to be featured in the *Journal of Emergency Medicine*."

Which is true. I got the letter confirming my acceptance this morning. As thrilled as I was that someone else thought my research was worthy, that feeling had been partially lost to my hyperawareness of Caleb today.

"Really?" He brightens. "That's great. Congratulations."

I laugh, mostly from relief that he doesn't know I was thinking about kissing him, but also from his interested expression. "Thanks. I wasn't sure they would take it, so I was excited when I got the news. This is just the first step. It still needs to pass through the final evaluation process, but I'm hopeful."

"Can I ask, what's your research about? Would I understand it?"

"It's not hard to understand. It's a pilot program that I started when I was a medical student and finally completed this year. I offered free screening for colon cancer to patients entering the ER, no matter what symptoms they were there for. Even if they came in because they broke an arm or something totally unrelated, they could get the screening test. Thousands agreed and because of that I found a couple hundred who had cancer, so small that they didn't have symptoms yet. Being able to treat them that early has a big impact. We're more likely to cure them."

If only my father had been diagnosed sooner, maybe he'd still be here with me today.

"That's cool. Why don't they always do that? If it saves lives?" There's a gleam of admiration in how he's looking at me, warming my cheeks.

"I have to prove that it's worth the money and time to offer it in the ER. Right now, anyone can get the test from their family doctor. It's easy. It doesn't include drawing your blood or anything. They just test your stool. But my argument is that many people don't have a family doctor or they don't see them regularly. If we have another place to test them, the ER, then we can find more cancer earlier."

"That makes sense to me."

I sigh. "I think so too. Now I just have to convince everyone else."

"Wow." Caleb leans back. "That's cool. You're going to be famous. A big-time academic physician. I bet your work gets lots of awards."

"We don't have fancy doctor red carpets like you do," I tease him.

He's serious when he answers, "You should, though. There should be a parade every time you save someone's life. Not just for doctors, but for police offi-cers, firefighters, teachers. Everyone whose job protects people from the things that harm them. You're the ones who should get the golden trophies. Not me."

I mostly agree with him but feel a need to say, "Your job is important, too. Everyone needs the arts, theater, movies, music, books. People have to express themselves and to escape the stress of their everyday worries. You pro-vide them with that outlet. To be someone different for a couple of hours. To live a million lives without leaving their hometown."

Caleb blows out a breath and runs a hand through his hair, uncomfort-able with my praise. "I guess so." He shifts, not meeting my eyes. "Anyway, I'm glad you're excited about the journal article. I was worried that you might be upset with me."

"Upset?" I repeat, confused. "Why would I be upset?"

"Upset might not be the right word." He's hesitant. "Maybe, uncomfort-able? I worried I was making you uncomfortable. You know, after all the stuff I told you last night." Caleb ducks his head, awkwardly staring at his feet.

It hits me then, how it must have looked to him. He exposed himself last night, allowed me to take a peek behind the curtain. And today I've been unavailable, distant even. Inwardly, I curse at myself.

He didn't need me thinking about kissing him. He needed me to show him that being honest won't lead to rejection. That someone sees beyond his face and reputation. I'm supposed to be that someone, and I let him down.

"Caleb," I wait until he looks up at me. "I'm sorry. What you told me last night didn't make me upset or uncomfortable or anything bad. It made me understand you better. And I liked that, knowing you."

"You did?" Disbelief on his face, as if he can't accept it. That someone could like those broken, imperfect bits of him.

But I do. I like all his shadows just as much as I like his light. "Yeah. I like who you are. I see it, all of you."

The smile he gives me is so pure, so genuine, that it catches me off guard. When he says, "I like who you are, too," something turns over deep inside me. A new feeling.

t's after lunch, and we're at the pool. Caleb swims, while Jenny and I spread our towels over lounge chairs along the side. Even with the towel, the sun-scorched metal of the chair seeps into my legs, warming them.

Caleb only wears a pair of swim trunks. The muscles in his powerful back and arms contract and then relax as he torpedoes through the water, doing laps. Water splashes, spilling over the edge of the pool.

"He's a good swimmer. Don't you think?" I ask, unable to tear my gaze away from him.

"He should be." Jenny slips on her sunglasses. "Did you ever see that movie he was in? The one where he had to escape from Alcatraz and swim across San Francisco Bay?"

I shake my head no.

"I once read that he did the swimming stunts for the movie himself. It wasn't really in the Bay, of course. No one could survive that. He was in the Atlantic and had to swim for up to ten hours a day. Can you imagine?"

"No," I answer honestly. "I can't." Before, I hadn't thought much about what it takes to be an actor. If anything, I figured it was easy. Just a lot of sitting around and spewing out lines that someone else wrote for you. Now, a kernel of admiration for Caleb and how hard he works grows inside of me.

Jenny and I go back to staring at Caleb, mesmerized. We might have drooled a little.

Pip runs back and forth along the edge of the pool, yipping like she's a lifeguard dog ready to jump in and save Caleb. She hasn't left his side over the past few days. I'm almost jealous, thinking she likes him more than me.

Changing the subject, Jenny pulls her sunglasses down her nose so she can look over their top at me. "Are you coming tonight or what?"

I sigh, understanding immediately what she means. "I don't know, Jenny. I'm not sure I want to."

In the food court, I had daydreamed about seeing Jax again, about getting back together with him, but now that doesn't seem as appealing. An image of Caleb, sparkling in the sunlight with Pip in his lap, flashes in my mind's eye. I push it away, not wanting to look too closely.

"What don't you want to do?" Caleb has swum over to us. He folds his tan arms over the edge of the pool and hangs there, kicking his legs slowly to keep himself afloat. Water droplets glitter like stars on his long eyelashes and run in streaks down his muscular chest.

Jenny answers before I can. "A bunch of our old classmates are going to Shooter's tonight. It's a tradition, but little Miss Scaredy Cat here doesn't want to go."

A line forms between Caleb's brows. "What's Shooter's?" he asks Jenny, "and why are you scared?" he asks me.

"Shooter's is a bar," I explain. "A small dive bar, nothing fancy, but for some reason alumni from our high school have been meeting up there during holiday breaks for ages. Anytime you go to Shooter's, you're basically guaranteed to see someone you know."

"What's so frightening about that?" Caleb asks.

"There's a high probability that Gwen's ex will be there tonight. His name's Jax." Jenny shoots me a disappointed glare, knowing I'll try to weasel out of going. "That's what's got her running for the hills."

I can sense Caleb's gaze warm on my cheek, but I refuse to glance over. This isn't a conversation I want to have with him around.

"What happened? End badly?" Since I won't look at him, I can't tell if Caleb is asking me or Jenny.

"You could say that." My voice is grim, but I don't elaborate.

Jenny fills in the blanks for me. "It was our senior year. Gwen lost her dad the summer before." I flinch, hating that she framed it that way. It makes me remember that time after my dad died. Walking around like a zombie, like I was missing the most integral piece of my puzzle.

How can I blame Jenny for saying it like that, though? Isn't that how I define my life as well? The time before and after dad? His death a jagged line down the middle of my world, breaking it into two separate halves.

"It was like something out of an '80s rom-com, a John Hughes movie," Jenny continues as she waves her hands across the sky in a grand gesture, like she's pointing out a theater marquee.

"Jenny," I warn, but I already know that once she gets into storytelling mode, there's no stopping her.

"Picture this. A shy, but attractive, nerd." She points to me, and I roll my eyes. "Meets the brawny, but brainless, football quarterback."

"He was a receiver," I correct.

Jenny waves me away. "The football, whatever his position was, guy has a problem. He's failing trigonometry. Oh, no!" She clasps her hands to her cheeks, like the kid from *Home Alone*. "Whatever shall we do?" Jenny says overdramatically, while I give a frustrated groan next to her. She ignores me and continues. "Ah-ha! An idea! Jock Boy asks Nerd Girl to tutor him."

A flashback comes to me. It had been such a role reversal. Jax, usually so confident, standing before me with his hands shoved into his pockets, feet scuffing the ground. "Will you help me, Gwen? I can't fail trig and lose my spot on the team." Me, usually so shy around guys like him but suddenly confident in my trigonometry skills, telling him, "You won't fail, Jax. I promise."

What a stupid, stupid girl I'd been. I'd given him everything: my heart and years of my life.

Jenny has continued on with her story. "Nerd Girl has had a secret crush on Jock Boy for years, so this tutoring proposition is like winning the lottery for her. Plus, Jock Guy just broke up with…wait for it, because it doesn't get any more predictable than this…the head cheerleader." Jenny makes a drum roll motion with her hands.

"Sophie was a regular cheerleader, remember? Sarah was the head cheerleader that year," I interject.

Jenny puts her finger over her lips. "Hush."

I spare a glance at Caleb to see how he's taking all this in. His arms are still resting on the edge of the pool, and his eyes are wide, his expression rapt. "What happened?" he asks, like he's hanging onto every word Jenny says.

Wanting this torture to stop as quickly as possible, I take over. "Nerd Girl fell for Jock Boy. He passed trig. They stayed together for six years. But next came the plot twist. Turned out that Jock Boy got tired of dating boring, too serious Nerd Girl, so Jock Boy dumped her, then got back with Cheerleader Chick and broke Nerd Girl's heart. The end." The words rush out of me, so fast I'm not even sure if they made sense. I barely have a chance to see Caleb and Jenny's stunned faces before I'm up and striding into the kitchen.

I open the refrigerator door to feel the cool air on my overheated cheeks. If I could crawl inside the arctic of the refrigerator, I would. Just curl up in there like a penguin, so I wouldn't have to face anyone, especially Caleb, again.

"Gwen, I'm so, so, sorry." Jenny is behind me. I close the door and turn to see her wringing her hands. "I'm a terrible friend. Forgive me."

"It's okay." I gather my long hair off my neck into a high ponytail, letting the air dry the sweat that's gathered there. "It's a good story, and if it wasn't my life I'd find it entertaining, too." I pull a hair tie off my wrist to secure the ponytail, winding it around and around.

Jenny's mouth tugs down. "But it is your life, and I know how Jax hurt you. I'm the one who helped pick up the pieces, after all. I shouldn't have made light of it."

"Honestly," I shrug. "I like how you tell it. Much easier than me having to explain what happened. Mostly, I'm embarrassed because Caleb heard."

"I doubt anything Caleb hears about you is going to change the way he feels." Jenny laughs softly. "Seeing how he can't stay more than an arm's length away from you today." She smiles at me gently. "I'm telling you. I'm *sure* of it. He's into you."

She steps forward, placing her hands on my shoulders, which she squeezes and gives a little shake, as if she's trying to wake me up. "I think you like him, too. The question is, are you brave enough to do anything about it? You leave for New York in less than three weeks. Tick tock, Gwen. Time's running out."

She taps her watch for emphasis as Caleb enters the room, rubbing a towel over his damp hair.

"Hey, Caleb. Any chance you want to go to Shooter's with us tonight?" Jenny asks brightly.

Caleb halts, mid rub of his towel. His eyes glance cautiously between Jenny and me, then linger on me. "I don't think that's such a good idea." He runs a hand through his hair, separating the damp strands.

Just like that, any hope that Caleb likes me in a romantic way comes crashing down. Guess Jenny is wrong. If he really likes me, wouldn't he stop me from spending time with Jax? Demand I stay home? Or wouldn't he want to be at Shooter's to claim me?

"It's okay," I tell Caleb. "You don't have to come. You'd be bored anyway, surrounded by a bunch of people you don't know. We'll be fine on our own."

With that, Jenny grins at me. "Did I just hear you say you're coming with me tonight?"

"I guess I am."

20

ax isn't at the bar when we first arrive, which is a relief. I wonder if this will be my lucky night. Maybe all this buildup has been for nothing, and I can avoid him for one more year. Jenny and I join several old friends sitting at tables along the back wall. They share their pitcher of frothy amber beer, sloshing it into my cup, while we catch up with each other.

The room is dark, mostly illuminated by neon beer signs that hang on every wood-paneled wall. In honor of the holiday, Christmas lights have been added. They've been strung across the ceiling and surround the bar, twinkling merrily.

The lacquered wooden table where we sit is scarred with hundreds of tiny scratches across its surface. It's a tradition to carve your name and the date when you have your first drink into these tables. Somewhere are my initials and Jenny's. I had felt like such a criminal, using a ballpoint pen to scratch my G. Running over and over the letter, until it was deep enough.

The graffiti isn't limited to first drinks, though. Lovers have etched their names into the tabletops too. T loves L forever 2022 is written under my glass. I trace another with my fingertip. A + M '09. Jax and my initials are on a different table, one that I make sure never to sit at.

Along the opposite wall is the bar, with swiveling stools all occupied by either hardened alcoholics or former alumni from my high school. A picture of our mascot, a wolf, is painted over the bar.

In the center of the room is a small dance floor with a tacky silver disco ball spinning overhead. It's empty for now, but as the night wears on and more alcohol is consumed, sweaty bodies will wander into the space to press close together, moving to the beat.

I'm having a great time. Beer and easy conversation loosen the tension in my limbs as I move from one set of friends to another. Last time I saw Jenny she was talking to Sarah, her friend who used to be on the cheer team. Now, I've lost sight of her, but I'm not worried. We have a pact to never leave a place without telling each other.

The door swings open, and the jocks enter. A large group of them. Some of Jax's old teammates are there. In the middle of the crowd, Sophie's red hair flashes like a beacon. No sign of Jax, though. Is it possible they broke up? Their crew takes a table across the room. They must have pre-partied. Already some of them sway on their feet, clearly drunk.

I shouldn't care. There's no reason to stare at them. Their loudness, brashness, the way they take up space and act entitled to every inch of it, makes me feel insecure. Reduced to that shy Nerd Girl I was all those years ago. In my regular life, I'm not that person anymore. But here, she whispers, *You're not good enough. You never will be.*

That's when I see it. The flash of a diamond ring on Sophie's left hand. A rock so huge that its sparkle reaches all the way over to me. My gaze snags on that ring, my stomach sinking at the sight of it.

I can't believe it.

They're engaged.

"Jax!" their group shouts. There he is, in the doorway, his hand raised in greeting. That same megawatt smile, the one he used to give me, now shining on their table. Same puppy dog eyes and curly brown hair.

It all comes back to me then. The day we broke up.

"You know this has been coming for a long time," he'd said, standing in the parking lot outside of the apartment we shared. An apartment he would never step foot in again.

But I hadn't known. I was so stupid to be blindsided like that. How could I have not seen the signs? Sure, I had been busy, consumed with classes and studying. It was my first year of medical school, after all.

Still, I had been caught unaware. I stood there with my mouth hanging open while he said, "The engagement was a mistake. We're too different. You and I. You've got your whole life planned out. You're always so serious, so focused. You're brilliant, and I'm just along for the ride. I wouldn't even have gotten into UCLA if you hadn't filled out my application for me. It's time for me to go off on my own. Figure things out without you leading the way. We're no good for each other."

What a lie. He must have meant *I* wasn't good for him, since I was sure that he was good for me. I adored him. Looked up to him. Couldn't believe that he picked me. When he proposed, I had been so excited that I had gone out and bought a wedding dress the very next day. At least we never got as far as booking a venue.

Within a month of our breakup, he was back together with Sophie, and I was all alone.

Now, with Jax in the same room, I try to ignore him. I really do, but I watch out of the corner of my eye as he moves through his friends, exchanging high fives and hugs. When he reaches Sophie, they kiss.

I can't take it anymore. I snatch my purse from the table, and, with my head down, push my way through the crowd. I don't have a plan. Jenny drove us here, so it's not like I can leave without her, but I have to get outside. My lungs are burning for fresh air. My eyes are burning, too.

I rush out the door, past a sharp-faced man smoking a cigarette and into the cramped parking lot.

Jax follows me out. I'm five steps from Jenny's car when I hear him behind me, calling out my name. "Gwen. Gwen. Stop." It's the first time he has said my name in years. For some reason, it doesn't sound right on his tongue anymore. I find myself wishing it was someone else saying it. Someone who rounds the G and flattens the N.

I halt and turn to him, spitting out, "Leave me alone." I spin on my heel, but his hand is on my arm, twisting me back.

"No, I want to talk to you." He's frowning, his brows heavy. I have no idea what he has to be upset about. I'm the one who was wronged.

"Well, I don't want to talk to you, so go away." I attempt to wrench myself out of his grasp, pulling against him so hard that it hurts. I can feel bruises forming, which infuriates me even more. "Jax. Stop it. Let me go." I scowl and yank my arm harder, but still he holds on.

A deep, husky voice says coolly behind me, "I suggest you listen to her." Jax and I both freeze at the sound. Jax's eyes shift above my head, and his face goes slack in awe. His fingers loosen enough for me to shake free.

I turn to see Caleb standing there. Freshly showered, his hair is styled and his jaw is clean shaven. He's darkly handsome in black jeans and a gray T-shirt. A leather jacket hangs from one finger, casually thrown over his shoulder like he's about to walk the runway in Milan.

There's nothing casual in his expression, though. Those aqua eyes glitter with cold menace. He's coiled tight, jaw clenched, a lion about to pounce.

Caleb doesn't look at me. All his icy fury is focused on Jax. "I once won an Oscar for playing an Olympic boxer. To prepare for that role, I trained every day with the world's best fighters. I don't think you want to see what my right hook can do." The only thing that moves is his mouth, which transforms into a cruel smile.

Jax takes a step back and then another. He turns and rushes back into the bar.

My heart is pounding. I'm walking, almost falling into Caleb. He catches me in his arms, crushing me against his firm chest. I start to cry, which is silly. The danger has passed. I don't know what Jax intended, but he never put his hands on me like that when we were together.

"Shh." Caleb's hand smooths down my hair and trails down to my cheek, as I soak his shirt with my tears. "Shh. It's okay. You're safe, Gwen." He says my name for the sixth time, this time with gentle tenderness.

Eventually, I quiet. "Sorry." I wipe my nose and look up at him, my knight in shining armor. "Can we go home, please?" I just want to crawl into my bed and forget this day ever happened. All of the confidence I've built up over the years, all of my accomplishments, have vanished with Jax's touch. I feel small and defeated. A little mouse, ready to run into her hole in the wall.

Caleb looks from me to the bar and then to me again. His mouth tightens. "No."

"No?" I reel out of his arms.

He's firm. "No. You're going to go back in there."

"What?" Panic is setting in. "Why?"

Caleb sets his lips in a thin line. "Because that's not who you are. You're not someone who gives up when things get hard. I know since you haven't given up on me yet."

He takes my hand and marches me back into Shooter's.

21

Caleb leads me past the smoking man and back into the building. We don't go to my friends. Instead, he chooses the darkest corner of the bar. Every seat is taken, so we squeeze in between a couple of patrons. He puts his back to the rest of the crowd, angling his body so it only faces the bartender and me. We're pressed together, shoulder to shoulder.

I take in a shuddering breath, still upset from Jax and unnerved to be so close to Caleb. His spicy scent invades my nose, warm and inviting.

"Are you worried about being recognized?" It hits me then, the risk he's taking, being out in public like this. He's worked so hard to keep his location a secret. He tries to reassure me with a confident smile, but I don't miss the tightness of his jaw. A surge of guilt twists inside of me for putting him in this position.

Sometimes I forget he's famous, that he can't interact with the world the same way I can. It's hard to reconcile that Caleb with the one I know, the one who cooks and does laundry and sometimes forgets to put the cap back on his toothpaste.

Caleb moves closer, hunching his body around me. It's loud in here, but when he drops his mouth close to my ear, I can hear him well enough. His breath stirs the hair at my temple, and a shiver runs through me.

"So…that was Jax?" He eyes me intently.

"Yeah, my ex-fiancé." I can't quite meet his eyes, not wanting to see what's in them.

He sucks in a breath. "Fiancé? Jenny didn't mention that part."

"It didn't work out. We broke up, and he went back to his ex-girlfriend, the redhead, over there." Caleb's gaze darts over my shoulder to where Sophie sits.

When he looks back at me, I lift a shoulder in a half-shrug and deliberately change the subject. "I owe you a drink. You know, for saving me." I tilt my head up so I can see him better. "What do you want?"

"Just a soda water with a slice of lime for me."

I'm taken aback. For some reason, I assumed he drank alcohol, but now that I think about it, we've never had any in all the days we've lived together.

I wave the bartender down and give him Caleb's order, with a beer for me. Out of the corner of my eye, I watch Caleb raise his hand, as if to scratch his forehead, the gesture obscuring his face. He's good at hiding in plain sight. He must have done it many times before.

"I'm sorry," I say awkwardly after the bartender walks away. "Do you not drink?"

"I used to drink, but I liked it a little too much." He pauses, as if weighing how much to tell me, then continues. "I get...obsessive about some things. Once I start, I can't stop. Drinking is like that for me. That's one reason why I said no when Jenny asked me to come here tonight." In a soft voice, he admits, "I haven't had a drink in five months now."

"Was it hard? Stopping?" I can't imagine the strength it must take. To quit cold turkey. I admire his discipline.

"Some days are harder than others."

"How'd you do it? Did you join Alcoholics Anonymous or something?" I don't intend to drill him, but I'm curious.

"Nah. I mean, I was never totally out of control, but I was heading in that direction. If I didn't quit, I worried what my life would be like ten years from now." He tilts his head, gazing down at me.

I frown, thinking of all the alcoholics I've seen in the hospital. How they lie, break their promises. They swear they'll stop and then end up right back in the ER, drunk again with their failing livers, organs shutting down. Of course, I only see the worst cases. The ones where the damage is irreparable.

Remembering what Jenny had mentioned the day before Caleb arrived, I ask, "Was that how you wrecked your car?"

He jerks back like I've slapped him.

"Jenny told me about it. I'm sorry. She had read an article," I say hastily, fearful he will think I've been researching him. I haven't Googled him once, even though recently I've been tempted. In the end, I resist because I don't want to learn about him through some biased media piece. That won't give me a clear picture, to view him through someone else's lens. I want to know Caleb through my own observations, with my own eyes, my own heart.

My explanation seems to calm him. He's silent for a minute. It's hard for me to be patient, but I wait to see if he'll answer.

He runs a hand through his hair. "No, I wasn't drunk the night that I crashed. I was about a month sober at that point and hadn't been drinking at all. It had been raining, and the road was slick. The car in front of me took the turn too fast and went out of control. It was fishtailing all over the place." He shakes his head, lost in the memory. "I couldn't get away from it. Our cars were nose to tail, bumping into each other."

The bartender stops by to drop off our drinks. Caleb is silent, ducking his head and waiting for the man to leave before he resumes. "We were on Pacific Coast Highway, on the cliffs high above the ocean. In the daytime, the view from there is gorgeous. You can see blue water stretching all the way to the horizon. But at night, there aren't any lights and it's black all around."

Caleb's eyes are vacant, looking at a time in the past. I move closer to his warmth, suddenly chilled.

"On that stretch of road, with the car in front of me swerving, I had three choices. Drive off the cliff to my left, fall into the ocean, and probably die. Hit the car in front of me and probably kill us both. Or I could drive into the rocky cliff on my right, have my car explode, and probably die."

I'm breathless, waiting to hear what happened. "What did you do?"

"I didn't want to kill anyone, so I couldn't crash into the car in front of me. I didn't like the thought of drowning, so I couldn't go left. I chose the cliff on my right. Figured an explosion would be a quick death at least."

He meets my eyes, and, even though his words are calm, there's a residual terror in them, a trapped scream, left over from that night. "You have to understand. This was all going through my head in a split second. But it was that weird thing, where time slows down. Like you always read about—it really happened to me. I had time to think about which direction to turn. I thought about all the mistakes I've made in my life. The dreams I've never realized."

I'm completely sucked into his story, immersed in that moment with him. The crowded bar around me fades and instead I'm on a rain-swept road. Two lanes twist endlessly before and behind me, high above the crashing waves. I can hear the squeal of tires on wet pavement. The thump of windshield wipers. The wrench of metal as his car collides with the mountain.

He could have died, I realize. He *should* have died, given how bad that crash had been. The thought of him hurt and bleeding on the ground, his light lost forever, is unbearable. To think of a world without Caleb.

"What happened?" My voice rasps, tears threatening.

"My car hit the cliff. It was like when a bird flies into a window. One minute I was in motion and the next I just…stopped. There was a loud crash. All of my windows shattered at once. The airbag deployed and hit my face. It broke my nose and gave me two black eyes, but I wouldn't know that until later. I didn't mind, though. A broken nose is a lot better than being dead. It took the emergency crew three hours to cut through my car and get me out. They shut down the entire highway. Traffic backed all the way up to Malibu."

My eyes are wide with horror. "What about the other car?"

"They almost died, too. When I went right, they went left. Ended up with their front wheels hanging off the cliff. Just a few more inches and they would have plunged into the sea. I met up with them later, after we got released from the hospital. Nice couple in their fifties, vacationing from the Midwest. They thanked me for not rear-ending them, pushing them over the edge." His eyes slice over to me and then away. "It's embarrassing, but we cried together. It was like we had been through a collective trauma. One that only we could understand."

It all makes sense to me now. How moody Caleb has been. How he's changed his life so dramatically. Near-death experiences tend to do that to people. They make you reevaluate your priorities. Another piece of his puzzle.

Caleb straightens. "Anyway, one of the ambulance drivers took a picture of my car and then sold that photo to the tabloids. They splashed the image all over their front covers. Everyone assumed I was drunk because, frankly, I drank a lot in the months before I decided to stop." He shrugs and looks at me over the top of his soda water, waiting to see my reaction.

Surprising both of us, I throw my arms around his neck and squeeze tight. Rising up on my toes, I whisper in his ear, "I'm so happy you're alive."

Caleb holds me close, his hands on the small of my back.

His voice rasps low. "Right now, I'm happy I'm alive, too."

We pull apart, and I'm looking up at him and he's looking down at me with an intensity that sets my nerves buzzing. The noise of the bar fades to nothing. He's so close I can see the individual hairs in his famous eyebrows. I can see the tiny mark in his hairline, the still healing scar from where I hit him. I can see the depths in his beautiful eyes, which drop to linger on my lips. Then the most incredible thing happens.

He kisses me.

Caleb Freaking Lawson kisses *me,* Gwen Totally Ordinary Wright.

In all the history of kisses, this is the best one. I just know it. It's soft, a gentle brush of his lips and his tongue. He tastes like lime, like a beach with white sand and drinks with tiny umbrellas.

I kiss him back, clinging to him, my hands gripping his shirt. White flashes of light penetrate through my eyelids, blinding me, leaving bright afterimages as my lashes flutter open.

We're both breathless when we break apart. It's like I got smacked over the head by a two-by-four. Like little cartoon character birds should be flying in a circle above me tweeting. Given the dazed expression on Caleb's face, I'm hoping he feels the same.

aleb hums along with Christmas music on the car radio, singing softly under his breath. His voice is beautiful, even in a whisper.

When I had explained to Jenny that I was catching a ride back with Caleb, she had jumped up and down. "He actually came here? He showed up?" She gave me her best "I told you so" look. She's gonna freak out tomorrow when I tell her about the kiss.

Now in the car, he holds my hand, with his other hand loose on the steering wheel. I give him a little squeeze, reveling in the sensation of his skin against mine. It's one thing to see Caleb on the big screen or on a magazine cover, but something totally different to touch him, to feel the shift and pull of tendons and muscles as he squeezes me back.

"You said when your car was crashing you thought of the things you hadn't accomplished yet. Was singing one of them? Because you really are talented, and I personally think it's a shame not to share that with the world."

His thumb has been stroking the back of my hand. It stills with my question. I have to strain to hear his answer. "Music was the first thing that came to my mind. I've always wanted to try."

"Why don't you?"

He turns down the volume of the radio, so we won't have to shout. "I told you before. I'm scared."

"I was afraid to walk back into that bar tonight, but you didn't let me run away. You made me face all that pain. It was hard, but I'm glad I did it. I wouldn't have gone in there without you holding my hand, though. Maybe I can do that for you. I'll hold your hand if you want to try singing. You could start out small, just friends and family, then work your way up to bigger and bigger venues."

Two lines appear between his brows. "You'd do that? Be there for me? Be patient while I worked it out?"

"Of course."

He pulls his hand away, leaving my palm cold and bereft without his heat. "Why would you do that?" Full mouth turned down. He runs his fingers through his hair, tugging on the ends.

I don't understand his reaction. "Why would I not?" It hurts, how he's looking at me, and I have to fight past the roaring in my head to think it through from his perspective.

Caleb parks the car on the sidewalk in front of my house and faces me, still frowning.

After a tense silence when we stare at each other, it comes to me. I realize Caleb is searching for my angle. What I want from him in return for my kindness. Most of Caleb's life is transactional. His agent talks to him to make a commission. Reporters flatter him to get a sound bite. Girls date him to end up on a magazine cover.

But I'm not like that. I don't want anything, except to see him happy. I reach over the center console and retake his hand in mine.

"It's whatever you're comfortable with, Caleb. I'm just telling you my thoughts, but I'll support you either way. As for the reason I'd do that…" *Tick tock, Gwen. Time's running out.* I take in a deep breath and blow it back out. "I would do it because I like you. Like I really like you."

Squinting my eyes closed, I brace for the inevitable rejection. I'm so tense that when his hand lightly brushes my cheek, I flinch, and my eyes fly open. Caleb has moved toward me, his frostiness melted. His eyes are tender and eager as they search my face, like he's trying to peer into my soul.

His thumb strokes along my jaw and then down to brush my lips, sending a tingle through my body. Caleb unbuckles his seat belt and scoots closer, half sitting on the center console in a position that can't be comfortable.

With a hand on each of my cheeks, he holds me still and touches his mouth to mine in a gentle kiss. Hands slipping back into my hair, he continues to kiss me, each touch divine, awakening a million butterflies who beat their wings in my chest and in my belly. My lips part, and a breathy little sigh escapes me.

We stay like that, kissing in the car like teenagers, for another fifteen minutes before we finally pull apart. I stare glassy-eyed at him in the glow of the streetlights.

"We should probably go inside." His chest is heaving the same way that mine is.

Hoping that he means go inside and kiss some more, I'm highly disappointed when Caleb stops at the bottom of the stairs, says goodnight, and walks away.

23

The next morning a bleary-eyed Caleb is in the kitchen when I come down. It takes me a minute to notice the mug of coffee that he wordlessly holds out to me. With a start, I grab it and watch as he carries his cup of tea over to sit at the puzzle-covered table.

I hang back, not quite sure if I should join him. I'm worried things will be awkward between us. What if he regrets kissing me? What if he wants to leave now that we've crossed that invisible divide between being friends to…I don't know what we are.

It was easy to be brave in the heat of the moment, in the darkness of that cheap dive bar, in the dim of the car, but my courage is nowhere to be seen in the light of this sun-splashed kitchen.

Before I can decide if I should sit or stand, a loud banging comes from the front door. "Open up," someone yells and then kicks the door, making it rattle in its frame. "I need some help out here."

Caleb and I both go to answer. When the door opens, Jenny's there, bowed under the weight of an enormous Christmas tree. Twigs and pine needles are caught in her hair and sweater.

"Jenny!" I exclaim. "What is this?"

She snorts, unladylike. "You need to get your eyes checked, Gwendolen. It's obviously a Christmas tree. One that I got for you. Surprise!" She takes a few steps forward, lugging the tree after her.

A snigger next to me. I turn to see Caleb's amused smirk. "Gwendolen?" he whispers and raises a taunting eyebrow.

"What did you think Gwen was short for?" I hiss back, already feeling off balance with him this morning.

"I'm not sure, but it definitely wasn't Gwendolen." He chuckles as he moves forward to help Jenny.

With her at one end and him at the other, they drag the tree into the house. I scurry ahead of them, moving chairs and books out of the way to clear a path.

Once we place the tree on its side in front of the fireplace, Jenny turns to examine each of us. Her sharp eyes sweep over to Caleb. "You look awful this morning," she tells him, heading into the kitchen to grab herself a cup of coffee.

Caleb runs a hand through his thick golden hair. His eyes shift to me. Voice rough, he says, "I couldn't sleep last night."

Please. Please let me be the reason for his sleeplessness.

If that's the case, he wasn't alone. I laid awake for eons last night. The master bed had felt much too big, while, conversely, the room had felt much too small. My window was lightening with dawn by the time my eyes finally dropped closed.

Jenny paws through the cupboards, looking for something to eat.

Caleb yawns, stretches, and scratches his chest. Every motion makes those muscles and that tan skin shift in ways that make me stare.

Oblivious, he blinks sleepily. "I'm going to go take a quick shower. Don't start on the tree without me."

Once his footsteps have gone up the stairs, I turn to Jenny. She's holding her mug of coffee to her lips, staring at me over the rim. "Please, please tell me that you touched that man last night."

Embarrassed, I clap my hand over my eyes, and plop down on the couch. I peek through my fingers at her. "Yes. I kissed him."

She flies over to me, a grin splitting her face. "You did?" She grabs my forearms and shakes me. "Tell me everything. Everything!" Her voice pitches high with excitement.

I laugh, swatting her away. "It was just some kissing. In the bar and outside in the car."

"Who stopped it? Him? Or you?"

"I don't know. Him, I guess?" I sigh. "I didn't push it, though." I turn to her. "It was amazing," I confess. "Hands down, the best kisses of my life."

Her laughter rises into the air, joyful and light. "Of course it was. Wow! I can't believe you kissed Caleb Lawson."

"Me either. It seems a bit like a dream."

"You have to do it again. You just have to!"

I laugh at her impassioned speech, but then grow serious. "I don't know, Jenny. What if he doesn't want to? What if he wishes he hadn't kissed me?"

She scoffs. "Impossible. No one could ever regret kissing you."

"You say that because you're my best friend."

"No. I say that because you are smart and pretty and kind and loyal. You're the most loyal person I know. Forget Caleb Lawson. He's lucky to have *you* kiss him. Not the other way around."

Her mouth slams shut as Caleb comes back down the stairs.

He looks at us, expectant, and rubs his hands together. "Let's start. I want to decorate my first-ever tree."

Jenny gasps. "You've never decorated a tree before?"

"Never."

"Tragic. Just tragic," she declares and shakes her head sadly. "We need to fix that immediately."

I get out the tree stand, and the three us wrestle the tree into it. The smell of pine is all over my sap-sticky hands.

Caleb puts Christmas music on his phone, the way he did when we decorated before.

I open the boxes in the corner of the room. The one on top still has some of my things in it. I pick up the watercolor paints and hold them for a minute, wondering if maybe I should try again. It might be fun to access that creative side of my brain. To paint something, try to breathe life into paper with a swirl of colors. I put the box of paints away, telling myself to be realistic. When would I have time for a hobby like that? I spend all my hours working in the hospital.

That's who I am. A doctor. Not a painter.

The third box in the stack holds the Christmas ornaments. I place the box on the floor and sit down in front of it. Recognition washes over me as I get out a silver heart ornament my mom made when I was a baby. I brush my finger over the engraving etched into its surface.

Gwen's First Christmas. Love, Mom, Dad, and Brandon.

Caleb comes up behind me. He reaches over and plucks the heart out of my hand. "This is yours?" he asks as he traces the words with one fingertip the way I did.

I nod, overwhelmed with nostalgia.

"Show me some more." He sits down next to me, crossing his legs gracefully.

I pull the ornaments out and tell him about my favorite ones.

"Here's the starfish ornament we got on a family trip to Hawaii when I was ten. This tiny stethoscope Brandon and Liv gave me when I graduated from medical school. This is the paper snowman Teddy made when he was in kindergarten."

Caleb picks up the last one, Teddy's snowman, and inspects it carefully, turning it this way and that. His gaze moves to the Christmas tree and then the stockings that hang by the fireplace with all our names on them: Mom, Seth, Brandon, Liv, Teddy, Gwen, Maddie, and Megan. When he finally looks back at me, there's something forlorn in his expression.

"What is it?" I ask, concerned by the shift in his emotions.

"It's just..." He trails off, shoulders drooping. A long sigh, then he tries again. "It's just being here and seeing all this." He holds up Teddy's snowman, with its crudely drawn mouth and Q-Tip arms. "It makes me see everything I missed out on, and I guess that hurts. I mean, I've had some amazing experiences. I've done things and been to places that most people would envy. But most Christmases I've been by myself or with acquaintances. Not with family. I never made an ornament in school. I've never even *owned* a stocking to hang. I don't know…Christmas with you, learning how your family does it, makes me think that maybe I'd like to have a box like this one day, full of memories made with the people I love."

I place my hand on his tense upper arm and squeeze gently. "I don't see why you can't have that, Caleb. If that's what you want."

"No." Each word is laced with melancholy. "That life's not for me. Not with the way I'm living now."

I open my mouth, about to say something comforting, when he gives himself a small shake and cuts me off with a gruff, "Show me some more."

Okay. Conversation over. Got it.

Digging deep into the box, I pull out a rough wooden reindeer, crudely painted brown with white-tipped hooves and a red nose. I swallow thickly, thinking about how a minute ago Caleb was sad and now, apparently, it's my turn. "My dad made this. Hand carved it. He and my mom didn't have any money when they got married. For their first Christmas living together, he created this, so they'd have at least one ornament on their tree. My mom painted it."

I have a flashback to when I was in middle school, Mom holding the reindeer up and laughing at her horrible paint job. "Look, honey," she said to me, "you're a much better painter than I ever was."

Jenny, who knows me so well, breaks in before I get too lost in my memories. "Come on, Gwen," she says, coming to stand behind me. "Help me put on the tinsel."

Her distraction works. While we decorate, I deliberately let go of the conversation Caleb and I just had and instead embrace the spirit of the holiday. *Focus on the present,* I remind myself. Jenny and I dance around to the music, sprinkling tinsel on the tree branches like we're fairies doling out pixie dust until the whole tree sparkles.

"Crank up the music," we shout to Caleb, who complies. The two of us croon along to the Christmas songs loudly and off key. We try to get Caleb to sing with us, but he's obstinate, crossing his arms across his chest and shaking his head with a bemused smile on his face. "It's more fun to listen to you butcher the songs," he says, laughing.

We *all* laugh and talk, the three of us, as we work on the tree. There's an easy familiarity growing between us. It's a feeling of friendship, and I love to see Caleb relax into it. He smiles more now than he did when he first arrived. He laughs more freely. There's something loosening in him. Knots coming untied, the way I untangled those Christmas lights with his help.

Jenny's changed, too. She talks to Caleb like he's human now, like one of us, and it makes me proud. She had a lot more invested in the false dream of movie star Caleb than I did, so I know it was hard for her to let go of that. To accept the reality of him, messy as it is.

After the ornaments have been carefully hung, we step back to admire the results. It's a beautiful tree, deep green and tall. The top almost scrapes the ceiling. Colorful lights twinkle, reflecting off ornaments that dangle and twirl from the branches. My family's history is in this tree. All of our fondest memories are commemorated here.

"Where's your special star?" Jenny asks me.

"What star?" Caleb looks at me curiously as he bends down to scratch Pip's head. She's under his feet as usual.

"We have this old, battered star for the top of the tree. We got it when Teddy was born," I explain. "Every year, my dad would put me on his shoulders and lift me to place it up there." I smile at the memory. "It made me feel special, that *I* was the one to carry the star. Never Brandon or Teddy, just me."

I turn to Jenny, answering her question. "Mom took it with her to Japan. She didn't expect me to get a tree here all by myself."

I pause, looking around the room and thinking. So many times in my life I've felt out of place. Insecure with Jax and his friends, believing I wasn't cute or charming enough. Too consumed with grief to share the same carefree joy that my classmates had in college.

Today, I haven't experienced that uncomfortable twinge once. That little voice questioning if I'm good enough has remained silent. Which is strange. I'm living with and kissing one of the most famous actors in America. I'd guess that if anything could trigger my insecurities, that would be it.

But I don't feel unworthy when I'm with Caleb. I feel empowered, knowing that he has his flaws just as I have mine. I'm understanding that people may seem perfect from the outside, but that many people are struggling inside. All those times I compared myself to others and came up short, I was seeing the image they presented, not the real person underneath.

"I'm not all by myself like my mom thought I would be." Looking at Caleb and Jenny, a sense of warmth and belonging fills me up. "I've got you guys."

I give Jenny a hug, wrapping my arms around her. "Thank you for the tree. It's wonderful."

She squeezes me back, a little too tight, just like usual.

Caleb echoes my sentiment. "Yeah, thanks, Jenny."

His eyes find me, skewering me with their sincerity. "Thanks to you, too, Gwen. For letting me stay here, welcoming me into your world."

His smile is devastating.

I'll never recover from it.

24

Still tired, Caleb and I separate to take naps after Jenny leaves. When I wake, it's early evening. I watch out of my window as the sun gives one last kiss to the horizon before it sinks from view. There's the comforting sounds of banging pots and water running from downstairs.

I take off my sweater and jeans, now wrinkled from my nap. Rifling through my luggage, I find my pretty short green dress with the belted waist and pockets. I had thrown it in at the last minute when I packed, anticipating that Jenny and I might go to a fancy restaurant while I was home.

Downstairs may not be an upscale restaurant, but the food sure tastes like it and I really want to impress the chef.

Pulling my hair up into a loose bun, dusting on some shimmery eyeshadow, and adding a layer of mascara completes my look. I stare at myself in the mirror.

Not too shabby.

The tantalizing smell of baking bread rises up the stairs when I leave the bedroom. I trace it down to the kitchen. Caleb is humming, bent over, peering into the oven, with Pip at his feet. He's wearing a fresh pair of jeans and my favorite dark gray T-shirt. Adorably, he's tied an apron around his neck and waist. It's my mom's, and it says "Kiss the Chef" in bold letters. I want to follow the advice but hold back, still unsure where we stand.

When he turns from the oven, he sees me and does a double take. "You look nice," he breathes out, eyes sparking.

"Thanks." I fumble, tripping slightly, as I move farther into the kitchen. "Can I help you?"

"Nope. I've got everything under control. It's a steak and potatoes kind of night. With homemade candy cane fudge for dessert. Oh! I made sourdough dinner rolls, too. Is that all right with you?"

"Mmm. That sounds great." I'm already salivating, mentally skipping ahead to dessert and picturing that minty-chocolaty fudge.

"You could do one thing for me, though." He wipes his hands on a towel and throws it over his shoulder.

"What's that?"

"We need some tunes. Take my phone and pick something out." He pulls his phone out of his back pocket and passes it to me. It's still warm from his body heat.

Caleb chops fresh rosemary, releasing its heady fragrance into the air while I thumb through the music on his phone. He's got quite a selection. Everything from classical to show tunes to hard rock.

"What are you in the mood for?" I ask. "You have so much music on here that it's difficult to choose."

He pauses and tilts his head thoughtfully. "How about some jazz? Try John Coltrane, My Favorite Things."

"You mean the song from *The Sound of Music?*"

He smiles, and it warms me from the inside out. I enjoy seeing him like this, relaxed, content.

"Yeah, that's the song, but you've never heard it the way Coltrane plays it."

With a push of the button, I turn it on. Caleb's right. The clarinet mixes with the saxophone to make something magical. A snare drum sets the beat in the background. The music spilling out of his tiny phone speakers is light and sophisticated and lovely.

I feel like a real grownup, with this handsome man making me dinner and jazz playing. I almost offer him a glass of wine but catch myself at the last minute, remembering that alcohol and Caleb don't mix. It's no big loss to me. Beyond the occasional beer or glass of wine, I've never been much of a drinker.

Caleb's phone buzzes in my hands. His mom's name lights up the screen. I hold it out for him. He reaches over and declines the call.

"You do that a lot," I note. "Avoid her calls."

An uncomfortable twist of his mouth. "We have a…complicated relationship." He turns away from me, busying himself with the food.

"You seem like you're close to your mom," he says, talking over his shoulder.

"We are, but we have a few sore spots between us. Mostly from around the time when my dad died. In the end, I know she loves me."

Caleb's quiet for so long I think he won't respond, but then he says, "I guess I know my mom loves me too. She just has a strange way of showing it sometimes."

I wait to see if there's more, but when he remains silent, I decide not to press the issue. This is feeling almost like a date, and I don't want to ruin the mood.

"Any update on the house renovations?" He changes the topic of conversation.

"I talked to the foreman today. He says it's coming along. They'll have some bedrooms upstairs done by the end of the week. You can finally move off the couch and into a real bed."

"Food's ready," he announces a few minutes later, placing a sizzling steak, salad, rolls, and loaded baked potatoes on the table. Bending, he puts a small plate with cut-up pieces of steak on the floor for Pip, who runs over eagerly. Caleb gives her an affectionate pat on the head and then we sit down together.

"You must really like music to have so many songs on your phone?" I ask, curious.

A bashful shrug. "I've moved a lot. Set to set. Location to location. More than any other thing or person, music has been my one constant. I take it with me no matter where I go. I find it soothing. Even heavy metal can be a lullaby, given the right circumstances."

Caleb's voice drops like he's telling me a secret. "There's music playing all the time in my head. It's like I have my own 24/7 soundtrack going on. I thought for years that everyone was like that. Just assumed it. It wasn't until I was an adult that I realized not everyone hears a song while they brush their teeth or walk down the sidewalk."

The steak is cooked perfectly with a slight char on the outside and a tender pink center. My fork pierces it easily. As I bring it to my lips, I ask, "What's your toothbrushing song?"

His laugh has a rumble to it, the sound the ocean makes as it tumbles over the shore at low tide. "It changes constantly, but recently it's been Uptown Funk. It used to be Every Breath You Take."

I pick up my spoon and mock sing into it. "Every breath you take will be so minty from the toothpaste."

He's laughing harder now. "That was *terrible*. Don't quit your day job."

"What?" I place my hand over my chest in feigned disbelief. "You don't think I should give up this doctor gig to run off and join a band?"

Caleb pretends to think for a minute, scrunching up his face and tapping his chin with his finger. "I'd say definitely no." He leans back in his chair and gives me an assessing stare. "Stay being a doctor. It suits you."

There's admiration in the way he says it, as if I've done something big and worthwhile. It causes a little fizz of pride to bubble up in my chest.

"We've established that I enjoy music," he says. "How about you? What do you like to do when you're not busy doctoring?"

"Doctoring?" I giggle at the word. "I used to have hobbies—reading and painting—but honestly, medicine has taken over my life. Even the hours when I'm not at the hospital I spend studying or working on research. I get this guilty feeling if I do anything else. Like I'm letting the patients down."

My brain scrambles, trying to find something interesting about myself. I don't want Caleb to see how boring and predictable I am. Finally, a nonmedical activity occurs to me. "I do like horror movies."

He gives me a look like he can't tell if I'm joking or not. "Horror movies?"

I nod. "I watch them at night when I can't fall asleep."

"That's…unexpected. What do you like about them?"

I trace a circle in the condensation of my water glass, my forehead creasing as I figure out the best way to answer. "I like the thrill they give me. It makes me feel alive, to have my heart pound. To experience that zing of fear. It's hard to explain, but in the ER I see a lot of horrible things. Car accidents, assaults, overdoses. After a day of real-life horror, it's nice to escape into fake horror. Makes the real stuff seem more manageable by comparison, I guess."

Ugh, he's going to think I'm a psycho.

I peer at him through my lashes, trying to gauge his response, and am surprised to find that he's looking at me like I've said something interesting. I ask him, "Have you ever acted in a horror movie?"

Caleb's attention narrows in on me. "How many of my movies have you seen, exactly?"

I hesitate before I answer, not wanting to hurt his feelings. "Maybe one where you were a detective?" I add, "Sorry, I don't watch a lot of movies. It's not because I don't enjoy them. I just never have time. Even the horror ones I hardly ever finish. Usually, I fall asleep halfway through."

"Don't apologize. It's oddly charming, how you haven't seen me like that." He looks pleased, a small smile playing at his lips.

Done with dinner and dessert, we gather the plates and silverware and carry them to the sink. "You cooked, so I'll wash up," I tell him, moving aside a red poinsettia that sits on the counter.

"That's okay. I'll help." He puts the plug in the drain, turns the hot water on, and adds a squirt of dish soap.

"Are you sure that's the right soap?" I taunt.

Caleb mock frowns and flicks a soapy finger at me, tiny water droplets landing on my dress. I splash him back, and we both laugh.

It's a double sink. Once Caleb's side is filled with bubbly soapy water, we fill my side with clean water. He scrubs the dirty dishes, then hands them to me for rinsing and drying. We're quiet as we work, finding a natural rhythm with each other. Every time he finishes a dish, my hand is there outstretched, waiting to take it.

When we're done, Caleb turns to me. "So?" His voice carries a note of uncertainty. "What do you want to do now?"

Kiss you.

That's what my brain supplies, but my mouth is smart enough to say, "I don't know. Watch a movie? We could watch one of yours?"

A firm shake of his head. "I *hate* watching my own movies. It feels weird, like seeing my ghost. Plus, I spend the whole time analyzing it. Thinking about how I should have delivered the line differently, how I could have made it better."

A beat of silence, then he says, "I know. Let's watch a horror movie. You pick it out. The one you like best."

After a moment of debate, I choose *The Shining*, which I've seen many times before. We turn off the lights. Caleb and I settle next to each other on the couch. Pip curls against Caleb on the side opposite of me. The movie begins with the iconic aerial shots of a car winding through the forest on its way to the haunted Overlook hotel.

I watch Caleb out of the corner of my eye. The flickering light from the TV screen plays over his features, highlighting those long eyelashes and sharp cheekbones. His cinnamon scent layers around me.

Like some inexperienced teenager, I shift and yawn, trying to subtly scoot closer to him.

He notices, but not in the way I intended. "Are you tired?" he asks. "We can finish this movie tomorrow."

"No!" I say, a bit too forcibly. "No. That's okay. I'm awake."

I'm awful at this. How is it that I can set a broken femur but am unable to make a move on a man I like?

I hold still after that, trying to watch the film but unable to concentrate, too distracted by Caleb next to me. The longer the movie goes on, the louder my insecurities become.

It's been an entire day, and he hasn't touched me. Sure, there were times it seemed like he was flirting, but what if I misinterpreted those? Was he just being friendly? The more I think about it, the more convinced I am that he must regret last night. Otherwise, he would have kissed me again by now.

Perhaps, after seeing how upset I was over Jax, he had kissed me out of pity. Or maybe he was tired of kissing the most beautiful actresses in the world. Maybe he had been curious about what it was like to kiss an "ordinary person" and once that curiosity was satisfied, he had no reason to do it again. Or maybe, I realize, my stomach sinking, maybe I'm a really, *really* bad kisser.

By the end of the movie, I'm convinced that Caleb thinks of me as just a friend and wishes he had a time machine to go back and unkiss me. He turns on the light next to the couch, and I stumble to my feet, my face flaming.

He notices that something's off right away. "Are you okay?"

"Fine. I'm fine. Just tired. I'm going to bed."

I start to brush past a wide-eyed Caleb, but he steps in front of me, blocking my path. We're close, standing chest to chest. I look down at the floor, feeling timid.

"Hey," he says softly.

Slowly, my gaze rises to his.

His serious aqua eyes search my face, looking for I don't know what. Slowly, his hand comes up, like he might caress my cheek. I lean toward that touch, rise onto my toes to be closer to it. My body pulls tight, filled with yearning.

I'm an arrow, notched in his bow. He just has to release me, and I'll fly to him.

After a long, heavy pause, his hand drops down to his side. I sink back onto my heels, and we break eye contact.

Caleb's voice is rough. "Well, goodnight, I guess."

There's a tightening behind my eyes like I might cry. "Goodnight," I choke out and spin away.

The whole time I go up the stairs, I'm hoping he'll stop me.

Call out my name. Ask me to come back.

But he doesn't.

can't sleep that night. Tossing and turning. Upset with myself for being so foolish. Upset with Caleb for being so irresistible. Upset with both of us for kissing. What was the point of that if we were only going to do it for one night?

Finally, past two a.m., I give up and pad downstairs to get a glass of water. On the very last step, the floorboard creaks under my weight.

Caleb's head pops up from the couch, his hair tousled. "Gwen?"

"Sorry," I whisper. "Didn't mean to wake you."

"I wasn't asleep."

Without thinking, I take a step toward that raspy voice, drawn to it like a moth to flame.

"Me either," I admit. "Could you not sleep because you were worried some creepy little twin girl ghosts were going to murder you with an ax?"

A sandpaper laugh from him, the sound scraping down my spine. "No, that's not it." There's a long pause, and then he asks, "Do you...do you want to come over here?" He whispers it so softly that for a minute I wonder if I'm back in bed dreaming. That's how this moment feels.

Dreamlike.

The Christmas tree lights are on, sending their rainbow of colors over the room, casting a stained-glass pattern across the floor. The light shifts over Caleb's face as I move closer, painting him in shades of red, blue, and green.

There's a hush in the air. Like the house, the whole world is holding its breath, waiting to see what happens next.

I stop a few feet away, uncertain. We stare at each other warily, the only motion the rise and fall of our chests as we breathe. Caleb's the first to break that tension.

"Please." He holds his hand out to me...and I take it.

He pulls me down onto the couch next to him. His hand comes up to gently brush my cheek. "Please," he begs again and then bends over me, placing a delicate kiss on my lips. I reach for him, sliding my hands up his neck and slipping my fingers into his feather-soft hair.

"I can't sleep. Haven't slept in days," he murmurs. "You. It's you. Keeping me up." He kisses me, soft and sweet. "Can't stop thinking about you. Dreaming about you." He continues to kiss me until I'm dizzy. Until I lose sense of time and self. I'm a bee, drowning in his honey and not even minding because it tastes so sweet.

After a few minutes, I wake up enough to ask the questions I need answers to. With gentle pressure, I push him away, far enough that I can look up into his face. "I don't understand. You didn't touch me all day. I was starting to think you weren't interested."

The shadows in the room exaggerate his grimace. "That just shows what a good actor I am. I was worried you wouldn't want me to. That it would be awkward, but I've been lying awake thinking about it. I kept wishing I could do the night over. Except this time, after the movie, I would kiss you like I should have. Like this." He kisses me passionately, like he wants to know all of my secrets.

Before I can get lost in the sensation, I push him away. "You need to quit doing that."

It takes a minute for him to respond. "What do you mean?"

"I mean acting with me. Hiding how you feel or what you think. I don't want you to do that anymore." I'm still upset with him for how tortured I'd been during the movie.

Caleb moves back, gazing down at me in the moonlight, his eyes clearing like he's really seeing me. "You're right," he agrees. "So, *is* it okay? This?" He gestures between us. "I can stop."

I pull him into me, "Don't you dare."

White teeth flash in the darkness and the thrill of it, of witnessing him truly pleased, has my heart singing.

I did this. I'm the one making him happy.

This time I take charge. Staring into his ocean eyes, I whisper fiercely, "I don't want to stop."

Caleb wraps his arms around me. His hand burrows into my hair, fingertips massaging the back of my scalp. His lips skim along my jaw and then up to my ear.

With a sudden movement, he presses his nose into my hair and inhales deeply. A soft exhale. "Your hair smells so good, like strawberry pie. I'm always sniffing it when I think you won't notice."

His admission and the adoring way he looks at me melts my heart.

We kiss some more, until I have no choice but to break it off. "Um. Caleb? I'm so sorry, but I have to use the restroom."

He laughs softly and releases me. "Okay. Promise to come right back, though?"

I place my hand over my heart and solemnly say, "I promise."

This earns another laugh from him.

A quick peck on his lips, and I run to the bathroom.

When I see myself in the mirror, I come to a screeching halt, barely recognizing my reflection. My eyes are feverish. My lips are red and puffy. I can't believe this is me, dependable, predictable Gwen running around the house in the middle of the night. Kissing famous movie stars.

No one would recognize me, and maybe there's something wrong with me because that thought gives me a thrill. It feels good to be reckless for once. To chase only what *I* desire with no thoughts about anyone else. After all, there's nothing sensible about wanting Caleb Lawson.

When I return from the bathroom, Caleb reaches for me but stops when I hold up my hand. "Is it weird that we're kissing in Mom and Seth's house?"

Caleb drops his voice. "Am I a bad person? Because I actually like it. I had my own apartment by the time I was fifteen, so I never got that making out in my girlfriend's parents' house experience until now."

The only word I heard in that whole sentence was girlfriend, and I cling to it like a life raft. I could listen to Caleb say that word all day. *Girlfriend.* Is that what I will be after this? I'm not naive enough to believe that kissing equates love or that it binds us together forever. My experience with Jax taught me that wasn't true.

We spend the next hour talking and kissing on the couch. It's the most natural feeling to be this way with Caleb. Like I don't have to be awkward or uncomfortable.

After a while he breaks off an especially long kiss and laughingly says, "I swear my heart just stopped for a second. That's how nice it is to touch you."

I giggle and lean against his chest, telling him, "Good thing for you I know CPR."

26

Caleb is happy. So, so happy.

A happy Caleb, well, he *shines*. He glows. So bright it almost hurts to look at him.

He reads to me, cooks for me, dances across the living room floor with me. He pets Pip and doesn't grimace when she slobbers on him.

He sits next to Jenny and me on the couch, watching cheesy horror movies. He laughs when I get scared and bury my face in his shoulder. "You're the one who picked this movie," he gently scolds, but doesn't force me to watch the gory parts.

He touches me constantly. A hand on my knee under the table at dinner. A kiss stolen on the stairwell. His arm around my shoulders while we read together on the couch.

We kiss each other good night before we part ways to go to our rooms. We kiss good morning over coffee and tea. He makes me so happy. The world could be burning down outside our door, and I wouldn't know or care.

That's when my mother calls.

know I'm in trouble right away.

It's in the tone of her voice. The voice that all mothers have, the sharp one. The one where they use your middle name, like, "Gwendolen Jane Wright. You get over here immediately."

That voice.

That's the one she uses when I pick up the phone. I'm lying in bed, with my head on Caleb's chest as he reads the last Twilight novel and I read a medical journal. Pip is curled into a furry ball at Caleb's feet.

As soon as I hear that voice, I'm up, shooting Caleb a "sorry" look and rushing out the door.

Halfway down the stairs, Caleb's phone rings behind me. I finally convinced him to unmute it, arguing that I might need to call him if Jenny and I got into trouble. Like if a baby goat fell on me and pinned me to the ground, for example.

I hear Caleb answer the phone with a warm, "John!" I recognize that name. It's Caleb's old trainer. Caleb's been wanting to ask him about what exercises he can do here in the house, without having to go to the gym.

"What's up, Mom?" I ask cautiously as I make my way to the living room.

"I don't know, Gwendolen," she says in *that* voice. "Why don't *you* tell me what's up?"

It's a trap. My body knows it, flushing immediately. Heat runs from my head to my toes, followed quickly by a frigid chill. My heart hammers as my nervous system goes into fight-or-flight mode.

"Umm," I hedge nervously.

"Anything you want to tell me?" she asks. "Anything about you or Teddy?"

My mind whirs in a million directions, searching for a way out. There are so many different things she could be referring to. Caleb and me? Teddy and college? Something else entirely?

"Teddy?" I repeat. "Have you talked to Teddy?" Maybe he's the one that's got her all riled up.

"Yes, as a matter of fact. I had a long and very interesting conversation with your brother."

Oh, boy. What did Teddy tell her? I decide to be proactive. Hopefully, my guess is correct and I'm not spilling my brother's secrets. "I talked to him, too. I don't think he's very happy at college."

"Exactly!" she cries out. "How could you have known that and not told me, Gwen? I expect you to share information like that with me. Don't you think I need to know if my son is struggling in school? He said he told you a week ago, but this is the first time I'm hearing about it. I trust you to help me with Teddy," she scolds. It's such a familiar phrase that nausea rises within me, a gut response to all those times she said something similar.

Help me with Teddy while I go to work.

Help me with Teddy. Make his dinner while I'm gone.

Help me with Teddy. I don't have time to go over his homework.

Help me with Teddy. Drive him to basketball practice.

It wasn't her fault. I know it wasn't. We had no other options. She was working, sacrificing everything to keep us afloat. All the resentment I felt back then had to be suppressed. Shoved down. Swallow my depression, my grief, my anger.

Teddy needs me, and I can't let him down.

I can't let *her* down.

"I'm sorry, Mom, but he asked me not to tell. I didn't want to betray his trust."

"Oh, so it was okay to betray *my* trust?" she asks angrily.

Closing my eyes, I rub the space between them. "You said it yourself,

Mom, when you left for Japan. Teddy's grown now. We all are. You can't have it both ways. We can't be old enough to leave but so young that you have to micromanage us."

There's a hurt silence from her end of the phone, followed by a stiff cough. "Someday," she says, "you'll have kids of your own. When you do, you'll realize that no matter how old they are, you'll always worry about them, want to help them."

A spasm of guilt clenches in my belly because she's right. I never really want her to stop worrying about me and caring for me, and she has helped me. I remember after Dad died, when things were bad, how she sent me to a therapist. I remember all the times she held me when I cried, after Dad and after Jax. How her own tears had mingled with mine.

Mom's voice has become more gravelly over time. It's a terrible moment to notice it, but she sounds older. It surprises me, that telltale mark of age. I still think of her as the young mom who picked me up from elementary school, but she's not that person anymore.

She's a grandmother now.

The thought of her aging frightens me. I've already lost one parent. As defensive as I feel in this moment, I can't stand the knowledge that someday I'll lose her too. I take my anger and turn down the heat, reducing it to a low simmer of regret and resentment.

My mind goes eerily silent when she adds, "Your brother told me another thing. About Caleb."

Teddy. You little tattletale.

She's waiting for me to say something, but I have no idea how much she knows, so I stay quiet.

A disappointed huff from her. "Is it true that he's living with you?"

"Yes," I answer her honestly. "Caleb's been here for a while. I'm sorry I didn't tell you. He's hiding out. Doesn't want anyone to know."

"Caleb tells you to lie to your own mother and you just do it? Really, Gwen. I raised you better than that." Suspiciously, she asks, "Is this because you resent me for moving to Japan? Are you lying as a way to punish me?" She's angry and, even worse, hurt.

"What? No! That's not it at all." Guilt mixes in with all of my other bad feelings. "I'm sorry. I didn't want you to worry about me."

"Like I just told you, I'm your mother. I'll always worry about you. It's my job." There's quiet on the phone for a long minute. "How's he been? Caleb? Is he being kind? Respectful? Seth says that we can trust him with you, but he doesn't understand what it's like to have a daughter."

"Caleb's fine Mom. He's nice and cooks all my meals. He's a talented chef."

I stop, thinking about my brother and how he ratted me out. "Teddy told you Caleb's here?"

"Don't be mad at Teddy. He had just told me he wants to quit school. I was yelling at him, and he blurted your secret out in a moment of panic. He felt bad. Tried to take it back, but I can always tell when he's lying."

She adds, "Seth was in on that phone call, too. He told Marjorie where Caleb was. He thought she had a right to know."

Uh-oh. I glance at the door, almost expecting to see Marjorie there, about to break it down. No one stands on our front step, though.

Mom's still talking. "I prefer that you don't get too close to Caleb."

I keep my tone neutral. "Oh yeah? Why's that?"

I can practically hear her fidget through the phone. "It's not my place to tell you the details, but he's had some…problems. Things I don't want you involved in—"

Before she can say anything else, I interrupt. "What problems? You mean his drinking?"

She halts mid-sentence, clearly thrown off guard that I know. "Yes, mostly that, but also some other stuff."

I want so badly to ask about the other things, but she'll see that as a sign of weakness and use it as a wedge to split Caleb and me apart.

"He's stopped drinking. Hasn't done it in months. He hasn't had a single drink since he's been here." Pip brushes against my leg. I scratch her ears.

"Well, that's good to hear," Mom says reluctantly.

I wait for her to go on.

Mom hesitates, debating something. "When Seth called Marjorie, she already knew that Caleb was staying with you."

Shocked, I sit down heavily on the couch. "She did? How?"

"You know Caleb has a whole management team, right? He has agents and publicists, even lawyers on retainers. I guess some young girls got pictures of Caleb while you were out caroling? Do you know what I'm talking about?"

"Yeah. What about them?" There's trepidation in my voice. Warning bells ring faintly in the back of my brain.

My mother is a good-enough person that she sounds regretful. "Those girls tried to post the pictures on the internet. Caleb's team intercepted the photos before they went viral. Marjorie and Ben talked to the girls and their family."

She pauses, waiting for my reaction, but I don't know what to say because I haven't figured it out yet. What is she getting at?

"They paid those girls, honey. Gave them money to stay silent. Made them sign an agreement not to post the pictures. They want to protect Caleb and give him the privacy he needs. Haven't you wondered why it's been so quiet around there? Why there aren't reporters and paparazzi knocking down your door?" She speaks slowly, giving space between each word so they can sink in.

I feel dumb because I haven't wondered about that. It didn't occur to me. "I just assumed we were doing a stellar job of hiding Caleb. Keeping it quiet that he was here," I tell her in a small voice, realizing that I've been naive.

I'm not powerful enough to keep Caleb safe on my own.

His team had been working in the background, sheltering him.

"Marjorie and Ben are trying to protect him. Give Caleb some space and quiet. He has things he needs to figure out. He doesn't need complications right now."

That's me. I'm the complication.

I don't tell her about how Caleb quit his entire career. I wonder if his parents are already aware. It's possible that I haven't given Marjorie and Ben enough credit. I see that in their own way they're trying to be good parents to Caleb. To give him the time he needs to heal. It must have been terrifying for them too when he almost died in that car crash.

"Does Caleb know about that? The money and those girls?" I ask quietly, wondering why he never mentioned it to me. Is he hiding it or is that just such a common occurrence in his life that he thinks it's not noteworthy enough to bring up?

"I'm not sure," Mom says. "I'm glad they paid those girls, though. It not only protected Caleb, but you too. You need to be careful around him. You have your future to think about."

She continues. "In a few years, you'll apply for a fellowship program. How would it look to them if you got caught in a scandal with Caleb? Every girl he's seen with ends up on a magazine's cover, even if they're just friends and not dating."

She doesn't know about the kissing. My first thought is, *Good, I don't want her to know.* When I think about it some more, I start to get angry again. Why does my mom assume that Caleb and I are only friends? It doesn't even occur to her that we could be something more. Does she believe I couldn't attract someone like him? Like I'm too far beneath him?

She goes on, oblivious to how I might be feeling. "It's dangerous, Gwen. Your life is too different from his. He's all drama, and you're…"

"What, Mom?" I demand. "I'm what?"

My rage builds slowly, a kettle on the stove about to boil over.

She sighs. "You're just Gwen. Sweet, smart, dependable Gwen."

I know she says it with love, but it makes me want to scream. I want to stamp my foot, throw myself on the ground like a toddler.

"What if I don't want to be sweet and dependable?" I snap. "What if there are different parts of me, ones that even you've never seen, that I want to explore? How would that make you feel?"

A shocked silence from the other end of the phone. I've *never* spoken to my mother that way. Especially after Dad died, my whole family has tiptoed around each other, scared to crack the eggshells at our feet.

Through her quiet, I can sense her hurt grow. Guilt and regret slice through my fury. This is my mom. She's loved me, sacrificed for me, suffered more tragedy than most. Who am I to add to her misery?

"Sorry." I soften my tone. "I shouldn't have said that. It's just that you're overreacting. Caleb is a good person, and I enjoy spending time with him."

"I don't want you to be hurt." Her voice becomes pleading. "Promise me you won't do anything stupid with him. That you'll keep your distance."

It's a vow I can't keep. One that I've already broken, but if I tell the truth, I know she'll try to break us up. The entire family will get involved. All of them butting in, giving their opinion of *our* relationship.

I only have a few more weeks with Caleb before I go back to New York. Selfishly, I want to keep him all to myself. To stay in this bliss-filled bubble we've created together. If I'm honest with Mom, that bubble will pop.

So I lie.

"Don't worry. I won't get close to him. I promise."

28

Once I hang up with my mom, her words bounce around in my head, as heavy and loud as bowling balls. The concern and fear in her voice replays in my mind. I flop on the couch, laying on my back with my eyes closed, and go over everything she said.

I hate to admit it, but she did have some points.

Caleb and I are very different people, from very different backgrounds. We've been sheltered, living in this Christmas-themed snow globe of a house. It's let the tendrils of our new relationship take root and grow. A tiny seedling, thriving on a diet of good conversation and laughter.

But what happens if that little plant is taken out of this greenhouse and exposed to true daylight? How will it respond with the sun glaring down and no place to hide? Will it wither? Be burned by the harsh atmosphere?

What about the secrets Caleb hides from me? Why didn't he tell me about those girls? Why has he never mentioned this Lola chick, who, if Jenny is to be believed, he was in a relationship with? What's in the notebook he's always writing in?

That's when I do something bad.

Something I swore I would never ever do.

I Google him.

Typing Caleb Lawson into the search bar brings up literally thousands of results. He's *all* over the internet. Articles about his movies, biographies about his rise to fame, exposés about his drinking and relationships. It's all there in gory Technicolor detail.

I glance at the stairs, worried about getting caught, as guilty as a kid looking at pornography. Caleb's voice murmurs above me. He's still on the phone.

In a rush, I skip the articles and go straight to the images. The page fills with tiny thumbnail pictures of Caleb. Photos ranging from him as a little kid to the present day.

The most recent photos are at the top. I see the one that Jenny showed me, the wreck of his car. There's another picture of him, obviously drunk, his shirt half-unbuttoned. His arm is thrown around the shoulder of another famous actor as they stumble out of a club in West Hollywood.

Many of the photos are of Caleb with a gorgeous woman, a total bombshell. She's tall, even taller than Caleb in her heels, which are all spiked stilettos, the kind I could never wear. I would break my ankle for sure in those shoes. The woman has an exotic look to her, like she's of Italian or maybe Mediterranean descent.

She has glossy black hair that hangs in perfect beachy waves down to her low back. Deep brown eyes are framed by lashes so long they have to be fake. Her lips are so plump that I imagine kissing them would be like falling into a soft, memory foam pillow.

She's exquisite.

I check the name under her picture.

Lola Monroe.

Darn it.

How am I ever going to compete with *that?*

With a thunk, I slam the computer shut and slump onto my back, throwing an arm over my face, unable to look at any more pictures of Caleb's life.

His *real* life.

He's never lied to me about any of this, but I still feel betrayed. I keep my eyes closed, those photos playing like a movie through my mind as my thoughts descend into panic and despair.

The more I think about it, the more I realize that maybe Caleb didn't lie, but there are things he hasn't mentioned. Like those girls from caroling or this stunning ex-girlfriend.

What *else* is he not telling me? I roll over onto my belly and stare at the bottom of the couch.

There it is.

That little black-and-white checkered notebook, one of its corners barely sticking out. I glance again at the ceiling and listen. Caleb's low, muffled voice drifts down the stairs.

Good. Still on the phone.

My attention is drug like a magnet to the notebook. It's practically begging me to come take a peek. Without a doubt, I know I shouldn't. It completely violates Caleb's privacy, an invasion I wouldn't want directed at me. A tiny voice in the back of my head tells me it's only fair. That this is his punishment for withholding from me when I've been so open and honest with him.

I almost convince myself that I'm doing it for us. To strengthen our relationship. To know him better so I'll be prepared for any more sneak attacks, like the one my mother just sprung on me.

With the devil's voice whispering in my ear, I lean over and pick up the notebook. I stand up with it in my hand and pace, slowly flipping through the book.

At first, it looks like what Caleb told me. Notes about appointments and flight times in his unruly cursive script flows over the pages. I have to squint to read it.

And they say doctors have bad handwriting.

After a while, the writing changes. Snippets of sentences that make no sense when taken together. Some of them rhyme, and I wonder if Caleb's trying to be a poet.

Toward the middle of the book, everything transforms. Those fragmented words align. They develop a rhythm, a cadence. Musical notes appear under some verses. That's when I finally understand.

Caleb is writing music.

This must be song lyrics and some musical notes that go along with them. I read fast, quickly scanning each line, scared of getting caught. But when I see my name at the top of a page, I slow down and take in each word like it's essential to my survival. Somewhere in these sentences that he's written about me is the key to Caleb's soul. The window to see myself through his eyes.

The song is beautiful, sweet with a hint of melancholy. It's the chorus that hooks me, though.

I read it over and over, tears gathering in my eyes.

My lips against yours
I've fallen under your spell
Never known anyone quite like you
No one's ever known me quite so well

I'm so engrossed in the song, trying to piece it together with the tune he's written under the lyrics, that I completely miss the creak of footsteps on the stairs.

It's not until he clears his throat that I look up to see Caleb standing on the bottom step, staring at the notebook in my hand.

The first of my tears fall.

29

W hat are you doing?" he asks, emotionless.

His face is blank, which scares me. I think I'd have a better chance of surviving this if he was yelling at me, ranting and raving.

I sniffle, quickly wiping the rest of my tears away with the back of my hand. There's a tremor in my voice when I answer, "I—I. It was sticking out, your book, so I looked at it." I know how lame that sounds, like I'm trying to blame the notebook for my treachery. I hold it out to him, but he doesn't take it.

In a low tone, he says. "I wasn't ready to show you that yet."

His words spark a tiny flame of anger in me. "When were you going to be ready, Caleb? Never?" I raise my chin, staring at him in defiance.

"Not never, but not now," he argues back, a whip of anger to match mine. "I can't believe you looked at it. You knew it was important to me. You knew I was keeping it private. I thought you would respect that."

I carry on, secretly thinking that if I can keep him fighting with me, then at least we're talking. My greatest fear at this moment is that he's going to leave. Turn tail and walk out on me. Shut down like he's done before. I'd take an angry Caleb over no Caleb any day.

"Private! Exactly! You keep yourself private from me. I'm tired of your secrets, okay?" I toss the notebook down on the couch, unable to look at it anymore. "I'm sorry. I shouldn't have read it. It was wrong to betray you like that, and I take full responsibility. But I did it out of desperation. In an effort to understand you better."

My words make him even more irate. "What do you mean, get to know me better? In just a couple of weeks, you've gotten to know me, the *real* me, more than anyone else in my life."

I place my hands on my hips. "There's a lot I don't know, though, isn't there? Like those girls from caroling and the money your parents gave them. Is that common for you? Having to throw money around to fix your problems? Because it's not something I've dealt with before."

I'm on a roll now, my insecurities providing me with an endless supply of complaints. "What about the future, huh? What happens to us after Christmas? Are you ever going to sing, because you should? This music is amazing. How about your girlfriend? What's her name, Lola Mon—, Mon—?" I sputter out everything all at once, ending with her.

It's bothering me now that I've seen her picture. I want to know more about this woman who held Caleb's heart before I ever got to feel it beat beneath my palm.

He's confused for a second, overwhelmed by all the things I just threw at him. His eyes narrow as he addresses the last item on my list. "You mean Lola? Lola Monroe?" His voice drips venom as he says, "Gee, Gwen. It's funny. For someone who claims to have never checked into my background, you seem to know a lot about me."

I throw my hands into the air. "You caught me. Okay? The only reason I know about Lola is because Jenny told me. You never mentioned her, so I had to look it up. I finally broke down and Googled you. I'm not proud of it, but how else was I supposed to learn about her?"

Sarcasm pours off of him, hot and biting. "Oh, I don't know. How about you ask me about her like a normal person? Tell me, did you like what you saw about me on the internet? Did I look famous enough for you? Is that why you've been so nice to me? So you can gloat to all your friends that you kissed a movie star?"

Now he's done it. I unleash. "You arrogant man. I've barely even seen any of your movies. I don't care about all that. I don't care about what a big shot you're supposed to be. I don't care about how many Academy Awards are on your mantle. I don't care about how many millions are in your bank account."

It's getting harder to yell at him because I'm crying. My sobs break my words into pieces too small to comprehend. "I don't care." My voice is choked. "Not about any of it. I only care about you. Only think of how I feel when I'm around you. About how I'm falling for you, you stupid gorgeous jerk." I sink onto the couch and wrap my arms over my head, curling into a ball of misery.

I sob, my shoulders shuddering.

His hands are on my arms, prying them apart. His fingers are under my chin, tilting my head until I look at him. "Gwen," he whispers, and I'm sure it will be the last time he says my name.

But then he's got me in his arms. He scoops me up and sits me on his lap, rocking me like you would a small child. I shove my nose into his neck and cry until I can't anymore.

"I'm sorry," I whisper to his sternum. "I'm sorry," I tell the shell of his ear. "So sorry," I say into his lips as I kiss him, praying to any god who might listen that he'll kiss me back.

His lips respond to mine, and my relief is so intense I almost pass out. We kiss for forever, pain and forgiveness passing between us without words.

Eventually, he pulls away, tenderly tucking my hair behind my ear. "What do you want to know?"

I hold him close, amazed by this human in my arms. By the capacity of his kindness. How could I have doubted him? I wince saying it, wishing I was a bigger person, "Start with Lola, and after that, I have more questions."

That famous eyebrow raises. A sardonic smile. "Oh, you do now? Well, I've got some questions of my own."

I don't like it, being on the receiving end of his questions, but I accept that it's only fair.

Tit for tat.

"Okay. Fine. I ask a question and then you ask a question." I move to sit next to him, so I can see his face better.

"Hmm. This might actually be fun." Caleb leans in to run his nose along my cheek and down my jaw. He nips softly at my neck.

His touch distracts me from what I was about to say. With firm hands,

I push him away. "I know what you're doing." I wag my finger at his face, which brims with false innocence.

He blinks slowly, one corner of his mouth curling up. "What exactly is that?"

"Trying to use your kisses as mind control. That way, I'll forget to ask you anything. Well, it won't work, mister." I make my tone as uncompromising as possible.

Caleb leans his head back and laughs, a full hearty laugh, and the last of my fear vanishes. That laugh means that he really has forgiven me for Googling him and stealing his notebook.

I grin with relief.

We're going to be okay.

"Mind control?" He laughs again and shakes his head at me, smiling like I'm the funniest person he's ever met. Which I'm not, but somehow when I'm with him I feel like I can be anyone I want to be. Maybe even funny or outgoing or beautiful.

I straighten my smile until it's a serious line across my face. Caleb sobers when he sees my expression, but a twinkle of mirth remains.

"Lola," I remind him with a stern glare.

He sighs and crosses one ankle over his knee, leaning against the sloped back of the couch. "She was my girlfriend. We dated for almost a year."

Darn it. I had no idea they had been together for that long. The way Jenny had said it, I had hoped for a fling. Not this, something serious.

"You cared for her?" I ask, bracing myself for his answer.

His mouth turns down. He nods once, not looking me in the eye.

Jealousy hisses through my teeth. I want to jump on him like a wild animal, claim him as my own and no one else's. "What went wrong?"

He meets my eyes then, letting me see his pain. "She thought I was more fun drunk than sober, so she dumped me."

"Oh, Caleb." I kneel and fold myself around him, wanting to protect him. Ready to fight anyone who hurts him.

After a minute, I disentangle myself.

"What about you and Jax?" Caleb takes his turn. "Do you still have feelings for him? You were engaged to him. That's a much bigger deal than me dating Lola for a year." His guard is up, and I see that he's scared I'll hurt him the same way I'm scared he'll hurt me.

I stare off into the distance, thinking, wanting to give him an honest answer. "I think I'll always have some feelings for Jax." I hold my voice steady, even as Caleb recoils. "He was my first everything, but recently I've realized that first doesn't have to be my last. That I'm ready for something new. I've been waiting without knowing it." I glance down, too shy to see the impact of my words.

He kisses me, a reward for being truthful.

"Were you ever going to show me your songs?" I ask, taking my turn.

Caleb blushes, suddenly awkward. "Eventually, but probably not for a long time. It's too vulnerable to have you see them."

"Well, you know what makes me feel vulnerable?" I counter.

"What?"

"Being romantic with you. Kissing you. To me, that's opening myself up, letting you see me weak, defenseless." I pause as another thought occurs to me. "But maybe you don't think of it that way. Maybe you're so used to having women throw themselves at you that you don't even think of this as a genuine relationship. Maybe to you this is just a fling."

Caleb watches out of the corner of his eye, evaluating me. "I won't lie. I've had relationships like that. Meaningless, easy to get."

Just when I think he's going to say that's all there is between us, he changes course. "That's not what it's like with you. I don't take what's happening between us lightly or for granted. This isn't a fling or some mindless way to fill my time. Being with you is deeper than that. My emotions are more involved. This relationship means a lot to me."

I can't stop the thrill his words bring. "It means a lot me, too."

Then he asks me the hardest question of them all. "Tell me about your dad."

30

hang my head and sigh. "We might need to lie down for this one."

We move upstairs to the bed, and I lay pressed against Caleb, taking comfort in his body. Pip follows and tucks herself between us, as if she wants to offer support as well.

How to describe someone as big and wonderful as my father? "He was charming, outgoing, the life of the party, my dad. Had the loudest laugh. Loved my mom something fierce." I smile, remembering how my parents' love was the sun that my brothers and I orbited around. "He adored Christmas, like I told you before. It was his favorite holiday. I think of him every day, but even more during this time of year.

"I was extremely close with him. A total Daddy's girl. I'd wait by the doorway until he'd come home from work. Then I'd tackle him and demand he play with me. Even though I'm sure he was tired, he'd throw his briefcase down and chase me through the house, tickling me mercilessly until I screamed with laughter."

My smile fades away. "When I was a junior in high school, he went to the ER with belly pain. Back then, I didn't realize that he had been constipated and his stool had blood in it."

I sigh, remembering back to those initial days. When the news was bad, but we had hope. And then later, when the news got worse, and we lost that hard-earned hope.

"They did a CT scan and saw a tumor the size of a cantaloupe blocking his colon. Of course, they did biopsies and labs to confirm that he had colon cancer, but it was that initial scan that found it."

I grow quiet for a moment. "All the testing showed it had already spread. The surgeons operated. They cut out the bad parts and stuck him back together. He did chemo and radiation, but I could tell from the way they talked to us, all full of pity, that it was no use. They wanted us to feel like we had done something. That we hadn't just given up on him."

Caleb bends his ear down to my mouth so he can hear as I whisper, "He was dead six months later."

I have more words, but they don't want to escape. They clump in my throat, piling into each other like cars in a traffic jam.

Caleb waits patiently.

"I had a hard time after he passed. Wouldn't get out of bed. I had no desire to see my friends. I started having panic attacks, so bad that I missed days and days of school. Mom forced me to see a therapist. She took me in, kicking and screaming. I know I shouldn't have felt this way, but I was *so* ashamed. I thought it was weak, that I couldn't handle everything on my own. Therapy helped. Honestly, it probably saved me. My therapist wanted me to go to a special grief counselor, but I stopped treatment once I left for college. I was too busy studying, trying to get into medical school."

It comes back to me in a rush, how scared I had been that someone from high school might find out I was in therapy. At that time, it had seemed like social suicide to let anyone witness how I was struggling. Only Jenny had known the truth. I didn't even tell Jax.

I'm much smarter now. I understand the importance of mental health. How it should be guarded as if it's something precious. And yet, I still can't look at Caleb. I don't want to see the judgment in his eyes.

He takes my chin in his fingers, forcing me to meet his gaze, full of sympathy and understanding. Slowly, he leans down and puts his lips to mine.

A kiss to make me feel better.

I'm almost at the end of my story and happy to be done with it. I don't enjoy reliving those days, but I understand it's important for Caleb to know.

That time in my life had a big impact on who I am now. If I can't show him that trauma, then he'll never really understand me.

As much as I've accused him of having secrets, there are parts of me I've held back as well. I want them gone. Any ghosts that stand between us—Lola, Jax, my dad. It's time to shine a light into those dark corners of ourselves, to let each other see all the pain, fear, and rejection.

"Is that when you decided to become a doctor?"

I lift one shoulder. "Kinda. I had thought about it before, going to medical school. I always loved math and science. After what my family went through with Dad, it seemed the natural choice. I think about him a lot, my dad, when I'm with patients. Try to remember what it feels like to be on the other side of that stethoscope."

"I'm sure you're amazing at it, being a doctor."

"I hope so. It's important to me. For many years, that was all I cared about, getting into medical school, then residency. Studying so much was a way to bury my grief and yet honor my dad at the same time. Now that I've done it, gotten into residency, I'm at a bit of a loss. I find myself wondering, what's my next big goal? What else do I see for my future?"

His lips brush against my hair. "What did you decide? What do you want?"

You. I want you.

That's what I wish I could say, but it's too soon and I'm too scared.

Instead, I shake my head. "Not sure, still figuring that out."

Caleb goes back to talking about my past. "What happened after your dad died? How did you all get by?"

"My mom had stayed at home with us kids when dad was alive. After he passed away, she had to work to pay our bills, especially the medical bills, which were insanely expensive. It was like we lost both our parents at the same time. Our dad was gone, and Mom was barely around, too busy working as a teacher during the day and taking side gigs like waitressing at night. Brandon was in community college by then, which he resented. He had wanted to go to a private university, but after Dad died we couldn't afford it. He was angry, hardly ever home.

"It was mostly Teddy and me. We took care of each other. In a way, I helped raise him."

Caleb rolls over onto his side, facing me, and scoots down until we are eye to eye. He rests his hand on my cheek, the pad of his thumb slowly stroking my skin. I close my eyes, focusing on that sensation. Letting his touch ground me in the here and now, where I am safe and loved. "Sometimes, I try to picture what my family would look like if Dad had never died, and it's sad because I don't think I would recognize us. That's how much it changed us."

"I know words will never be enough, but I'm sorry." His voice is as soft as his caress.

I sniffle and nod. "I'm sorry too. For everything you went through with the accident. And I'm *so* sorry for reading your notebook. That wasn't mine to take."

His smile is full of emotion. "Gwen, don't you know by now...anything of mine is yours. You just have to ask."

31

t's evening and we're in the living room. Caleb stretches over me to retrieve a blanket from the corner of the couch. He tucks it around us, creating a nest for two, nice and cozy. Cuddling with him, burrowing into his warmth, has my muscles stretched out like warm taffy, all loose and relaxed. Nestling closer, I press my face in the crook of his neck. He smells like cinnamon and some kind of manly scent I can't define.

His words rumble against my ear. "You asked about the future the other day."

I pull out of his embrace and prop myself up on one elbow against the back of the couch so I can see him better. "Do you think about it? A future for us?" I gulp, nervous to hear his answer. I can't bear it if he says no.

The somber expression on his face scares me, even though his words are reassuring. "I think about it a lot." Absentmindedly, Caleb plays with the end of my hair, winding it tight around his finger and then releasing it, only to repeat the motion. "There's a price to being with me, though. I'm not sure it's fair to ask you to pay it."

"I'm not scared, Caleb." I lift my chin.

He chuckles, "Oh, I know. You're not scared of anything." He sobers. "It's a six-hour flight from L.A. to New York. With the three-hour time difference, it takes all day to travel from one to the other."

"True, but maybe if we saw each other once a month or meet up somewhere in the middle, we could make it work?" It sounds daunting, even as I say it.

"You don't understand." He blows out a frustrated breath. "Eventually, I have to go back to acting. It's the only thing I'm good at. When I'm filming on location, I can be gone six, up to nine months. In places that are hard to get to. The African desert. The Bering Sea. One time I froze my butt off in the Arctic for almost a year."

"I get it. Sometimes I go a whole month in the hospital without a single day of vacation." Using my knuckles, I rub at my eyes, trying to take away the sting. "But acting isn't the only thing you're good at. What about your songwriting? Singing? You're good at that, too. I think you should try."

"Maybe," he says cautiously. "I could talk to my agent about it. Just open the conversation. My lead PR person, Nicole, has been with me for over a decade. I could float the idea by her, too. I can trust her to be honest and keep it quiet."

I have to restrain myself from jumping up and down. It's not much, but this is the first time I've heard Caleb even consider a music career.

"Could you transfer to a different residency?" He pushes himself up on the pillow. "We have hospitals in L.A., you know."

"Are you kidding me? Do you have any idea how hard it was to get into my ER residency? I'm lucky to have that spot." I think back to all those long days in the library studying. All the time I spent doing research in the labs. The hundreds of hours volunteering in the hospital.

"I know, I know." Caleb reaches out to run his hand down my arm. "Have I told you how proud I am of you? How amazing it is that my girlfriend is a doctor." His eyes shine, full of admiration. "Smart and sexy, that's what you are. The complete package."

Right now, I could float away. Caleb Freaking Lawson just called me his girlfriend *and* sexy all in the same sentence. My heart might burst. There's too much happiness for it to hold.

"I've already given up my career." He grows wistful. "I could stay with you in New York. Do your laundry, cook for you, and take out the trash."

He feels so good, sitting next to me, that I almost take him up on the offer. "Do you really think you could be happy doing that?" I ask him. "I mean realistically."

He runs his hand through his hair. "No, probably not."

Around and around, we go. Trying to fit our lives together like the puzzle pieces on the kitchen table. No matter which way we turn them, the edges bump up against each other, not sliding easily into place.

We're too involved with our careers. Both of us have worked too hard, put in too many years. I'm not Gwen without medicine. He's not Caleb without acting. They're a part of our identity. To rip that away from either of us would remove something essential. Would we still be falling for each other if those parts ceased to exist? If we were different people without those titles, would we still be attracted to each other?

Finally, I ask, "Is it hopeless? You and me together? Should we just give up now?" I choke on the sob that's trying to claw its way up my throat. Life without Caleb is the very worst thing I can imagine.

He pulls me close and kisses me. "No. No," he repeats in my ear, his hand rubbing small circles on my back. "It's okay if you're scared or if this gets hard, but I'm never giving up on us, Gwen. Never."

32

Tired of getting nowhere with our future plans, I decide to focus on the present. Which to me means Caleb's music.

"Please," I beg. "Sing for me. I'll be the only one who hears, and I'll love it no matter how you sound."

Just like I love you.

I say the words in my head but not out loud, worried it'll scare him away.

As for the music, he makes lots of excuses. He's not ready. He wants more time to perfect this song he's working on. His throat is scratchy. He needs his guitar.

"Guitar?" I perk up. "How did I not know that you play guitar?"

"Not many people do. I have a couple at my place downtown. Acoustic and electric, too. Started lessons when I was fourteen." We're sitting on the couch in the living room. He's lounging, legs splayed, a book loosely clasped in his hand and Pip curled up by his feet.

"You must be pretty good, then?"

He shrugs. "I guess."

Excited now, I jump up. "I'll be right back."

There's a storage space under the staircase, full of cobwebs and dusty boxes. The door that leads in is a tiny square, like it was made for elves, cut out of the wall and hung on silver hinges. I open it with a creak and crawl in on my hands and knees. The scent of dry paper and mothballs assaults my nose, making me sneeze.

Deep in the space, I find what I'm looking for. It's in the corner, the case coated gray with dust. I drag it out and return to Caleb.

"Ta-da!" I announce proudly and shove it into his arms.

He stares at it, perplexed. "A guitar? Where did you get this?"

"It was my dad's. He played for us, mostly on holidays. He was pretty talented." I can almost hear it. Frosty the Snowman strummed in front of the fireplace on Christmas Eve while we all sang along. My voice, tiny and young, with the lisp of early childhood. My brothers' voices not yet deepened from puberty.

"I can't use this. Not your dad's guitar." Caleb tries to hand it back, but I cross my arms over my chest, tucking my hands away, and shake my head firmly. "He'd want someone to play it, not have it stuck forever in a dark closet."

There's a tightening in my throat. Voice shaking, I say, "I wish you could have met him, Caleb. He would have loved you."

He comes to me, placing a soft kiss on my temple, then leans his forehead against mine. "I wish I could have met him, too."

When he steps away, he releases a heavy breath. "I'm worried I can't do this. I've been saying other people's lines for so long that I don't have any of my own. I'm an actor. Not a singer. Not a songwriter. What if I fail? I'm not strong like you, Gwen."

"I get it. You're frightened. But guess what? I'm scared too. Every day when I walk into the Emergency Room, I'm scared. Every time I don't hear from my family for a while, I'm scared that something bad has happened to them. I'm worried about losing them, the way I lost my dad."

"But still you go on. You do the things that need to be done." He looks at me as if he thinks I'm hiding some secret. Something that will magically make it okay for him to take a risk. To put himself out there. But I don't have any special potion. Just some grief and a whole lot of stubbornness.

I shrug. "What other choice is there, Caleb? I know better than most people that we only get one life to live."

He surprises me by leaning down and pressing his ear against my chest.

The gesture is so unexpected that I laugh. "What are you doing?"

When he straightens, he's smiling. "Just like I thought. There's a lion's heart beating in there."

Blushing, overcome by so many emotions I can't name them all, I playfully shove him away.

One more grin for me, then Caleb sits down on the couch and unzips the case. With reverence, he brings the guitar out and gazes at it.

I wince when I see the shape it's in. There are discolored, worn patches on the body, and a couple of frets are uneven. Heart aching, I run my fingers over the guitar's imperfections, thinking about how upset my dad would be to see it in this condition. "Sorry, I didn't know it is in such bad shape. Can you still play it?"

He looks over the damage carefully before responding. "It'll be fine. At least this way, if a note is off, I can blame the instrument instead of my lack of skill."

"No more stalling," I chide. "And no more putting yourself down. You're talented, Caleb. Everyone should hear it."

I give him a kiss for encouragement.

He places the guitar on his knee and strums lightly. It takes a while for him to tune it, gently twanging and adjusting each string one by one until they all ring true.

He asks me, "What should I sing?"

I rock on my feet and say in a small voice, "What about my song?" I know it's too much to ask. He's never going to play that for me. But one corner of his mouth twitches up, giving me hope.

Cradling the guitar like a lover, he bends over it and strikes the first chord. His eyes squeezed shut, Caleb sings. His voice is just as I remember, deep and husky but rising up like morning dew from the grass, becoming higher and softer during the sweet parts of the song. I drop onto the couch, my legs suddenly unable to support me.

It's only when he reaches the last chorus that Caleb opens his eyes and looks at me. Staring straight into my soul, he sings, "Never known anyone quite like you. No one's ever known me quite so well." The ending note hangs in the air between us.

Tears in my eyes, I burst into applause. Clapping so loud that my hands hurt. He sets the guitar on the ground, and I fly to him, clambering onto his lap. He laughs as I cover his face with a million kisses. "That was so good, Caleb," I say between kisses. "So, so good."

He kisses me back. "We're so good, Gwen. It's you. It's us. That's what's good."

33

enny has dragged me out of the house to do water aerobics. It's only been an hour and already I'm missing Caleb. It seems wrong to be away from him, like I've lost an essential part of my own body, an arm or a leg. If this is how I feel now, when I go back to New York after Christmas it will be devastating.

I don't want to think about that. This is time I've dedicated to spend with Jenny. I'm going to miss her just as much.

"How's the research paper coming along?" she asks, treading water.

"Good. The *Journal of Emergency Medicine* confirmed they'll put it in the summer issue." My chest swells with pride. I did it. I'll be a published author in a respected medical magazine. My goal for the month has been a success.

Jenny swims over to give me a too-tight hug. "I'm so proud of you, Gwen! That's great." She's always been my biggest cheerleader.

"How about you? Any leads on interesting news articles for you to write?" I adjust a pair of goggles over my eyes, loosening the strap.

"How about the fact that my best friend is kissing America's sweetheart?" She wiggles her eyebrows.

I shoot her a withering glare.

"Never mind." She laughs. "I already know I can't publish that one." She adds, "Remember that editor I told you about?"

I nod. "The jerk?"

Her cheeks tinge pink. "Yeah, him. He asked me out, and I might say yes."

"Jenny!" I splash her, laughing. "I thought we're supposed to hate him. You said he is mean and bossy."

It's so rare for Jenny to be embarrassed that I hardly recognize the expression on her face. "He *is* bossy, but sometimes he can be kind of sweet, too, and he's awfully good looking."

I want to tease her some more, but the instructor is at the front of the class, ready to begin.

"You didn't mention that we needed to be retired to come here," I joke under my breath, surveying all the elderly women who surround us. They float with pool noodles tucked under their arms, blue-gray hair shining in the bright California sun.

Jenny whispers from the corner of her mouth, "Don't underestimate them. Last time I did this, I was gasping like a fish out of water and those ladies had hardly broken a sweat."

"Seriously?"

She nods. "They come here every day." She lowers her voice even more. "I'm pretty sure they're part mermaid."

I laugh, liking the idea of grandma mermaids wrinkled by the pool rather than wrinkled by time.

Jenny's right. Halfway through the class, my arms and legs are burning from using resistance weights to drag my limbs through the water. My eyes sting, blinded by the splashing of the septuagenarian in front of me.

"Jenny," I pant. "I'm not going to make it. Put me out of my misery. Please, let me drown."

She isn't doing much better, sputtering, her head drifting below the waterline as her legs give out. "I told you," she wheezes. "These ladies aren't human."

"When you mentioned mermaids earlier, I assumed you meant the Ariel kind, not Ursula."

The elderly lady to my right must be eavesdropping because she corrects me. "Ursula was a sea witch. Not a mermaid." She shoots me a scathing look and snaps out, "More paddling and less talking, girlies."

She doesn't need to tell me twice. I don't have enough breath left to speak.

After forty-five minutes of this torture, we're done. Jenny and I crawl out of the pool and collapse onto the concrete deck. The older women politely step over our prone bodies on their way to the showers.

"I can't move," I groan.

Jenny opens one eye to look at me. "I thought with all the kissing you've been doing with Caleb, you'd have more stamina by now," she teases.

In retaliation, I sit up and shake my head like a wet dog, sending a spray of cold water over her.

"Eew. Okay. Okay. Stop." Laughing, she puts up one hand to block the spray.

I laugh too and collapse back to the ground.

She rolls over on her side toward me. "How is Mr. Famous doing, anyway?"

My cheeks heat from more than just the sun overhead. "He's good. Great, actually."

"Great, huh?" She raises an eyebrow.

My smile stretches my face so far that it almost hurts. I can't seem to stop grinning recently. "Great in every way. You wouldn't believe how wonderful he is. He's smart and sweet and kind, and I already told you how well he cooks."

"Wow." She shakes her head at me. "It's like someone switched on a flashlight inside you. I've never seen you so bright and loose and giggly. Usually you're more serious."

Dependable Gwen. Mom's words come back to me. *Predictable, serious,* said Jenny. This is how my family and best friend view me. I had spent years studying to get through medical school, and I suppose you had to be those things, serious and dependable, to accomplish all that I have. Those traits had helped me when dad died, too. When I took over for mom while she was working.

But it's difficult hearing those descriptions now. I don't want to be serious and dependable. I want to be fun and spontaneous. I want to be passionate about medicine but about other things too.

Caleb brings that light-hearted side out in me. That's what Jenny is talking about. The changes that she's describing are all from him. He makes me feel free. Like the burden of the hospital and the misery I see there isn't quite as heavy. Like I'm not betraying my dad's memory by being happy again. Like there's a future where I can take risks. A future where I can't fall because he'll catch me.

Jenny says, "You've got it bad, don't you?"

"I love him," I tell her, stating it like the simple truth it is.

I expect her to hug me or congratulate me, but instead her smile dims. "Love?" she repeats as if the word is foreign to her. "Gwen. You aren't supposed to love him."

"What do you mean?" I'm puzzled.

"Caleb's supposed to be a fling. A rebound from Jax."

"What? You were the one who told me to pursue him. You kept encouraging me, remember?" My head swims, baffled that we could be so out of sync.

"I encouraged you, that's true. I wanted you to have some fun. You know, get some attention and then move on."

"Caleb is more to me than that."

She shakes her head like she can't believe what she's hearing. "You've known him for a month, Gwen. *A month.* What would you say if I came to you and said I was in love with a guy after one month? You're the one who always complains about that in romance books. Insta-love. Where the characters fall madly in love at first sight. You say how unrealistic it is, but now you're telling me that you love Caleb? It makes no sense."

I flinch. It does sound insane when she says it out loud. I hate to admit it, but the truth is that if she told me she loved someone after such a short time, I would try to talk her out of it.

But this is Caleb and me. I have no doubts about my feelings for him. Since our blowup over his notebook, we've been growing closer, talking nonstop, holding nothing back. Every day I've learned more about him, seen how his past has shaped him. Heard what he wants for the future. In return I have let him see me, even the parts I'm ashamed of.

"It's been quick, that's for sure, but I've never felt so much like myself as I do when I'm with him." I say it with certainty, trying to reassure her, and maybe myself as well.

"Oh, yeah? You think you know him? Then tell me, what's his middle name? What's his favorite color? Where was he born?" Jenny challenges.

My confidence takes a step and falters. I don't have the answers to her questions.

She lets my silence hang there, ominous, before she says, "His middle name is Augustus. His favorite color is blue, and he's from Illinois. Don't you think it's a problem that I know more about the man you're supposedly in love with than you do?"

Outwardly I scoff, but inside I'm unsettled. Jenny's blow landed exactly where she intended. "Those are trivial details you read in a magazine," I argue. "Memorizing random facts doesn't mean that you know Caleb, not like I do."

Jenny softens. "It's not that I don't believe you have real feelings for each other. That's not what I'm saying. If you had more time together, you would eventually learn those things. My worry is that everything has been so fast. What if you put all your trust in Caleb and end up disappointed? I saw you do that with Jax. It was awful when you two broke up. I can't *ever* see you miserable like that again." The line between her brows deepens. "What does Caleb say? Has he said that he loves you back?"

Uncertainty lodges deep in my bones, weakening me. "Well, no, but I haven't mentioned it to him yet, either."

He *has* to love me, right? The other night I looked up from reading to find him staring at me. I swear I saw it then, love sparkling in his eyes.

"Christmas is in two days. Then you go back to New York." There's something like pity in her tone. "What're you going to do?"

It hurts to even imagine a life where I don't live under the same roof as Caleb. Where he's not the first and last thing I see every day.

"Caleb has some loose ends to tie up in L.A., then he'll fly out to visit me. We'll talk on the phone, of course, until we're together again."

A worried side glance from Jenny unsettles me. I want, need her to believe that what Caleb and I have is real. "I know it sounds crazy, but it's like that puzzle you saw on my kitchen table when we decorated the tree. I'm telling you. Caleb's it. He's my missing piece."

34

A plate of frosted sugar cookies that Caleb made rests high on the kitchen counter, well out of Pip's reach, but she can smell them and the scent has her tongue lolling. Mugs of steaming hot chocolate with tiny marshmallows sit next to the cookies, cooling, so we can drink them without scalding our mouths. We've set the TV to a channel that shows a red brick fireplace with a yule log burning on an endless loop.

It's Christmas Eve. Caleb and I are in the kitchen, at the table with our chairs pulled close together, our elbows touching. He rests his chin in his hand, surveying the puzzle spread out before us. Only five pieces remain. I'm momentarily distracted by Caleb's white-socked foot, which strokes my leg under the table.

One by one, the puzzle pieces go in. Caleb holds the last one out to me, his eyes bright. "You do it, Gwen. Finish it." When it slides easily into place, we sigh and smile at each other. There's a sense of accomplishment in looking at the completed puzzle. Dolphins, sharks, and turtles sway next to billowing tendrils of kelp. Colorful fish dart and peek around rough coral. A starfish lies on the pebbled sandy ocean floor.

"I can't believe it's done," I say with wonder.

We're silent for a minute, both staring at the puzzle. Then Caleb bounces his knee, jittery with excitement he can no longer suppress. "Let's open our presents now. Please?" he begs, eager like a little kid.

He's been asking all day, and all day I've said no.

"Caleb," I chide again gently. "Wait until Christmas."

He stares into my face, eyes earnest. "Come on, Gwen. I'm so excited for you to see your gift. I need to know if you like it or not."

"If it's from you, then I'm sure I'll love it." I'm incredibly curious to see what it is. Caleb had done all of his shopping online. For the past week, whenever a package had been delivered he had snatched it away and taken it upstairs so I couldn't see what was inside.

Leaning closer, Caleb takes my lips in a long, breathless kiss. "Please," he draws out the word, murmuring it one last time against my mouth. My resolve wavers…and breaks.

Who can resist this man?

Not me.

Besides, it's been sensible, predictable, responsible Gwen telling him no all along. I'm not that woman anymore. The new spontaneous, fun Gwen is the kind of person who goes crazy and opens presents a day early. *That's* who I am now.

"Okay." My smile melts into his lips. "I can't wait for you to open your gift, too."

He whoops and pulls me to my feet, grinning recklessly. We sit down on the floor in front of the Christmas tree, where only two presents remain. I had given Jenny hers before she left for Hawaii, and we had mailed the rest to our families days ago.

"Here you go." Caleb hands over mine. The bright paper covering is wrinkled and secured with multiple heavy layers of tape. A red bow sits off center. "Sorry," he winces. "It was my first time wrapping."

My heart melts at this beautifully imperfect gift given to me by this beautifully imperfect man.

The box I hand him is smaller. I had taken extra care when I wrapped it, thinking of all the Christmases he had missed out on and wanting so badly for this one to be special.

"Let's open them together," I suggest. "On the count of three. One, two, three."

Wrapping paper is shredded, ribbons are pushed aside.

"Oh, Caleb," is all I can say as I stare at the box in my hands. It's a paint set, watercolors in every color of the rainbow. The kit includes fresh paint-brushes and a palette for mixing. Tears blur my vision as I lift my gaze to him. "How did you know?"

"Did you think I wouldn't notice?" he asks me tenderly. "How every time you would get out those old paints. The way you looked at them, with such longing, it wasn't hard to figure out they meant something to you. You've accepted me. The past versions of me and new versions, too. I'll do the same for you. If you want to paint, then I say paint. You can be anyone you want to be. My beautiful, strong, lion-heart Gwen."

I go to him then, crushing my mouth against his, trying to lock this moment in my memory. Put it next to that other room, the one when I first started to fall in love with him, when he sat in the sun with Pip in his lap. How lucky am I? To have rooms full of Caleb in my heart?

When we break apart, he asks, "Does that kiss mean that I guessed right? That you wanted the paints?"

"You guessed perfectly." I take his hand in mine and look down at it, loving how our fingers intertwine. "After my dad died, I gave up so many pieces of myself. When Jax left, I swore off happiness because I thought it only led to pain, but then you came along and everything changed."

Another kiss, this one searing through my body like a bolt of lightning.

He inspects his present as I explain, "It's a portable speaker. A small one that connects to your phone, so you can take it with you anywhere. I made sure to get one with good sound quality."

He's delighted, immediately jumping up to try it out. Within minutes, Caleb has music flowing out of the speaker. It's amazing. Each note is clear and true. The melody winds around us, as Caleb holds out his hand to where I sit on the floor. "Dance with me?"

His hand is warm in mine as he pulls me close. He guides my arms up to his neck and settles his hands at my waist, the position reminding me of my mom's wedding all those months ago.

"Remember when I first came to this house?" Caleb murmurs against my temple.

"You mean when I hit you with the wrench? Yeah, it was kind of unforgettable." I chuckle, resting my cheek on his chest.

"You said the only present I would get here was you." He pulls back slightly, and the way he looks at me, as if I'm something precious, gives me the sense that I'm not just dancing but flying.

"Turns out you were right," he whispers huskily. "You're the best gift I could ever have. I love you, Gwen. When we're together, I feel you with my body but also my mind and my heart. You've got me all wrapped up, every part of me obsessing over you." He grabs my hand and places a soft kiss on my palm, before curling my fingers in like he wants me to hold his love there forever.

With relief, I release the words that have been on the tip of my tongue so many times. "I love you too, Caleb. I have for a while now."

Love.

I'll never tire of hearing, or saying, that word.

Not when it's with Caleb.

As we sway to the music, he kisses me slowly. The imprint of his lips against mine burns like I've kissed the sun.

"We're really doing this?" I pull apart and ask, my eyes locked on his. "You and me? Together? Promise?"

A kiss to my forehead, his lips silk soft. "Promise. You and me. Always."

t's early Christmas morning, the dawn only recently arrived. I'm awake, worrying about what will happen next. Tomorrow, I go back to New York.

Just one more day to spend with Caleb. To tattoo his love onto my skin, so I never forget.

Last night, we fell asleep cuddled together watching a movie on the couch. Now, I lift my eyes to stare at him. He's stretched out with one arm thrown above his head and the other wrapped around me. It's the most beautiful view, to see him lying there with his face soft and unguarded. His hair runs smooth as silk through my fingers as I brush it aside. I press a whisper of a kiss to his forehead, careful not to wake him.

My phone buzzes on the end table, stirring a flash of irritation. Who's calling so early? The screen shows it's Jenny. Her voice is frantic when I pick up. "Did you see the news?"

Stifling a yawn, I answer hoarsely, "What news?"

"Gwen, I need you to Google your name immediately."

Her obvious alarm has me sitting up straight. "What? Why?"

I've literally never Googled myself in my entire life. I'm not important enough for that.

"Just do it now."

After I put her on speaker, I open the internet browser on my phone and do as she asks. The minute I hit enter, hundreds of responses pop up. They are all the same words said in different ways, but I only skim what is written. The thing my eyes zero in on is the picture that pops up with each article.

It's grainy because the room where the photo was shot was dim. The image shows a crowd of people, pressed tightly together, but in the middle of them a couple stands out like there's a spotlight shining down just for them.

It's a man and a woman caught the second after they have kissed. Their lips hang inches apart. They gaze at each other with identical expressions of surprise, wonder, and desire. The depth of their emotion leaps off the page. The woman's hands are fisted in his shirt, holding on like she'll never let go. The man's arms are wrapped possessively around her back.

I recognize the wood-topped bar with the wolf painted over it.

It's Caleb and me.

The first time we kissed at Shooter's.

And it's all over every newspaper, magazine, and social media page.

I remember it then, that burst of white when Caleb kissed me, the after-image still blinding me as I opened my eyes to look at him. In that moment, I had thought it was my brain short circuiting from amazement, but now I realize it was the flash of a camera. Someone in the bar captured us and then sold the picture, probably for a tidy profit.

Darn you, whoever you are.

"Jenny, I've got to go." I hang up before she has a chance to respond.

My gaze returns to Caleb, sleeping peacefully. It pains me to wake him, but this is an emergency. I shove his shoulder roughly.

He sits up with a start. Immediately, his hands are on my arms, eyes full of concern as he searches my expression. "Gwen? Gwen, what's wrong? Are you okay?"

I shake my head no and thrust my phone at him. He takes it from me and swings his legs over the side of the couch to sit up more fully. Emotions flicker over his face as he scrolls through the articles. Shock, anger, and finally fear.

"I don't understand," I rasp, my voice rough. "That picture is from weeks ago. Why is it coming up now?"

Caleb gives my phone back and pushes his hands through his hair, leaving it sticking up all spiky. "It takes time for whoever took it to negotiate with the magazines. Or maybe the person who took the photo initially gave it to someone else who sold it. I've had photos that were over a year-old pop up out of nowhere, and the press acted like it was stuff that had just happened."

I run my hand over his unruly hair, smoothing it back in place. Caleb captures that hand and kisses it absentmindedly, then keeps it loosely clasped in his. "Listen, this is—"

Pounding on the front door drowns out whatever he was about to say. Caleb's wide eyes meet mine as fear spikes through my veins, icy cold. Together, still holding hands, we go to the door. As soon as it swings open, Marjorie comes rushing into the room, gripping her phone tightly. Ben trails behind uncertainly.

"Caleb!" she screeches. "What have you done? Your PR agent just called, and she's furious." Marjorie halts and goes wild-eyed when she sees me, my hand still held by her son.

"You!" She jabs a finger my way. "You sneaky girl. Under our noses, you've taken advantage of him. And at Christmas of all times." Her face twists with disgust.

"Me?" I drop Caleb's hand and point to myself, shocked that someone just called me sneaky. *That's a first.*

Before I can say anything else, Caleb steps in. "Mom, stop! Gwen did nothing wrong. Why are you talking to my PR people? Why isn't Nicole calling me directly?"

Marjorie drops her eyes and fidgets with her phone. "I told Nicole to run things through me." When she sees that Caleb is upset, she adds, "It was only for a little while. I instructed *all* your staff to call me. You said that you needed some rest, darling. You've been so exhausted recently, overworked and stressed from that horrible crash. I was trying to protect you."

The emotions of shock and anger war with each other on Caleb's face. "I should have known. I wondered why my phone's been so quiet." He shakes his head like he's as furious with himself as he is with her. "I've been distracted. Otherwise, I would've figured out what you did sooner."

Ouch. I'm a distraction.

Something about hearing me in those terms makes my stomach turn sour.

Caleb steps closer to Marjorie. "You have to stop doing this, Mother. Stop smothering me, trying to control me. You had no right to give orders to my team without my permission."

"What was I supposed to do?" Marjorie cries out. "You had disappeared. Stopped talking to all of us. It took me forever to find you. Don't you know I worry about you, Caleb? Don't you know I love you?" She continues, "And now this! You and Gwen? Everyone knows about you two." She darts a glare my way, brandishing her phone with the picture of us kissing like it's a weapon. "It's all over the internet."

Caleb narrows his eyes at his mother. "Mom, stop. I'm a grown man. I can do whatever I want with my career. I can date whoever I want. I —"

There's the sound outside of car doors slamming and the murmur of voices.

Caleb swears under his breath. He leaves me and rushes to the window, peeking through the curtains. He turns back to us, but it isn't me he looks at. It's his mother. "The press," he says grimly. "They're here."

Marjorie pales, clutching her chest.

My phone rings in my hand, my mom's name lighting up the screen. Frightened by the dire expression on Caleb and Marjorie's faces, I pick up. "Mom?"

My mom's voice is tight with worry. "Gwen, what's going on? I turned on my computer this morning, and I see a picture that looks like you and Caleb kissing. Is this real?"

Shoot.

"Yes, it's true. Caleb and I are together."

Baffled, Mom says, "I don't understand. We talked about this."

Caleb must guess why my mom is calling. We exchange glances filled with dismay.

"I know it's a shock for you all to find out this way," I tell Mom. "But we're together, and I love him."

Caleb's looking right into my eyes as I say the last part. He gives me a small proud smile, and, for a minute, I think everything is going to be okay.

My mother's voice is pure steel, a tone I've never heard from her before. "Absolutely *not*. You are not in love. Not after a month of hiding, keeping secrets. This is not love. It's lust and foolishness. I will not stand for it. I won't let you do it. Ruin your future. I'm so disappointed in you, Gwen. I can't believe you would lie to your parents like this."

"Seth's not my parent!" I interject, which my mom ignores.

She continues, full of judgment. "I told Seth I didn't trust Caleb, but no, Seth thinks the world of him. Well, I've read the articles about him. I've seen the magazine pictures of him out partying, women hanging off him like jewelry. After all this, even Seth will have to see the truth. Like *you* need to see that Caleb's changing you. You used to have such a good head on your shoulders and now look what's happened."

I fight back. "He's not changing me, Mom, at least not in a bad way. I know it makes you more comfortable when I'm predictable and reliable. The person you needed me to be after Dad died. You needed my help to raise Teddy and contain Brandon's anger. I became the good girl who never challenged you." Tears gather in my eyes and spill, scalding down my cheeks.

Caleb goes stiff when he sees that I'm crying, tension radiating off him in waves.

I continue talking to Mom. "I'm tired of being that person. I've never felt more whole than I do when I'm with Caleb. More myself. There are parts of me I've hidden because I was scared to hurt you. I can show those things to him, and he still loves me."

Mom is livid. "I'm sorry that I was busy working to keep a roof over your head. I get that you were forced to grow up quickly and take on a lot of responsibility. It's not what I wanted, but your dad dying wasn't what I wanted, either. We play the hand we're dealt the best way we can. You had to be mature, and I had to put my life on hold."

What a nightmare. I squeeze my eyes closed, wishing this mess would disappear. When I open them, I see Marjorie and Ben glaring at me. Their anger and distrust hits like a sucker punch to the stomach, knocking the wind out of me. As I watch, they pull Caleb to the side of the room and begin a frantic whispered conversation with him. I wish I knew what they're saying.

Mom continues her rant. "What about your brothers? Don't you think this will affect them, too? Already they're getting phone calls asking what's going on. Everyone will talk about *all* of us. This isn't only about you. We're all going to suffer the consequences when this relationship blows up in your face. I can't believe you're being so self-centered."

Her words make anger trickle up from deep inside of me. It rises to the surface and stays there, simmering in my veins. "I'm sorry I'm not taking everyone else's feelings into consideration for once, but it's time I lived life for myself. I can't keep putting what I want aside for the rest of you."

"Why not? That's what I did for years, Gwen. Years!" Mom fires back.

"Because you're the mom. You're *supposed* to sacrifice for your kids. I'm your daughter. Not your husband. Not your co-parent. I'm the child. I'm supposed to focus on building *my* life. To decide what's best for me."

"Congratulations, then. You're being unbelievably selfish. Bravo." She's pure ice, cold and bitter. "The fact is that you lied to me. After your dad died, you were the one person I could rely on. Now, how can I ever trust you?"

The thought of Mom hating me forever has me trembling. This has been my biggest fear all along. That if I change and become the woman I want to be, it will disrupt the delicate balance in my family. That my mother and brothers won't accept any version of me except the one they've known. I can't stand the idea of them rejecting me.

Mom falters, choked with emotion before speaking again, but this time I sense her concern. "It scares me how much you're risking right now. Don't you see how dangerous this is? You could destroy everything. Your job. Your reputation." A hitching sob comes through the phone, piercing me. I never could stand to hear her cry.

I send Caleb a pleading look full of desperation, wishing he could save me from this pain. He returns my stare with his own expression of agony, his dilated eyes panic-stricken. He rips his hands through his hair, tugging at the ends. The motion reveals where his scar should be, the one in his hairline from where I hit him. But it's gone, fully healed.

In this moment of extreme stress, the sight makes me irrationally sad. I know it's wrong, but I want to leave a permanent mark on him. The way he's left a mark on my soul. I'm frightened I'll fade, just like that scar.

"I have to go," Caleb says. The rush of his words makes my chest tighten painfully. "Don't worry. I'll draw them away. The journalists. The paparazzi. They'll follow me."

I shake my head, whipping it so wildly from side to side that my hair flies out. "No, Caleb. No."

Someone knocks on the front door. Voices rise from outside, and is that the sound of a...helicopter? Have they sent one of the news helicopters to hover above my house? Our neighbors are going to lose their minds over this.

With horror, I watch Caleb grab the quilt off the couch. He moves to the front door with his parents.

The phone drops from my ear as my mother's voice continues to spill out of it.

Caleb can't leave. Not when I need him the most. Less than twenty-four hours ago, we promised to love each other, and now everything is falling apart. If he walks out, when will he come back? How are we going to handle the press outside? How can we make this relationship work? My tears fall faster, a torrent raining down to splatter the tile floor at my feet.

"Caleb, wait!" I shout as he opens the door. The flash of cameras is blinding, whiting out my vision, so I miss the exact minute he exits. By the time my eyes clear, the door swings shut.

He's gone.

It's Christmas, and I'm alone.

36

H and shaking, I bring the phone back to my ear. "Mom," I interrupt, "I've got to go." With a click of the button, I hang up.

In a haze, I run upstairs and slam the master bedroom door. My heart rending itself apart, I fling myself onto the bed, sobbing for hours, my body wracked by tears.

I must have fallen asleep, a month of late nights with Caleb finally catching up, because when I open my salt-crusted eyes, the sky outside is dark and my phone is ringing.

Groggily, I answer, "Hello?"

"Gwen." Caleb's voice sounds weird, lower than usual. I realize with a start that this is the first time I've ever spoken on the phone with him. All the moments we've shared have been in person.

I don't understand how to communicate without being able to read his face, to sense his touch. It's like someone cut off one of my hands and asked me to tie a shoelace. That's how I feel talking to Caleb over the phone.

Mind whirring, I pace. "Caleb, where are you? Why'd you leave?"

"We're staying at the Four Seasons downtown. I had to go. It was the only way to get them off your front lawn. I knew they'd come here with me."

He doesn't have to say who they are. It's the press. The paparazzi that follow him everywhere. I peek out my window. Only a couple of cars and vans remain parked by our house now, a few stragglers hoping that Caleb will come back.

I can already tell from the sound of his voice that he won't.

The silence that follows is thick with unanswered questions. "When am I going to see you?" I work hard to keep my words steady, not wanting to seem desperate for him, even though I am.

"I don't think that's a good idea," he rasps out.

Something dies in me then. That little plant, with its flowers just about to bloom, withers before my eyes. "Like never?"

A heavy sigh. I know his mannerisms so well I can picture him sitting in the hotel room with his body curled around the phone. I bet his hand is running through his hair, mussing it until it sticks up all over the place.

Caleb swallows so loud I hear it. "We need to separate."

What? He's speaking a language I can't translate. I don't understand. What about all our plans? Our promises? He said that he would never give up on me, on us, but now he's going back on that. Numb disbelief spreads through my veins, flowing through each crack in my emotional armor, the armor *he* made me disassemble.

This doesn't make sense. I search for a reasonable explanation. "Is it *you* saying these things, Caleb? Or is it your mom? Or all the people who make money off you?"

"It's not just them. It's me, too. I don't want you to live this life. I won't do it to you." He's strained, each word high and tight. "When I saw all those cars out of your window, I knew it wasn't right. You can't fathom what it's like to be hounded by them."

A flare of anger fights against the numbness, momentarily pushing it aside. "It's true. I don't know what it's like. But that doesn't mean I can't handle it." It's one thing for my family to underestimate me, but a whole different thing for Caleb to treat me this way. As if I'm too fragile for the world he lives in.

"No one can handle it," he insists. "It'll drive you insane."

I begin to argue, but he cuts me off. "They'll criticize everything about you, Gwen. They won't pull any punches. They'll talk badly about your clothing, your hair, your car, your friends. Nothing is off limits. If you lose weight, they'll say you have an eating disorder. If you gain weight, they'll say you're pregnant."

I suck in my breath. That's a low blow, mentioning pregnancy. I'd be a liar if I said that I hadn't already pictured it. What our children would look like. If they would have his eyes or mine. Those dreams are shattered, blown up by the grenade of his words.

"What about your work?" he goes on, relentless. "You think the hospital will tolerate it? One of their doctors attracting all that negative attention. It's bad publicity, and you had better believe they'll take it out on you. You could lose it all. Everything you worked so hard for."

He's telling the truth, but I'm too stubborn and idealistic to listen. "You don't know that, Caleb. You can't see the future. Maybe I could talk to the reporters. Get them to stay away from the hospital."

His laugh is harsh. "Actually, I *do* know. Since I was a kid, I've been dealing with them. So much that I recognize most of them. I can tell you their names, that's how well I know them. They're like terrorists, impossible to negotiate with."

"I'll take the chance," I persist, and even I'm surprised that I mean what I say. After my father died, I used to be so risk-averse. *Dependable. Predictable.* But Caleb has changed me. He's made me bold. Let me be myself enough to find my own strength. If only he'd let me show him that side.

"No," he says firmly. "I love you too much to let you throw it all away."

How *dare* he use the word love right now? Fury heats my bloodstream until it boils.

"This is all wrong," I yell into the telephone. "I'm a grown woman. You don't get to decide for me. How can you sit there and tell me you love me and then leave? If you really love me, you stay and we fight together." I'm shaking. That's how angry I am.

A part of my mind is in denial, screaming that this isn't happening. He can't be slipping through my fingers. This entire day is a nightmare I'll wake up from soon. The other part of me is furious, that this is my reward for being vulnerable. For putting my tender heart out there, only to have it stomped on by the person I trusted the most. He might as well shove a knife in my back and give it a twist.

I can practically hear him shaking his head through the receiver. "No,"

Caleb repeats. "I spend all my time in my house, too worried about the fans and the reporters to go outside. Since the accident, I barely drive anywhere. You should be out in the world, traveling, working, sharing your gifts. Even a castle becomes a cage when you can't leave." There's a rough intake of breath on the other end of the line, followed by a series of soft exhalations.

Caleb is crying.

That suppressed sob makes me worry about him. As he eviscerates my heart, there's still a part of me that wonders who will take care of him if he cuts me out of his life. Who will help him become the person he wants to be? His parents, whom he doesn't fully trust? The staff he pays, who prioritize his career over the real human Caleb?

"Please," I beg. "Please don't do this. You promised you loved me."

He can't speak, struggling to get himself under control. After several excruciating minutes, his voice shuddering, he says, "I do love you, and that is exactly why I have to let you go. This is the hardest thing I've ever done. I'm sorry, Gwen. It's over."

That's it. The last time he speaks my name.

37

The next morning, I wake to the sound of a car door slamming. Pip barks downstairs. The deep timber of a man's voice floats up to my room as someone from outside the house calls up to my window. "Gwen?"

He's changed his mind.

I barrel down the stairs, still in my PJs, hair unbrushed and wild.

It's not Caleb who stands in the doorway, but Jax, his baseball hat gripped tightly in his hands. I let him in, my face falling with disappointment. Pip sniffs around Jax's feet as Jax gives me a tentative smile, which I don't return.

"How did you find me?" I ask, my voice raspy from exhaustion and from the tears I've shed.

"Everyone knows where you are. The whole town is talking about how Caleb Lawson has been hiding out here with you."

Oh, fabulous. Just what I need.

"Well, Caleb's not here anymore." Even saying his name hurts, each syllable a shard of broken glass in my throat.

I head to the kitchen, with Jax on my heels, as he says, "I know you probably don't want me here, but I need to talk to you." I ignore him, dropping into a seat at the kitchen table, where I stare vacantly at nothing. The table is empty. I put the puzzle away late last night, unable to stomach looking at it. The white tabletop is boring and bare without that splash of color. Much like my life without Caleb.

Jax coughs nervously into his hand. I wait silently for him to speak, not in the mood to ease his discomfort. Another change in me. I used to be so quick to help people out, even those who had hurt me.

After several minutes, he says, "I wanted to come here and apologize to you. First, for grabbing you at Shooter's. I shouldn't have touched you like that."

I have a flashback then, of Caleb bathed in moonlight. His mouth on my arm, kissing fingerprint-shaped bruises in purple and blue. His voice, growling, "I'll kill Jax if he ever comes near you again."

But Caleb is a liar. He's not here to protect me now. *Is he?*

Jax keeps talking. "Second is the thing I wanted to talk to you about at Shooter's. It's long overdue, but I need to say sorry for our breakup. I was awful to you." He sneaks a look over at me while I keep my face impassive. "The worst part is that I left you thinking it was all fake. That I didn't care."

He stares openly at me, willing me to meet his eyes. "I cared. All those emotions I had for you were real. I just…got caught up in old feelings when Sophie said she wanted to get back together. Honestly, I always felt like you were out of my league. You're so smart that I was convinced it was only a matter of time before you would dump me. She seemed the safer choice."

I'm stunned because, as much as I hate to admit it, I *have* believed I'm smarter than Jax. Our entire relationship was built around the difference in our intelligence. I was the tutor, and he was the student. I had no idea he thought about that as well, didn't know it bothered him. This admission doesn't stop the burn of my anger, remembering how he broke up with me and how quickly he got together with Sophie afterward.

"I see you're engaged to her. Congratulations. I don't understand why you need to come tell me all this when you're clearly happy." Old resentment tastes sour on my tongue.

There's a question that I've been wanting to ask but haven't. I've been too afraid, not sure if I can trust him to answer honestly. But today my heart is already ruptured, the blood pouring out of all my emotional wounds, so I might as well add another cut to the collection. "Did you cheat on me with Sophie? You got together with her pretty fast after we broke up." I can't believe I've waited so long to say it.

His voice stays steady, as do his eyes. "No. I was talking to her when we were together, but I didn't touch her until after we broke up."

Not sure if that answer makes things better or worse. "You may not have cheated, but you still betrayed me," I tell him evenly, and it's good. To speak my truth for once. Not worried about how he might take it. Not worried about hurting his feelings. After all, my feelings matter, too.

I sit with his answer for a moment, letting it sink in. The more I think about it, the more I realize that he might not have physically cheated on me, but he was emotionally cheating. That makes me furious. The rage feeds into my devastation over Caleb, making it easy to lash out.

"I can't stand how you used me, Jax. First for tutoring, but then for the rest of our relationship, I was the steady one. I listened to your dreams and complaining while you went out pursuing whatever passion project you were into. When I told you my worries, like my fear that I wouldn't get into medical school, you dismissed my concerns. Acted as if my goals didn't matter."

"That's because I was sure you'd make it into medical school. You studied so hard for it." Jax crumples the hat still held in his hands. "About my engagement to Sophie, I'm not here to rub it in your face. It's just when I saw you at Shooter's, it all came back to me. Our history together."

There's an awkward silence, while I get hold of myself and calm down. Then I say, "I didn't think that I was too good or smart for you. I thought the opposite."

He snorts, incredulous. "Why?"

It's embarrassing to talk about my insecurities, but I try. "You were so handsome and popular. I was a nobody. People only noticed me because I dated you."

"Let me ask you a question." He leans into my space. "Did *I* make you feel special?"

I remember all our years together and come up…blank? Jax hadn't been an awful boyfriend, never abusive or cruel, but he could be shallow and selfish. Most of the activities we did were ones that interested him, not me. Now I can't remember whose fault that was. Did he demand we do those things, or was I too timid to suggest alternatives? Either way, the result was that he rarely made me feel special.

The internal debate I'm having must show on my face, because he leans back with a look of bitter satisfaction. "Let me rephrase," he says, frowning. "Did I make you feel special or was it the *idea* of me? The part of me that was good at sports and was chosen as prom king?"

That drops like a brick on my head.

I've told myself a story about our relationship. How it was pure, and I lost it. How he'd used me, and I was the victim. Jax's questions challenge that belief. Back in high school, was I using him partly as a stepping stone to reach for popularity and acceptance? Yes. Am I using Caleb the same way? Absolutely not. I was telling the truth when I said I don't care about Caleb's fame.

"Honestly?" I ask, and he nods. "A little of both. It was nice to be seen, and that didn't happen until we started dating, but I also liked *you*. I admired you, how easily you get along with everyone."

He smiles then, his eyes crinkling in the corners, exactly like I remembered. That smile used to send butterflies swirling through my body, but their wings don't flutter now.

I stop to think about it and realize I used Jax in more ways than just for high school acceptance. He was an escape from my grief over Dad. A way to distract myself, to lose myself in another person so I wouldn't be alone in my head.

Maybe I had it all wrong. Maybe I wasn't the victim in our relationship. *Jax was.*

"You know how my dad died before we started dating?"

He nods solemnly.

"I never told you, but I had a rough time dealing with my grief. To be honest, I'm still struggling with it. I even went to see a therapist back in high school."

"Why didn't you say anything?" Those brown eyes grow soft with concern.

"Not sure." I look away and shrug. "Ashamed, I guess."

"I knew it was hard for you."

I whip my head toward him. "You did?" After all those years together, I hadn't thought Jax could surprise me, but today's conversation has been full of revelations.

"Gwen, seriously." He blows out a breath, fond exasperation etched into his features. "We dated for a long time. You think I couldn't see how bummed you would get around Christmas every year? It was clear how much you missed your dad."

"Why didn't you say anything?"

"I did, remember? In the beginning, I would ask you about it, but you never wanted to talk, so after a while I let it go."

What a lost opportunity. Jax could have comforted me during those dark days, but I hadn't let him in. In all the time that we dated, I hadn't fully let him see the real me. "Sorry, I could have handled that better. I should have been honest about what was going on with me."

I make a promise to myself, right then, to not hide my true self anymore. If I ever get a chance at love again, I will speak my mind, even if my thoughts and feelings are ugly or imperfect.

"It's okay," he says with a sad smile. "We both made mistakes."

Smile fading, Jax becomes serious. "Do you think it would have worked out between us? If we had gotten married?"

"I don't know." I let my gaze grow distant, looking into a future that will never happen. What I see frightens me. I imagine how people-pleasing me would have sacrificed myself to him. How I would have lost myself, disappearing a little more each day to meet his needs.

With Caleb, I had met his needs, but he had satisfied mine equally. There had been a steady back and forth between us. The tide of the ocean, pushing and pulling.

"I think the old me would have made marriage with you work. Cobbled a life together, even if it meant sacrificing things that were important to me. But I've changed recently, and the new me wouldn't have been happy. I'm not willing to compromise any longer. I won't change myself to conform to someone else's standards."

I swallow, realizing it was Caleb who had taught me that. Watching him struggle to write and sing, to be his own authentic self, had inspired me. He had played a role his whole life, that of the famous actor.

I had been playing a role, too. The dutiful daughter. The dependable girlfriend. I held onto those titles even when they became painful. I'm sick of all that, ready to let it go and write my own lines.

Respect shines in Jax's eyes. "I believe you. You seem different to me, bolder and more confident somehow. I like it. The change in you."

"Thanks." We have enough shared history that his praise still matters to me. "I don't think I could have said this to you before you came over here today, but I hope that you'll be happy with Sophie."

"Really? It means a lot to hear you say that." He lights up with pleasure, shoulders moving back and chest pushing out.

There's a release of the tension between us. It's good to be at peace with him. A kind of closure.

"What's up with you and Caleb Lawson?" Jax asks the question casually, but there's a hard focus to the way he watches me. His expression has transformed into something sneaky, almost sly. "I saw you kissing him. Never thought of you as a groupie."

The characterization as a groupie stings. Suddenly, I wonder if he would be here today if he hadn't seen Caleb kiss me. Jealousy can be a powerful motivator.

An even more sinister idea occurs to me. The hair rises on the back of my arms, a deep primitive part of my brain sensing a threat. I lean back to better survey Jax, noting how his eyes shift left to right and how he taps his fingers on the tabletop.

"Tell me Jax…why are you *really* here?"

"What do you mean? I wanted to talk to you. Put things to rest between us." He's acting innocent, but I dated the man for six years.

I know when he's lying.

"Jax." My tone is full of warning. "It's one thing for you to come over and talk about us, but why are you asking about Caleb and me?"

His mask falls away, revealing cold-hearted cunning beneath. It's a look I don't recognize. Before he could be hurtful in a thoughtless way, but now, this new Jax, there's a sense of jealousy from him, of bitterness. This is not the man I dated.

"What's the big deal?" he spits out. "People are curious about what's going on with you two. They have a right to know."

Fury tightens my spine, pulling it straighter. "Who wants to know?" I demand. "The reporters outside?"

His silence is his confession.

"Guess what, Jax. No one, and I mean *no one,* has the right to know what I do in my own house. Not you and not them. How much money are they offering you for the inside scoop, huh? In those articles, they always say a 'source close to the couple reveals.' Is that you? Do you want to be that snitch? Tell me, what's the starting salary for that job?"

I've gotten under his skin. He snaps out, defensively, "It's not like I came over here thinking about that. I just wanted to talk to you. When I was walking up to your front door, a few reporters approached me and asked if I was friends with you."

I stand up, my body vibrating with anger. "We're not friends, because friends don't sell each other out."

"I'm sorry," he says, not sounding sorry at all. "But I've got expenses. You wouldn't understand how hard it is to pay for a wedding on a teacher's salary, *Dr. Wright,*" he sneers. "Tell me what's going on with Caleb. A few details. That's all I need."

I point my index finger at the front door. "You know what? You were right earlier. It never was about you. I loved the idea of you, and clearly that man never existed. Now, get out."

"Gwen, listen, it's no big deal."

He doesn't budge, so I grab his shoulder and yank him up. One quick shove sends him toward the front door. He hesitates on the threshold, and something snaps inside me. Enraged, I shout, "I said, get out!"

So he does.

Jax leaves, just like he's left me before.

Just like Caleb left me yesterday.

Just like Dad left me years ago.

38

NEW YORK

January in New York suits my mood just fine. Cold and dark. The leaves stripped bare from the trees. Sounds muffled by the blanket of snow under my feet.

I trudge back and forth the three blocks that separate my apartment from the hospital, with my footprints trailing behind me. Sometimes I look back and pretend they belong to another person walking along with me. Someone with eyes like the ocean.

Mostly, I try not to think of him. It's a hard task because I'm rarely alone. The paparazzi have found me. Cameras flash and reporters scream when I open the front door.

"Where's Caleb, Gwen?"

"Have you spoken to him?"

"When are you going to make up?"

All great questions that I'd like to know the answer to as well. Some things they ask are more ridiculous, though.

"Is it true that you're secretly married?"

"Are you carrying his love child?"

"How did it feel, sleeping with your cousin?"

That last one gets to me. "He's *not* my cousin," I growl so ferociously that they all take a step back. To ward away the glare of their flashes, I throw my hand over my eyes. I shoulder past them and stomp to the hospital as they surround me, my own unwanted entourage.

After the first day of this chaos, I had opened my door to a burly man who had introduced himself as Dean, my new bodyguard.

"Bodyguard?" I scoffed. "I don't need a bodyguard. Who hired you?"

"Mr. Lawson did, ma'am. I'm here to protect you." The man stood ramrod straight, probably ex-military. He had that kind of bearing.

A red haze of fury had clouded my vision. On my doorstep, in front of all the cameras, I lost it. I screamed, "You can tell Caleb Lawson to get lost. I don't need you or him. Now get out of my face."

There must have been madness in my eyes. I certainly felt like I was losing my mind. The bodyguard had paled and backed away.

Click, click, click went the cameras. The reporters had twittered, turning to talk rapidly into their phones and recording devices, all trying to beat each other to the headline.

A lone paparazzi caught my eye when I looked through that crowd. The only one still watching me rather than his screen. The tip of his cigarette glowed red as snow fell down all around us.

Needless to say, I made the front page. I stared at it in the grocery store checkout line. A picture of me with my mouth a jagged gasp and my hair tangled. On my toes, I'm jabbing my finger into the face of the scary-looking bodyguard, who lurches away from me in fear. The headline reads, "Caleb Lawson's ex-girlfriend tells him to get lost."

I mean, how can I complain? It was an accurate quote.

Caleb was wrong. I can handle the press. It's easy to tune out their noise. What's harder to deal with is work. Those first weeks back in the hospital, I'm bombarded with questions. Nurses and techs I've never met before call out my name like we're old friends.

They ask about Caleb, about me, about us. They ask how he takes his coffee (he prefers tea, but I don't tell them that) and how he kisses (fantastic, but thinking about that makes it hard to breathe).

I deny, deny, deny. "Oh, that was a mistake," I say. "That's not me in the picture." I try for a lighthearted laugh and end up choking. "He's a distant relative. I've only met him a handful of times."

No one believes me. They all saw the photo, but my lies are enough to stop their questions. After a month, things start to quiet down. The number of microphones in my face each morning dwindles. The whispers and stares in the hospital hallways diminish.

That's why I'm extra-irritated to be called into the office of the hospital's chief medical officer, my boss's boss. Top of the doctor food chain.

"Dr. Benson." I swallow nervously when I shake his hand and take the seat he offers. We're in his corner office, with a view of the Hudson River out of his window. Wooden framed diplomas with shiny gold seals line the wall. I find myself distracted, reading them rather than listening to what he has to say. There are so many intimidating letters after his name on those certificates. M.D., Ph.D, FACP, FAHA, FACC. Even I don't know what they all mean.

"Is it going to continue to be a problem?" he asks, and, judging by the scowl on his face, he has repeated this question several times.

"I'm sorry. Is what a problem?" I cross my legs, think better of it, and uncross them.

"Your involvement with celebrity personalities. The press that waits for you outside of our hospital's doors every day. The exposé published by the newspapers."

Shoot. He saw that one.

"No, sir. Dr. Benson. It—I won't be a problem." I shake my head. This meeting is terrifying. Will this man fire me?

Caleb's voice whispers in my mind. *You could lose it all. Everything you worked so hard for.*

Shut up, I snarl at imaginary Caleb, willing myself to hold still and not fidget.

"It's going to be fine," I say, not sure who needs more reassurance, Dr. Benson or myself. "This is a tiny blip. Those reporters will get bored soon. In fact, every day, more of them leave."

He looks doubtful, but I'm just one more unpleasant meeting in his day, so he releases me with a vague warning to "try to stay out of trouble."

Whatever that means. Trouble is following me these days, not the other way around. If I could avoid it, I would.

39

Stupid things trick me into thinking about him. They come out of nowhere, slap me in the face, and run away before I can hit back. A quaint used bookshop, with a battered copy of Twilight in the window. The smell of a man's cologne in the hospital elevator. Sunlight filtering through clouds, its golden beams the same color as his hair.

I think of him during a particularly difficult shift. I'd just transferred a forty-year-old mother up to the ICU when we lost her pulse, and she stopped breathing. We coded her for over an hour, but all her heart monitor showed us was a flat green line. We couldn't get a single beep of life back. Every death is hard, but the young ones, like her, always hit closer to home.

As I sit next to her body and write out the death certificate, I glance up at the TV mounted on the wall. I do a double take when I see Caleb on the rectangular screen. It's a rerun of one of his old movies. His face was still rounded with teenage youth in this film, those cheekbones not so sharp yet.

The sound is off so I can't hear his lines, but the movie must be a romance because he's smiling at a gorgeous actress and she's smiling back at him. He closes his eyes and leans toward her. The camera zooms in for a closeup as their lips touch. Caleb kisses her passionately as I watch, unable to rip my gaze away.

Gagging, I bolt for the doctor's lounge, sprinting down the long beige hallways until I reach it. It's past three a.m. and I'm all alone, so there's no one to see me vomit noisily into the trash can.

At a round table, I collapse and bury my head in my folded arms. I burst into heaving, body-shuddering tears. Bawling so hard that I can't catch my breath. I'm hyperventilating, wheezing, struggling for oxygen so much that tiny white spots float in front of my eyes. This a full-on panic attack. Like the ones I used to have after Dad died.

I'm going to pass out. Dimly, I imagine some other doctor finding me unconscious on the floor. It'll be so humiliating, all the hospital gossip stirring up again. Dr. Benson will fire me for causing more drama.

A hand is on my shoulder, shaking gently, but I refuse to open my eyes. I don't want anyone to see me like this, so undone.

A woman's voice, honey-smooth, says my name over and over. "Dr. Wright. Dr. Wright. Come on. You're okay."

As I gasp desperately for air, she becomes sterner, more commanding. "Stop that caterwauling right now, little missy," she snaps. "You need to breathe."

The force of her words has me cracking my eyelids open. It's Alvina, one of the charge nurses from the ICU. She must have followed me, or maybe she heard me crying from out in the hallway.

She's in her fifties, with wide brown eyes the same color as her skin. Her hands are on her hips. Her face is stern, almost angry, like she won't tolerate any more of my nonsense.

"Take some deep breaths with me," she demands, her gaze never leaving mine. Alvina sucks in a sharp, loud breath through her nose and whooshes it out through her open mouth. I mimic her, trying to slow down my breathing.

Once I have it under enough control that I won't faint, she says firmly, "Now, tell me what's wrong."

I'm breathing better, but I still haven't stopped crying. "I m—miss him. So, so much," I stutter out in between my tears. "So much. So much." I rock back and forth, my arms hugging my chest.

At that moment, I'm thinking about Caleb, but also about my dad and even a little about Jax. Not the jerk that I kicked out of the house, but the soft-hearted boy I tutored in high school. The loss of all of them amplifies, echoing off one another until my grief over one becomes indistinguishable from the others.

She doesn't ask who I'm talking about. Instead, she pats me on the shoulder and makes quiet shushing noises, like you would to a baby. Eventually, my tears slow and dissolve into hiccups.

"Sorry," I mumble to her, mortified that she witnessed my meltdown.

Alvina sighs heavily, as if she knows the burden of sadness. "You're hardly the first doctor to cry in front of me."

That makes me feel a little better.

She looks me up and down, assessing, then makes a tut-tut noise with her tongue like I've disappointed her. "You're nothing but skin and bones. How much weight have you lost?"

Uh, not sure. Food tastes like dust, so I've been eating only when I get lightheaded. Maybe that's why I almost passed out, besides the crying and vomiting, of course. I glance down at my body and see for the first time how tightly the drawstring of my scrubs is knotted. How my pants hang off my hips, and my wrist bones stick out all pointy.

"Wait here." Alvina leaves. I put my head back down on my arms. I still have eight hours left in my twenty-four–hour shift, and I honestly don't know how I'm going to make it.

She returns with a cookie in her hand, chocolate chip. The kind with the big ooey-gooey chocolate chunks. "Here." She hands it to me. "Made it myself. Old family recipe. You eat that, and I *dare* you to tell me it isn't the best you've ever had."

It's a bold statement to make. My curiosity piqued for the first time since Caleb left, I bite into the soft cookie, its crumbs falling like rain onto the table. It's absolutely delicious. Like I actually moan. That's how good this cookie is. Sugar infuses into my bloodstream as if I injected it directly into my veins. "Oh, my goodness!" I exclaim, not caring that I'm speaking with my mouth full.

She rocks back in her seat, grinning smugly. "See? Told you so."

Out of thin air, another cookie appears in her hand. I vacuum it into my mouth. "What do you put in these? They're amazing."

"Uh-uh." She shakes her head, still smiling. "I'll never tell. Family secret." She winks and hands me a napkin so I can wipe the chocolate from my lips. "You working tomorrow?"

"Not tomorrow, but the day after." I pat the napkin to my mouth, hoping that I'm getting it all. I can't walk out of here tear- *and* chocolate-stained.

"Good. Me too. I'll bring you some more."

It shows what a bad place I'm in. That a couple of cookies and kindness from a woman I barely know makes me cry again. Alvina pulls me into her ample bosom, which I should resist because it's unprofessional, but I don't because it reminds me of Mom, whom I'm still barely speaking to. I paint Alvina's shirt with my tears, crying more quietly now.

I'm a mess.

"How can I live without him?" I cry, broken-hearted, again thinking of Dad, Jax, and Caleb all rolled into one.

She pats my shoulder. "Oh honey, you'll do it like you do all hard things. One day at a time."

40

That night, I go home and sit on my couch staring at nothing. A soft lick at my fingertips interrupts my trance. I look down into Pip's soulful brown eyes and swear I see sympathy in them.

Scooping her up into my arms, I burrow my cheek into her short fur, thankful that Mom agreed to let me bring her back to New York. Having her with me has been one bright spot in an otherwise bleak winter. I've arranged for a high-school student down the hall to take her out for walks when I'm stuck at the hospital.

"Oh, Pip." Her ears perk up at the sound of her name. "What should I do? I obviously can't keep going on like this. I've got to get over him." I don't even know which "him" I'm talking about.

She cocks her head at a ridiculous angle, like she's listening to me. "You're right," I tell her, as if we're having an actual conversation. "Boys are dumb. Who needs them."

She lets out a small yip, clearly agreeing.

Smart dog.

"Okay. Things need to change." I square my shoulders. "Where to start?"

With my hand on my forehead, I think until it finally comes to me. I've already said my peace to Jax. Someday down the road, I'll have to deal with Caleb, but for now it's time to put my father to rest.

I grab my phone off the table and search through my emails until I find what I'm looking for. It's from my old therapist, the one who took care of

225

me back in high school. She sent me this email when I left for college, but I never followed up. In the email she strongly advised I see a dedicated grief counselor. I didn't listen to her back then, but it's time to change that. After a bit of research to find the best therapist, I dial a number and leave a message, asking to make an appointment.

That phone call done, I go to my suitcase, with Pip trailing behind me, her tail wagging. I've only partially unpacked since returning from California. Digging to the bottom, my fingers find the edges of a rectangular package. I pull it out and stand there, an ache in the back of my throat, staring at the box for a very long time.

It's the paint set that Caleb gave me for Christmas. At the last minute, I threw it into my bag without much thought.

After my panic attack earlier, I had remembered how painting used to soothe me, before Dad died. On my way home from the hospital, I had ducked into an art supply store. In a daze, I bought a large framed blank canvas, pretending that I didn't know why I was buying it.

Now, I stare from the paints to the canvas, which leans against the wall of my small apartment. It's late, but I won't be able to sleep tonight anyway.

I glance down at Pip, who sits by my feet. "What do you think?" I ask her. "Should I try?"

Her tail wags even harder, which I take as a yes.

I get out the watercolors, set the canvas on the table, and paint.

41

lvina makes it her life's mission to fatten me up. During my next shift, I take a break from the ER and go to see her in the ICU. When I arrive, a paper plate covered with aluminum foil is waiting. My name is written on a piece of scotch tape across the top. When I pick it up, I almost drop it. The thing weighs as much as a brick.

"What's in this?" I ask her, lifting one edge of the foil to peek underneath. The mouth-watering aroma of fresh-baked cornbread comes wafting out. I was going to wait and eat it later, but once that smell hits me, it's game over.

The foil rips easily to reveal a full Thanksgiving-style dinner. There's thick-sliced turkey, homemade mac 'n' cheese, sweet potatoes with mini marshmallows toasted brown on top, and, of course, chocolate chip cookies. Everything is delicious.

"Wow," I tell her in between mouthfuls of food. "You sure can cook. This is amazing."

Alvina tosses her hair and smiles proudly. "Cooking for five children makes you learn mighty quick. I've been missing it, cooking for someone else, so I'm happy to do it for you."

Caleb used to cook for me, too. I push that thought aside.

"Five children?" My brows hit my hairline. "What moisturizer are you using because you look too good."

That makes her laugh, hearty and loud, the sound bouncing off the harsh white walls and linoleum floors of the ICU. "I started young. My kids are mostly grown now. Got my first grandbaby on the way."

"That's one lucky baby, if you feed your family the way you're feeding me. Your husband is lucky, too." I smile around the food in my mouth, the gesture rusty from the last month.

Her smile falters. "My husband passed away two years ago. Heart attack." Now I know why she understands sadness so well. Alvina's had her own fair share of heartbreak.

"I'm sorry," I whisper into the silence that follows.

She nods and her eyes sweep over my face. She harrumphs softly. "You got a little more color to your cheeks, Dr. Wright, but not enough. I expect you to finish that plate."

I give her a mock salute. "Yes, ma'am." My smile comes easier this time.

My pager beeps. Time to go back to the ER. "Thanks, Alvina. I mean it, thanks a lot." Smiling, she waves her hand, shooing me away. Down the hall I go, hoping to save someone else's life the way that Alvina just saved mine.

42

Weeks pass, and most of the reporters go with them. Eventually, only one stands outside my doorstep. The older man, who I first noticed on the day I fired the bodyguard. The one who's always smoking.

He's probably in his late fifties, judging by the gray hair at his temples. His eyes are gray, too. Sharp, like they see too much. It's unsettling when they focus on me. In honor of *The X-Files* and my secret crush on David Duchovny, I name him the Smoking Man in my mind.

In rain, snow, and sunshine, he stands with unnatural stillness, as if it's all the same to him. Only his eyes shift, roving over the cars and people who pass by.

I ignore him, stalking past each day, and he leaves me alone. Until one stormy morning when he falls in step several paces behind me as I walk to the hospital. He follows me home the same way that night.

The next morning, he moves in close, and I whirl around. "Go away or I'll call the police," I spit out, my hands balling into fists.

Smoking Man is unfazed by my threats. Using two fingers, he pulls the cigarette out of his mouth. A smoky tendril curls from its tip. "There was a mugging on this block last week. Young lady like you."

"So, you're what," I tilt my head, my voice rising in disbelief, "protecting me?"

Smoking Man's eyes shift away as he takes in a long drag and blows it back out of his nose.

Glaring at his cigarette, I warn, "You shouldn't smoke so much. Those things will kill you. I see it every day."

He shrugs his shoulders unevenly, the right rising more than the left. "At least it'll be a death of my choosing."

I don't bother telling him that working in a hospital has taught me that we rarely get to handpick the method of our death. Everyone thinks it's going to be lung cancer, but it's the drunk driver instead. That prostate cancer is easy to treat, but all those years of eating greasy food brings on the widow-maker heart attack. Death can be as sneaky as love. You never see either one coming.

Now that I'm facing him, it strikes me that I've seen this man before, but that can't be right. I sift through my memories until it hits like a bolt of lightning. "You!" I cry out. My finger points accusingly. "I saw you that night. At Shooter's." I remember it, the sharp-faced man smoking a cigarette outside the door of the bar as I exited with Jax hot on my heels.

He doesn't deny it, only says nonchalantly, "That picture was some of my best work."

Rage surges, burning through my veins. It's *his* fault, this man. All the things I lost. Caleb. His love. I draw in a deep breath. "Explain one thing," I grind out. "How'd you know Caleb would be there that night?" It's been driving me crazy, the not knowing.

A glint appears in his eye, almost like pity, but gone so quickly I can't be sure. "Don't ask questions you don't want the answers to."

"Don't you dare tell me what I want," I practically shriek at him.

The Smoking Man remains calm, probably used to being yelled at. I'd guess it's a hazard of his job. He answers my question with some of his own. "Who knew Caleb was with you? Who knew he might come that night?"

"No one," I insist. Hand to my forehead, I rub it, thinking back to those days in my mother's house. "I mean, one person knew."

He gives me a knowing look, and my heart sinks down to my feet.

Jenny.

43

That night, I call Jenny.

She answers with her usual cheerfulness, her tone chirpy. It makes the boulder in my chest that much heavier.

"Did you tell anyone that Caleb was at my house?" I try to keep the accusation out of my voice but can't.

There's a long silence when all I hear is her breathing. It goes on for so long that I already know what she'll say.

"It might have slipped out to Sarah—just once."

My eyes squeeze closed, trapping any tears that want to escape.

Her words become harried. "I'm so sorry, Gwen. You know how I get. I was talking about you, and, before I knew it, I mentioned him. I didn't mean to. Is that how the paparazzi found out Caleb would be at Shooter's? Did I ruin everything for you?"

There's panic in her voice, the choked sound of her crying.

I don't even know how to respond.

I told her. She *knew* how crucial it was to keep Caleb a secret. We had multiple discussions about it. And yet, she went ahead and told the secret to Sarah. It was an accident, a momentary lapse. I get that. Jenny would never knowingly hurt me. But that doesn't make it any less devastating.

"Please," she begs. "Please talk to me. I'm so sorry. I had no idea it would turn out like it did."

My chest aches so badly that I look down, expecting to see a gaping hole where my heart should be. "I needed you to be on my side, needed you to keep it a secret," I tell her. "Maybe it was unfair of me to ask that of you. And I totally understand that if it wasn't you, eventually someone else would have found out. I get that, but darn it, Jenny, losing Caleb has nearly killed me. Now I can't think of that pain without also thinking of you. It's all tied up together."

I drag in a ragged breath, my emotions spiraling into a dark place. "You were my safe space. My whole life, when Dad died and when Jax left, you were there for me. I need you again now, but I...I can't do it like those other times."

My own chest reverberates with her harsh sobs.

"Can you ever forgive me?" she cries. "I don't want to lose you."

My throat tightens at the thought of stepping away from Jenny. I've already lost so many people in my life. I can't give her up too, not completely.

"You won't," I tell her. "Our friendship isn't that fragile, but I have to be honest with you. I'm hurt, and it'll take some time to get past that."

I can barely make out her garbled, "Okay. I'm so sorry, Gwen."

"I know you are."

Struggling not to break down completely, I say good-bye and hang up. Once I'm off the phone, I kick myself for being such a fool. I should have known this would happen.

Caleb was too big a secret to keep.

44

The grief counselor tells me to call her Dr. Jill.

Her office is full of plants. They sit in a row on the windowsill, on the corners of her desk, even in the nooks and crannies of her bookshelves. She likes the leafy ones, with vinelike branches that trail and tumble down the sides of the pots.

I stare at them, the plants, rather than at her as I settle into the chair she offers across from her desk. This is my first appointment, and I've been anxious about it all day.

"It's nice to meet you," she says pleasantly. "Why don't you tell me why you're here today?"

"Well," I hesitate, my knee jiggling with nervous energy. "My dad died when I was in high school. Colon cancer. The rest of my family has moved on. My older brother is married with his own kids. My younger brother is going to community college. Even my mother has remarried. But for me, I'm stuck. Still sad and angry like I was when it happened nine years ago."

"You mention being sad and angry." She takes notes.

I wonder what she's writing. It's irrational, but I worry it's something like "This woman is unhinged. A total lost cause." Surely, that's not it. Right? I'm not hopeless. Is that why Jax and Caleb left me? Because they sensed that I was broken? Damaged beyond repair?

Dr. Jill is still talking. "Most people would understand the sad part, but can you tell me a little more about why you're angry?"

"Because it was so unfair," I blurt out, the force of the words startling in the quiet office, where the only other sound is the hum of the heater. "He was only forty-five. He wasn't supposed to get sick, definitely wasn't supposed to die and leave us behind."

My throat tightens, and I swallow around the lump growing there. "If the world is that cruel, to take him from me, how can I ever trust it? How can I ever believe that anything—life, love, happiness—will last? I'm angry because his death took away my faith in the future." My chest heaving, I cut myself off, feeling overly exposed, raw, and ragged. I hadn't meant to reveal so much so quickly.

Her pen makes a rustling noise as she writes. "I see," she says as she looks up from the page. "Do you feel like this cynicism about the future, your lack of trust in it, has affected other areas of your life?"

She had made me a cup of tea before we started the session. Chamomile. Supposed to be calming. I'm anything but calm, so I take a gulp, hoping it will soothe me.

"My relationship with my first boyfriend was in some ways a distraction from my grief," I admit. "The whole time we were together, which was a long time, I kept expecting it to fail. Partly, I realize now in hindsight, because he was the wrong guy, but also because I couldn't imagine anything lasting, not after Dad."

"You mention that he was the wrong guy, so why did you stay?"

"I became risk-averse after Dad died. Set in my routines." *Serious, dependable, predictable, boring.* "Back then, I didn't fully realize that we weren't a great fit. I was too busy clinging to him to take an honest look at our relationship. He represented stability to me at a time when I couldn't take any more change. I almost married him."

I take a deep breath. "More recently, I fell for a guy." The flash of ocean eyes and hair like the sun whirs through my memory, making my heart speed. If she knows who I'm talking about, she doesn't show it. I had double-checked that everything I tell her is confidential before I booked this appointment. The last thing I need is for the things I say in this room to end up in the newspapers.

"It all happened pretty fast. I believed he was the right man, but even with him, a part of me worried it wouldn't work out. That nothing will stick to me. No one will stay. When he left, it just proved I was correct, and that makes me angry. Furious, really. That all my fears keep coming true." My thumb rubs over the handle of the mug. The warmth of the tea seeps into my palms.

"Hmm," she murmurs, taking her own small sip of tea. "I'm sensing some problematic thought processes. You're making connections that might not exist. Your father's death may have nothing to do with these failed relationships. After all, lots of people break up with their boyfriends, people who haven't had a death in their family. The only way you would be correct is if you were subconsciously sabotaging these romances. Are you doing that?"

With my chin in my hand, I consider the question. "Maybe with the first boyfriend, but I don't think I did with the second."

"Okay. We can explore that in future sessions. I have some techniques I can teach you to help cope with these thoughts." More writing. "When you have this sadness, anger, and doubt, what do you do to distract yourself or make yourself feel better?"

"I talk to my best friend." *The one I'm barely talking to right now.*

"Call my mom." *The one who is barely talking to me.*

I sigh, wondering when my life became such a disaster.

"I also watch horror movies, and, recently, I've been painting."

She quirks a brow, looking interested.

"Painting is something I did a lot when I was younger, and now I've picked it up again. My mind is…I don't know, quieter, when I do it?"

Dr. Jill taps her pen on the paper. "Have you heard of art therapy?"

"Only vaguely. I'm not really sure what it is."

"You work with a trained art therapist. They usually have a master's degree or higher. Composing artwork stimulates symbolic processing centers in the brain. It's an alternative way to express and explore your issues. Studies show that, when used with our talk therapy sessions, it can be quite beneficial. I'll give you a referral."

"Okay, thanks," I say politely, while I remain unconvinced. How much could it help, really, to do some doodling?

We speak for a while longer, touching on my resentment over my mother's new marriage and my lukewarm reception toward Seth.

When Dr. Jill announces that my time is up, I lift my watch to look, surprised it had gone by so quickly. I leave a little shaky, but also a little lighter.

A lvina and I are on the upper east side of Manhattan today, checking out a local bakery. She gets a blueberry muffin, and I grab almond cookies, wrapped in a cellophane bag with a twist tie at the top. As a native New Yorker, she's decided to show me around the city, stopping at all of her favorite places.

We've become friends. It all started with her feeding me. When we discovered a mutual love of cheesy horror movies, I took a risk and invited her to a matinee. After that, it was dinner at her place in Chelsea.

We might be a bit of an odd couple, with me in my twenties and her in her fifties, but Alvina has a young spirit. Full of energy, she absolutely refuses to let me wallow in my apartment.

"You had your first art therapy thing, right?" she asks, as a flock of pigeons scatter at her feet, cooing loudly.

"Yeah. It was weird in the beginning, but then I kind of got into it. The therapist was great. Super knowledgeable, both about art in general and also about how to apply it to therapy. She had me cut words out of a magazine that resonated with my emotions and make them into a collage."

I picture how it looked when I was done. That paper full of terms like *death, anxiety, fear, depression, abandoned, unworthy.* Each word a splinter in my soul. It had been hard to look at that collage, but I'd forced myself to not turn away.

"The therapist gave me homework to try something similar, except this time to paint it with images and symbols at home, instead of using words. I'm going to work on it during my next day off. Of course, that's like two weeks from now." I roll my eyes, and she laughs softly, understanding how packed my work schedule is.

As I chew on a soft cookie, we stroll down the street. It's a warmer day. The winter snow has finally melted away, leaving behind dirty puddles in the gutters. The city sings its constant song of jackhammers. There's always construction going on, with orange detour signs pointing everywhere.

"This cookie is tasty, but not as good as your chocolate chip ones," I tell her for the twentieth time. "I swear, you should open your own restaurant or food truck."

She turns her face to the sun, basking in its warmth. "Now, you're talking crazy again. I've got five more years in the hospital, and then I'm retiring. Will have enough saved up by then to kick my feet up on the coffee table and watch TV for the rest of my life."

I sigh. "That would be heaven." I try hard not to think about my future. It yawns like a gaping hole before me. I've been piling things into that hole—extra shifts at work, therapy appointments, outings like this one with Alvina—so it won't swallow me up.

She chuckles. "You're just at the start of your career. No resting on the couch for you yet."

"Don't remind me," I grumble. "Two more years until I graduate from my residency. I'll probably do a fellowship after that, so tack on another year or two. I'll be old as dirt by the time I'm finished. Too bad I can't hit the fast-forward button. Just be done with it."

"Now, don't be saying that." Her voice turns admonishing. I call this Alvina's "mother hen voice." "You should never skip parts of your life. Each one is too important. Life is already too short." I sense she's thinking about her husband with that last part.

Tick tock, Gwen. Time's running out.

I shake my head. "I'm sure you're correct, but right now my days are so full of drudgery that I want to get through this hard part and move on. Working over a hundred hours a week in the hospital is exhausting."

She gives me a knowing look. "Is it work that's bothering you or something else?"

I almost choke on my cookie. Alvina's been great so far, never outright mentioning my panic attack in the doctor's lounge. I guess that changes today.

"It's the hospital…and other stuff, too." I'm mostly lying. The long hours at the hospital are brutal, but I continue to love medicine. I find it rewarding to care for my patients, to be there when they are scared or hurt.

It's Caleb that's bothering me. Still, after two months, I can't totally shake him.

He doesn't have the same problem, based on the celebrity gossip magazines at the grocery store. He's gone back to acting, picking up a leading role in some police drama on one of the major networks. "*Lawson's triumphant return!*" the magazine had exclaimed. I looked away as quickly as I could, fighting the lead ball in my chest.

"Hmmm." Alvina seems doubtful. "About that other stuff. Maybe you should call him. Say all the things you need to so you can get it out of your system."

I wish she wouldn't bring it up. Now I'm thinking about Caleb, his hand on my cheek, his eyes sparking with something that I had mistaken for love. The memory hurts, sharp and piercing.

How could I have been so stupid? I should have known he was a liar. It's his literal job, convincing people he's someone he's not. Playing the role. Speaking his lines.

But he was such a pretty liar and so, so good at it that he had me convinced. I had closed my eyes, not looking at our reality. Let him sweep me away. Let him cast me as his leading lady. Let him play my Prince Charming. It had been easy to accept his whispered falsehoods, to trust in the story he spun.

So easy to fall for him.

But now, as the time I've spent apart from him becomes longer than the time we spent together, my doubt grows, tainting all of my memories.

What was real? Any of it?

"Never," I vow. "There's nothing I didn't already say." I mentally dig in my heels, determined that I'm not the one who should call. I'm not the one who walked away, after all.

"You know, Gwen. Sometimes people need to hear something more than once before it sinks in," she says with the wisdom of a veteran ICU nurse. "Even more, *you* might need to say it again, so you'll actually believe it yourself."

"Believe what?" I gruff, gripping my cookies so tightly that I've crushed them into tiny crumbs that rattle around in the bottom of the bag.

"That you two are finished."

moking Man's name turns out to be Wayne, but I still like to call him Smoking Man in my mind. I Google him and find out that in the world of sleazy underdog reporters he's kind of a big deal. He's gotten the scoop on many celebrity dramas, everything from divorces and drugs to infidelities. Lots of articles from him about Caleb.

Interesting guy, this Wayne. He has a knack for being in the right place at the right time.

We're not friends, like Alvina and I are, but I don't hate him as much as I used to. Sometimes we have mundane conversations about the weather or how my shift at the hospital went as we walk together.

One day, curiosity wins out. It's twilight, colors bleeding out of the sky into shades of gray. We're standing on the sidewalk in front of my apartment. I'd just gotten home from a dinner out with Alvina where I hadn't felt normal, but I had been a little less unhappy.

"Why are you still here?" I ask him. There had been hundreds of reporters initially, now whittled down to this single slim man.

Wayne takes a puff of his cigarette. His answer comes out along with the smoke. "Same as you. Waiting for Caleb."

A harsh laugh from me. I can't believe he just said that. It may be the stupidest thing I've ever heard. "Well, you're going to be waiting a long time. Forever, probably."

His gaze pins me, sharp with foxlike cunning. "I don't think so."

I snort in disbelief. "Why not?"

Another puff of smoke before he answers. "I've been covering Caleb Lawson since he was nine years old. Know him better than my own son. Never seen him look like this."

He pulls out his cell phone and flashes the picture of Caleb and me at Shooter's, passionately embracing.

"That's over," I tell him definitively, barely glancing at the photo. I've looked at it enough. Have every inch of it memorized. I analyzed it a million times in the days right after we broke up, searching for what went wrong. How those two lovers, so intertwined in the picture, could be torn apart.

"No. A man looking like that." He glances down at the image, takes another drag. "That's not something he's going to give up. I'm good at this job because I play the long game. That's you, Dr. Wright. You're Caleb's long game. I want the exclusive when he comes crawling back."

"He won't," I scoff. "He doesn't care. I was just a distraction from his problems. A chance to pretend to be someone else for a change."

Wayne doesn't even blink. "I know what Caleb is going to do. The thing I'm not sure about is *you*. You're the wild card. Will you take him back? No matter how broken he is?"

He pulls his phone in close to his face and, using the hand holding his cigarette, scrolls through pictures with his pinkie. "Let me show you another." He finds the one he's looking for and holds it out to me.

It's a photo taken in front of my mom's house. I recognize the brown stucco and double front doors. Caleb is rushing down the front steps with Marjorie right beside him. Her hand is gripped so tightly around his upper arm that I can see where the fabric indents under her fingers. My grandmother's quilt is thrown over his head to hide his face, but it's slipped enough that I see his profile and the fear stamped across his features. Eyes so wide they are mostly white and his mouth twisted.

Caleb looks terrified.

"Caleb's been dealing with the paparazzi since he was a kid," Wayne says. "Never seen him frightened before. Annoyed? Yes. Angry? Sure. But not frightened. Answer me this, Doctor, who do you think he's scared for in this picture?"

Me. He's worried about me.

I brush that thought aside, not willing to examine it in front of Wayne's prying eyes. "He was just mad he got caught."

Wayne shrugs. "Okay, then. I have one more for you. It'll be in the paper tomorrow, but you may want the first peek."

It only takes a second for him to find what he's looking for. This time, he hands his phone to me. I hold it up to the streetlight. The image is dark, slightly distorted, as if it was taken at night through a window. The setting is a bar with a long granite countertop.

A lone man sits with his back partially turned to the camera, shrouded in an air of melancholy. He's hunched over a glass, the short kind that holds hard alcohol like bourbon or scotch. His hands curl loosely around it, caressing it. Head hanging heavily, a lock of hair falls into his eyes. He gazes into the drink like all the love left in his world resides at its bottom.

It's Caleb.

"Oh no," I whisper, tears springing unbidden in my eyes. "No. No. What have you done?" I ask the man on the screen. The first tear slips down my cheek as I touch my fingers to his image, wishing I could reach through the phone and grab him. Lift him out of that bar and bring him home to me.

I barely notice Wayne studying me carefully. Barely hear him whisper, "Maybe not such a wild card after all."

More loudly, he says, "There are other photos, too. Ones that his parents and PR team have suppressed. A bar fight in Calabasas. Passed out in Santa Monica. You knocked him off the wagon, Dr. Wright. How do you feel about that?"

Each word is a blow, hitting behind my knees until I want to crumple to the ground. I stay standing, though. I stroke my thumb over Caleb's face on the tiny screen. "Can you not print it? Please," I beg, understanding the damage this picture will do to Caleb's career.

"Sorry, sweetheart. Business is business."

I hate him in that moment. Hate the whole world for being so cold, so cruel. Hate all the people, myself included, who buy those magazines and read about other people's lives. Thrilling when celebrities fail because it makes us feel better about our own meager existence.

The dirty look I send Wayne has no effect. I hand him his phone and wordlessly go up the stairs to my apartment, where I sit on my lumpy second-hand couch. Pulling out my phone, I stare at Caleb's number for a long time.

The picture of him at the bar keeps flashing through my mind. The misery in the droop of his shoulders is burned on my eyelids, a stain I'll never be able to remove.

Heart in my throat, I dial.

Somewhere in California, his phone rings and rings.

No one answers.

47

The next morning, with the first rays of dawn skimming the horizon, I charge down my apartment stairs. Wayne falters when he sees me, pausing with his Styrofoam coffee cup halfway to his lips.

"He's still in L.A.?" I bark out my question, the airline website already open on the phone in my hands. Caleb may not care about me, but as much as I wish it were different, I still care about him. In that picture, he looks like someone who needs saving.

That's my job. I save people. Heal them.

Wayne takes a sip, wincing like the coffee tastes terrible. "You're too late. He's gone."

Tick tock, Gwen.

"What? Where?"

He eyes me shrewdly, taking note of my desperation. I can practically see him writing the article in his mind.

Lawson's ex goes berserk trying to find him.

I don't care what he, or anyone else, wants to say about me.

"Don't know. Disappeared like last Christmas when he went to your house. His parents came into town, not a good sign." He sighs. "They've never let him grow up, you know? His parents, his agents, all his handlers. He's easier to control that way, helpless without them." His words remind me of when I first met Caleb, how he couldn't even turn on the washing machine.

"Careful. You almost sound like you care," I warn.

"Let me tell you a story," Wayne begins, and as he talks I see why he's such a good reporter. He has a way of capturing my attention, painting a picture with his words.

"When Caleb was about nineteen or so, I was outside his building waiting for him to come out. My third wife, now ex-wife, was on the phone, complaining about how I was missing my son's baseball game. I was always missing those games back then. Too busy working."

"Anyway, Caleb comes out and tells me to get lost like usual. I tell him off, like I always do, but then I get upset because it's bugging me, missing my kid's game. I keep thinking of how my son looked at me that morning. How he didn't even bother to ask if I'd make the game, something he used to do. It was like he'd given up on me, his workaholic dad."

"I don't mention any of this to Caleb, but, somehow, he knows. We've been together a long time, like I told you. He asks what's wrong, and for some stupid reason I have a moment of weakness and tell him."

"Caleb rolls his eyes and tells me, 'Okay. Let's go.' And I'm like, 'Go where?' He says, 'To your son's game. I'll go too so you can watch him and me at the same time.'"

Wayne gets uncomfortable at this point, as if he regrets bringing it up. He rushes to the ending. "We go, and my kid freaking loves it. Tells all his friends, 'Check out my dad sitting over there with Caleb Lawson. They came to see *me* play.'" Wayne shrugs. "My son still talks about it, all these years later."

I look at him with fresh eyes, seeing the attachment you must make when you spend so much time together, the way that he and Caleb have, even if most of it is at a distance.

He glares at me. "Don't go getting all sappy-eyed, sweetheart. There's no heart of gold under this shirt."

"Yeah, yeah." I wave him off, thinking about how his heart may not be gold, but he did just prove that it's still beating.

"That's a good story. Sounds like the Caleb I thought I knew." Sadness tinges my words.

Wayne's sharp eyes are evaluating me again. "That is Caleb. So is the drunk.

So is the jerk. So is the guy who donated hundreds of thousands of dollars to charities last year without telling anyone about it."

"Exactly!" I throw my hands up. "Isn't everyone like that? Aren't we all a million contradictions? Sad one day. Happy the next. Sometimes kind and other times selfish. The only sure thing about us all is our inconsistency. I don't understand why we expect celebrities to be any different. Why must they be only one person? Never changing. Always frozen in time."

He shakes his head. "That's not what people want. It's too confusing. They want the simple story. Good versus evil. They want the celebrity wearing the white cowboy hat to never put on the black one. Caleb's been painted as a golden boy. It's a long way to fall off his pedestal."

Turns out Wayne is right. I start paying attention to the magazines I used to detest. I watch the entertainment shows on the TV. That picture of Caleb at the bar is everywhere. His sudden disappearance doesn't help. It makes him seem guilty. No new shiny photos of him to replace that incriminating one. The news anchors repeat over and over, "Caleb Lawson's representatives decline to comment."

With Pip sitting next to me on the couch, I call Caleb's phone again that night and the next and the next.

No answer.

I don't leave a message.

Instead, I paint.

ehab," Wayne announces a few days later as I emerge from the hospital after a twelve-hour shift. He hands me a cup of coffee. Starbucks this time. Not the cheap stuff. It must be bad news if he's bringing me caffeine.

"A facility up in Santa Barbara." He takes a sip from his own cup.

"Is he okay?" I open my lid a crack and blow on the steaming liquid, watching it swirl under my breath. The drink warms my paint-stained fingers.

"Don't know. That place is locked up tighter than Fort Knox. It caters to celebrities. Prides itself on keeping things confidential. You wouldn't believe the strings I had to pull just to confirm he really is in there."

"Will you publish it? That he's in rehab."

Wayne sends me a look, showing he's disappointed that I even asked. Like I should know better. But when he sees the frown lines in my forehead, he softens and gives me a begrudging, "Sorry, sweetheart."

He usually says sweetheart sarcastically, like the word was caustic, but today he says it without irony, the gentle way a father would to his daughter.

He must be worried about Caleb, too.

"When is he getting out?"

"No clue."

That night, I give Pip a pat on the head and call Caleb's phone. This time, when I get his voicemail, I leave a brief message. "Hey. It's me, Gwen. Just hoping you're okay."

49

stride forward with my hand outstretched and my head held high, trying to project confidence. I'm hoping Dr. Benson won't remember the last time I was here. Back when he was angry with me for the Caleb fallout.

"Dr. Wright." He greets me with a firm handshake and a flat smile that doesn't make the journey to his eyes. "How nice to see you...again," he says dryly.

Uh-oh. Guess he remembers.

Not off to a good start.

We take our respective seats, him at his desk and me in the stiff chair in front of it. Just like last time, I find the framed degrees on the wall behind him distracting, but I wrench my gaze away from them and focus instead on the gray-haired doctor.

"I want to come to you today with a proposal." I hand over the binder that contains all of my carefully compiled research and preliminary budgets. Dr. Benson flips through the pages briefly before placing it on his desk and returning his attention to me.

Although my hands tremble where I hold them folded in my lap, my voice is steady. "I believe this hospital would benefit from instituting an art therapy program."

He raises a brow.

After taking a deep breath, I launch into the speech that I practiced this morning in my mirror. "Art therapy has many proven benefits. I've included the research in the material I gave you." I gesture to the binder. "Among the positive effects are elevated patient mood, faster healing times, and quicker discharge from the hospital."

Dr. Benson steeples his hands and leans forward on that last one, just as I knew he would. At the end of the day, the hospital is, sadly, a business. The more patients who pass through our doors, the more money there is to be made.

"How would that work, exactly?" he asks.

"A team of therapists could visit the patients and do art with them in their rooms. I'm estimating that for the size of this hospital and the number of appropriate patients, we would need to hire three full-time therapists."

The lines on each side of his mouth deepen as he frowns. "Where would the money to pay their salaries come from?"

"The insurance companies reimburse for this treatment but not enough to pay for the entire cost. Combined, the payments from insurance providers would cover one therapist's salary. I found a grant provided by the federal government that would fund another of the positions."

"That's enough for two therapists. What about the third that you seem to think we need?" he interjects, running a hand over his chin.

This will be the most difficult part, getting the hospital to shell money out of its own pocket. Pulling myself as tall as I can, I answer, "That's where you come in, sir. The hospital would have to budget for that cost."

He's quiet for a few minutes, staring at me with a critical eye. I fidget, straightening my already straight white lab coat.

"It's a cute idea." A glance at the clock on the wall behind me. "But we're going to have to pass."

Cute? Did he just say cute?

I give it another try. "But, sir, as you can see from the information I have provided, I've identified a subset of patients who could truly benefit."

He sighs, puffing out his cheeks like I'm annoying him. The look at the clock lasts longer this time, and I know I've lost him. He rises from the desk and leans over its shining mahogany surface with a politician's handshake. "Sorry, Dr. Wright. Maybe we can reassess when we're compiling the budget for next year."

Reassess, yeah right. This man has no intention of promoting my idea. He might as well tell me not to let the door hit me on the way out.

The knowledge sends me into a tailspin. Old feelings of depression and inadequacy rear up. *Was I stupid to believe this could work? Is it an inherently flawed plan?*

No, I decide as I trudge down the five sets of stairs that lead me back to the ER. I've looked at my patients over the past few weeks. I've seen ones that would benefit from the extra boost art therapy gives. Patients teetering on the border between health and simply giving up on life. Those are the ones who could transform with the change in mindset that art therapy provides. I see those people, and I yearn to help them.

Well, you know what?

Forget Dr. Benson and his lack of forward thinking. It's a good plan. I feel it in my bones.

Now I need to find someone who agrees with me.

ow's the weather in California?" I ask Teddy, straining to hear his answer through the tiny speaker in my cell phone.

We're back to mostly superficial conversations. It hurts my heart, but after seeing how Marjorie smothered Caleb and how that backfired, I'm retreating a step. Let Teddy have his space and figure out some things on his own. He knows I'm here to help whenever he wants me.

Besides, I'm sure Mom is nagging him enough for the both of us.

My phone sits propped up on the kitchen counter. I need my hands free to work. Tonight's canvas is filled with the face of one of my patients, an elderly lady with fluffy white hair that floats around her head like a snowy cloud. I had asked her permission to sketch and then paint her. Once she agreed, I'd used my lunch break to run up to her room and do a rough drawing.

All day, I've been looking forward to working on this. Painting, along with my near weekly sessions with the grief counselor and art therapist, has been a balm to my soul. I'm starting to feel more like my old self. Not just the person I was before Caleb left, but the person I was before my father died. The person who saw a multitude of possibilities when she looked in the mirror.

"The usual. Cold in the morning and night. Warm in the middle of the day. Have to dress in layers." Teddy sighs. "I'm not complaining, though. It's a lot better than the snow at the University of Michigan."

He had followed up on his plan and dropped out of college after Christmas. He's taken over my old position as house sitter at Mom and Seth's place.

Now he's the one who gets to listen to the distant sound of hammers and wood saws. At my urging, he's started enrollment at the local community college and picked up some bartending work for money.

He's doing okay, but not great. A little lost, lacking purpose.

I've added him to my list of worries. It goes something like this. Teddy. Caleb. The slowly shrinking, but not yet gone, hole in my heart.

"How're things going with you and Mom?" he asks.

"Better. At least we're talking, but she gave me a big lecture about being more honest in the future."

"No offense, Sissy, but you kind of deserve that. You did lie to her."

"I realize that, and I feel guilty about it. I figure I'll be making it up to Mom for, oh, I don't know…the next forty or fifty years of my life."

Teddy's laugh is good to hear. It hits me how rarely I had heard it while he was in Michigan.

"At least we'll get to watch you grovel to Mom next summer. I can't wait to go to Japan," Teddy says, mentioning the trip my entire family has planned to visit Mom and Seth.

"Liv told me the twins want to see every Pokémon store there. They won't stop talking about it." I smile, thinking about those two girls tearing through all the toy and card shops in Tokyo. "I can't wait for Japan, either."

"What about Caleb? Any news?"

Now it's my turn to sigh. "None."

Thanks to Wayne, everyone has figured out that Caleb's in rehab. They've eaten it up, casting him as a fallen star. Another cautionary tale of a child celebrity gone off the rails.

"I shouldn't care, anyway. It's not like I'll ever see him again."

"Unless he turns up at some family event," Teddy counters.

Ugh. I hadn't thought of that. I would hope that Caleb at least had enough respect for me to spare me from that horror. I'm still trying to forget him.

Then why are you leaving messages on his phone? a tiny voice that sounds suspiciously like mine asks in the back of my head.

Why am I? Since Caleb's been in rehab, I've developed a nasty habit of calling his phone every night. At first it was just to hear his voice on the voicemail greeting. "Hey, it's Caleb. Drop a message and I'll hit you back." *Beep.* I would leave a quick generic voicemail like, "Hi. Hope you're doing okay," or "Thinking of you."

But like every junkie, I've increased my dose. Now my messages are longer. I tell him about my day at the hospital. Talk about funny things that Alvina said or that Wayne still won't leave me alone.

Pathetic, I know.

Since he never picks up, it feels as if it's a safe space. Like I'm throwing my words into a void, letting them get whisked away into the ether. Gone to wherever cell phone signals go. It's nice to unburden my soul that way.

A little less lonely.

'm rushing to meet Alvina and a few other co-workers for happy hour when I see it. There, in large gold letters on the marquee at the Prestige Theater on 49th Street, the sign reads: "Caleb Lawson Stars in Crazy for You, a Musical."

I skid to a stop, staring up at the sign with my mouth agape. My heart plummets down to the ground, sinking into the pavement.

What. The. Actual. Heck?

Even Wayne is speechless when I tell him about it the next morning. "I swear I had no idea," he says as we walk to the hospital. He's angry. Mad that someone beat him at his own game. "Don't worry," he assures me. "I'll figure it out."

We've become conspirators over the past month, Wayne and I.

An update from him the next day. "It was arranged when Caleb was finishing rehab. The producers auditioned him from there. Must have gone well because they gave him the lead role." Wayne looks at me suspiciously. "I didn't even know he can sing. Did you?"

"Umm." The sidewalk is suddenly very interesting.

"Gwen," he warns, and I understand that I'm about to lose my daily vanilla latte if I don't start talking.

"He's actually really good. At singing. Like *really good.*" I spill like a pinata at a kids' birthday party. I don't tell him about the stage fright, though. No need to give away all of Caleb's secrets. There must be no more stage fright.

Not if he's playing on Broadway, right? Even thinking about that, about staring into an enormous crowd a few feet away from the stage, frightens me for him.

    I hope you know what you're doing, Caleb.

lvina talks me into going to the musical. She says that I need to see Caleb to get over him, and this is the perfect way. I can hide in the crowd and watch him anonymously. Prove to myself that he's alive and okay. That I don't have to worry about him anymore. Even Wayne agrees when I mention the idea.

I'm doubtful that it'll work, but I go along anyway. Since Caleb's reappearance, I've been too scared to leave messages on his phone. I'm exhausted by the end of the day, frustrated without the outlet of talking to his voicemail.

It's ridiculous. *I'm* ridiculous. It's been almost three months now. I seriously need to move on…find a healthy relationship where I talk to a real person instead of an empty voice mailbox.

We're running twenty minutes late. Alvina had taken forever to get ready. As we rush down the street, my heel lodges in a crack in the sidewalk. I wrench it free, then run to catch up to her. She's holding the large wooden door to the theater open. "Hurry," she says frantically.

The lobby is empty. Everyone must have already gone in. The lilt of music drifts out through the gap in the doors that lead inside.

"I have to stop at the restroom," Alvina says in a harried tone, her features drawn tight.

"Really? Right now?" I grit out, annoyed that she can't wait. This is seriously the worst timing.

She pushes me toward the entrance. "Go! Get our seats before someone else takes them."

"Okay. Okay. Geez." I frown at her, not appreciating the shove. I don't need her being bossy on top of the nerves I'm already feeling. Now that we're here, this doesn't seem like such a brilliant plan.

Not wanting to bother anyone, I push the doors open a tiny bit and turn sideways to slip through. It takes a few minutes for my eyes to adjust to the low light inside.

Once they do, I can't make sense of what I see.

Built during more opulent times, the theater is gorgeous. It's painted in tones of red and gold, with soaring curtain-draped balconies. Elaborate gilded chandeliers hang, dimmed and glittering, from the ceiling. Fancy golden scrollwork runs over the walls and surrounds the large dais where the actors perform, framing it like a picture.

It's beautiful, and it's…empty.

Rows and rows of deep red velvet seats stretch out before me. All leading down to the stage, where a single spotlight illuminates a man sitting on a plain wooden stool with a guitar in his hands.

Caleb.

And he's looking right at me. "Hi, Gwen." He says my name for the 229th time. Okay, I'm not sure about the number—I lost track—but it doesn't matter because he's here and he said it.

I swallow, my throat suddenly full of too many emotions. Fear, sadness, joy at seeing him again.

"Come closer." His hand beckons, and then he adds quietly, "Please."

My numb feet automatically respond to his call, leading me down the aisle until I'm standing at the edge of the stage, my head tilted up to see him.

I search his beautiful familiar face for any changes since I saw him last. Mostly, he looks the same. Same aqua eyes and tousled golden hair. But there's a seriousness to him now, a quiet stillness. Like he's matured in the time we've been apart.

Glancing around again, I see no one in the wings of the theater. No one in the orchestra pit. We're completely alone.

"Caleb?" I stutter. "Wh—what's going on? I thought I heard music."

"It was me, practicing before you came in." He brushes a single lock of hair off his forehead, only to have it fall back into the same position.

"But…why?" Have I tumbled into a rabbit hole and come out in an alternative reality? Caleb belongs in L.A., not New York. He should be on a movie screen, not alone on a stage with me as his only audience.

Yet he looks so good up there with the guitar in his hands, so confident and powerful. His eyes are steady, focused solely on me. The familiar timbre of his voice, low and smoky, sends a shiver of longing down my spine.

"I had you brought here because I wanted to play you a song. *Your song.* It comes out on the radio tomorrow, and I didn't want that to be the way you first heard it."

"What?" My jaw drops with shock. The old Caleb wouldn't have been able to release his music like that. To send it out into the world for mass consumption. It would have terrified him.

"Your songs are going to be on the radio?" A thrill of excitement for him rushes through me. "That's great. I'm so proud of you." I snap my mouth shut, sure I've gone too far. Why would he care if I'm proud of him or not?

His smile is sweet but sad, as if he's lost something. He breaks eye contact with me and bends over the guitar. Eyes closed tight, he strums the first chord and then the rest. Playing along with the music, Caleb sings my song.

His voice lifts like a bird soaring into the rafters of the theatre. The melody echoes through the room until the lyrics surround me, a soft caress.

> *My lips against yours*
> *I've fallen under your spell*
> *Never known anyone quite like you*
> *No one's ever known me quite so well*

I've heard my song before, but never like this. Each word is filled with pure, raw emotion. You can tell that he loves this woman he's singing about. That every single thing about her is precious to him.

There are tears in my eyes when he finishes. It breaks my heart to know that he used to feel that way about me. All these months apart I've doubted him, doubted that what we had together was real. Hearing him sing puts all those fears to rest. There's no way he could compose a song like that if he hadn't felt the connection between us. The love that I *still* hold in a room hidden deep in my heart.

Once he's done, Caleb walks down the stairs to the level where I stand. He's so vibrant and gorgeous standing before me. I want to reach out and touch him. To run my fingers through his hair and brush my hand across those sharp cheekbones and down his firm body. All to prove he isn't a dream. I don't dare do any of those things, though. It's too combustible, this tension I feel whenever we are close. I thought after all these months that fire would fade, but it's still here in me, igniting at the sight of him.

It frightens me.

"Let's sit." He leads me to the front row. "Best seats in the house," he jokes as we sit next to each other, my body sinking into the plush velvet. He's so close that I can smell his spicy cinnamon scent. I can see the variations of blue in his eyes, like in the puzzle we once completed together.

He bends over to lean the guitar against the seat on the other side of him. My gaze snaps from the guitar, then to Caleb, and back to the guitar. "Is that?" I ask uncertainly. "Is that my *dad's* guitar?"

He nods. "Yeah, your mom said I could borrow it. Just for a little while. She made sure I understood she wasn't giving it to me permanently."

My face screws up in confusion. "But Mom made me ship that guitar to Japan. I did it right after Christmas." I distinctly remember her telling me she wanted it sent by express mail from California to Japan. She said something about Seth wanting to take lessons so he could play with Caleb the next time they were together. It had been such an awkward conversation. Mom was still furious with me at that point, angry that I had lied to her about Caleb's and my relationship.

Caleb straightens and meets my eyes. "It was a long flight there and back."

"Wait." I shake my head, trying to clear it. "Are you saying that you went to Japan and talked to my *mother*?"

This time, his smile has some of the old swagger in it. That little fizz of cockiness, like he's enjoying my befuddlement. "Yes, Gwen. I went to Japan. Figured I owed your mom a big apology for ruining her Christmas."

I can't imagine that. Caleb flying all the way to Japan. Caleb and my mom in a room together without me. The thought is surreal.

He interrupts my thoughts. "The main reason I visited your mom was because I had some questions."

"Questions?"

Caleb searches my face intently. "Questions about you. About what to do. How to win you back."

I'm too stunned to respond. What is he talking about? Win me back?

"Of course, your mom didn't make it easy on me. Took a couple of days before she would see me, let alone talk to me. Took even longer to convince her that I was still crazy about you."

His hand settles against the back of mine, sitting on the armrest. Electricity bursts across my skin where he touches it, waking up an entire flock of butterflies in my stomach.

"Eventually, I got your mom to see my point of view," he says softly, never taking his eyes off me. "That's when she lent me the guitar."

I inspect the guitar more closely and notice that someone has replaced its discolored patches and worn-out frets. It looks as shiny and new as it did when my dad first bought it. Questioningly, I lift my gaze to Caleb.

He understands instantly. "I know a guy who does guitar restoration. Hope you don't mind that I had it worked on. Your mom said it was okay."

It touches me that he took the time to get my dad's guitar fixed. To return it to its original glory. In a daze, I let him flip my hand over, palm up, so he can link his fingers with mine.

I blink, trying to piece the timeline together. How long has he been out of rehab? When did he go to Japan? Why didn't my mother mention his visit to me? "I'm so confused. How did this happen? Alvina told me that there was going to be a performance of the musical tonight."

"The show doesn't start for another four months. We're just doing rehearsals now."

I frown, unable to fit these puzzle pieces together. "But Alvina?"

Caleb clears his throat, a rare blush on his cheeks. "Yeah, about that…I got your messages on my phone."

I gasp, and the blush jumps from his face to mine. "You never answered. I didn't think you'd ever hear them."

"For a while, I couldn't access my phone." His gaze grows distant, looking over my shoulder. I know he means when he was in rehab, but he doesn't use that word. A deliberate choice.

He refocuses on my face. "Once my phone was returned, your messages were there, waiting for me. You can't understand what a gift that was. I had thought about you every day. Wondered how you were, what you were doing. I listened to those recordings, and it was like magic, your voice leading me back into your world. When I got to New York, I reached out to Alvina. You had talked about her and where she worked, so I knew how to contact her."

He lets out a sharp whistle. "I'll tell you she was even harder on me than your mom. You should have heard the tongue lashing she gave me. I considered going to the hospital or your apartment, but I worried it would be too much too soon. I needed her to bring you here, to me." Bashful now, he ducks his head. "Don't be mad at her for tricking you, though. It was my idea."

Caleb takes a forceful breath, dragging the air from deep inside and blowing it out in a quick burst. He straightens his shoulders and leans over the armrest, his face earnest.

"I'm *so* sorry, Gwen. So, so sorry. I messed everything up. You were the only good pure thing I'd found in a really long time, and I didn't want you to be changed by all the craziness that surrounds me. I felt this insane need to protect you, shelter you the way no one ever sheltered me, even when I was a kid. I was trying to keep you safe, but I ended up being the person to hurt you."

A shuddering breath and then he continues. "It was arrogant of me to take that choice away from you. You'd already proven you can handle the hard stuff, that you're not scared. Remember? I told you that after Jax grabbed you outside of Shooter's? I said that, and then I forgot it at the most crucial time. Clearly, I'm an idiot, but if you give me a second chance, I swear I won't make that mistake again. I promise."

I can't believe it. Here he is, saying exactly what I've wanted to hear for so long. I thought I'd be jumping into his arms by now, but I'm not. The weight of my pain, all my sadness from the past couple of months hangs between us, a curtain that's too heavy to part.

I think about that panic attack in the doctor's lounge and how it terrified me. Gasping for breath, I felt like I was *dying*. I can't go through that again.

I think about how I let Jax pick me and then throw me away. I let him dictate the path of my life, like I had no control over it. Like he was the river, and I was a leaf floating in his current, powerless to chart my own course.

But that's not true. I have choices. I can choose to put myself first for once.

I've been trying so hard to shed my old persona, *predictable, dependable*. But I'm learning that there is some worth to being predictable and dependable. Those qualities aren't all I want to be, but some of them in moderation are actually good. They make me feel safe, and not only do I need them in myself but also in my partner.

Caleb sure hasn't been dependable or predictable. He's the opposite of that. At first it thrilled me, the chaotic energy of his lifestyle, but now I see that maybe he's not a great match for me, not if he can't make me feel secure.

I get to choose. I control who I'm with and how they make me feel. I hold the power to my own happiness.

I hesitate, trying to find the right words. The ones that will organize all my random thoughts and force them into an orderly line. "I don't know, Caleb. It's been a rough few months. I was in so deep with you that when you walked away, it was really painful. I grieved for you, almost like grieving for my dad again and for my broken engagement. It brought up a lot of that old sorrow, which isn't fair to you. I get that. You aren't responsible for Dad dying or for Jax abandoning me, but I think it made me extra sensitive to the rejection of your leaving."

Pausing, I draw in a breath. "I've been working hard to rebuild my life. I'm not sure I can risk it, getting hurt and having everything fall apart. What if a few months from now you change your mind? You promised you'd never give up on us, but then you did. It could happen again."

There are tears in my eyes by the time I'm done talking. I'm sad for not just me, but also for him, to be saying these things. I don't wish to hurt Caleb, especially after everything he's been through. If he relapses back into drinking because of me, I would feel so guilty. No matter what happens between us, I will always want the best for him. Isn't that what true love is all about?

He grips my hand even harder, gazing intently into my eyes. "I *won't* change my mind. I swear it. I never did, although I told you differently."

Gently, I pull my hand away. "You shouldn't say that. Things change. People change. You can't promise forever."

He flinches. I've injured him, and the realization makes me sick. "I understand," he says. A little part of me deflates, sad that he gave up so easily, but then he recaptures my hand and grips it, not letting go.

Eyes narrowed with steely determination; he rasps out, "Gwen, what *you* have to understand is that I'm not done with you. I don't care how many days, months, or years it takes. I don't care what I have to do. I *am* going to change your mind. Prove that you can trust me." He squeezes my hand once, hard, to punctuate his next words. "I'm going to teach you that forever isn't long enough for the two of us."

Whoa. Was not expecting that.

My traitorous little heart kicks up a beat. I have a brief argument with it, demanding that it listen to reason while it ignores me, pitter pattering away in my chest. But I let it lead me last time, and all I got was misery. I need to be strong now, not allow those full lips to draw me in with their pretty promises.

I shake my head. "I'm not saying that you were right to break up with me at Christmas, but some of your points were valid. Our problems are the same now as they were then. How can we combine our lives when you have to travel and I'm stuck here? How does an ordinary person date someone famous?"

Caleb's quick to correct me. "There's nothing ordinary about you. That's why I can't let you walk away. Do we have issues we need to work out? Sure, but I'm willing to try."

A sharp jab of anger then. Where was this Caleb when I needed him? When he abandoned me in California and left me alone to pick up the pieces?

"I'm sorry, but it's best if I go." I remember talking to my mother. Months ago, I told her I wouldn't do anything stupid with Caleb. If I stay here any longer, I'll break that vow. Already my resolve wavers. Before he can say another word, I'm up, running along the aisle to burst through the double doors into the lobby.

I don't even glance back to see if Caleb watches me leave.

53

slink down my apartment stairs the next morning, barely able to open my eyes. Last night, I hadn't slept at all. I had just hugged Pip and alternated between crying into her wiry fur and staring blankly into the darkness of my room, running over the reunion with Caleb. Questioning if I made the right choice.

Now, I have an early shift at the hospital to slog through. Twelve hours of charts and patients. At least it should help take my mind off him.

Dawn is just breaking as I stumble out into the street and then freeze. Wayne is waiting for me as usual. But so is Caleb. They talk to each other with the familiarity of old friends. Caleb must say something funny because Wayne throws his head back and laughs in a full-bellied way I didn't think he was capable of.

Caleb's facing away from me. He hasn't seen me yet. I take the time to drink him in. My gaze lingers on the angle of his jaw, the curve of his ear with the tiny scar at the bottom, how his golden hair peaks out from under his baseball cap, glinting in the early morning light.

When I glance up, I see Wayne watching me. He smirks. The look of a man who reads the last chapter in a book before starting at the beginning. I frown, sending him my most piercing glare, but that just makes him grin wider.

Caleb follows Wayne's smile, tracing it back to me. When he sees me, his own sunny grin lifts the corners of his mouth. "Gwen." Darn it, my name sounds so good coming from those lips.

Round G. Flat N.

Caleb plucks the steaming coffee cup out of Wayne's grip. Ignoring Wayne's vocal protests, he walks over and hands it to me.

"Good morning." His gaze roams over my body, head to toe and back again, lingering on my red, puffy eyes. Concern darkens his expression, but he quickly smooths it away. "I know Wayne has been walking you to work, but I'm going to take over for him today."

Wayne makes an indignant sound, telling me this is news to him as well, but he doesn't stop Caleb.

More hesitant now, his voice tight with trepidation, Caleb asks. "If that's okay with you, that is…if you'll let me walk you?"

My emotions are all over the place. Relieved to see Caleb here when last night I had convinced myself I would never see him again. Scared that his presence will lead to more heartache. Proud of him, that he's taking this risk, being out in public just to take *me* to work. I'm still angry that he left me, hurt me. My thoughts are too tumultuous to speak, so I shrug and turn away, not wanting him to read the conflict on my face.

Caleb falls easily in step beside me. He's quiet for the first few moments, then he looks at the cup I'm holding. He laughs softly. "I see you somehow tamed the infamous Wayne. Leave it to you to have him bringing coffee every morning. Most people are terrified of him. Not you, though. You've got him eating out of your hand."

He shakes his head ruefully. Quietly, he says, "I can't blame him. I'm the same way when it comes to you."

The confession makes me swallow hard, something hot and full blooming in my chest. I don't trust myself enough to respond.

Humming to himself, we continue down the street. I steal glances at Caleb when he looks away, noting how his face and body have filled out again. How healthy he seems compared to when he first showed up at my mom's house before Christmas.

He changes the tune of his humming, and it reminds me of how he once said that he has a soundtrack always running in his head, even when he's walking down the street. I listen more closely, trying to make out the tune. My heart does a somersault when I place it.

It's my song.

That's what Caleb is singing under his breath.

All too soon, we're at the hospital doors. I still haven't said a word to him. It doesn't seem to matter. Caleb is happy, undeterred by my silence. "Have a good day at work," he tells me cheerfully.

I go in the hospital and stand hiding off to the side where he can't see me. Peering out the glass door, I watch him walk away. I stay there, not moving, staring as his form grows smaller and smaller until eventually he disappears.

54

The hospital is slammed with patients. There's a multi-car pileup on the freeway, a nasty stomach virus going around, a lady who comes in and gives birth in the elevator. It's pure insanity, just like every other day.

Even though I'm distracted by work, in the back of my mind I keep picturing Caleb from this morning. I see him standing there with his easy smile, holding that coffee out to me.

Ever the scientist, I analyze what little data I have. Caleb seems different. The moody man from my mom's house at Christmas is gone. This version of him is calm and confident. Like he's more at home in his own skin. But I've only seen him twice. I need more information before I can confirm these changes are real.

All day, I wonder if walking me to work today includes walking me home too. Will he be there waiting for me? My hopes rise against my will. A dangerous feeling.

After twelve long hours, the revolving front door of the hospital spits me out onto the sidewalk. My head swivels, searching for Caleb, but he's not there. I've just given up, let my shoulders fall to the ground, when he separates from the shadows of the wall he's been leaning against.

"Gwen." My name again, from those lips. I can't deny the relief that floods my body, but, still scared, I remind myself of all the ways we are better off apart.

He left you for months without a single phone call. Don't be a fool twice.

"How was your day?" He shoves his hands into his pockets, loping along casually next to me.

I don't answer his question, too busy thinking about all those long, empty months. I'm also remembering what Jenny said, way back before Christmas, when we did water aerobics.

"What's your favorite color?" I ask abruptly.

Caleb blinks, perplexed. "Um, blue?" he says, giving me a strange look.

"Middle name?" I fire out.

"Augustus. After my great-grandfather."

"Where were you born?"

"Marion. Small town in southern Illinois. What's up with the twenty questions?"

We've reached the sidewalk in front of my apartment. I cross my arms over my chest, keeping my face stern. "After everything that happened, I realize I don't know you as well as I thought."

His mouth turns down, hurt. "I've told you before. You know the real me better than anyone." He shoves his hands even deeper into his pockets, looks over my shoulder, and blows out a frustrated breath.

After a beat, he relaxes. "But if this is what you need, then we'll do it. You have to answer the same questions, though. Like we did that one time back in California." He sends me a piercing look.

Oh, yeah. Tit for tat.

"Fine," I huff, determined to hold on to my outrage over our breakup. "Pink. Jane. Santa Monica, California." I spin on my heel and march angrily into my apartment, slamming the door in his face.

55

He's waiting for me the next morning, coffee in hand. My heart wants to lift at the sight of him, but I won't let it.

Today, as we walk, I ask, "Favorite food?"

"Chocolate."

"Favorite movie?"

"Well, it was a TV series instead of a movie, but my favorite is *Band of Brothers*. I like the way those guys supported each other. I've always been moving around and so busy with work that I've never really had a chance to make friends like that."

It's impossible to miss the note of longing in his voice. "Were you lonely?" I ask before I can stop myself.

He glances at me out of the corner of his eye. "I was until I met you."

We're at the hospital doors. I walk in before he sees how much that last answer affected me.

The ER is running behind all day. Overflowing with patients until they spill out of the waiting room and onto the sidewalk. I stay late to finish my charting. By the time I'm done, it's an hour after the official end of my shift.

Still, when I exit the revolving doors, Caleb is lurking in the shadows with his hat pulled low and a newspaper in front of his face so no one can recognize him.

I breeze past, and he runs to catch up to me.

"What are your questions tonight? Oh, and, by the way, I noticed you never answered mine this morning." He says it lightly, as if he's liking this game.

I think back, trying to remember. "Favorite food is also chocolate."

"See." He bumps me with his elbow, grinning. "We have so much in common."

My lips twitch, but I suppress my smile. "Favorite movie, *When Harry met Sally.*" I look fondly around me, at the tree-lined street and rushing cars. "That movie made me fall in love with New York before I'd ever set foot here."

We're halfway to my apartment. "The last question was if I'm lonely, and the answer is that I was when you left me." I cut my eyes over to him with a glare.

Caleb blanches visibly, and the people-pleasing part of me wants badly to take it back. But new Gwen lets it lie there between us. He hurt me, and it's okay to acknowledge that.

"Next set of questions," I declare after a sorrowful pause. "Favorite book?"

"Hmm." Caleb scratches his chin. "Tough one. I like *Ready Player One.* How about you?"

"That's easy. Any novel by Stephen King."

He laughs. "I should've guessed."

"Favorite song?"

He doesn't hesitate. "The one I wrote about you."

My heart spasms.

"Last question. You said earlier that you didn't have time to make a lot of friends, but do you have a best friend? Like Jenny is to me?" I ask, genuinely curious.

Again, no hesitation. "I do have friends, but none of them know me the way you do. So I guess that means it's you, Gwen. You're my best friend."

Darn Caleb Freaking Lawson. He makes it so difficult to stay mad at him.

56

The next morning, I discover that Caleb is allergic to bee stings, likes dogs better than cats—a new decision based solely on his experience with Pip—and has a fear of creepy clowns who live in sewers. By the time he drops me off at the hospital, I'm smiling, just a little.

When he picks me up that night, we walk in a companionable silence.

"What? No questions tonight?" he asks teasingly after the second block.

"No," I sigh, tired after an extra-draining shift. "I don't have the energy."

"Okay." He swings his arms as he strolls along. "Can you tell me about your day?"

Slowly at first, but gathering more speed, I share stories from the hospital with him. All about the most interesting cases and the hard ones, too. Caleb listens intently, asking questions about the parts he doesn't understand.

As we continue, my curiosity builds. I want to know more about what's going on in his life. How he ended up here in New York. "You'll be in a musical? I'm assuming that means you have to sing? And you said something about your song being on the radio?"

Caleb stretches out his neck, cracking it to one side and then the other with loud popping sounds. "I recorded a few tracks before I left L.A. Mostly stuff I worked on over Christmas at your house."

He sighs sadly, and I know we are both remembering those times, all the love and how it ended.

"Anyway, the producers liked them. They want to make a full-length album once I get enough material. The showrunners of the musical got hold of some early releases from those tracks. They called my agent to audition me. I figured they were considering me for a supporting part, something little. You can't imagine my shock when they offered me the lead role."

Our conversation pauses as an ambulance rushes by, its sirens wailing. Once it's moved farther down the street, I ask. "Are you nervous? Singing in front of a crowd?"

"Absolutely terrified. Going to the recording studio was fine, fun even. It was like a movie set. Small space. Not many people were around. Everyone was a professional. My manager knows I'm worried, so she brought in more and more people to watch me record. It was okay, but I still haven't sung in front of a crowd as big as at the theater."

When Caleb turns his face to me, there's a haunted look to him. Fear shining in those fine blue eyes. His voice drops low and raspy. "I'm scared I can't do it. Everyone keeps telling me I can. I want to believe them, I really do, but what if they're wrong?"

I'm puzzled by his confession. "Why did you agree to do it? The musical? If you weren't sure?"

Caleb widens his eyes and gives me a pointed stare, his silence speaking volumes.

"Oh," I say and then with deeper understanding, "*Oh.*"

Me? He came here for me?

He shrugs. "I heard the words New York, and I jumped at the chance."

He makes it sound so simple when, clearly, it's not.

57

This goes on for two more days, Caleb waiting for me before and after work. Just Caleb, no Wayne. He must have told Wayne he wasn't needed anymore. I almost miss that grumpy, smoke-tinged reporter. He had been one of the most consistent people in my life for the past few months. I might even call him my friend.

Each of those days I rush out of the hospital with my heart in my throat, sure Caleb will be gone. That he'll let me down. But every time, he's there, waiting for me with a smile, small and tender, one I've never seen on the movie screen or in a magazine. A smile that he's designed only for me.

As we walk home on the fifth day, Caleb sighs loudly. "This has been so…" He pauses, scrunching his nose in a way that I try not to find adorable. "Nice isn't a big enough word, but I'm not sure what to call it. Great. Wonderful. I don't know. I really love spending time with you."

Though the words are kind, there's something mournful in his tone. I curse myself, thinking this is it. Just when I'm starting to trust him again, this is when he leaves.

But that's not what he says. "They'll find us soon. The paparazzi. The fans. I'm surprised they haven't already, even with Wayne helping." He laughs lightly when he sees my quizzical expression. "Wayne has a lot of sway with the rest of them. I promised him an exclusive if he could keep everyone away for a little while, so I could be alone with you."

Ah, I think. Clever Wayne. Business is business, after all.

Caleb continues, "Wayne kept his promise. But even he can't hold them off forever." He shakes his head. "I think Wayne's really doing it for you, keeping them away. That's how much he likes you. Which is crazy because he doesn't like anyone."

"I think he's lonely," I say softly, picturing the wiry reporter.

"He would hate to hear you say that." Caleb gives me a sideways glance.

"Doesn't make it any less true."

We're in front of my apartment now. We face each other, and I'm momentarily overcome by Caleb's proximity. He's so close I could reach out and touch him. Wind my arms around his neck. Lift my lips up to meet his, soft and full. Fold myself into the warmth and comfort of his body.

But I don't.

Fear and the memory of what it's like to lose him holds me back.

Caleb stares down at me, his mouth and the corners of his eyes turned down as if he's worried. "It can get a little out of control with the press, but I know you can handle it. If you can't, that's all right, too. Just tell me. Okay?"

"Okay." I nod, thinking I understand.

I have no clue.

A little crazy is the understatement of the year. By the next week there are at least eighty people waiting outside my door, a mixture of press and fans. All screaming Caleb's name. Even more oddly, some of them scream my name too.

The week after that, the group swells to well over a hundred people. The police are out front, keeping the crowd off the street and directing traffic when the cars slow down to gawk.

Before, right after Christmas, the reporters had left a respectful bubble around me. Never actually making contact with my body as they walked along beside me.

Now, with Caleb here, that barrier has been broken down. People jostle against each other and against us, slowing our progress until it takes almost twenty minutes to walk the three blocks to work. Caleb wraps a protective arm around my shoulders, holding me close and steadying me. Flashes pop as photos are taken of us, the bright light making me squint.

Caleb stops before the last block. He leans over, placing his mouth to my ear, and shouts, "Dean's going to take you the rest of the way. I'll lead the reporters in the opposite direction." He gestures to Dean, his personal bodyguard, and the man that I told to get out of my face months ago. The brooding guard hulks a few steps away, glaring threateningly at anyone who comes too close.

I nod, sadly grateful he's come up with this plan. As much as I like him taking me to work, I can't bring this circus to the front door of my hospital. I'm already scared that I'll get called into Dr. Benson's office again.

Caleb had warned me that loving him could make me lose everything I had worked for. As the number of reporters who follow us grows, I'm beginning to truly understand what he meant. It's terrifying to think of all my years of medical training going down the drain.

I'm halfway down the next block when I stop and turn to look back at Caleb. He stands facing away from me. He raises his arms to the sky, and the group before him hushes. Outlined by the sun, he's like an Olympic god about to make some great proclamation. There's such power in his stance, it radiates out of him in waves, spreading over the crowd, over the entire street.

I see it then, the charisma he wields. How he can turn it on and off like a light switch. It's indescribable, the nebulous quality that makes one person more famous than another. Whatever that trait is, Caleb has it in spades. It's in the fans' adoration. In the rapt way the reporters drop their notepads to stare at him open-mouthed. I've never truly appreciated it before, how dim his spark was back before Christmas, but now he lets it shine. The full force of Caleb's talent, his charm, is absolutely blinding.

In a loud voice he roars, "Who wants to go to Central Park and sign autographs?" The crowd goes wild, cheering, hooting, clapping. His fans light up like it's Christmas and he's Santa bringing them presents. Off he saunters down the street as everyone follows.

Only I notice, because I know him so well, the weariness in his arms as they drop back to his sides. The tilt of his head, as if it's just a little too heavy. I see the cost of his gifts, the pieces of himself he signs away. The worst part is that he's doing it for me. Leading them far from my hospital. Trying to protect me.

Oh, Caleb.

I have a sudden urge to run after him. Drag him into my apartment where they can't touch him. Hide him forever. But we did that before, back in my mom's house in California, and it wasn't sustainable.

If I want to keep him, which I'm becoming more and more convinced that I do, we have to find a way to make this work. Find a way to merge his public life with our private one. I need to help him find that balance.

For him, and for me, too.

58

D r. Patel." I catch up to her outside the hospital cafeteria, breathing heavily from my dash down the hallway.

Brown eyes framed by arched black brows regard me with curiosity. She's still wearing her blue paper cap and matching scrubs from the operating room. A gaggle of surgery residents surround her, but she nods them on.

Once they've moved into the cafeteria, she glances at my name badge. "How can I help you, Dr. Wright?" She has a soft voice, which is in direct contrast to her hard-eyed gaze.

I've never spoken to her before, although I have talked to her residents countless times. Dr. Patel is the highest-ranking surgeon in the hospital. She's an orthopedic surgeon, and her department brings in more money than many others combined. More importantly to me, she's the vice-chair of the executive committee, second only to Dr. Benson.

"Sorry to interrupt you," I start off, a bit nervous because she has a reputation for being stern. I can't blame her for that, though. I don't see how you can rise to her position in such a male-dominated specialty without having balls, or ovaries, of steel.

She purses her lips and blinks, waiting for me to speak. I have a flashback to Dr. Benson checking the clock on the wall as if I was wasting his time.

Hurry up, Gwen.

"I have an idea I want to bounce off you. It's about bringing an art therapy program to the hospital. I believe it would help many of our patients," I blurt out.

Her slim shoulders lift. "Sounds interesting. Why don't you submit it to the executive committee for consideration?" She turns away, dismissing me.

"Wait!" I call out. Her back stiffens, and she slowly spins around as I explain. "I already did that. I had a meeting with Dr. Benson and everything, but he didn't think there was money in the budget for the three therapists we need."

She tugs the surgical cap off her head, and a tumble of wavy black hair flows over her shoulders. I had assumed she was older, but with her hair down, I'd place her in her mid- to late-forties.

"That's odd," she says sharply. "We haven't finalized the third-quarter budget yet." My knees quake when she narrows her eyes at me, her jaw tight with anger. I'm not sure if that ire is directed at me or Dr. Benson.

"Let me guess," she drawls. "Benson said something demeaning when you talked to him. Something designed to make you feel small."

My mouth drops open as I sputter, "He said my idea was *cute*."

"Of course, he did." Her eyes roll. "That man drives me crazy. Would he ever tell a male resident that his idea was *cute*?" She motions with her hands, putting air quotes around the word "cute."

I shake my head slowly because she's right. No one would say that kind of thing to a male resident.

With a disgruntled groan, she tips her chin back and closes her eyes, breathing deeply like she's attempting to maintain control. After a beat of silence, her eyes snap open. "Walk with me," she barks and spins to go into the cafeteria. I follow at her heels, as obedient as Pip was when we took her to doggie training classes.

We hurry through the line, picking out salads and sandwiches. "I've only got twenty minutes before my next case, so you'd better be quick," she calls over her shoulder.

I launch into my art therapy presentation, talking fast as we pay for our food and find seats at a small, round table. A couple of surgery residents approach like they're going to sit with us, but Dr. Patel gives a firm shake of her head and they scurry off.

By the time I'm done with my speech, we're walking over to the trash can to dump our crumpled napkins into it and place the now-empty plastic trays on top.

Dr. Patel has been silent while I gave my spiel. The woman has a great poker face. I have no idea what she thinks about my proposition.

"You've found money for two out of the three spots?" she confirms, musing out loud.

"Yes, that's right."

Tapping a finger on her lips, she tilts her head to the side and regards me. "How do you know this therapy will work?"

"It will," I assure her. "I'm certain because I've done it myself and found it immensely helpful." My fingers find the buttons of my white lab coat. I fiddle with them, wondering how much to divulge. Showing weakness, especially in the form of mental health, is highly frowned on in medicine, but I decide to be honest. It's time to break down those old stigmas. "My father died when I was a teenager. Art therapy helps me cope with my grief."

My explanation must make sense, because Dr. Patel purses her lips, debating. "You have all this information written down somewhere?"

I promise to drop the binder off at her office later today.

"It might look good for our advertising." Her gaze grows distant. "We could spin it as a way to show that we treat the whole mind-body connection. That sort of thing."

I nod encouragingly, feeling hopeful.

"There's a meeting of the executive committee in two weeks. I can take this to them and see what they say." She pins me with a serious look. "No promises, but I'll try."

I beam, resisting the urge to bounce on my feet. "That's wonderful. You won't regret it."

59

It's two a.m., and I'm in the ER, suturing a nasty cut in a twenty-year-old's shoulder. He's passed out, drooling slightly. I wrinkle my nose from the alcohol stench that's expelled every time he breathes. He smells like he went swimming in a vat of tequila.

"Tell me again how this happened?" I ask his friend, who sways drunkenly in a chair next to me.

"We were partying," he slurs, answering my question.

"Yes," I say dryly. "I can see that."

"It was a costume party."

"Yes, I can see that, too," I say, eyeing his skin-tight Spiderman costume that leaves nothing to the imagination.

"Anyway. We were having a gr-gr-great time," he continues, hiccupping and stuttering his way through the tale. "Steve here was dressed up like Superman. He was su-su-super, hiccup, drunk."

He swipes at his nose with the back of his hand and misses. I resist the urge to roll my eyes. "Steve decided he could f-f-fly, so he jumped out of a second-story window, hiccup, at our friend's apartment." He ends the story with a wide yawn, releasing his own blast of toxic alcohol breath.

My hand clutches the needle that I've just pushed through his friend's skin. "That's it!" I breathe out, an idea sparking in my mind and taking off like wildfire. "That's what Caleb needs." I'm so excited I don't realize I've spoken out loud until the drunk friend says, "Huh? Who's Caleb?"

I'm not even listening, because I'm a mastermind and I've come up with a plan.

The next day, when Caleb walks me home, I initiate phase one of my top-secret mission. I grab his hand and pull him stumbling into the lobby at the bottom of my apartment building.

It's a small space, with just enough room for a row of mailboxes in the wall and an umbrella stand by the stairs. The door thumps closed behind us, muffling the sound of the crowd still buzzing like bees around him. Caleb's the picture of surprise, his mouth a round O and eyes wide. He's never been inside my building before. His head swivels, taking in each detail before settling back on me.

"Ask me out," I demand, my chin lifted in challenge.

He blinks and shakes his head like he's heard me wrong. "Wh—what?"

I push my index finger against his chest, poking him hard enough to set his tall frame swaying. "I said, Ask. Me. Out." I glare up at him. When he still looks confused, I clarify, "like on a date."

That snaps him out of it. "Oh!" he exclaims. "Oh! I see." He gathers himself together. With a glint of humor in his eyes, he relaxes back onto his heels. Overly dramatic, he clears his throat and lowers his eyebrows. In an unnaturally deep voice, he says, "Dr. Gwen Wright. Will you do me the honor of going on a date with me?"

I huff, annoyed that he's not taking this seriously even though I've waited days to tell him, even though I'm nervous as heck, not sure if this is the right thing to do. "Well, if that's how you're going to ask me, the answer is no."

Spinning on my heel, I lunge for the stairs, but Caleb catches my elbow and drags me back, laughing so hard his eyes water. "Wait! Wait. I'm sorry. I was just so stunned. After all this time, I'd almost given up hope that you'd ever say those words. I've been wanting to ask but promised myself not to rush you."

Mad, and a little embarrassed, I cross my arms over my chest, petulant like a child.

Caleb is still chuckling as he reels me into his body. He envelops me in a hug, surrounding me with his familiar cinnamon scent. At first, I stay stiff and unyielding, but slowly his warmth melts away all my bad feelings, leaving a sense of relief to be there in his arms. I sigh and snuggle closer.

Caleb's sigh matches mine as he buries his nose in my hair and inhales deeply. "I missed how you smell, like strawberry sunshine." His grip on me tightens. "Will you *please* let me take you out? I've been wanting to for so long."

I nod, liking the way his stubble scratches against my scalp with the movement. "This doesn't mean we're getting back together," I warn. "I still haven't gotten over everything. This is more like a test...a chance to see if we can merge our worlds a little better." Hastily, I add, "Also, you have to meet me here, at my place."

"I'll meet you anywhere you want." He pulls away to stare at me, his aqua eyes deep enough to drown in. His expression solemn, Caleb speaks slowly, like he wants to make sure I absorb each word. He says, "As long as you are there, that's where I'll go."

60

P hase two of my plan requires some help from Alvina and Wayne, but they are quick to pitch in and deliver on my requests.

That Sunday morning, Caleb rings the bell from my apartment lobby. I buzz him in and wait nervously, chewing on my bottom lip. Glancing around my small studio, I wonder what he will think of it.

Everything is in one room. My queen bed, nightstand, loveseat couch, and old bulky TV. Beyond that is my tiny kitchen with its undersized refrigerator and two-burner stove. I've paired a round bistro table with a couple of mismatched chairs.

My place is a far cry from whatever luxury penthouse Caleb no doubt lives in. I don't worry about it too much, though. He's never struck me as the snooty type.

At his knock, I open the door and almost fall over. Caleb wears a pair of tight dark washed jeans that cling to every muscular bulge of his legs. He's got on a form-fitting gray shirt that I recognize because I helped him wash it in my mother's laundry room about a hundred times.

The sight of that shirt brings back so many memories. How it felt under my palms when we kissed.

Recently, he's been wearing a baseball cap, pulled down low, to limit how much of his face the reporters can see. But today, he wears no hat. His hair shines brightly, the sun coming in through the window highlighting its subtle wave.

He's perfect. Utterly beautifully perfect. It makes me catch my breath, and the craziest part of it all is that he's looking at me the way I'm looking at him. Like *I'm* the miracle, the one he can't quite believe exists.

A bashful "Hello" and that tender smile he made for me as he walks into the room.

There's a flash of tan fur at my feet, followed by loud barking. Pip runs in circles around Caleb's legs, yipping happily.

"Pip!" Caleb exclaims with a joyous grin. He reaches down to pick up the tiny dog. Once she's in his arms, Pip covers his chin with slobbery dog kisses while Caleb laughs loudly, the sound ringing like a bell through my small space.

Pip shoots a big doggie smile over to me, clearly thrilled to see Caleb. In response, I narrow my eyes at her.

Traitor dog.

I'm trying to hold on to my anger at Caleb, but it's getting slippery. Its twisted red knots are fraying in my hands and in my heart. Another thread unravels as I watch them together. Caleb and Pip. Friends reunited.

After Caleb finally lowers Pip to the floor and gives her one last petting, he rises and then stills, realizing we aren't alone. He sends me a questioning glance. "Um. You didn't mention this is a double date?"

I laugh, not recognizing myself in that moment. How light and airy that sound is. It's been a long time since I laughed like that.

"It's not a double date, silly. This is Jacob, who works in the special effects department of the Empire Theater and knows Wayne." A burly Asian man holds up a hand in greeting.

"And this is Joal, Alvina's cousin. She does make-up, mostly for weddings, but she can do it for anything." I point to a woman who looks like a skinner version of Alvina.

"Hey," she drawls with a half wave from where she sits on my tiny couch, scrolling through her phone.

"Okay." Caleb draws the syllables out, his forehead puckered with questions.

I laugh again, liking how it sounds coming out of my mouth. "They're going to do our make-up."

"Our make-up? For what?"

"For our date. These two will transform us, Caleb, make us into someone else. Someone unrecognizable."

Understanding dawns on his face. "Ah, you mean like a disguise?"

"Exactly. Like a disguise. Like the scarves you wore when we went caroling, but even better. So, tell me. Who do you want to be today?"

Caleb grins at me, happy with this plan. His smile fades into an expression of wonder when he sees the dozen or so paintings that lean stacked against the wall behind my kitchen table.

"Gwen," he breathes out, going over and crouching down to view them better. "You painted these?"

I nod and look at the pictures, trying to see them through his eyes. There's no rhyme or reason to what I've painted. I've let inspiration lead whenever I have reached for the set of watercolors he gave me at Christmas.

I've painted landscapes of Central Park, a colorful picture of Pip, the faces of my patients. There's even one abstract painting, a splash of random colors and shapes.

He looks the paintings over so thoroughly and for so long that it makes me nervous. It's like exposing a piece of my soul every time I paint. I might not be ready to have Caleb see me that way, open and raw. The pain of our breakup is still sharp, making me want to protect myself.

My doubts fade when he says over his shoulder, "They're amazing. I didn't know you're so talented."

I hadn't realized how much I craved his praise until that moment. His words bring a rush of confidence to me, a sense of possibility. It's that same feeling, the one I had when my dad beamed at me after I won the science fair back in seventh grade.

"Thanks," I murmur and glance away, overcome by emotion.

"Have you shown your mom or Uncle Seth these?"

"No. You're the first person who's seen them."

"Well, I'm honored. Do you mind if I take a picture of this one?" He points to the painting I did of my patient, the elderly lady with hair like snow. "I want to have it, to look at sometimes. Would that be all right?"

I nod, as a swell of pride rises from my belly to fill my chest. To think that Caleb likes my work so much that he wants to carry it with him.

That's a good feeling.

He goes back to the paintings, again flipping through the canvases slowly. A smaller one was hidden behind the others the first time he looked, but now it peeks out from the stack. I had forgotten it was there. Caleb draws it out and sinks onto his knees, running his fingers lightly over the words that I glued onto it months ago.

It's the original art therapy project I did. The collage where I wrote down all the words that spoke to me.

Death, anxiety, fear, depression, abandoned, unworthy.

Caleb looks up at me, his features a blend of bafflement and compassion all mixed together. "*This?* This is how you feel?"

I nod, my eyes dropping to the floor. It's too much to see that tortured twist of his mouth. I stare at the picture instead, where his finger strokes the word unworthy over and over.

My hands twitch by my sides as embarrassment washes over me, burning up my neck and splashing across my face. I want to rip that collage out of his hands and light it on fire. I want to crawl out of my skin, but I don't. I'm trying to be real. To let him, and everyone important to me, see the person I am with all her flaws.

Just darn. It's too painful to be vulnerable.

"I don't really want to talk about it. I…it's too hard to be this open with you right now," I tell him honestly.

He looks away, his throat working, but he nods with understanding.

"Makeover time. Let's go," I say with false brightness, relieved to change the subject.

It takes over an hour to complete our metamorphosis, but when I look at my reflection afterward, I know it was worth every minute.

Caleb joins me in the bathroom, staring into the full-length mirror on the back of the door. He's dressed the same, but his face is different. A prosthesis glued to his skin and painted with make-up makes his slim nose bigger. It flattens his sharp cheekbones so they look generic. He wears a dark wig, fit so closely to his head that you would never question if it's real. That black hair sets off his eyes, the contrast making them spark even more brightly blue.

My wig is red and long, hanging in glossy waves down to my mid-back. They didn't use a prosthesis on my face since I'm not so recognizable, but Joal is a genius with make-up. She's given me wide, smoky eyes. Outlining my lips with a thick red pencil and filling them in with the same color of lipstick has them looking as luscious as a ripe cherry.

Phase two complete. My plan is finished.

"Well, heck," Caleb says. "This has to be the best date in the world, and we haven't even left yet."

We smile at each other in the mirror.

Caleb's eyes run over my body with admiration, sparking into flaming heat. "You look hot," he purrs close to my ear. The resulting jolt of longing shocks me, making my limbs twitch. "Like a superhero, that's how you look. Like you're ready to go kick some butt."

"That's because I am," I tease. "Your butt."

rmed with our new appearances, we leave my apartment, exiting out the back door and into the warmth of spring.

I shake my head languidly from side to side, liking how my wig swishes prettily over my shoulders. Caleb laughs and gives a quick tweak of the artificial hair. "Red looks good on you."

His comment brings up an old memory. "When I was doing my interviews for medical school, I had one in Ohio. A radiology resident interviewed me there. She had gorgeous, long, red hair. I'll never forget it. Her name was Tiffany Hart. Isn't that a funny name? Dr. Hart?"

"Hmm," he murmurs lazily. "That is a funny name. No matter how nice her hair was, though, there's no way she's more gorgeous than you are right now."

I blush from the compliment and how Caleb can't keep his eyes off me. "Maybe this is a bad idea. I don't want you to be disappointed when I go back to blonde."

"Your hair could be indigo for all I care, and I'd still think you're the most beautiful woman in the world."

I have to stop myself from skipping down the sidewalk, reminding myself that this is *not* my boyfriend. No matter how sweet he's being, I can't endanger my heart just yet. He was nice in California too…right before he dumped me.

Take it slow.

"What's your plan?" I quirk an eyebrow at Caleb, daring him. "I'm the only one contributing to this date so far. It's time for you to take over."

He smirks back and says vaguely, "I've got some ideas."

"Oh? Do you now?" I'm trying to act cool but failing miserably. I want to shake him and demand that he tell me everything, but I attempt to contain my enthusiasm.

"I may or may not have arranged some things." He's all mysterious.

"First activity is close by, right here in the park," Caleb announces. He grabs my hand, and I let him. Swinging it between us, we cross the street and head into the leafy greenery that is Central Park.

It's as if we have walked into an enchanted wood. Now that winter has passed, the rain and melted snow have brought out all the flowers. Fields of tulips bloom, red, pink, and yellow. The cherry trees arch over our heads, their pale blossoms falling like colorful rain to land in our hair and on our shoulders.

Caleb picks one out of my wig and hands it to me with a flourish. I tuck the tiny flower into my pocket. Later I'll press it between the pages of a book so I can keep it as a memento.

We wander the curving paths, nodding hello to the strangers we pass. Our disguises must be working because nobody gives us a second glance. We're just two nondescript people taking a stroll in the park. Totally normal. Nothing to see here.

I had thought our route was random, but when we arrive at the lake and Caleb sends me a satisfied smirk, I realize that he's been leading me all along. Guiding me to this place, the Loeb boathouse.

It's a long building with white columns, striped awnings, and a green patina-coated roof. The structure's reflection wavers in the mossy water of the large lake in front of it. At the shoreline there are paddle boats, rowboats, and gondolas, all tied together in a neat line. Their noses bob gently in the wake.

Caleb speaks with a man at the counter, and, before I know it, the staff pulls a shallow, weathered rowboat out for us. Caleb holds my hand, steadying me as I climb in. The boat wobbles, tipping dangerously to the side until we find our balance, sitting on rough wooden benches directly across from each other.

"If I'd known I was going to work out today, I would have worn my exercise gear," I grumble good-naturedly, smiling to let him see I'm joking.

"Don't worry. I promise to do all the rowing." He settles on the bench that has paddles attached to its side. With a mighty heave of his shoulders, he pushes us away from the shore and moves us out, heading deeper into the lake.

"What else don't I know about you?" I ask, thinking of our game from earlier as I watch the shore recede, the people who walk along it becoming so small they look like toy figurines.

Caleb tilts his head, squinting in the sunshine. "Je parle un peu Francais, ma cherie," he says in perfectly accented French.

"What does that mean?" I laugh in surprise, the sound echoing across the surface of the water.

"I said, 'I speak a little French, my dear.'"

"Don't tell me." I hold my hand up to him, still chuckling. "You once played a famous physicist who lived in Paris, and you had to learn French for the role."

Caleb laughs with me. "Not quite. My on-set tutor lived in France for a while, so he had a pretty good accent."

Imagining what it was like for him as a kid makes the laughter die in my throat. I'm somber as I ask, "That must have been lonely? Just having a tutor and not going to school with a bunch of other kids?"

He shrugs, his gaze skittering along the tree line. "It was lonely, but I was so busy I didn't really notice. Filming means long days. We'd shoot for sometimes fifteen, eighteen hours in a row."

"Kind of like my shifts in the hospital, when I'm there for up to twenty-four hours."

Blue eyes meet mine. One corner of his mouth lifts into a teasing smirk. "See. I told you we have a lot in common."

"Hmm. If you say so." I remain noncommittal but can't stop the smile that slips past my lips.

I lean backward, letting my hands on the bench take my weight, and close my eyes. The sun is warm on my skin. The air is filled with birdsong and the rhythmic sound of Caleb's paddling. A serene feeling comes over me.

I keep my eyes closed for so long that Caleb says, "Hey. No falling asleep over there." He uses the tip of the paddle to splash a bit of water my way. Droplets stain my pants, darkening them from navy blue to black.

Opening my eyes, I blink in the sunlight, dappled by clouds that pass overhead. "I'm awake. I'm awake." I laugh, holding up my hand in case he splashes again.

We've reached the center of the lake now. Caleb drops the paddles and lets us drift. He looks around at the wall of green trees that surround us. The trees are tall but dwarfed by skyscrapers that rise behind them, sending spires of brick and concrete high into the air.

"It really is beautiful here." His gaze rests on my face as he ends the sentence. My skin warms from more than just the sun overhead.

"Have you never been here before? On this lake?" I ask.

"No. You?"

I shake my head no. "I've been so busy working that I haven't gotten to explore all the places in the city I want to see yet. Alvina's been showing me some things, though. She's an excellent tour guide. Have you spent a lot of time in New York before this?"

"I actually have a place here, a condo on the Upper East Side. I don't spend as much time in New York as L.A., but I come for premieres, press parties, interviews, that kind of stuff." Caleb leans forward, his elbows resting comfortably on his knees. His mirror image ripples, dancing in the water next to the boat.

"Oh, I see." I widen my eyes dramatically. "Fancy stuff."

That makes him smile, a small grin. "Exactly. Fancy, that's me."

I tilt my head, gazing at him through my lashes as I gently taunt, "Are you going to show me something fancy, Caleb?"

His grin widens into a smirk. "I'm sure going to try."

We're flirting with each other. It's dangerous but delicious in a tantalizing way. Like the appetizer before the main course. The opening overture before the symphony starts. The anticipation of what comes next is painfully sweet.

Caleb must sense it too because he's up and crossing slowly over to me. His movement makes the boat tip wildly.

"Careful!" I cry out, grasping my seat with both hands. "Don't capsize us."

We're both laughing by the time he sits next to me, squeezed in tight on the small bench. The boat rocks back and forth, bumping us up against each other with the motion.

Our laughter fades as Caleb stares down at me, so close that I could count each individual eyelash framing wide, serious eyes. My heartbeat seems to halt, hitch, and then speed up in response.

We lean toward each other, magnets drawn together. I watch as his lips part and feel mine do the same. The boat bounces and sways beneath me. My eyes flutter closed, and that's when it hits me.

The memory of the doctor's lounge and the panic attack.

The nights I cried myself to sleep.

The picture of him broken at the bar.

I jump back so quickly the boat jerks and water splashes over the side, soaking Caleb's pant leg. "Shoot. Sorry." My heart jackhammers from a mixture of lust, anguish, and embarrassment.

"It's okay." Caleb runs his hand down his leg, squeezing the extra moisture out of the fabric like a squeegee. "A little water won't melt me."

Moving back out of my orbit, he shifts and braces himself with his hands behind him, in the same position I used earlier. Our shoulders touch, brushing against each other with the motion of the waves.

We're quiet for a while then, listening to the water slap the hull of our boat and to the laughter of children at the playground across the lake.

Slowly I let my head relax, tilting to the side until it lies on Caleb's shoulder. He feels firm under my cheek, solid and warm. A heartbeat later, Caleb's head drops down, his temple resting gently on the side of my head.

We stay a long time like that, leaning against each other.

62

After we return the rowboat, Caleb shows me his next surprise. He reaches behind the podium of the boat rental place and retrieves a large picnic basket, the wicker kind with the lids that flap open.

"What's this?" I ask, eyes wide as he brings it over.

"This," he says proudly, "is lunch. I had them hold it for me while we were out on the lake."

We sit on a red checkered blanket in the lush grass of the Great Lawn in the center of the park. Caleb has music playing softly, running through the portable speaker I gave him for Christmas. "I take it with me everywhere. It's the best gift," he told me when he first pulled it out, the comment filling me with pride.

After lunch, I groan and say, "I think I ate too much. That was all so delicious." He had brought a wide selection of imported cheeses and thin-sliced meats, along with crusty sourdough bread he baked himself. Strawberries dipped in chocolate had been dessert.

Sucking the last drop of chocolate off my finger, I lift my gaze to find him watching me closely. A swirl of yearning stirs in my belly. I drag my eyes off him and lay down on my side, facing Caleb, who is sitting with his legs crossed yoga style.

As my attention wanders, I notice a group of teenage girls a few blankets away ogling him, giggling whispers coming from behind their raised hands. I push up onto my elbow and look around. Multiple groups of strangers shoot looks over at Caleb, mostly women but some men too.

"Are you aware that even with your disguise, people are looking at you?" I ask, arching a brow.

"Are they?" he asks absently, shredding a napkin into tiny pieces. He puts the scraps of paper aside and surveys the crowd around us with a small frown.

I shake my head. "What is it about you that's so magnetic? Even now, you attract attention."

He lays down next to me and rolls onto his side with his eyes level to mine. "I honestly don't know. It's always been that way."

I like this. Laying with Caleb right in front of me, his body blocking out the rest of the world until there's only the two of us.

"My mom says that's why she brought me to L.A. That everyone kept stopping her in stores or on the street when I was a baby saying I should model or be on TV. I don't know, though, probably lots of people say that about babies."

He sighs, reaches out and hesitantly touches my arm, fingers fluttering over my skin, leaving a prickling sensation behind. It's too much, too overwhelming. I move away and attempt to ignore the hurt that runs across his face.

"How old were you when she moved you to L.A?" I ask, hoping to distract him.

"Two years old. We're from a tiny farm town. At first, Mom moved with just me. My dad stayed home to keep his job so he could send us money. It was like that for three years, with my parents apart, although they would visit back and forth."

"Once I started consistently booking roles, Dad quit and moved out to L.A. Not that it really mattered if he was here or there. My dad is pretty passive. He always lets Mom take the lead. I don't remember much of those early days. I was too little, but Mom talks about it a lot. How we lived in tiny apartments and spent all our time going to auditions."

"That must have been hard. Your mom on her own with a young child in a strange city."

"I suppose it was." He angles his head and stares up into the sky. Fluffy white clouds drift overhead, swirling into different shapes. I turn to watch the clouds with him, naming them in my mind as they transform into a rabbit, a lion, a swan.

"When I was young, we were close. My mom and me. She was always with me on set. As my career took off and I got older, things became more difficult. She was busy negotiating my contracts and arranging my next role."

"At fourteen, I had my first big breakout movie. After that, it was too much for her. She was bitter about it, but I had to fire her and hire a professional management company. Everything has been strained between us ever since."

It's a terrible thing to think about, having to fire your own mother. I've had struggles with my mom, but nothing like what Caleb's been through. "I'm sorry it's rough between you two."

"I'm supposed to talk to her about it. That's part of my..." He pauses, and I fill in the blank, knowing he means rehab for his alcoholism. I want to ask him about it so badly, but I'm trying to be patient and wait until he's ready. Predictably, he dodges the subject and says "treatment. I'm required to go apologize to all the people I've hurt. She's coming for a visit next week. I'll do it then."

He doesn't sound happy about it.

"What about you?" Caleb asks, startling me. "I saw that you looked upset at the wedding. You should give Uncle Seth a shot. He can be a little shy, but once you get to know him, you'll see how amazing he is."

"I'm sure he's great. My mom wouldn't have married him otherwise. I just don't think we have much in common."

A frisbee flies over our head, chased by a barking dog. The dog leaps up high. Midair, it snatches the toy in its jaws and lands gracefully, tail wagging.

"Can you imagine Pip trying to catch a frisbee like that?" I ask Caleb. We both laugh at the thought of tiny Pip chasing a frisbee bigger than she is.

"What happened with your art therapy proposal?" Caleb yawns sleepily, tucking his hand under his head and snuggling down into the blanket as if he'd like to take a nap.

The combination of a food coma and a day in the sun has sapped my energy as well. Eyelids heavy, I blink. "Dr. Patel said the committee was interested but had questions for me. They meet again in a few weeks, and I'm supposed to be there." His yawn was contagious, passing over to me.

"You'll do great at that, answering their questions." His body slackens, muscles relaxing, hands unfurling.

It feels like a lazy Sunday where you never really wake up. Where you live in a daydream, a place where things slow and everything is colored in pastels.

The sun retreats behind a cloud. A breeze whips out of nowhere, ruffling Caleb's hair, blowing a stray piece across his forehead. Before I can stop myself, I brush that soft strand out of the way. My fingers graze his skin and freeze, buzzing from that simple contact.

He's so handsome with his skin darkened by a tan, sun kissed from being outside all day. Without even knowing it, I've inched closer, my hand moving from his hair to skim along his cheek, testing the sharp angle of his cheekbone.

A minute ago, I didn't want him to touch me, but now *I* want to touch him. I want to curl into his warmth, like a cat into a sunbeam.

What is wrong with me that I can't resist this man? Am I no better than those girls giggling over him earlier? I don't care. This is *my* desire driving me.

I'm in charge now.

My fingers continue their journey downward. I outline the full cupid's bow of his mouth, and Caleb's eyes slide closed with pleasure. He lets out the slightest sigh, so quiet I read it from the motion of his parted lips rather than hear it with my ears. I suck in a shuddering breath, imagining my fingers replaced with my kiss. Remembering how he tastes, spicy and yet somehow sweet.

The alarm on my phone beeps, waking me like a bucket of ice dumped over my head. My breathing choppy, I snatch my hand away and sit up. "I've got to go. My next shift starts in an hour." There's an odd ache in my chest. The hollow of unfulfilled longing.

Caleb lays still, staring at me with brooding hooded eyes. "You know, Gwen," he says darkly. "I messed up when I left you. It's a mistake I won't make again. I'm willing to wait for now, but I have to warn you, eventually I'll grow impatient and then I'll simply claim what's mine."

My body processes his words before my brain does, and it must like what it hears because my heart rate speeds up alarmingly. My mouth slackens, taken aback by the possessive glint in his eyes.

I mean, wow. That was kind of hot.

My brain catches up, and I close my mouth. I attempt to appear offended, narrowing my eyes to glare, but the effort is half-hearted. Caleb ignores me and stands up. He calmly places our empty containers into the picnic basket. I roll up the blanket and pass it to him. The breeze is cooling as we leave the park and walk back to my apartment.

When we reach my door, I stand there awkwardly, not sure how to end the evening. "Well, thanks for the date." I dig into my pocket, fishing around for my key. "I had a good time."

"When are we going out again?" he asks with a squint.

I arch an eyebrow. "My, that's rather presumptive of you, isn't it? Assuming I'll go on another date with you?"

He stares at me, deadpan. The silence lengthens, and he doesn't even blink.

Darn it, he's way better at this game than I am. My shoulders slump with defeat. "My next day off isn't for a week and a half."

The pleased guttural rumble in the back of his throat makes me lightheaded. There's extra weight when he says, "That's okay. I'll wait for you."

He starts to walk away, then hesitates and turns back to face me. "You know that picture I saw this morning with all those words on it?"

I flush and glance sideways, picturing all of those sad and ugly words. *Death, anxiety, fear, depression, abandoned, unworthy.*

"You may not be ready to hear this from me." Caleb's stormy gaze pins me in place, but then it softens. More gently, he says, "I understand that you see those things in yourself, but I need to tell you who *I* see. You are the most strong, brave, smart, beautiful, lovable person I've ever met. You deserve the best of everything, and I couldn't walk away until you knew."

I let his voice reach me, sink into me like a stone. To ground me for the next time I'm uncertain or insecure. I'll replay his words in those moments of weakness, like a record. Use that music to soothe my soul.

'm worried about taking Caleb to a bar," I whisper to Alvina in the back seat of the taxi. "Is it a stupid idea? To take a recovering alcoholic to a place where the main thing they serve is alcohol?"

She has rimmed her eyes in black, making them appear even bigger than usual. The wave in her hair gleams ebony under the shifting streetlights. "Did he say anything about it when you told him where we were going?"

"No. He's coming straight from rehearsal, so he just said he'd meet us there."

Caleb's growing more anxious about performing in the Broadway musical. After some thought, I had come up with tonight's excursion as a way to ease his fears. I clasp my hands together in my lap and look out the window, wondering if this is a bad decision.

It's past eleven at night, and the streets are teeming with people. Twenty- and thirty-year-olds hop from one bar to another in the trendy meat-packing district. A warm late spring breeze ruffles the hair and clothing of the crowd, who wait in long lines outside the most popular clubs.

I stifle a yawn, tired from my ER shift earlier today. It always amazes me to see all these people out at night. I'm usually so exhausted that I fall into bed as soon as I get home. I forget that there's a huge part of the population out here living normal lives where they go out with friends and stay up late. They aren't worried about working twenty-four–hour shifts the next day. They aren't worried that fatigue could cause them to make a mistake at work, a mistake with deadly consequences. Sometimes, I envy them.

The taxicab makes a sharp turn to the left. I wobble in my seat, trying not to fall over into Alvina. A pine-tree–shaped air freshener hanging from the driver's rear-view mirror sways with the motion. Within minutes, we pull up to the neon-lit bar with its red-painted door. A bouncer dressed all in black checks our IDs, and we're in.

I blink, my eyes adjusting to the shadowy interior. With my hand on Alvina's shoulder, I shout into her ear, "Wayne said he's holding a table for us in the back."

Rising onto my toes, I search through the crowd until I find the thin-faced reporter tucked into the corner of the room. A cone-shaped light hangs low over the table, casting a focused yellow glow on my enemy turned friend.

"There he is!" I yell over the loud singing and point. I lead the way, winding through the throng that clusters by the bar, with Alvina trailing behind me.

Wayne half-stands when we reach him. He lets out a grunt of surprise as I throw my arms around his scrawny frame to give him a brief hug. "I haven't seen you in forever," I yell, grinning as the singer on the stage hits an off-key note.

Alvina comes to stand beside me. "Alvina, this is Wayne. Wayne, Alvina," I introduce them, my gaze bouncing from one to the other.

Wayne's stare travels appreciatively over Alvina. "Well, hello there," he drawls with an expression that can only be described as lecherous.

Alvina narrows her eyes at him. "Not happening," she snips, and his face falls.

I hide my snort of laughter behind my hand.

A husky voice speaks from my left, saying, "What's a pretty lady like you doing in a place like this?"

I whip around, ready to reject whoever is hitting on me, but freeze when I see a pair of deep aqua eyes. "Caleb!" My heart does a triple beat at the sight of him. "I barely recognized you."

Temporary dye has transformed Caleb's hair from golden into a dark auburn hue. His nose prosthesis is back in place. "I know." He runs a hand lightly over the top of his head. "Maren did a pretty great job, didn't she?" he says, referring to the make-up artist at the theater who had helped him get ready tonight.

I have a flashback to when I first suggested this idea. I had told Caleb I thought he should use his disguise. I said, "What do you think? How about being 'not Caleb' again?"

It had broken my heart when he had sighed and dropped his head. He had answered, "Sometimes being not Caleb sounds really good to me."

I shake off the memory to refocus on the bar and the man before me. "You're right. Maren really came through." I touch his hair and look at my fingers to see if the dye rubs off. It doesn't. "Just hope you can wash that out before you go back to rehearsal tomorrow. Your director might have a heart attack if he sees you. He hired a blond Caleb Lawson, not a redhead."

Caleb places his index finger lightly against my lips, his touch sending a tendril of desire spiraling through me. "Shh. No using my real name, remember?" He presses in close, our chests brushing together in the crowded bar. My breath catches from that simple friction. A dart of longing hits when his gaze drops to linger on my mouth.

"You said tonight was about practicing singing *without* the pressure of my fame." Hunger builds between us as we stare into each other's eyes. It's an exquisite kind of torture, having him close enough to smell his seductive cinnamon scent but still too exposed in this packed bar to kiss him.

"Good grief. Please tell me they're not going to make googly eyes at each other all night long. It's disgusting," Wayne says loudly to Alvina, slamming his beer on the table.

"Hope not. I didn't sign up for that either." Alvina shoots me a disapproving glare.

They share a look of commiseration.

I take a quick step away from Caleb, grateful for the darkness of the bar. I'm hoping it masks the flush that colors my cheeks.

Wayne takes a long pull on his beer. I glance at Caleb to see how he's responding to Wayne's drinking, but he doesn't notice. He's too busy staring at the raised stage in the front of the room.

A bachelorette party is currently singing a disjointed version of "Girls Just Want to Have Fun," next to an enormous sign that reads "Karaoke night. Half-price draft beers." One woman hits a pitchy note, and the rest of them giggle, drunkenly leaning on each other.

I guide the subject away from Caleb and me. "What are we going to sing?" There's a list of karaoke songs on the table to choose from. I pick it up and hand it to Alvina. "Let's do a duet."

"You and me? A duet?" Her lips purse as she considers the idea.

"Yeah." I've been thinking about it all day, how we could sing together. "It'll be fun."

She shrugs lightly. "Okay, I guess."

I clap my hands, delighted she's humoring me. "How about Taylor Swift? She has a ton of songs on that list."

Alvina's perfectly arched brow lowers. "Taylor Swift?"

"Please," I wheedle, giving her my best puppy dog eyes. "She's my absolute favorite. Please, Alvina?"

"Okay. Okay." She waves me off. "I don't know her as well, so you pick the song."

I choose Blank Space, and we put in our request. There's just one group waiting to sing in front of us.

Caleb keeps glancing at me while he drums his fingers nervously on the table. I assume he's worried about his upcoming performance, but then he steps closer. "I did something." His brow furrows with concern. "I'm scared you'll be mad at me."

My mind races, sifting through all the possibilities. "What is it?" I shift my weight as I brace for his answer.

"I showed that picture, the one of the painting you did, to an art gallery owner that I know."

Wait. What?

"Why?" I'm bewildered. "Why would you do that?" The implications of what he just said hit me. Eagerly, I press for more details. "What did they say? Did they like it? Hate it? Think it was any good? Oh no, they thought it was awful, didn't they? Did they ask if a third grader painted it?" I bury my face in my hands, peeking out from between my fingers.

A slow smile spreads across his face. "Whoa, Gwen. Calm down." He holds up his hand, laughing. "He loved it. My friend, the gallery owner, wants to talk to you. He's interested in seeing more of your work."

I drop my hands from my face and grin, my excitement almost unbearable. "*Really?* I can't believe it. That's amazing."

"You're not mad at me?"

Am I angry with him? I should be based on principles alone. Caleb went behind my back and showed the gallery owner my painting. But it's hard to be upset when the result is beyond my wildest expectations. It's a dream I never dared to hope for, that someone at an actual gallery could be interested in me and my artwork.

I'm saved from answering Caleb's question by the MC calling my name.

Alvina and I ascend the raised dais in the front of the room. Standing before the rowdy bar, I have a newfound appreciation for the stage fright Caleb has described. It's just as he said. The spotlights are hot and blinding. Magnified by my fear, the crowd expands, like there are thousands of people about to watch me make a fool of myself.

Instinctively, my eyes search the audience for Caleb. He's there. His bright blue gaze and encouraging smile calm me.

Alvina shows no sign of nerves. I guess when you help run one of the busiest ICUs in the country, karaoke might seem tame in comparison. I swallow around the lump in my throat. The spotlights dim, then flare into red as the first beats of the song pour from the speakers. As we had planned, we trade off singing each verse and sing the chorus together.

I'm not delusional. My singing voice is awful, high and warbling. I sing along, at first cautious but slowly becoming more carefree. Besides my friends, I'll probably never see anyone from this bar again. Why should I care what these strangers think about me?

This is karaoke night, not *American Idol.*

Alvina, on the other hand, has nothing to be ashamed about. Her singing voice isn't professional grade, but it's pretty good, smooth and rich. She's able to hit those tough to reach high notes.

We are halfway through the song when the computer screen that shows the lyrics glitches and goes blank. Inwardly, I groan, but I'm not scared for me. I know all the words. It's Alvina I worry about.

She flashes a bewildered glance in my direction. I make a "keep going" motion with my hand as the song bridges into her section to sing. There's a pause, and she picks up from where I left off. She gets all the words in the verse correct, but at the chorus, when she should say, "I've got a long list of ex-lovers," she fumbles. She's clearly searching for the right phrase and not finding it. Finally, Alvina stutters out, "a long list of...of...eggs and butter."

I almost stop her but don't want to ruin the rhythm. The crowd is initially taken aback. As they catch on, they begin to laugh uproariously. They think it's hilarious. Soon the whole bar sings along with us, screaming out the words "eggs and butter" especially loud. By the end of the song, even I'm singing "eggs and butter," while I pretend to crack an imaginary egg and mix it in an imaginary bowl.

Raucous applause breaks out when we are done, with people high-fiving us all the way back to our seats.

"It's ex-lovers," I tell her, laughing as we sit down.

She smacks her hand to her forehead. "I couldn't remember. I had to make something up."

I pat her on the shoulder. "I like your version better, anyway."

At the table, Caleb is shifting nervously on his feet, waiting to be called onto the stage. "Don't forget, this is supposed to be fun," I tell him. "You love music more than anyone I've ever met, Caleb. If you struggle, just remember that. Tap into that passion and let the melody carry you away."

The last words leave my mouth as the MC shouts for Caleb to come up, using his fake name.

I hold my breath as he ascends the steps and takes the microphone. His voice quavers slightly. "I'm going to be singing Don't Stop Believing by Journey."

The audience claps loudly, pleased by his choice.

The opening bars start. Caleb clears his throat and runs a quick hand through his hair. I can tell he's nervous, with the way he taps his fingers along his thigh. He closes his eyes and begins to sing with that distinctive husky voice.

It's like when we were caroling. At first, he's hesitant, his voice subdued. As he gets about halfway through, Caleb loosens up, his words swelling, gaining strength with each passing note. The noise from the bar quiets as strangers pause their conversations. They turn in their chairs to listen.

Close to the end of the song, his eyes open wide, searching through the crowd until he finds me. He lands his stare on me and completely lets go, belting out the music. Singing like we're the only two people in the room. He sings, "The movie never ends. It goes on and on and on and on," sounding so good that I suck in my breath, my chest expanding with pride.

The whispers begin during the last verse, starting at the back of the bar and spreading forward. "Lawson?" I hear the woman at the table next to me ask her friend, her tone questioning.

Without breaking eye contact with Caleb, I speak out of the side of my mouth. "Wayne, you drove here, right?"

"Yeah."

"Go get your car and park it by the door. Keep the engine running."

I don't need to tell him twice. Alvina is already moving, getting my purse and hers off the backs of our chairs.

Caleb finishes the song, and a group of people rush the stage, led by the bachelorette party. "Aren't you Caleb Lawson?" a woman demands when she reaches him.

Caleb's eyes fly wide. "Me?" He points at himself, shaking his head. "No. You've got the wrong guy."

The lady won't give up. She's adamant. "You *are*. I recognize your voice. It's like that new song on the radio. What's the name? Gwen?"

I move up behind her and motion to Caleb, reaching my hand out to him. He takes it. I pull, dragging him down the steps. As soon as we hit the ground, we're running. Hand in hand, Caleb and I burst through the doors and rush out onto the busy sidewalk. Wayne's car is at the curb, engine running, with Alvina in the passenger seat. We jump in the back, and Wayne roars off down the street.

"Whew." I watch over my shoulder, making sure no one follows us. "That was crazy. They recognized you just from your voice."

Alvina looks behind her to Caleb. "You were great in there."

His hand is shaky as he runs it through his hair. "Thanks. It was pretty terrifying in the beginning, but I felt more confident by the end."

"You sounded decent." Wayne's tone is casual, but he can't hide that he looks at Caleb with respect.

"Better than decent," I'm quick to correct. I beam at Caleb and tell him honestly, "You were wonderful."

"Thanks. It was a good idea you had. To do karaoke." The back of his hand brushes against mine, the sensation burning my skin. My heart lurches as the touch turns more deliberate and he strokes along the length of my fingers. I flip my palm and hold still as his hand settles down on top of mine, as light as a butterfly landing on a flower petal. My nerve endings fire, sending thrilled fizzy signals to my brain, highlighting every point where we connect.

I glance up to see my special smile on his lips, the one that's small and tender. Something broken inside of me slips back into place. It's hard to describe, but when Caleb looks at me like this, the world becomes brighter, more vivid. The stoplights and street signs are more colorful. The laughter from the people on the sidewalk as we drive past is more joyful.

When he looks at me like this, everything…almost…makes sense.

64

The hospital stairwell looks like a scene from one of my horror movies. Utilitarian with cracked white paint and rough metal handrails. Thick silver pipes fitted with valves and rusted joints rise along the walls. The heavy doors clang shut with a sense of finality behind me.

Most staff take the elevators, but, whenever I can, I take the stairs. Ugly as they are, it's my one place of occasional solitude. The only time during my current twenty-four–hour shift that I'm not surrounded by beeping monitors, shouted orders, and other…people.

Always *so* many people down in the ER.

I reach the seventh floor and exit. Ten minutes into my thirty-minute break, and I've decided to visit Alvina.

My phone vibrates with a text from Caleb. He's out to dinner with his mom. I had texted earlier asking how he was doing, knowing he was anxious.

I glance down at my phone as I walk into the ICU.

Caleb writes, "We talked. Told Mom I need her more as a parent than as a manager. She cried twice and hugged me five times, so it's going okay, I guess?"

My chest fills with pride. Marjorie is a tough cookie. She had to be to bring her baby to L.A. and propel him to stardom. Her crying and hugging Caleb gives me hope that they've had a genuine breakthrough.

"You're doing awesome," I text back. "Keep it up. Also, get the chocolate cake for dessert. I had it from that restaurant before, and it's yummy."

"Already ordered it," he writes. "Great minds think alike." The winking emoji, drooling emoji, and cake emoji combo he texts has me grinning.

I round the corner and go to the center of the ICU, where Alvina sits at her desk.

"What's up with that face?" she asks warmly, looking up from behind her computer.

"What face?"

Her eyebrow quirks, semi-amused. "The cat ate the canary face or perhaps I should call it the 'I'm texting with Caleb' face."

I fight to stop my smile from climbing higher up my cheeks. "Maybe I was texting with him and maybe not," I tease, attempting to seem mysterious.

I can't pull it off. Alvina rolls her eyes and says sarcastically, "Keep on talking to your boyfriend. Go ahead and ignore poor old Alvina."

"Hey!" I lean on my elbows on her desk, bending at the waist to be closer. "I walked up seven flights of steps for you. If that isn't love, then I don't know what is. Anyway, he's not my boyfriend. We're just dating."

If incredulous had a picture in the dictionary, then Alvina's face would be right under it. "*Right*. If you say so."

"I'm telling the truth," I object. "We haven't even kissed since he's been back."

She rolls away from her desk at that, the wheels of her chair emitting a loud, high-pitched squeak. "Why not?" she demands, crossing her arms over her chest like she needs them there, otherwise she might strangle me.

"Why not what?"

"Why aren't you kissing that handsome boy who's been following you around like a lovesick puppy?" Only Alvina could get away with calling Caleb a boy.

Her question lodges in my rib cage and sits there. I've been asking myself the same thing. Ever since the near-perfect date in Central Park and then how Caleb held my hand in Wayne's car, it's gotten harder to ignore how much I want him.

"Don't know." I pick up a pen from her desk and click it several times, staring at it as an excuse to not look her in the eye. "I'm still getting over how he left and trying to figure out if there's a future for us."

Alvina looks like she wants to scold me, but she pauses, and her expression softens. "What's scaring you?" she asks softly, striking right to the core of my problems. "And don't bother telling me it's about your work and schedules and blah-blah-blah. You can figure out those things, given enough effort and time."

I want to argue that those are real concerns, but, as usual, she's correct. That's not what is holding me back, not with how kind and flexible Caleb has been recently.

"I'm scared of getting hurt again," I admit, my voice hushed. "Terrified, actually. Alvina, what should I do?"

"Get over it," she says without an ounce of compassion. "He will hurt you, and you'll hurt him. In big ways and small. It's called being in a relationship. But hurting doesn't mean leaving, and I think that's what you're really afraid of. Do you believe he'll leave you again?"

"How can I know?" With a groan, I flop into the chair next to her and swivel aimlessly side to side, my feet dragging along the floor. "I didn't think my dad would die or Jax would dump me. I didn't think Mom would remarry and move out of the country. Apparently, I suck at predicting the future."

Squeezing my eyes closed, I focus on her question. Casting my mind back to how Caleb has acted since he's been in New York. All the things he's said and done.

As long as you are there, that's where I'll go.

The sincerity in his gaze as he told me that. The determined set of his shoulders. "It's hard to be sure, but I don't think he'll leave. Not if he can help it."

She lets the warmth seep back into her face. "Well then," her voice is molasses, sweet and slowly poured. "Sounds like you've got your answer."

65

The executive committee meets in a bland conference room at the back of the hospital. The view out of the windows is of the physician parking lot, which is only half-full since evening has fallen. A lone doctor, her white coat gleaming in the lamp light, tromps from her car to the hospital entrance, preparing for a night shift.

I feel for her, having just finished a week of nights myself. Fatigue has left the sensation of sandpaper grit in my eyes. I can practically hear it scrape every time I blink.

I turn away from the window and walk through the conference room. There's a chair pressed against the wall where I sit, tucking the tails of my white lab coat over my knees like a blanket.

Dr. Benson has seen me enter. A shadow of annoyance ripples over his features. He stands and makes his way over to me. "Dr. Wright," he says stiffly. "What are you doing here?"

"I'm here to present my art therapy plan to the committee."

An angry glower from him. "I already told you there's no money for that."

Refusing to back down, I tilt my chin up and say calmly, "I'm hoping the rest of the committee comes to a different conclusion. I'm sure with the combined intelligence in this room, we can come up with creative solutions to any budgetary restrictions."

Dr. Benson splutters, "You're wasting both your time and ours."

Now he's making me angry. I stand to my full height, which still only reaches his chin, but whatever, and spit out, "It's never a waste of time to improve the quality of life for our patients."

He opens his mouth to respond but is cut off by the secretary calling on everyone to begin. There's an angry stomp to his footfalls as he stalks back to his seat. I sit down, settling in until it's my turn to present.

Surprisingly, the meeting is riveting. This week's topic is renewal of physician privileges and censure of inappropriate behavior, which sounds boring as heck but turns out to be General Hospital–level drama.

I hear about a surgeon who is being penalized for angrily throwing a scalpel in the operating room. Then about a doctor who's getting fired for slapping the butt of his female resident. And finally, about an administrator who got caught for petty embezzlement and is being placed on leave.

Who knew these sessions are so full of juicy gossip?

Jenny would love it.

The thought sends a pang through me. Jenny and I have been talking daily just like usual, but I find myself editing what I tell her, especially when it comes to Caleb.

I know I have to let it go. She's apologized many times, but I'm not quite ready to allow her full access to that part of my life yet. For my sake, but even more for Caleb's. He's only now regaining some credibility with his fans and the press. I don't want to be the one who messes that up for him.

"Dr. Wright will give us a briefing about her art therapy proposal," Dr. Patel announces, introducing me.

I take my place at the front of the room. Staring into all of those faces, the most powerful doctors and hospital administrators all gathered together, sets my heart racing. I exhale a shaky breath and replay what Caleb said to me after our Central Park date. When he talked about how I'm smart and brave and deserving. Those words fortify me, giving me the strength to speak.

"Thank you for the opportunity to present to you today." My voice rings out loud and clear as I outline the plan I explained to Dr. Benson in his office weeks ago.

As I talk, I carefully gauge the reactions, reading the faces of the individuals who sit around the table. That old need to impress them, these authority figures, hits me with a vengeance. I want them to like me and my ideas. People-pleasing Gwen craves their approval.

Stop! I command myself. *This art therapy is a great idea. Something that can help so many of your patients. These people should appreciate it for its own merits. If they don't, then it's their loss.*

I make a solemn promise to myself. *Someday* I *will be in a position of power.* I *will be the one making these choices. If the program doesn't get accepted now, then* I *will make it a reality in the future.*

A sense of control fills me where before there had only been nerves. My jaw firms, my shoulders straighten. With calm precision, I go through each detail in my plan, talking about it like it's already a foregone conclusion that they will approve the program. In the audience, heads nod, and some of the friendlier members smile. Their nonverbal cues fuel my confidence.

There's one face not smiling at me, though. Dr. Benson. He sits with his arms crossed like a shield over his chest, glaring at me angrily. It's obvious now that Dr. Patel and I undercut him.

Too bad. I don't like him…or the patriarchy.

Once I'm done with my presentation, the doctors ask me a couple of simple questions. I refer to the handout that I've provided, citing the most recent data about the therapy's effectiveness and discussing the federal grant money available to support the program.

"Thank you, Dr. Wright." Dr. Patel inclines her head, appearing nonchalant, but I can't miss the triumphant look she flashes over to Dr. Benson. She's using me to annoy him, but if it benefits the patients and brings him down a notch, then I don't mind being a pawn in her game. "Dr. Wright, please step out. We'll discuss the program and then vote on it."

Pacing back and forth, I wait anxiously in the hallway. I chew on my bottom lip, wondering what the committee will decide. They seemed to like my ideas, so I'm hopeful. As long as they can outvote Dr. Benson, I might have a chance.

Ten minutes later, Dr. Patel sticks her head out the door. "Dr. Wright, come back inside, please."

I reenter the room and examine the faces around me, trying to guess the outcome of the vote. Most of the members smile openly at me, raising my hopes even further.

"We're still meeting to discuss some other unrelated issues," Dr. Patel states. "But I wanted to bring you back in here to officially announce that we approved your plan. This hospital will institute a brand-new art therapy program. We'd like you to be involved in the hiring and design process as we develop it."

I have an urge to hoot and holler but swallow it down. Instead, I smile politely and thank the committee, reassuring them that I'll be available to assist in any way I can.

There's a spring in my step as I walk out of the hospital. Adrenaline from the meeting surges through my veins, supercharging me until I feel invincible. I dance down the sidewalk, pumping my fist in the air and letting out a relieved burst of laughter.

I did it! I had a vision, a way to contribute to the well-being of my patients, and I brought that idea to life. I pushed through my own insecurities, through my fear of risk and failure, and made it happen.

I don't think I've ever been so proud of myself.

"You're going to change the world." Dad's words come back to me, which would usually make me sad, but today they cause my chest to swell.

In the middle of the sidewalk, I stop to stare into the stars. "I'm doing it, Dad," I speak into the evening air. "It's taken me a while to find my strength, but I'm going to make the world a better place. I promise you."

With my words fading into the wind, a burst of happiness rushes through me, making me buoyant. I need to share this joyous feeling, to tell someone else about my accomplishment. I run through all the important people in my life: my family, Jenny, Alvina, and even Wayne.

In the end, there's really only one person I want to talk to right now. One person who I want to share my highs and lows.

The knowledge hits me like a battering ram when I realize who that person is, but there's no questioning it. It's undeniable.

I call Caleb.

He answers right away, his voice warm and smoky, the sound making me smile.

"I did it!" I squeal, grinning like mad. "They approved the art therapy program."

A happy sigh from him. "Oh, Gwen!" he exclaims. *Round G. Flat N.* "That's wonderful. I'm not surprised, though. I always believed in you."

A few months ago, I would have called him a liar. Pointed out how he didn't believe in me, in us, when he broke up with me at Christmas. But now, I'm starting to see that he did believe in me. The person he didn't believe in was himself. He didn't trust that he could keep me safe.

But I don't need him to keep me safe. I can do that on my own.

After all, I'm Gwen Freaking Wright.

"here are we going?" I ask for the tenth time, clutching Caleb's arm as he drags me along.

"No peeking," he orders, like he has every other time I've asked. The sliding sound of an elevator door opening and then we're moving again.

The blindfold he's placed over my eyes itches, the black fabric blocking out all light.

"A little further." His voice rises, all amused excitement, reminding me of the man who begged to open his Christmas gift early.

His spare hand comes around to clutch my waist. "Up this staircase now." His fingertips dig in lightly as he helps me ascend. From the reverberations under my feet, it seems like we're climbing a long set of metal stairs.

With my free hand, I tug down my short skirt. I had gone all out on my appearance tonight, full make-up and hair done. I'm hoping I can be brave and finally kiss Caleb.

My efforts had been rewarded when he picked me up and his jaw hit the floor as he took in the tight, red dress I'm wearing.

With a dazed expression, he had drawled, "My, my. You're a pretty little thing, aren't you?"

At his comment I had blushed, my face matching the dress, but I didn't mind the heat.

Caleb is looking good as well, in his navy suit jacket and pants. A trim black leather belt accentuates his narrow waist. His white button-down shirt is open at the top, exposing a sculpted throat and upper chest.

Pining filled my chest as I took in his broad shoulders and the curve of his collarbones. I had to stop from touching that divot at the bottom of his neck, right above his breastbone. *Suprasternal notch.* I repeated the medical name to myself, thinking it had never sounded so sexy before.

Now, the screech of a heavy metal door opening. A brisk wind hits along with a repetitive stuttering noise so loud it makes me want to cover my ears. Caleb tugs at my arm, jolting me to a stop. His breath is hot on my cheek as he shouts, "You mentioned during our last date that you wanted something fancy, so here we are." With that, he whips off the blindfold and yells out, "Surprise!"

Rising before me is a gleaming midnight black helicopter. It's so sleek it looks like it should belong to Batman. The twin propellers on top spin faster and faster until they blur into one.

Spring has passed the baton to summer. The wind generated by the propellers is humid hot. It sends my unbound hair flying, tangling into my round, shocked eyes.

Caleb's laughing, his hands moving to catch my hair. He gathers it gently in his hand and holds it to the side. He leans in close. "You should see your face right now." He laughs again, the sound low and rumbling. "Have you ever been in a helicopter before?"

I can't speak, can only shake my head no.

Craning my neck, I find that we are on top of a skyscraper. One so big that it towers over all the other buildings. The wind whipping around me isn't just from the helicopter, it's from the fact that I'm up so high.

I take a few steps toward the building's edge, and a wave of dizziness hits as I look down the vertical miles that separate me from the street below.

"Whoa." I stumble slightly, off balance from vertigo. "What is all this?" I turn to Caleb, wonderstruck.

He keeps one hand on my arm, steadying me. "I'm taking you on a sunset flight over Manhattan. You said that you hadn't seen as much of it as you wanted, so I thought this way I could show you all of it."

Wow. Just wow.

Caleb pivots and heads to the helicopter, but I call to him, "Wait."

He returns to me, eyebrows raised questioningly.

"This isn't *your* helicopter, is it?"

No way he has a helicopter, right?

Caleb laughs like I'm being ridiculous, and I feel a sense of relief. Of course, he doesn't own this beast of a machine. That would be crazy.

Shouting to be heard above the roar of the engine, he answers, "No, this isn't mine. I just have the jet. It's back in L.A."

He grins merrily and waves at me, curling his fingers into his hand. A come-hither gesture. "Let's go, Gwen." There's a single metal rung that he steps on to haul himself into the cockpit.

I'm left standing on the concrete circle of the helipad, my mouth unhinged.

Did I hear that right? Caleb owns a *jet*?

I bend low and rush under the rotating propellers to board. The pilot sits in the front seat. Caleb and I are in the back. Caleb helps me adjust heavy, padded earphones over my head. He points to the small microphone that sticks out in front of my mouth.

"You can talk into here, and we'll be able to hear you, the pilot and I," he says, his headset picking up the words and transmitting them to mine.

I press the microphone closer to my lips. "Like this?"

"Yes, that's it." He squeezes my thigh encouragingly. "Are you ready?" Static slightly distorts what he says.

My heart is a hummingbird's wings, beating fast with nervous excitement. "Ready," I answer, trying to keep the quaver out of my voice.

The helicopter tilts at an alarming angle, and I throw my hand out to brace myself against the bubble-like window to my right. Then we are lifting straight up into the sky. I give a startled yelp as the ground plummets away below us.

We hover, holding still for a minute, and then shoot forward. The motion presses my body into the cushion behind me. There's a feeling of weightlessness as the helicopter flies, tilting and swaying as it enters the city.

It keeps low, with tall buildings rushing by on either side. Our reflection soars along with us, rippling in the mirrored windowpanes of the skyscrapers we pass. The pilot speaks over his microphone as he navigates, pointing out landmarks and offering interesting tidbits of history.

I'm held captive by the view, my face pressed up against the window. My hands splay across its surface as if I could grab hold of the beauty I see. We go by old brick buildings and new glass ones, too. We fly over grassy parks with splashing fountains and then to the East River.

The sun is setting, sinking low over the water. The stone of the Brooklyn Bridge catches one last flash of golden sunlight before fading into deep purple-black shadows.

The natural light of day has been replaced by the colorful nighttime lights of the city, which twinkle like the Christmas tree I decorated with Jenny and Caleb many months ago. It's gorgeous, this shimmering tapestry I now call home.

The joy bubbling in me overflows. I face Caleb. "It's so incredibly beautiful," I tell him, breathless, my smile wide.

He's been staring at me rather than out the window, watching me the whole time.

Our eyes lock onto each other.

"Darn," Caleb says thickly. "That smile. I missed that smile. Those lips." He blows out a frustrated sigh and shoves his hands through his hair. "Do you think you'll ever forgive me? Because it's torture sitting next to you and not being able to kiss you. I'm trying to be patient. I swear I am, but I need to put my hands on you."

My stomach clenches low and tight, desire and fear warring in my gut. "I'm not sure, Caleb. Maybe we're better off as friends?" I don't believe a word that's coming out of my mouth.

"That's not true, and you know it," he grits out.

Guess he doesn't believe it either.

"You're mine, Gwen. It's as inevitable as that sun going down and rising back up again tomorrow." His jaw clenches. Once. Twice.

My eyes flick to the pilot, who's kept his head forward through this entire exchange. "Shh," I tell Caleb. "He'll hear you."

Caleb's voice gets even louder. "I don't care who hears me. I'll shout it out to the whole city if I need to. I love you, and I want you back. *Now.*"

Love. He said love.

Caleb rips his headphones off and throws them to the floor. He reaches over and takes my headset off as well. "What do you say?"

My lips are already falling open, barely able to murmur, "Yes," before he's all around me. His lips crush against mine. A man starving, deprived for far too long. His hands are in my hair, his upper body straining against his seatbelt in an effort to reach me.

I'm breathless, gasping softly, giddy with each touch. Unlocking my seatbelt, I move to encircle my arms around the back of his neck. I scoot closer, practically climbing across the seat.

The helicopter banks, rises, and dips. Its propeller whirs on. I don't care if we fall out of the sky and into the river right now.

I'm already drowning in Caleb, in the sensation of his mouth, his hands as they wrap around my shoulders.

It feels amazing to touch him again.

It feels like coming home.

67

Now that we've started kissing again, we can't stop. On the limo ride to dinner, we kiss in the back seat. Soft kisses that build to hard. Caleb has pulled out all the stops. Making this the most romantic, the most *fancy*, date in the world.

In the elevator up to the restaurant my song plays through the speakers. I break off our kiss to listen, tilting my ear toward the sound, my hands resting on Caleb's broad shoulders.

The song, *my* song, is a hit. Since it was released, it's been steadily climbing the pop charts. The version he recorded is faster, more beat-laden, than the one he sung in my mother's house and on the stage when he returned to me, but it still has that mournful note of longing stitched through each verse.

I point to speakers in the ceiling as the elevator dings its way along, rising through hundreds of floors. "Oh, look," I tell Caleb, grinning from ear to ear. "It's my favorite song."

This earns me another kiss.

"What's the name of this restaurant we're going to?" I ask once we break apart. He's been cagey about where we're eating all night.

"It's called the Adelaide. One of my friends owns it. He's the chef."

"Wow. I've read about this place. It's impossible to get a reservation. You really are being fancy," I tease.

"That's the goal." He glides his nose down along mine, ending in a deep kiss.

On the 103rd floor, the elevator stops. The double doors slide open to reveal the most incredible view. The entire skyline of Manhattan is spread out before us. Its lights twinkle through the night like stars.

The far wall of the restaurant is pure glass, three stories high, leading out to a long balcony. This is where Caleb leads me, placing his hand on the small of my back and gently propelling me over plush carpet.

As we walk through the restaurant, I look around, confused.

"Caleb," I whisper. "Why isn't anyone else here? It's empty."

He whispers back, "Because I rented out the whole place. I wanted to be alone with my girlfriend."

Girlfriend. I like how that word falls from his lips.

His voice is low and silky as he confesses, "I don't want any distractions. I'm going to keep you all to myself." A wolfish grin, showing all of his teeth.

How can I resist Caleb Lawson when he's looking at me like that?

No one could. It's impossible.

He opens a glass door and motions me out onto the balcony. We stop before a single table set for two. It's laid out beautifully, with fine white porcelain plates and filigreed silverware. A centerpiece of simple pink rosebuds packed tightly together rests in a low vase.

Caleb holds my chair so I can sit. The glowing warmth of a nearby outdoor heater takes away the evening chill. After we are both seated, a server in a white tuxedo approaches our table with an enormous bottle of champagne.

Uh-oh. Alcohol served to someone freshly out of rehab seems like a terrible idea. I start to wave the man off, but Caleb takes it from him and calmly fills my glass. He leaves his glass glaringly empty. I try not to stare, but he catches me looking.

"No alcohol for me. You know…since rehab." His jaw tightens around that word.

"We haven't really talked about that yet," I say tentatively, unsure how to begin this conversation.

Caleb sighs heavily, his gaze slipping past me to focus on the sparkling city lights. "I've been avoiding it," he admits. "Didn't want you to think of me as weak."

It's more than sadness in his expression. It's shame, self-loathing, fear.

"Getting help if you need it is never weakness, Caleb. That's strength."

He fidgets, rearranging the silverware by his plate.

"Can you tell me about it?" I prompt gently.

His voice is so muted that I have to concentrate on each word. "I was a walking disaster. After the car crash and then losing you. I couldn't cope. It got bad…really bad. I went to a dark place, and I wasn't able to drag myself out. No matter how hard I tried." His hand darts up to run through his hair.

That picture flashes through my mind. Caleb at the bar bent over like he's broken in half, pouring his soul into that glass. How the image had shattered me.

"I'm an alcoholic. I realize that now. I'll always be one, even if I never have a drink again for the rest of my life." His eyes are on me, begging for forgiveness, but braced for rejection.

He turns his body away, hunches his shoulders, and mumbles sadly, "I understand if it's too much. If you don't want to deal with someone so messed up."

His dejection, that air of a lost boy, skewers me.

I scoot my chair closer and capture his hand in mine, tracing small circles over the back of his hand with my thumb. "I'm not scared of you, Caleb. Once before, I told you that revealing the imperfect parts of yourself won't ever make me upset. I like understanding you, *all* of you."

I take a minute to consider my next words. It's no easy thing to love someone with addiction. It takes a lifetime of patience and an iron will, to protect both them and yourself. Am I up to that challenge? I look deep inside myself, searching for the answer.

Once I'm sure I've found it, I continue, "I see alcoholics every day in the hospital. The ones in acute withdrawal, with their hallucinations and seizures. The ones with chronic liver failure, whose bodies have given up completely. I know how hard they struggle."

"You're going to have to fight this. It's a battle I can't do for you. I can sit next to you and cheer you on, but, ultimately, it's up to you. And if you can't…can't control it." I stop, choking back tears, unable to envision that future. The one where I lose this precious man to his demons. "I won't sit

by and watch you destroy yourself. I can't do that to you or to me. Understand?" I'm lecturing him, but it's something I need to do. He has to understand my boundaries.

It's hard for him to meet my eyes, but he does. "I understand, and I swear
I'm trying to change." He looks up like he's searching for words written in
the sky. "I joined Alcoholics Anonymous. They gave me a sponsor, and I'm
working through the steps." He confirms what I've already suspected. It's a
relief that he's ready to let me into this part of his life. Finally, he's letting me
see *all* of him, the good and the bad.

"I want you to know how much I appreciate it," Caleb continues. "That you
aren't disgusted or ashamed of me. You're the strongest person I've ever met."

"Me?" My eyebrows raise to my hairline. I've never thought of myself that
way before, as strong.

"Yes, you. Everything you went through with your dad. All the suffering
you see at the hospital." He lets out a low, shaky breath. "Everything I put
you through, and yet, you don't give up on any of us, humanity or me. I told
you before, you don't give up even when things get hard. There are a lot of
qualities I like about you, but that's one of the biggest. I've never met anyone who's more brave."

Huh. Brave. Perhaps I should add that to my list. *Dependable, predictable…and brave.*

Those aren't bad things to be.

68

Caleb pushes up from his chair.

"Where are you going?" I ask, surprised by his sudden movement.

A corner of his mouth lifts into a smirk. "You didn't think I would let just anyone cook your dinner, did you?"

"You're making my food?" I was already excited to eat at this restaurant, but knowing that Caleb will be my chef heightens my anticipation to a fever pitch.

"Can I come with you?" I place my napkin on the table and stand.

"Don't you want to stay here? Relax and enjoy the view?" He motions to the panoramic scene from the balcony.

"*You're* my favorite view."

Caleb's eyes soften as he takes my hand and draws me close. A searing kiss sends tingles throughout my body. It goes on until my toes curl in my high heels.

"I love you," he murmurs against my mouth.

"Love you back." It's the first time I've said it since our breakup. I expect it to feel awkward or forced, but it doesn't. Those words coming from my lips are as natural as breathing.

I love him.

I never stopped loving him.

I'll always love him.

Leading me by my hand, Caleb takes me to the back of the restaurant, where the kitchen lies behind a swinging metal door. It's massive, full of shining stainless steel appliances, some of which I don't recognize. Other appliances I've seen before, but they look like giant versions of the ones that are on my countertop at home. There's a mixer that is identical to mine, except that it sits on the floor and comes up to the top of my chest. You could make twenty cakes inside that thing.

A long-haired Asian man enters the room, his face breaking into a wide grin when he sees Caleb. "You made it!" He embraces Caleb, giving him a firm slap on the back.

"Gwen, this is Nick. He owns the restaurant."

I try to shake hands, but Nick goes in for a full body hug. "Caleb's told me so much about you. Great to finally meet you."

After we exchange pleasantries, Nick peers over Caleb's shoulder. "What are you making?"

"I'm thinking of a steak with a white wine reduction. Some bearnaise sauce on the side. Scalloped potatoes and asparagus." Pots and pans are taken from a drawer next to the oven, clattering as Caleb places them on the counter. He glances back at me. "Sound okay to you, Gwen?"

On cue, my stomach grumbles so loudly that it makes us all laugh. "I think that's a yes." Still laughing, my hand flies up to cover my complaining belly.

"Well, I'll let you get to it," Nick says. He and Caleb fist bump, then Nick hugs me lightly. A quick wave, and he takes off.

Caleb has all the ingredients laid out on the table behind him. He points out what he needs, and I bring it over. Soon, pots are bubbling, and the most tantalizing smells fill the room. I breathe it in—rosemary, garlic, a hint of oregano.

Caleb's taken off his suit jacket and rolled up his sleeves while he works. I'm entranced by the way his muscular forearms ripple with each practiced chop and stir.

He dips the frying pan into the fire of the stovetop, and the pan lights with a burst of flames. "Oh!" I cry out, squeezing my eyelids shut as the heat blasts against my face. With a bit of flare, Caleb clangs a lid on top of the pan, extinguishing the fire. His eyes dance with amusement. "Pretty *fancy* method to sear the steak, wouldn't you say?"

I nod my assent, impressed yet again by the man's culinary skills. I mean, seriously, is there anything hotter than a man who knows his way around a kitchen?

I think not.

"I enjoy seeing you like this," I tell him, taking in the relaxed set of his shoulders and how his eyes turn up in the corners.

"What? Cooking for you?" he teases lightly.

"Well, yes, but it's more than that. You look at home here, in the kitchen. Like this is the place where you can let go. Where you're the most authentic version of you."

He ducks his head, pleased and somehow embarrassed by what I've said.

I stay quiet after that, observing Caleb as he works. He hums, moving quickly from one dish to another. A few minutes later, Caleb spins to me, extending a spoonful of the sauce he's been working on. "Try this. Tell me if it's too salty."

I'm sitting on the kitchen counter, my legs dangling. Doing as he asks, I take the buttery mixture into my mouth, "Yum. Not too salty. It's perfect."

He moves closer, standing with his legs pressed to mine. "I'm glad you think it's good. I like making you happy," he leans in and whispers into my ear, his voice low.

"Oh, yeah?" I tip my lips up to his. Caleb's cinnamon taste mixes with the taste of the sauce in my mouth as we kiss. It's a delicious combination.

"If you like making me happy…then keep cooking for me," I say, my voice breathy.

A chuffing laugh from him ends as I pull him in for another passion-filled kiss.

There's a new smell mixing in. Something…burnt. Caleb swears and steps back so quickly that I end up kissing air for a second.

Once he's moved the lightly smoking pan with the potatoes out of the oven, he wags a finger at me and warns, "If we keep this up, the food's going to be ruined."

"Okay." I clasp my hands in my lap, attempting to look demure. "I'll behave myself."

I keep my promise and don't distract Caleb the rest of the time he's cooking. It doesn't take him long to have the meal completed. He somehow manages to have all the food finished at the same time, a trick I've never been able to master.

We carry the warm plates back out to the balcony.

"This looks amazing. I can't wait to dig in," I tell him. He holds my chair out for me and helps slide it in once I'm seated.

"Mmm. Me too." Caleb gives me a lazy smile. My stomach plunges, butterflies erupting when he flashes that slow, sexy smile and murmurs, "absolutely ravenous."

69

Dinner was delicious. We climb into the back of Caleb's limo, our date almost over. I glance to the front of the car, but our driver is hidden. The shiny black privacy divider is up, separating us from him.

"I still can't believe you have your own limousine, like you don't even rent it, you own it." I half walk, half crawl over the long bench seat to join Caleb on the other side. He opens one arm so I can tuck myself in next to him. Once I'm seated, that arm settles over me like a warm blanket.

"I hardly ever use it." His lips press a soft kiss into my temple. "Just brought it out tonight in an effort to impress you. You know, fancy and all that." Another kiss. "Did it work? Did I impress you?"

I screw my face up, pretending to think. "Impress is an awfully strong word," I say slowly. "I'd say that you were…adequate."

"Adequate!" He's mock indignant. Without warning, he scoops me up and places me in his lap. Staring down at me, Caleb growls, "I'll show you something I'm good at, a lot better than adequate." His mouth comes down on mine, demanding.

Yes, please.

After we kiss for a few minutes, I pull back to look at him. I had almost forgotten how beautiful he is like this, exposed in every way. The contours of his face are colored by passing streetlights. The naked emotion in his eyes is a heady combination of desire and something deeper, something that looks a lot like love.

346 Dr. Melissa Dymond

Caleb kisses my neck. I turn my head, and his lips find mine.

"You're good at this. Kissing. Your lips are so soft," I whisper against his mouth.

He chuckles darkly, arms wrapping tight around my waist. "What I'm hearing is that I'm more than adequate."

He tips my chin up for another kiss.

"More than adequate," I admit, my lips curling without permission. My head is heavy, thoughts scattered. I snuggle into him, my arms around his neck.

We stay like that, wound up in one another for minutes that pass into an hour.

Finally, I drag my head off Caleb's shoulder and peer out the window. "Hey. Shouldn't we be at your penthouse by now?"

He's sheepish. "I told the driver to keep driving us around. Not to go straight to my place."

"What?" I'm awake now, eyes popping open, pushing away to sit up in his lap. "Caleb!" I swat him on the arm. "Did you plan this? Limo kissing?"

He looks only mildly repentant. "If it didn't happen, that would have been fine. But I thought…well, I knew I couldn't make it all the way home before I wanted to hold you."

He gives a quick kiss to my shocked face. "It's a compliment when you think about it. You drive me so crazy, I just couldn't wait."

"Hmm," I murmur, skeptical.

"Come on, Gwen. Don't look at me like that." He peppers tiny kisses across my cheek until his mouth takes mine. He kisses me and keeps on kissing until I forget where we are and where we were going. All I want is to be here with him, in this perfect moment. Surrounded by his love.

aleb needs you." Dean, Caleb's long-time bodyguard, looks uncharacteristically rattled, his tie crooked and words clipped. I glance at Alvina, who sits next to me, and see my concern reflected in her face. Wayne leans around her, trying to figure out what's going on.

"Can you hold my jacket?" I ask Alvina. Before she can answer, I shove my coat into her arms and rise from my seat in the third row of the Prestige Theater.

It's opening night. Alvina and Wayne have agreed to be my dates so we can watch Caleb's big debut in the Broadway musical. A debut that, given the expression on Dean's face, isn't going well.

Muttering apologies, I clamber over the legs of the people in my row, holding my arms out for balance. I wave to Marjorie and Ben, who sit behind us. "Is everything okay?" Marjorie asks, half-rising from her seat like she's about to come with me. If Caleb is panicking, the last thing he needs is his mom adding to his stress.

"Yes! Yes. Everything's fine," I lie and stumble over the person in the end seat. I almost fall but pull myself upright at the last minute and land in the aisle.

Dean gestures wildly for me to follow him. We rush into the backstage and down the hallway to where the private dressing rooms are. One door is marked with Caleb's name.

I push inside to find Caleb sitting with his head in his hands. He looks up and I falter, caught between attraction at how handsome he is with his stage make-up on and distress over his obvious anxiety.

I crouch down in front of his chair.

"Hey," I use my most soothing tone. The one I've cultivated in the hospital for when I deal with agitated patients. "What's up?"

Caleb's hands are clasped, his knuckles white. His eyes roll wildly. "I can't do it." His leg jitters, sending tremors through his body. "I'm telling you, I can't."

I rest my hands over his tightly coiled fists. "It's okay. I know you're scared, and that's normal. Remember, we talked about this? It's your first night onstage. Once you get out there, it will all click into place."

I'm certain that Caleb can do this. I've run through his lines with him. Watched him dance until he mastered every move. Seen him shine in dress rehearsals.

"You're going to be okay, Caleb," I reassure him again.

"No," he insists, his chest heaving. "Tell them I'm not going out there. You tell them, Gwen."

No way am I doing that.

"Can you tell me what's going on? What's worrying you?"

Caleb answers right away. "I'm scared I'll be awful. That everyone will see what a fake I am. I shouldn't care about their opinions, the negative reviews. Most of the time, I convince myself that I don't. But in the end, I suppose I do. I depend on that…external validation, I guess you'd call it? I need that to know if I'm any good."

I rub my thumb over the back of his hand. "Okay, let me tell you. Listen to *me* when I say that you are good. You're amazing. So talented. I've seen it, and everyone else will, too. And if they don't. If you get a bad review. You know what? Forget 'em. It won't be the end of you. Your world won't crumble. You have a lot of people who love you. The *real* you. You don't need the worship of strangers. Your parents, your friends, my family, *me*. We'll all still be here if you succeed or if you fail. It won't change how we feel about you. Our love for you isn't dependent on how you perform." I stop, a little breathless from my big speech.

Caleb is staring at me, his eyes as round as saucers. I'm satisfied to note that his breathing has slowed somewhat.

"Tell me what else. What else scares you?"

He swallows thickly. "There's just so many of them. So many people are out there. I'm worried I'll look up and see them all, and it'll be too much. Too many people staring back at me."

I think for a minute, trying to figure out a solution. "What if you pretend it's only me out there in the crowd? You know where I'm sitting, right?"

He nods.

"When you look out at the audience, find me. Just like you did when we went to karaoke together. *Only* look at me. I'll be staring straight at you with a big smile on my face. Can you do that?"

"Maybe." Then more firmly, "I think I can." He's still frowning, but his foot has stopped jiggling and his shoulders have relaxed back in their normal position.

The door opens. A stagehand leans into the room. "You're on, Mr. Lawson. Time to take your place."

Caleb stiffens, but I keep rubbing my finger over his skin. "Breathe, Caleb, breathe. It's going to be okay. I promise."

He lets out the air he's been holding a soft whoosh. I've never been so proud of him as I am when he stands up, squares his shoulders, and steps toward the door. Right before he reaches it, Caleb whirls around and takes me into his arms. He kisses me once, quick and firm, before he leaves the room.

71

He's magnificent, of course. I had no doubt. Watching Caleb up on that stage is a thing of beauty. Every expression on his handsome face seems so genuine, so real. He has this way of sucking you in, making you invested in his character. So much that you feel like you are up there with him. Like it's your life being played out in that story.

And when he sings, oh my, it's the most breathtaking thing. At the end of his first song, the whole crowd hushes in awe of his voice. A split second after, the applause starts, everyone clapping so loudly that the sound swells, filling the entire theater.

Caleb stays true to his word, and so do I. Every time he looks out at the audience, his eyes seek mine. Searching until he finds me. He captures me in his stare as I grin my widest grin up at him. I will my strength into him, sending it across the space that separates us. Hoping it reaches his heart.

At the end of the show, he gets a standing ovation. The crowd surges to their feet, applauding wildly. I clap the loudest of all.

Caleb stands there with a bemused expression. For the first time, he allows his gaze to travel over the theater, taking in all the people cheering for him.

He grins then. A proud smile, lighting up his entire face.

Once the applause has died out, Caleb strides past the other actors. He descends the stairs by the side of the stage and pushes through the crowd that moves to surround him. People clap him on the back and shoulders, congratulating him.

He walks by all those fans until he reaches me. There, in front of the entire theater, Caleb Freaking Lawson lifts me into his arms and kisses me.

The best, sweetest, most thrilling kiss.

When he places me on my feet, Caleb looks down and gives me a smile, small and tender.

A smile for only one person in the crowd.

Just for me.

72

SIX MONTHS LATER, CALIFORNIA

Same as last year, it's Christmas day and I'm at my mom's house in California. Except that *nothing* is the same as last year. Back then, I felt alone and abandoned. Now, the renovations are complete, and my family has been reunited.

Seth, Mom, Ben, and Marjorie sit around the kitchen table talking and working on a new puzzle, a jungle scene this time.

Even though they still live in Japan, Mom and Seth used his vacation time to come home and host Christmas here. Mom said they still felt guilty for leaving me on my own last year.

I had reminded her that I was never alone because I had Caleb and Jenny.

From where I sit in the living room, my eyes catch on the painting that hangs on the wall above them. It's one of mine, the portrait I did of Pip. The rest had all sold at the gallery show I had last month, but I kept this particular piece to give to Mom and Seth as an early Christmas gift.

They had loved it, with Mom acting like I had painted the Mona Lisa.

"You know," she told me, "Seth was an art major in college."

My head had whipped to him. "You were?"

"Yep." He laughed at my disbelief. "I love art. Back in the day, I did some drawing and painting, just like you." A little shyly he said, "Maybe we could paint together sometime."

Out of the window, I watch Brandon toss a football with Teddy. Liv, the twins, and Jenny are in the pool, enjoying how the sun has warmed the water.

Jenny catches my eye through the window and waves enthusiastically. Things are back to normal between us. She cheers me up, drags me to torturous workout classes, and hugs too hard.

I love it.

I may not have all the answers in life, but I understand some people are worth fighting for, even through the difficult times. Jenny's not perfect. I'm not perfect either, but we're perfect together.

The sliding glass door squeaks open, drawing my attention. There he is, Caleb Freaking Lawson, walking straight to me with Pip trotting at his heels. His mouth quirks, a tender curl of a smile, when our eyes meet. He comes over and kisses my temple. As always, his touch is electric, sending a thrill of desire out to every corner of my body. I turn and wrap my arms around him, resting my cheek on his chest. We stay like that for a moment, locked in an embrace.

He pulls back to look down at me. "Thanks again for the stocking." His long fingers gesture to the mantle, where an extra stocking has been hung this year. One that has his name on it. I had surprised him with it last night, just in time for Santa to fill it with gifts.

"I remember you told me once that you didn't own a stocking, so I had to fix that. Besides, you need one so Santa can tell you if you've been naughty or nice." I glance around to make sure no one is looking and lower my voice, transforming it into a silky purr. Rising onto my toes, I whisper in his ear, "I personally think you've been very, very nice." Gently, I kiss his cheek. He turns to me, and we gaze into each other's eyes. I'm lost in those beautiful blue depths.

Mom rises from the kitchen table. "Time to decorate the tree." She claps her hands together with excitement.

Caleb and I jump apart, as guilty as teenagers caught sneaking home after curfew. We look at each other and burst into laughter.

Mom lifts her eyebrow, wondering why we're laughing like hyenas, but after a minute she shrugs and walks past us. She leans out the sliding glass door to tell the rest of the family to come back inside.

There's a flurry of activity as wet swimsuits get exchanged for dry clothing, and Pip runs around barking. Soon, everyone gathers in the living room.

"Thanks again for waiting to decorate the tree," Brandon says to Mom. His flight had been delayed yesterday, not getting in until past midnight.

"There was no way we would do it without the girls." Mom puts her hand on top of Maddie's head and tousles her granddaughter's blonde curls. "We know how much they enjoy it."

Seth and Caleb carry in the cardboard boxes that contain all our decorations. At least they're better organized now since I'm the one who put them away last year. Back when it was just Caleb and me sharing this space. I almost don't recognize the house without the sound of hammering.

We unpack the ornaments, tinsel, and garland. The twins laugh while they run in circles around the tree, letting the garland flow through their hands as they wind it from top to bottom.

Sipping hot cocoa with tiny marshmallows, we hang ornaments on the tree one by one. The twins place them in a random pattern, mostly clustered on the front, leaving the back of the tree bare. Mom's expression is strained. I can tell she's having a hard time stopping herself from rearranging everything, so it's more evenly spread out.

I pick up a round ornament that contains a small picture and hold it to the light. "Girls," I call to the twins, "Look at this." They come to stand by my side, peering at the photo in my hand. It's them, their infant faces chubby and tiny fists clenched.

"We had this made when you were just one-year-old. I have a similar one, but mine is heart-shaped." The twins gasp at the thought of it. That they were once little babies and that I was, too. They fight with each other over the ornament, each girl wanting to place it on the tree.

I sit down to take it all in. The magic of this day. Carefully, I memorize the chiming laughter of my nieces, the softness of my mother's sweater, the gleam in Caleb's eyes as he watches me from across the room.

My gaze lands on a present leaned up against the wall next to the tree, a decidedly guitar-shaped gift. The tag reads:

To: Caleb

From: Melinda and Uncle Seth.

It's my dad's old guitar. The one Caleb used to win me back.

Mom and Seth had decided to give it officially to Caleb, but in my mind I imagine it as a present from Dad himself. I know how much he would have loved Caleb. How they would have bonded over their mutual love of music and their mutual love of me.

A tear gathers in the corner of my eye, and I swipe it away. This is not a day for crying. Caleb is at my elbow immediately, lips puckered with concern. "What's wrong?" he whispers so the rest of the family can't hear.

I shake my head as more tears threaten, not knowing how to express my overwhelmed emotions. But I don't have to. He takes one look, and I have the sense he understands. Every unspoken joy, all my tiny heartbreaks. He gets it. He sits beside me, and his hand seeks mine.

"It's just that I love them so much, my family," I say finally, my voice choked.

He squeezes my hand, letting me know I'm not alone.

Eventually, all the ornaments get hung. Caleb pulls me up from the couch, calling out, "Maddie, Megan, where's the star for the top of the tree?"

Tissue paper rustles as the girls dig to the bottom of the ornament box. "Here!" Maddie jumps up and down, holding the star in her hand, the one that was in Japan last year.

We bought this star the year Teddy was born. I remember shopping for it with my parents, Brandon, and Teddy, who was a tiny bundle of blankets in the stroller, just home from the hospital.

I had held out the star to him, saying, "See, baby. Do you like it? It's a little star, like you. You're a little person. The real stars are much bigger, like Daddy is bigger than you and me." Eight-year-old me had recently learned that in science class and felt very wise, to already be teaching my baby brother such important facts. I remember being excited, thinking about all the things I wanted to share with him.

Back then the star was shiny and perfect, but now its gold has rubbed off in some places. There's a dent in one pointy corner from where I dropped it when I was ten. I had cried and cried when I had seen the damage from that fall.

Dad had kissed away my tears. "Don't you see?" he had told me. "It's more beautiful now. Each of the star's imperfections tells the story of our family, our Christmases together. When I look at that ding, I won't remember that it fell. I'll remember how high you held it."

Maddie places the star in my hands.

Caleb kneels down at my feet. I stare at him in confusion.

He grins. "What are you waiting for? Climb on." He motions toward his back. "I'll lift you up."

Understanding dawns and, with it, a thrill. For the first time since Dad died, *I'm* going to put the star on the tree. I clamber onto Caleb's back like he's giving me a piggyback ride. He hoists me high. With him on his toes and me reaching out as far as I can manage, I place the star on a spindly branch at the top of the tree. It bobs there for a second and then the branch straightens, holding the star steady.

He gently lowers me to the ground. With my family all around, I let myself stay in the circle of his arms, gazing up at him with wonder. "Thank you."

When Caleb first came into my life, I thought I had everything figured out. I thought he was the one who needed my help to heal, which he did. But now, as I stare at him in the colorful glow of the Christmas lights, I see I need him as much as he needs me. I've got long-neglected broken parts, too.

With each touch, each kiss, each whispered confession, Caleb mended me. Putting all my pieces back together. Just like the star, I won't be perfect, but those scars I carry tell my story. If he can love those flaws, then I can, too.

EPILOGUE

SIX MONTHS LATER, TOKYO, JAPAN

Whatever you do, don't look." Caleb is close, his hands tight on my face as he covers my eyes. Cinnamon scent swirls around, comforting me.

"If it's a helicopter, then I've already seen this trick," I tease.

There are so many noises to sort through. The unfamiliar syllables of people speaking a different language. The honk of cars and the occasional echo of a distant siren. I'm jostled when someone hits my shoulder as they rush past.

We've only been here a week, yet already I've learned that the sidewalks of Tokyo are always jam-packed, morning, noon, and night. There's no sense of personal space, not with the thousands of people crowding each other on the streets and in the subways.

"Almost there, Aunt Gwen," seven-year-old Megan sings out from somewhere close by. She and Maddie had been having the best summer visiting Mom and Seth. I swear we've been to every Pokémon store in town. The girls have thick binders full of colorful trading cards. Although I can't see them since my eyes are covered, the rest of my family is also here. I can hear them chattering around us. Caleb had insisted we all be present for his "big surprise."

After walking for what feels like forever, we stop.

Caleb's lips brush the rim of my ear as he removes his hands and says, "You can look now."

My eyes fly wide and then narrow in puzzlement when I see the red brick and dark tinted windows of the building before me. "It's your restaurant."

Caleb had invested with Nick, the restaurateur who owns Adelaide. Together, they had opened three new restaurants: Mallory in Boston, Sophia in Los Angeles, and Amelia in Chicago. Now, with this one they're opening in Tokyo, they own five restaurants.

"I've been to this place before, remember?" I say slowly to Caleb, not sure what's going on. "You brought me to see it yesterday."

He can't have forgotten, can he?

His eyes twinkle merrily. "You saw the restaurant, but you didn't see the sign." He points over my shoulder. I draw the line from his fingertip to the building with my eyes.

When I was here before, yellow scaffolding had covered most of the windows. The new front door had been only half painted. Now, all the paint cans and toolboxes have been removed. The restaurant rises whole and shining before me.

Caleb jabs his finger, forcing me to lift my eyes to the rectangular wooden sign over the door, which reads *Gwendolen*.

I gasp, my hand flying to my chest as I whip around to face him. "*Me?*" I question, my voice rising. "You named the restaurant after me?"

My special smile is on his lips, small and tender. He bows his head slightly, confirming, "You."

I can't see him anymore because my eyes are blurring with tears. "Caleb!" I throw myself into his arms, and he lifts me off my feet. He spins me around once, twice, before setting me back down. We're both laughing.

"It's wonderful! Thank you."

He bends his head down to kiss me, causing my heart to trip over itself.

"That's so cool!" exclaims Maddie from behind me.

"Wow. Now you're famous too, Sissy," Teddy jokes.

Even Brandon gives a begrudging, "Congratulations on the new restaurant."

Mom and Seth take turns hugging Caleb and then me.

I don't miss the way that Caleb's eyes moisten when Seth grips his shoulder and tells him, "You did good, kid."

I return my stare to the gleaming sign and can't help but grin. "It's going to be a huge success, like all the others," I assure Caleb. "Especially with you as the special guest chef, it'll sell out immediately."

It had been Caleb's idea when he and Nick started opening the other restaurants. Caleb had suggested setting aside a couple of nights a week when someone famous could come in and be the head chef. They could design the menu with their favorite foods, oversee the kitchen, and cook. Turns out, there are a lot of celebrities—athletes, authors, musicians, and actors like Caleb—who enjoy cooking.

Back in New York at the Adelaide, the evenings when Caleb will be the cook are so popular that they're already sold out for the entire upcoming year.

I shake my head fondly. "Between working in the restaurants, being on Broadway, and finalizing the music for your second album, you'll barely have time for me."

"That's why I'm not making any more movies," he reminds me. "So I can focus on those three things and on you. Although you're right. With the painting you made for my new album cover, it's sure to be a hit."

I smile, remembering how fun it had been to collaborate with him. Both of us had worked past midnight tweaking my artwork until it represented his new music perfectly. Luckily, the next day had been a night shift in the ER. Otherwise, I would have been too tired.

"You're the busy one," he says. "Practically running the art therapy program in addition to your residency. How long again until you get paid real money for those jobs?"

Even though I haven't graduated from my residency yet, the hospital has already offered me a job in the ER and as the administrator of the art therapy program. It's all of my career goals coming true.

"Just a few more years," I answer. I pat his shoulder, appreciating how patient he's been with my crazy work schedule.

I look again at my name emblazoned on the side of the building and curl my arm around his waist. Rising up onto my toes, I kiss Caleb's cheek. "I'm proud of you."

He turns his gaze to mine. "I'm proud of us."

"Look at you," I tighten my arm, squeezing him. "Actor, musician, songwriter, chef, not to mention amazing son and boyfriend. You've got it all going on, Caleb."

He brushes my hair away from my face. "What about you? Doctor, artist, sister, daughter, friend, and amazing girlfriend. You're a million kinds of wonderful, too."

"I guess it's good to know we can be so many different people at once. That you aren't *just* a movie star and I'm not *just* a doctor. We're so much more than that."

I think back over all the things I've learned over this year and a half, and I realize that I don't have to be one thing. I can be reliable, dependable, sensible *and* fun and spontaneous. I can be a doctor and a painter.

Caleb can be scared of some things and brave about others. He can be an actor, songwriter, and a chef.

In the past, I've limited myself with labels. Painted myself into boxes so small they felt like prison cells. It's been terrifying to pry open those doors and explore something new. There's so much fear of failure, but if I can be brave enough, if I can hear my lion's heart beating, then I can do it. The freedom on the other side has been worth it.

Stepping closer, Caleb cradles my face in his hands, interrupting my thoughts. He looks at me with a depth of tenderness beyond anything I've seen before.

"I'm wondering," he says with that husky voice, "if you want to add one more title to that list."

My forehead wrinkles, confused. "What do you mean?"

"I mean the title of wife." Right there, in the middle of the crowded sidewalk, in the middle of Tokyo, Japan, Caleb Freaking Lawson drops to one knee and pulls a tiny square box out of his pocket.

My heart skyrockets, and my vision tunnels down to focus only on the Tiffany blue box and Caleb's face as he asks, "Will you marry me, Gwen? Will you be my best friend forever? My wife? My love? My life?"

I've never been so happy. Couldn't even imagine this level of happiness was possible. Love is a balloon, inflating my chest, filling up every cell, until I'm nothing but lightness and joy. "Yes! Yes, I'll marry you!" I choke out, overcome by emotion.

For the second time today, Caleb sweeps me up in his arms and spins me around, while my family applauds, cheering us on.

I take this memory and lock it away in a special room in my heart. Next to rooms already full of Caleb and empty rooms that wait to be filled with the future we will build together.

He gently lowers me to the ground, whispering in my ear, "I love you, Gwen."

Round G. Flat N.

"You're the best Christmas gift I've ever gotten."

The End

N ow that you're at the end, let's go back to the beginning. Want to see what Caleb thought of Gwen the first time they met? Click this link or scan this QR code to join my newsletter and receive a bonus chapter featuring the opening wedding scene from Caleb's point of view.

THIS EXCLUSIVE CHAPTER IS ONLY AVAILABLE TO MY NEWSLETTER SUBSCRIBERS!

http://lnkiy.in/holidaystarbonuschapter

You are cordially invited to the wedding of
Dr. Gwen Jane Wright and Mr. Caleb Augustus Lawson.
Coming soon!

DO YOU LIKE GAMES?

Me, too!

In this story I have hidden references to three of my favorite things:

Twilight by Stephenie Meyer (Team Edward, all the way)
Taylor Swift (Die hard Swiftie here)
Stephen King (The man. The myth. The legend)

Can you find them? Email me if you do!
hello@melissadymondauthor.com
Occasionally, I'll give a special gift to the winners :)

THANKS FOR READING!

Can I please ask you, dear reader, for a BIG favor? If you enjoyed this book, pretty please leave a review.

I know that your time is precious, but reviews are what makes or breaks an author's career. They influence everything from reaching new readers to training Amazon's algorithms to put this book on the top of the page when you search for it.

I personally read every review and your feedback helps me write the books YOU want to read. We are in this together, you and I. :)

So, thank you a million times over for reading this book and for leaving a review. You are literally making my dreams come true.

Lots of love, Melissa

AVAILABLE FOR PREORDER ON AMAZON NOW!

PAGING DR. HART BY DR. MELISSA DYMOND

Her white coat hides a dark past, but his blazing touch makes her want to trade peril for passion.

Ice Queen. That's Dr. Tiffany Hart's nickname in the hospital but when she meets red-hot new hire Dr. Ethan Clark she loses her cool. He's arrogant, annoying, and stupidly handsome.

But that's okay. Frozen from a past filled with danger and betrayal, Tiffany is immune to charming men, even if they remember her favorite coffee and let her pick what to watch on TV.

Dr. Ethan Clark comes from a long line of famous doctors. Wanting to escape his legacy and forge his own path, he's happy to transfer to Tiffany's hospital. Especially, when he lays eyes on the fiery redhead doctor assigned to train him.

Sure, she looks like she wants to punch him most of the time, but he can't ignore the sparks between them, so he vows to thaw her icy heart.

When Ethan and Tiffany are sent back to his home hospital and then to a medical conference at Disney World, they're forced to share close quarters. And when Tiffany's past finally catches up to them, they have to fight for their lives.

Can this prescription for disaster turn into happily ever after?

Paging Dr. Hart is a swoon-inducing, page-turning, medical romance book set in the Mercy Hospital world. If you like enemies-to-lovers, forced proximity, slow-burn chemistry, and pulse pounding suspense, you'll love this book.

Paging Dr. Hart will diagnose desire!

READ BELOW FOR AN EXCERPT FROM PAGING DR. HEART

He picks up a single lock of hair from my shoulder. It blazes scarlet in the late morning light. Running it through his fingers, Ethan bends his head so that I'm staring straight into his smokey eyes.

He says softly, "You're no ice queen. You're pure fire."

With that, Ethan drops my hair and walks away. Calling over his shoulder as he goes, "See you back in Columbus. Drive safe in that death trap you call a car."

He leaves me there in the parking lot.

Speechless.

MEET MELISSA!

Melissa Dymond is a mom, doctor, and writer.

Born and raised in California, she did medical school and training in the Midwest. Now she lives in the Southwest surrounded by boys, including her doctor husband, three amazing sons, and adorable Siberian husky, Buddy.

When she's not working, you can find her drinking an iced white chocolate mocha while voraciously reading, scrolling social media, and planning her family's next Disney vacation.

She would love to connect with you on her website, www.melissadymond-author.com, where you can sign up for her newsletter, get free chapters and writing updates, see character art, get the best deals on bookish merchandise, and share book related memes.

Also, she would love to chat with you on social media, where she spends WAY too much time. :) Join her at:

Instagram: https://www.instagram.com/melissadymondauthor/
Facebook: https://www.facebook.com/melissadymondauthor
Tiktok: https://www.tiktok.com/@melissadymond6

ACKNOWLEDGMENTS

Dear reader, prepare yourself for the corny part. Ever since I was a little girl (told you it was corny), I wanted to be a writer. But it was a desire that seemed so unattainable that I never mentioned it to anyone, even my husband. Surprise, honey! (I don't actually call him honey in real life, but it seemed appropriate here.)

Even though I had done hard things in my life, like becoming a doctor and overcoming a decade of fertility treatments to have my beautiful children, this writing thing felt like the most difficult.

Yet here we are! I did it, and you, dear reader, can do it too. By it I don't necessarily mean writing. I mean the thing you've always wanted to do but have been too scared to try. There's a great freedom to letting go of your hesitation and jumping into something. Feeling that free fall lurch in your gut as you hurtle toward your destination.

I have faith in you, dear reader. I know that you are strong, and stubborn, and smart. Remember as long as you are trying, there is no failure. I can't wait to hear about your successes. Contact me at my website or on social media and tell me all about it!

Ok. Whew! Corny part over. Now on to the acknowledgments. As I said above, this writing thing can be hard, but it was made easier by a whole army of family, friends, and peers.

Thank you to my editor, Caroline Accbo, who made this book so much better with your insightful critic and suggestions. Thank you for formatting this book so the pages weren't a terrible scramble, Steve Kuhn. Thank you for designing my gorgeous website, Katharine Bolin. Seriously, you have to see this website. It's SO pretty! www.melissadymondauthor.com

My beta readers, Nicole Rempfer and Jackie Hernandez, offered so much great advice and encouragement.

Thank you to all of the wonderful and supportive friends I have had through the years. Michelle Center, Judy Fann, Karen Fann, Tricia Verhoeven, Charity Yarnal, Pam Noll, Janelle McDonald, Nicole Danner, Jen Julian, Jenn Hamilton, Marcie Lane, Julie Sallquist, Liz Martin, Jill Rother, Maren Umlauf, Collin Zaffery, Stephanie Horton, Parris Maxwell, Darren Todd, Dorene McLaughlin, Jenna Price, Laura Weiss Ross, and so many more.

Thanks to my family. My mom who inspired my love of writing. My dad who taught me to be brave enough to try. My beautiful sister-in-law Amelia and her awesome husband Steven.

Most of all, my deepest love to my three sons. You are the best part of all my dreams brought to life. You make me smile every single day. My love also to my husband, Andrew. Layered behind all of these pages is our love story. The best story of all.

Check out my website and join my newsletter for exciting updates about writing, book releases, great book deals, freebies, and more.

WWW.MELISSADYMONDAUTHOR.COM

Milton Keynes UK
Ingram Content Group UK Ltd.
UKHW020644041223
433752UK00018B/1216

9 798987 585047